A TASTE OF CHRISTMAS

The snap of the ginger, the dark sweetness of the treacle . . . he closed his eyes, and for an instant he was a little boy again, sitting at the table with his mother and grandmother, his fingers and toes still numb from his play outdoors, the spicy taste of ginger nipping at his tongue.

When he opened his eyes again, she was watching him, a faint line between her brows, and her lower lip caught between her teeth. "Do you . . . are they as you remembered them, Your Grace?"

He gazed at her through the gloom. "They're perfect."

There was nothing for him to do then but rise and make his way to the kitchen door. But he paused halfway there and turned back to her, and the next thing he knew, he'd taken her hand in his. "Thank you, Miss St. Claire, for . . ." He searched for the proper words, but they didn't come. How did you thank someone for giving you back a piece of yourself you'd thought was gone forever? "Thank you."

She smiled. "You're most welcome, Your Grace."

He raised her hand to his mouth. It was fleeting, not a kiss so much as a brush of his lips across her knuckles, but he lingered long enough to inhale her, to feel the silky glide of her skin against his lips . . .

BOOKS BY ANNA BRADLEY

The Sutherlands
LADY ELEANOR'S SEVENTH SUITOR
LADY CHARLOTTE'S FIRST LOVE
TWELFTH NIGHT WITH THE EARL

The Somerset Sisters
MORE OR LESS A MARCHIONESS
MORE OR LESS A COUNTESS
MORE OR LESS A TEMPTRESS

Besotted Scots
THE WAYWARD BRIDE
TO WED A WILD SCOT
FOR THE SAKE OF A SCOTTISH RAKE

The Swooning Virgins Society
THE VIRGIN WHO RUINED LORD GRAY
THE VIRGIN WHO VINDICATED LORD DARLINGTON
THE VIRGIN WHO HUMBLED LORD HASLEMERE
THE VIRGIN WHO BEWITCHED LORD LYMINGTON
THE VIRGIN WHO CAPTURED A VISCOUNT

Drop Dead Dukes
GIVE THE DEVIL HIS DUKE
DAMNED IF I DUKE
THE DUKE'S CHRISTMAS BRIDE

Published by Kensington Publishing Corp.

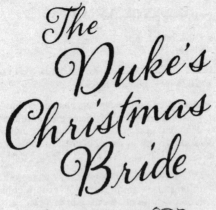

The Duke's Christmas Bride

DROP DEAD DUKES

ANNA BRADLEY

ZEBRA BOOKS
Kensington Publishing Corp.
www.kensingtonbooks.com

ZEBRA BOOKS are published by

Kensington Publishing Corp.
900 Third Avenue
New York, NY 10022

All Kensington titles, imprints, and distributed lines are available at special quantity discounts for bulk purchases for sales promotion, premiums, fund-raising, and educational or institutional use.

Special book excerpts or customized printings can also be created to fit specific needs. For details, write or phone the office of the Kensington Sales Manager: Kensington Publishing Corp., 900 Third Avenue, New York, NY 10022. Attn. Sales Department. Phone: 1-800-221-2647.

Zebra and the Z logo Reg. U.S. Pat. & TM Off.

First Printing: October 2024
ISBN-13: 978-1-4201-5541-9
ISBN-13: 978-1-4201-5544-0 (eBook)

10 9 8 7 6 5 4 3 2 1

Printed in the United States of America

PROLOGUE

He shouldn't have come here. He'd promised himself he wouldn't.

But he'd made that same promise before—last year, and the year before that—and every year, it turned out to be a lie. He always came, no matter how many times he swore he wouldn't.

Promises were sneaky that way, especially the ones you made to yourself.

In the end, they always became lies.

Shouldn't he know that by now?

The sun was just melting into the horizon when he slipped from his father's house and down the pathway toward the wood, fitful streaks of amber and crimson like bloody claw marks torn into the sky, but underneath the trees, it was as dark as midnight.

It didn't matter, though. He knew every stone, every jutting tree root, every dead leaf hidden in the mud under his feet. He'd trod this same path so many times he might have found his way blindfolded, memory guiding his steps.

Except it wasn't the same, no matter how familiar it felt. It would never be the same again. Pretending it could be was just another lie.

There was no snow this year. Only rain, an occasional grim drizzle since he'd come home from Eton, washing everything in shades of gray. The ground was wet still, the icy water seeping into his boots, and the mud sucking his feet into the earth, the darkness like the heel of a palm pressing into his eyes.

But not for long.

It was waiting for him when he emerged from the shelter of the trees, just as it always was. A burst of light, setting the inky sky above aglow, as if every star were shining down upon it at once. As if some great hand had scooped all the brightest ornaments in the sky up into a tight fist, and was squeezing them, squeezing until liquid streams of light spilled through its fingers directly over Hammond Court, bathing it in pale silver fire.

As if *here* was the only place that mattered. As if Ambrose St. Claire was the only man who mattered.

It was the same, every year.

Max kept to the shadows, outside the pool of golden light spilling into the drive. He was invisible to the party guests laughing and gossiping on the other side of the windows, a blur of satins and silks and glittering jewels, small silver cups of spiced cider in their hands.

The warmth and merriment unfolding behind those windows were as far away from him as the stars gleaming coldly in the black sky, but even from here, he could hear the laughter, the chatter, the singing. Christmas carols. The same songs, every year.

Boughs of holly. Silver bells. Partridges, pear trees, and golden rings.

He stuffed his hands into his coat pockets and kicked at the muddy ground. It had been four years since he'd been inside the house, four years since it had been his home.

Four years. He wasn't a boy anymore. He was sixteen, nearly a man, yet he still couldn't make himself stay away.

He didn't want to be here, didn't want to remember. If he could, he'd turn around and never come back, never set eyes on the house again, but he couldn't make himself forget what it had felt like to be on the other side of those windows. It would be easier if he could, but there was no forgetting such a betrayal.

No forgiving it, either.

It wasn't fair. It wasn't bloody *fair*.

Inside his coat, his hands clenched into fists. He hated Ambrose, hated him so much the bitterness scalded the back of his throat, making him cough and choke.

Ambrose might play at being lord of the manor, but that didn't change the truth. He wasn't a lord, and he'd *stolen* the manor. Stolen it from Max and his father.

He wasn't the only one. There had been others who'd taken what was once theirs. Over the past four years, they'd been picked clean of everything that wasn't entailed, until only the bare bones remained.

The other boys at Eton sneered at him over it, calling his father the Destitute Duke.

He'd make them pay for that, one day. He'd make them all pay, but none of them would pay as dearly as Ambrose St. Claire would, because of all the betrayals, his had cut the deepest. That wound was raw edged and bloody still, even four years later.

Once upon a time, before Max's mother died and everything fell apart, Ambrose had been their friend. He'd *trusted* Ambrose, had looked up to him. Worshipped him, even, but in the end, Ambrose hadn't been any different from the rest of them.

He was a thief and a liar.

Someday, when Max came here, he wouldn't hide in the woods under the dripping tree branches, cold water trickling down the back of his neck. No, he'd walk right up the front drive and through the door, and he'd take his father's house back.

For now, though, there was nothing to do but return home, where there were no garlands, no silver cups, no golden lamplight. His father would have fallen asleep on the worn leather chair in his study by now, an empty bottle of brandy lying on the floor beside him.

Max dragged the back of his arm over his damp cheeks, the wool of his coat prickling his skin, and turned to go—turned his back on the bright lights of Hammond Court, leaving it behind until next year.

He *wasn't* crying. Not over a villain like Ambrose St. Claire.

The dampness on his cheeks was just drops of water falling from the branches above, nothing more.

CHAPTER 1

Fairford, Gloucestershire
December 12, 1819

It was snowing inside Rose's bedchamber.

The chill woke her, the draught of wintery air biting at her nose and setting her toes atingle, rousing her from a fitful sleep. She struggled onto her elbows and peeked over the edge of the coverlet. Muted morning light filtered through the thin draperies, catching the pale gleam of downy snowflakes swirling through a jagged fissure in the window.

The snowflakes were pretty, but alas, it wouldn't do. A glittering flurry of harmless flakes could become a blizzard in the blink of an eye, and the steely gray clouds beyond the window promised more snow.

More snow, and here was Fairford, already half smothered in it as it was. It had begun snowing in early November and had hardly let up for a single day since.

Now the dratted flurries had found their way indoors.

She tossed the coverlet aside with a sigh. If it had been any window, in any other bedchamber, in any other manor house, an indoor squall would have been shocking indeed, but at Hammond Court, the boundary between indoors and outdoors had grown increasingly indistinct as the golden days of autumn slid into the deep chill of winter.

At least, that's how Ambrose would have put it. He'd always fancied himself something of a poet. It was one of the things she'd loved most about him.

A hot ache pressed behind her eyelids, but she shook off the tears that threatened with an impatient jerk of her head. He wouldn't have wanted her tears and mournful sighs. Why, if he could see her now, he'd scold until her ears burned.

Anyway, when had sniveling ever helped anything?

She rolled out of bed, snatched up the coverlet, and wrapped it around her shoulders, then skidded over the wooden floorboards in her stockinged feet to inspect the snowdrift gathering under her window.

Or puddle, rather. A large puddle. It had been snowing for some time then, likely most of the night. She jerked the worn draperies aside to get a better look at the damage to the glass. It was early still, the gray light too weak to dispel the shadows lingering in the corners of the bedchamber, but there was no missing the fracture splitting one of the upper panes.

Well, that explained that menacing crack that had woken her last night. It hadn't been a ghost after all, then. That was some comfort, at least. Not that she believed in ghosts, of course. She wasn't such a fool as that. But in the deepest dark of the night, with the house creaking and moaning around her, it had occurred to her that if there was ever a man who'd find a way to walk amongst the undead, it was Ambrose.

Yes, he'd take great delight in haunting her, the scoundrel.

She edged closer to the window, careful to avoid the puddle, and squinted at the crack in the gloomy light. Yes, it was certainly longer than it had been. She'd marked the end of it yesterday with a smudged thumbprint, and it was well past that point now. It reached the top edge of the windowsill and was surrounded by a spiderweb of finer cracks, like wrinkles fanning out from the corner of an eye.

It was spreading, along with the dozens of other cracks that decorated the walls.

She could stuff rags into the gap at the top, but already the windows were more rag than glass. It was a wonder the ceilings hadn't toppled down upon their heads by now. If she didn't come up with some way to put a stop to the deterioration, they'd have to leave.

"Well, that's a bit of a mess, isn't it?"

Rose turned around to find Abby hovering in the doorway, her grizzled gray hair standing on end. "It's just a bit of water, Abby. Nothing that can't be cleaned up."

"It's a miracle you haven't caught your death in this damp, drafty room."

"All the rooms are damp and drafty."

"None so much as this one." Abby pointed an accusing finger at the puddle. "For pity's sake, Rose, why won't you come and share my bed with me? It's dry, and we'd both be warmer that way."

Warmer, yes, but not safer. She'd taken to sleeping in

this room after one of their creditors in the village had appeared on their doorstep in a rage, demanding payment and making all manner of unpleasant threats. Fortunately, she'd managed to intercept him before he broke the door down, but he wouldn't be the last of them.

They had a great many creditors, and all of them as angry as spitting cats. She didn't fancy being caught unawares again. This bedchamber looked down onto the front drive, and so here she would stay. "I like this room. It's, er . . . cozy."

Abby snorted. "Cozy, is it?"

"Quite so, yes." The lie slipped easily enough from her tongue, but Rose took care not to meet Abby's eyes. Abby could always tell when she was lying, and she didn't fancy a blistering scold just now.

"Cozy, my eye." Abby turned on her heel and disappeared through the bedchamber door, her slow, heavy tread echoing down the hallway. When she returned she was carrying a bundle of dark red cloth in her arms. "Here, help me with these."

Rose skirted the puddle and crossed the bedchamber, taking up a fold of the cloth from the bundle, but she paused with it clutched in her hands. "This isn't a rag. It looks like—"

"It's one of the silk panels from Mr. St. Claire's bed hangings." Abby thrust her chin into the air. "Now, don't fuss, pet. We're nearly out of rags, and anyway, the silk is thicker. This will keep the draughts out much better than some old kitchen scrap."

"But it's *silk*." It was a ridiculous objection, of course. What use did they have for silk bed hangings? It was too old and worn to be of any value, and yet . . .

These had belonged to Ambrose, once. She resisted the urge to bury her face in it, knowing she'd get nothing but a nose full of dust for her troubles, but it seemed wrong that a person should leave so many odds and ends behind when they died—wrong, that all these things that had been so secondary to Ambrose during his lifetime, mere afterthoughts, should have somehow outlived him, and be all that remained of a once-vibrant man.

She expected Abby to scold, but when she looked up, Abby was staring down at the red silk panel, her faded blue eyes damp with tears. "Curse him, anyway," she whispered, dragging the back of her hand over her eyes. "I can't think why I miss him so much, the troublesome old villain."

"He was troublesome, wasn't he? And it's just like him to go off and die right before the weather turned foul. I daresay he planned it out that way. It's the sort of thing he'd do."

Abby gave a shaky laugh. "I daresay he did." She grabbed the other silk panel from the pile and made her way to the window.

"Mind the puddle there. Don't get your stockings wet." Rose trudged across the bedchamber and got down on her hands and knees to wipe up the puddle. The icy water soaked through the silk, turning her fingers numb.

Perhaps this would be the last of the snow for a

while. Perhaps she'd wake tomorrow to find the sun had emerged from behind the clouds. It would warm up a touch then, just enough to take the bitterest edge off the cold. Perhaps good fortune was just around the corner. Perhaps it would find them today, even, and then—

"My goodness, who can that be?"

Rose stilled, the dripping silk panel clutched in her hands. "What?" But she could already hear the carriage wheels rattling up the drive.

"There's a carriage." Abby peered through the glass, her brow creased. "How strange. It's not yet seven o'clock in the morning. Who would be coming here so early?"

Who, indeed? No one they wished to see, that was certain. Rose leaped to her feet, the puddle forgotten. "Come away from the window, Abby."

But Abby didn't come away from the window. She remained where she was, in plain sight of anyone who happened to look up at the house, staring down at the drive as the grind of the carriage wheels over the ruts grew louder. "Heavens. That's no ordinary carriage, but a right fancy one, and I think . . . Rose, come and look! Is that a crest on the door?"

A crest? Good Lord, she hoped not. Nothing good ever came in a crested carriage.

"We can finish this later." Rose took the silk panel from Abby's hand, then herded her away from the window toward the door. "Go on back to your bed-chamber now and let me take care of our visitors. No doubt they've come to offer their condolences and will be gone again in a trice."

Condolences, indeed. No one came to offer condolences at seven o'clock in the morning. No, they'd come for something else entirely.

Whatever it was, they'd almost certainly be obliged to leave without it.

"Did Ambrose know any lords?" Abby peered over Rose's shoulder, trying to see out the window. "Because I'm certain I saw a crest—"

"I daresay he must have known a lord or two. Ambrose knew everyone." More to the point, they knew *him*. "I'll come and tell you all about them once they've left. Go to your bedchamber until then, and stay there until I come and fetch you, all right?"

Abby gave her a worried look, but she shuffled toward the bedchamber door. "Yes, all right, but come up as soon as they're gone."

"I will, but promise me you won't venture out of the bedchamber until I come for you." Rose hesitated, then added, "No matter what you hear."

Abby's eyes widened. "My goodness. I don't like the sound of that."

No, but whatever was about to unfold downstairs, odds were she'd like the look of it even less. "Promise me, Abby."

"I promise, but you be careful, pet. You hear me?"

"Yes, I will." Rose waited in the doorway until Abby had hobbled down the hallway to her bedchamber and disappeared inside, closing the door behind her.

Then she flew back into her own bedchamber and peered out the window.

The carriage had come to a stop halfway up the drive. She stared down at it, her heart pounding hard enough to reduce her rib cage to a powder. Abby was right. It was no ordinary carriage, but a vision in glossy black lacquer, with shiny black wheels, gold spokes and fittings, and a sleek pair of matched bays dancing restlessly in the traces, their dainty feet pawing at the ground.

The word "grand" didn't even begin to describe it. It was the sort of elegant, fashionable equipage one might find promenading in Hyde Park. At least, she imagined it was, having never set foot in Hyde Park herself, or anywhere else in London.

There was a crest on the door, too, something in black, gold, and royal blue. She couldn't make it out from this angle, but that combination of colors was familiar. Hadn't she seen something similar on some of Ambrose's correspondence?

She waited for the occupants to emerge, her breath held, but no one came out. A minute passed, then another, but just as she'd begun muttering a prayer that they'd go away again, the driver descended from the box, leaped out onto the drive, and opened the carriage door.

Whoever was inside felt no urgency to alight, but left his coachman standing on the drive, his greatcoat flapping about in the wind, and snowflakes gathering on his shoulders, until finally, *finally*, a long leg encased in a pair of fitted, dark gray pantaloons appeared, ending in a shiny black boot with handsome gold tassels.

A large, immaculately gloved hand landed on the top edge of the door, and then the rest of the man unfolded himself from the carriage. He turned to say something to his coachman, then marched up the drive until he was standing directly below her window.

Rose sucked in a breath. This man was undoubtedly the owner of the carriage.

He was . . . goodness, she'd never seen anything like *him* before. His face was partially obscured by the brim of an elegant beaver hat, but she caught a glimpse of a straight, aristocratic nose and a mass of thick, dark hair. He was exceptionally tall and broad shouldered as well, perhaps the largest and most ideally formed gentleman she'd ever laid eyes on, the power of his body tightly leashed, like a coiled spring.

He marched toward the house, his stride loose limbed and confident, like a man who was accustomed to everyone scurrying out of his way. A moment later there was a brisk knock on the front door, the thud echoing throughout the house.

She waited, her every muscle tensed, her hands clenched, fingernails biting into her palms.

Go away, damn you. Just go—

Her only answer was a second thump, this one louder and more impatient than the first, and then, after a few moments of decidedly ominous silence, there was another thud, followed by a cracking noise like wood splintering.

Her hand flew to her mouth to smother a shriek. Was

he attempting to break down the door? No, surely not! Even the most determined of Ambrose's creditors wouldn't dare to force their way into—

Thump!

She gasped, her heart vaulting into her throat.

Dear God, he *was*! He was breaking into *her* house, forcing his way inside like a common criminal. She backed away from the window, her legs shaking, and crept toward the clothes press on the other side of the bedchamber.

Ambrose's pistol was already loaded. After their last unwelcome visitor, she always kept it so. She threw her cloak on over her nightdress, stuffed the pistol into the pocket, and slipped from her bedchamber in her stockinged feet.

She paused when she reached the landing, taking care to keep out of sight, and froze, listening, her fingers tight around the pistol.

The noise had ceased. She peeked around the corner, then darted back out of sight behind the edge of the wall. The front door was wide open. It appeared to be still intact, but goodness only knew what his next target would be. He hadn't barreled his way inside with such viciousness only to give up now.

This man . . . he was the sort accustomed to getting what he wanted. His carriage, with that elaborate crest, his arrogant stride, that costly beaver hat, and those gold-tasseled boots—anyone could see at a glance that he wasn't the sort to trifle with.

But then, neither was she.

CHAPTER 2

It had taken fifteen years, one battered carriage, two lost horseshoes, and irreparable damage to his right arse cheek for Maxwell Alastair Hammond Burke, the Tenth Duke of Grantham, Viscount Hammond, to return to the village of his birth.

Fifteen years and eight hours, that is. Eight interminable, bone-rattling hours of travel from London to Fairford, the carriage tilting crazily with every inch of rutted road that passed under its wheels, his body aching and his backside battered beyond the telling of it, only to find ruin at the end of his journey.

Not figurative ruin, either, but *actual* ruin.

A heavy blanket of snow covered the gardens, but choked weeds and gnarled roots jutted up from underneath the thick carpet of white like bony fingers, and the once-tidy pathways were now a wilderness of overgrown shrubs and untrimmed hedges.

It was positively uncivilized to a gentleman accustomed to the manicured grounds of Hyde Park, but if possible, the house was in even greater disarray than the gardens. Crumbling stone walls staggered under the weight of a sagging roof, and three of the four bedchamber windows on the third floor were cracked, the slashes in the glass like ugly scars on an otherwise smooth cheek, the raw edges glinting in the weak light.

If he'd had a smidgen of forbearance left, even the thinnest thread of good humor, the sight of the old place after all these years would have extinguished it in an instant.

He didn't, as it happened.

He'd lost any claim to proper human feeling when they'd reached Hermitage, and his flask of brandy had run dry. Why hadn't he thought to bring two flasks? Or the whole bottle, come to that? He wasn't given to heavy drinking, but a sojourn in the godforsaken village of Fairford could drive the soberest of men into his cups.

Was it any wonder his father had found his death at the bottom of a bottle?

But this was no time to think about his father's disgraceful end. There was never a proper time to think about *that*. He generally made a point of not doing so, but damned if the mere sight of Hammond Court didn't set all those old ghosts free again.

He'd only just arrived, and already he was growing mawkish.

But he was here now, and the sooner he got this over with, the sooner he could leave and forget about Fairford for another two decades. He stepped up to the front door, seized the knob, and gave it a hard twist, but for all that the rest of the house was falling to bits, the iron lock on the front door appeared to be maddeningly intact.

He backed up and scanned the front of the house. It was early, not yet seven o'clock, but there wasn't a flicker of light to be seen behind the windows, or a curl of smoke rising from any of the four soot-stained chimneys ranging across the lopsided roof.

Abandoned, of course, and just as well. The place was a bloody hazard.

Behind him, his coachman stirred. "All right, Your Grace?"

Max turned and glanced back at Bryce. He'd ordered him to stop halfway up the drive to save his carriage springs, which had been popping loose with every turn of the carriage wheels over the rutted drive. "Just a bit of trouble with the door, Bryce."

He grasped the knob again and gave it a vigorous shake. The lock held steady, but the same couldn't be said of the doorknob itself, which rattled in its setting, the wood around it cracked and shredding.

A hard kick would see the thing done. It wasn't quite the dignified entrance he'd envisioned, but he *had*, after all, been invited. He retreated a step, braced himself, and struck the knob with the side of his boot.

Nothing. The blasted thing held fast.

"Damn it." He struck it a second time, giving in to a fit of temper utterly unworthy of a gentleman, and most particularly a duke.

Bryce let out a startled gasp. "Your Grace?"

Max sucked in a deep draught of freezing air until he was able to face his driver with his usual sangfroid. "It's all right, Bryce. Remain with the carriage."

It was just as well if Bryce wasn't close enough to

witness what he intended to do next. Kicking doors down was not proper ducal behavior, but this was *his* house, *his* door, and *his* doorknob, or they would be, soon enough, and he may abuse them as he pleased.

"Can I help, Your Grace?" Bryce called out again, clearly alarmed.

Help? No, he was well past the point of help now. If he hadn't been, he would have returned to his carriage, ordered Bryce to take him to Grantham Lodge where a meal, a bath, and a comfortable bed awaited him, and return later with a few sturdy footmen in tow.

But where his past was concerned? He was a perfectly rational duke, run mad in the Cotswolds. "No. I've got it, Bryce."

"Yes, Your Grace." Bryce cast a dubious glance at him. "If you're quite sure, Your Grace."

He wasn't sure of a damned thing anymore, except that he *would* get into this house, one way or another. "I'm sure. Wait there."

He retreated a few steps, then ran at the door, aiming a kick at the doorknob. This time he struck it dead on with his heel. A crack echoed in the frosty air as the wood splintered, and the knob and the plate that affixed it to the door dropped to the ground like birds shot from the sky.

Ah, good. That would do.

He pushed the door open and ducked through it, coughing as a cloud of dust rained down on him, ruining a perfectly good beaver hat. He paused on the threshold, but there wasn't much to see with the dull gray sky above greedily hoarding what little light there was.

But he didn't need any light to know the way. Even after so many years, and with half the furnishings shrouded in dust cloths, he moved easily from room to room, memory guiding him.

It was strange, how little things changed.

It had been nineteen years since he'd set foot inside this house—fifteen since he'd set foot in Fairford itself—but he knew it as well as he knew the lines intersecting the palm of his hand. Every decorative plaster cornice, every one of the hundreds of pieces of crystal dangling from the heavy chandelier in the entryway, and every inch of the wooden floorboards under his feet.

Time had taken liberties with the cursed old place, but otherwise, it hadn't changed as much as he'd expected. It was still the same house in which he'd run wild as a small boy—or what was left of it, after nineteen years in Ambrose St. Claire's careless hands.

It wasn't surprising. Everything Ambrose touched, he ruined.

Not just houses, but people, too. Lives.

Ambrose was the reason he would never be able to truly come home again—the reason his boyish adoration for his once-beloved home had turned into a man's implacable hatred. But that was the way of things, wasn't it? Love and hate were inextricably linked, different sides of the same coin, a mere flick of a thumb the only thing separating one from the other.

He ambled through the rooms on the main floor, taking care to sidestep the floorboards that had swollen and warped with age and damp, wandering from the entryway with the grand, carved-wood staircase down the hallway toward his father's study, with the library on the left, and the drawing and music rooms on the right, each a faded version of what they'd once been, and everything hidden under a thick layer of dust.

He made his way down the corridor and the servants' staircase, the thud of his footsteps much too loud in the silent house. The kitchen hadn't changed. The same copper pots still hung from the rack over the stove, and the old table still took pride of place in the center of the room.

He rested his hand on the scrubbed wooden surface. He and his mother used to sit here together on cold winter afternoons, feasting on warm chocolate and her special ginger biscuits, the same recipe his grandmother had used to make for her when she was a girl. He'd never tasted any as delicious. Even Gunther's, for all that it offered the most celebrated sweets in London, couldn't produce a ginger biscuit to rival his mother's.

He cleared the sudden thickness from his throat. How absurd. That had been a lifetime ago, and his mother was long since dead and buried. Still, he couldn't resist running his hand under the edge of the table, a smile rising to his lips when he felt the familiar indentation under his fingertips.

Four letters—M, A, H, and B, for Maxwell Alastair Hammond Burke.

He'd carved them with one of the cook's sharp kitchen knives when he was seven years old. He'd wanted to carve his entire name, but it was too long, so he'd settled for his initials to save his backside from the thrashing he certainly would have gotten if

Mrs. Archibald had caught him abusing her precious knives. The letters weren't as distinct as they'd once been, the edges of each dulled with wear and time, but they were still here, the wood smooth and clean under his fingertips—

Clean? His head jerked up, the hair on the back of his neck rising as he glanced around the space. The table had been recently scrubbed clean. The polished copper pots gleamed in their place over the stove, and there wasn't a speck of ash in the massive stone fireplace that dominated the room. The iron kettle sat atop the stove, with coals stacked neatly in the firebox underneath it, and the flagstone floors were swept clean.

Nearly every stick of furniture on the main floor was shrouded with sheeting and coated with dust, but here in the kitchen, there wasn't a single streak of dirt or a cobweb to be seen. It was as spotless as it had been when Mrs. Archibald had presided over it, almost as if . . .

Someone had been in here.

He turned about in a circle, peering into the shadowy corners.

That was when he heard it.

It was so faint it would have been inaudible to anyone whose ears weren't straining against the silence. The soft scuff of a footfall over the floorboards, a creak, and then louder, from behind him, the unmistakable click of a pistol being cocked.

Then a voice, soft and steady. "I don't know who you are, or what you're doing here, but I demand you leave at once."

He whirled around, but by then it was already too late. A figure was advancing toward him from the deepest shadows hovering around the archway that led into the stillroom—a figure clad in a filmy white gown with a cloak thrown over the top of it.

She—for it was a *she*, and rather a small, slight *she* at that—was not at all an intimidating figure, aside from the pistol balanced in her hand. It was no pretty little muff pistol, either, but a double-barreled flintlock dueling pistol that was more than capable of blowing a sizable hole in his chest.

"Turn around, and go back out the way you came in." Her voice was calm, even polite, but there wasn't so much as a quiver in the hand that held the pistol, and her finger was steady on the trigger. "Now, if you please."

As assassins went, she was a remarkably courteous one. Surely, such a gracious, soft-spoken lady wouldn't actually fire on him? "If I don't, madam? What then?"

She raised the muzzle of the gun—higher, then higher still, until it was no longer aimed at his chest, but right between his eyes. "Then I'm afraid I'll have to shoot you."

CHAPTER 3

"Must you, indeed? How tiresome of you." Not as tiresome as a pistol ball lodged in his skull would be, but Max would have wagered his dukedom that when he did choose to leave, he'd do so with his head intact.

He'd faced enough violence in his lifetime to know an empty threat when he heard one.

He'd fought dozens of brawls before the end of his first year at Eton and endured countless thrashings from vengeful headmasters. He'd had his eyes blackened, his bones broken, and boot heels lodged in his ribs.

Oddly enough, however, not once in his thirty-one years had he ever found himself on the wrong end of a loaded pistol. He'd had a near miss or two, certainly—there'd been that footpad in Covent Garden who'd held a blade to his throat, and on one memorable occasion a former mistress had tried to smother him with a pillow—but those were isolated incidents, and they'd taken place years ago.

These days, there weren't many people in England who'd dare raise a fist or point a weapon at the Duke of Grantham.

"Did you not hear me, sir? I ordered you to leave my home this instant."

He squinted into the gloom, but aside from a sweep of floating white hems, he couldn't make out much of her. Her face was cast in shadows, but there was no mistaking the quiet menace in that soft voice.

Wasn't his past meant to flash before his eyes in such circumstances? Shouldn't he be overwhelmed with regrets over his misspent life? Shouldn't he fall to his knees and grovel for forgiveness for his sins, and beg for mercy from the depths of his blackened soul? Surely, the fleeting moments before death should be ones of perfect clarity, and divine thanks?

But he *wasn't* thankful, and the sudden racing of his heart and his sweat-slick palms weren't the result of fear, but of fury. The sun had only just struggled over the horizon, for God's sake. Surely, it was a bit early in the morning for such theatrics?

If he was destined to meet his end with a ball between his eyes, it wouldn't be in the kitchen of his childhood home before he'd even had his morning coffee, nor would it come at the hands of this . . . this . . . well, he didn't have the vaguest idea who she was, or what she was doing in his house.

"Don't trifle with me, sir." She inched closer, close enough so he could see her long, slender finger on the trigger. "It would be a great pity if I were obliged to shoot you."

She didn't *sound* like a murderess. Her voice was husky but sweet, and not at all the tone one might expect of a murderess. "Indeed, it would, but you're not going to do it."

At least, he hoped not, especially if Ambrose had been the one to teach her how to shoot. The man had been a liar and a degenerate of the first order—a trickster at best, a charlatan and thief at worst, but there was no denying he'd been an excellent marksman.

She shifted but remained hidden in the shadows, and the dainty hand holding the pistol didn't so much as twitch. "You appear quite confident of that, but it's not the sort of thing one wishes to be mistaken about, is it?"

"No, but I'm not mistaken." He leaned a hip against the table and crossed his arms over his chest. "You're the housekeeper here? A maidservant?"

"You're rather inquisitive for a man with a pistol aimed at his head." She tutted, a soft click of her tongue. "Presumptuous, as well."

"I do beg your pardon, miss . . . miss . . ." He raised an eyebrow inquiringly, but Ambrose's serving maid, or cook, or whoever the devil she was didn't deign to offer her name. "Perhaps I should explain. I was invited here. Surely, you don't intend to shoot a guest?"

She let out an incredulous laugh, the sound far sweeter than a lady with a pistol in her hand had any right to produce. He squinted into the darkness and caught a glimpse of a small, straight nose and a curved cheekbone, but otherwise, she was merely an indistinct shape in white.

Well, aside from the pistol pointed at his head. *That* was distinct enough.

"Invited? I rather doubt that."

"I have a letter that proves it. May I fetch it?" He reached a hand toward his coat pocket.

"No, I'd rather you didn't move, if you please. Who wrote the letter?"

"Ambrose St. Claire, of course. Who else?"

Ah, now that got her attention. She didn't move, or venture into the light, but the air between them changed, grew charged, the sudden deep hush crackling with tension. At last, she said, "Ambrose is dead."

He was, yes, and not a single bloody moment too soon. "I'm aware of that, madam. An unfortunate accident, I believe. Pity. But this is his house, or it was."

Except it hadn't been, had it? It hadn't been Ambrose's house at all, no matter if he'd been living in it these past nineteen years. Ambrose St. Claire was no better than a poacher with a brace of pilfered pheasant hidden under his coat. He'd *stolen* this house right out from under Max's father, and by the looks of things, he'd taken bloody poor care of it.

"It was his house, yes, but it's mine now, and I certainly didn't invite you here."

"*Yours?*" Like bloody hell it was. Hammond Court was the one remaining piece of his family's legacy that he had yet to reclaim, the missing jewel in the Grantham family's crown. It had eluded him for years, and he'd be damned if he'd let it slip through his fingers now.

"Mine, yes, and I don't want you here."

"I rather assumed that, madam, given you greeted me with a pistol in your hand."

"Are you complaining, sir? Because it might just as easily have been a ball between your eyes. If I were you, I'd consider myself fortunate, given I would have been well within my rights to shoot you."

"Shoot me? On what grounds? Just because I—"

"Kicked my door down, and broke into my house? You're an intruder, sir."

It wasn't *her* house, damn her, and he'd only kicked the doorknob, not the door, though admittedly he'd left it a trifle mangled. "I beg your pardon. I was under the impression the house had been abandoned." Anyone would have thought so, given the decrepit look of the place. Half the windows were cracked, for God's sake.

"It hasn't been," she said, her voice flat.

"Yes, well, I see that now. But be that as it may, Ambrose must have wanted me here, or else he wouldn't have invited me to come. One would think you'd choose to honor his wishes in that regard. Or do you mean to disregard the final, dying request of your, er . . . employer? Friend? Distant uncle, or second cousin, perhaps?"

Alas, the woman was too clever to be goaded or tricked into revealing herself, and his questions were met with a deafening silence.

"I've come all the way from London at Ambrose's summons, madam. You might at least agree to have a look at the letter," he said when the silence continued to stretch between them. "You'll see it's written in his hand."

There was another long, fraught silence, then she jerked the pistol toward the kitchen table. "Very well. Sit down, and take care to remain still, if you please."

Ah, at last, they were getting somewhere.

He drew a chair away from the table and sat, careful

not to make any sudden movements. He was almost certain she wouldn't dare shoot him, but *almost certain* wasn't quite good enough when it came to keeping one's brains from splattering onto the kitchen table, was it?

He reached into his coat pocket, withdrew the letter, and waited with some curiosity for her to emerge from her hiding place, but when she detached herself from the shadows and passed in front of the window, the gray morning light fell on her face, and he nearly bit his tongue in half.

This was no robust kitchen wench with raw, red hands and the thick neck he'd been expecting, but a slip of a girl with luminous green eyes, silky golden hair hanging in a long, loose braid down her back, and the hems of a white nightdress swirling around a pair of trim ankles.

This was his tormentor? This nymph, this woodland sprite, this dainty little pixie had threatened to put a ball between his eyes? He bit back a wild urge to laugh. Why, the chit couldn't be more than twenty years old, and she appeared as delicate as the porcelain figurines his mother used to collect.

Who the devil *was* she? And what was she doing here, alone in this house?

Could she have been Ambrose's lover? She was far too young for him, of course, but there was a certain type of man who allowed his cock to make decisions that were better left to his head. He wouldn't have thought Ambrose was one of them, but then he'd only been a boy when he'd known him, and he'd revered him then with the sort of blind adoration of a lonely child.

God knew Ambrose had proved himself a scoundrel in the end.

So, Ambrose had taken a much younger lover, and then he'd gone and died on her, leaving her alone in a ramshackle house? Yes, that sounded plausible.

If he'd been a better man, perhaps he might have felt some sympathy for her, but he *wasn't* a better man, nor did he aspire to be one. Whoever she was, she had no one to blame for her current predicament but herself. He'd save his sympathies for those who didn't cause their own problems with poor judgment.

She held out her hand. "The letter, sir, if you please."

He placed the scrap of paper in her hand, still taking care not to make any sudden movements. She might have an angel's face, but given the ease with which she wielded that pistol, the celestial began and ended there.

The letter was a paltry thing, one line only.

Come to Fairford, and claim your treasure.

It was characteristically cryptic, but then Ambrose had always had a flair for the dramatic. He never did a thing plainly, but surely there was only one way to interpret such a message? After all these years—a decade of offers of outrageous sums of money, and when that failed, threats, scheming, and bribes—at long last, Ambrose had decided to just hand Hammond Court over to him.

Rather surprising, as he hadn't shown the least qualm in stealing it in the first place, but perhaps his conscience had got the better of him, in the end. Such things tended to happen when a man was on his deathbed.

"Grantham."

He jerked his attention back to the nymph—that is, the chit with the pistol. She'd turned the letter over and was studying the direction.

"Yes. I'm Grantham. The Duke of Grantham," he added, rather unnecessarily. Everyone in England knew who he was. "I'm certain Ambrose must have mentioned me."

"Grantham," she repeated, staring down at the paper in her hands as if she couldn't quite believe what she was seeing. "His Grace, the Tenth Duke of Grantham."

"As I said." Good God, was the girl simple? "I do hope you're not going to claim you've never heard of me." He may not have set foot in this godforsaken corner of England in fifteen years, but there wasn't a single soul in the cursed village of Fairford who didn't know the name Grantham.

Knew it, and remembered, just as he did.

One never forgot where they came from, no matter how much they might wish to. You couldn't escape your past. It held you fast, like a butterfly pinned to a board.

She continued to gaze at him, her face giving nothing away.

"I think you know precisely who I am, madam, and why I'm here." Max rose to his feet, weary of her games. "Nineteen years ago, Ambrose St. Claire stole Hammond Court from my family, and I'm here to take it back."

* * *

Grantham. God above, Maxwell Burke, the Duke of Grantham, here at Hammond Court.

Ambrose hadn't merely mentioned this man, he'd *warned* her about him, on numerous occasions, most notably on the day he died. "I know who you are, Your Grace."

She'd known him forever, hadn't she? For as long as she could remember, Ambrose had spoken of him in a tone he seemed to reserve for Maxwell Burke alone, one of regret, fondness, affection, and resentment all at once.

A lost soul, Ambrose had called him, but the duke didn't look lost to *her*. He'd found his way through the front door of Hammond Court and into her house easily enough, hadn't he?

They'd seen their fair share of uninvited guests since Ambrose's passing, but none so brazen as the Duke of Grantham. Ambrose's creditors had been nasty enough, but they had at least contented themselves with pounding on the door and shouting curses at the windows, their hands fisted and threats on their lips. None of them had dared to attack her door, and then stroll into her kitchen as cool as you please, as if they had every right to be here.

Only a duke would be so shameless as that, so certain he wouldn't be held to account for his behavior. It was a wonder he hadn't plopped down at her kitchen table with a plate of biscuits and a cup of tea.

She eyed him. He'd risen to his feet despite her warning to remain seated and was lounging against the kitchen table as if he hadn't a care in the world. Dear God, the gall of the man! He was practically daring her to shoot him. Her wrists ached from the weight of the pistol, but she held it steady in clenched fingers, the grip tucked tightly against her palm.

She'd known he'd come, sooner or later, but she thought she'd have more time.

Ambrose was hardly cold in his grave, yet here was the duke, tall and broad and expensive, his shoulders nearly as wide as the doorway behind him, his head a mere foot from the heavy beams in the ceilings.

How could she not have known at once who he was? Ambrose's creditors were plain men with aprons under their serviceable coats, not sleek, elegant creatures like the one before her, with his gleaming dark hair, maddeningly perfect aristocratic nose, and gold watch chain dangling from the pocket of his richly embroidered silk waistcoat.

"Ah," he murmured. "I see Ambrose *did* mention me. You've gone quite pale." He pulled a chair away from the table. "Perhaps you'd better sit down. May I help you to a chair?"

She resisted the urge to back away from him, to throw the pistol at him, to turn and flee. Instead, she raised her chin, even as a tremor drifted down her spine at that cold, gray gaze. "Tell me, Your Grace. Is it now considered acceptable for a duke to enter a private home without so much as a by-your-leave? Have the laws of England changed without my knowing of it?"

One dark eyebrow rose. "Not that I'm aware, no."

"Then you do not, in fact, have any right to be here at all." Her voice was shaking, but only a little. "As that is the case, I must insist once again that you take your leave."

"We're back to this, are we?" His mouth curved in an amiable smile. "Come now, madam. You're not going to shoot a duke. I believe the Crown frowns upon that sort of thing."

"I believe the Crown also frowns upon strange men accosting defenseless young ladies in their homes." Especially men the size of the Duke of Grantham, whose sheer magnitude made her perfectly serviceable kitchen feel as if it belonged in a doll's house.

Why, the man's legs alone seemed to stretch for miles.

His gaze moved from the muzzle of the pistol to her face. "You're hardly defenseless. Still, if you did intend to shoot me, you'd have done so by now. Come now, madam. I mean you no harm. May we not sit down, and have a cup of tea?"

So polite, so charming. Ambrose had told her he would be.

Ambrose's voice had warmed with affection when he spoke of the Tenth Duke of Grantham, but he'd also taken care to caution her about the man. He'd told her the duke would present himself as an old friend of his, and thus as a friend of hers, and while that wasn't a lie, precisely—not quite—neither could she entirely trust him. He'd told her over and over again to be extremely cautious when it came to the Duke of Grantham.

What he *hadn't* said was that he'd summoned the duke here himself.

That letter the duke had produced—or the scrawled note, more accurately—she'd never laid eyes on it before, but there was no mistaking Ambrose's messy, slanting scrawl. He'd written it. He'd summoned Grantham to Fairford with a cryptic invitation to "seize his treasure."

What could he have meant? There was, alas, a shocking lack of treasure to seize at Hammond Court, unless one considered a mountain of debt a treasure.

The only thing of any value was the property itself, but surely Ambrose couldn't have meant for the Duke of Grantham to have Hammond Court. Why, the duke's country seat was a mere five or six miles from here, and a grander, more ducal residence she couldn't imagine.

What did the duke want with Hammond Court, when he had Grantham Lodge?

But why, then, would Ambrose lure the Duke of Grantham from London to Fairford with false promises of treasure? She couldn't begin to imagine, but Ambrose did have his secrets, and while she'd never known a kinder, more generous man than he, there was no denying this was just the sort of mystery he would have delighted in.

Whatever the reason, the duke was here, rather like a plague of locusts, and for all that she'd just as soon send him to the devil with a pistol ball to the head, the cursed man was right about one thing.

Ambrose had brought him here, and he must have had a reason to do so.

"I don't believe you've told me your name, madam.

Now that you know mine, it seems only fair I should know yours in return."

"I think not, Your Grace. You won't be here long enough to use it, in any case." She had no intention of telling him her name, no matter how sneakily he tried to squeeze the information out of her.

"In what capacity did you serve Ambrose? You don't look much like a maidservant to me." He cocked his head, studying her with cool silver eyes. "Were you his paramour?"

Paramour! Before she could stop it, an incredulous laugh burst from her lips. For pity's sake, Ambrose was—had been—three decades her senior! But then that sort of thing happened all the time within the aristocracy, with fathers sacrificing daughters scarcely out of pinafores on the altar of their ambitions.

But she wasn't about to explain herself to the Duke of Grantham. The less he knew about her, the better. "I'm afraid I must insist you be on your way, Your Grace." She gestured toward the kitchen door with her chin. "Now."

She waited, the only sound the drip of water falling into the pail she'd set under a leak in the adjacent still-room, yet the odious man didn't move. Dear God, was she really going to have to shoot him? She didn't fancy it at all, but perhaps a graze to his leg might convince him to—

"Very well, if you insist on it. Might I have my letter back?" He held out his hand.

Dash it, she was hoping she might get a better look at it, but she had no right to keep it. "Of course."

She held it out to him. His fingertips grazed the edge

of the paper, but then with the speed of a striking snake he seized her wrist, and with one quick tug, jerked her off balance. "Oh!" She stumbled into him, and for an instant they both froze, the long, hard lines of his body pressed against hers before they both shifted at once.

She scrambled backward in a panicked attempt to put some distance between them, but he held her fast, his gloved fingers wrapped around her wrist, and—no, *not* her wrist, but the barrel of the pistol! He was trying to snatch it from her hand!

A scream swelled in her throat, but it didn't make it past her lips before a deafening blast rent the air, the resounding crack bouncing off the walls of the kitchen, echoing long after the ball lodged itself . . . somewhere.

Dear God, had she actually *shot* him? Or had the gun discharged accidentally? Oh, she didn't know! She stared down at the gun in her hand, at the thin cloud of smoke drifting from the end of the barrel. The acrid stench of gunpowder filled her nose, and yet . . .

The duke was still standing upright. There weren't any massive holes in his person, and he still held her wrist, his grip too firm for a man whose lifeblood was gushing from a gaping wound.

The floor, alas, hadn't fared as well. The floorboards a mere hair's breadth from his foot were now a mess of pulverized wood. She wrenched her arm, struggling to loosen his grip. He released her at once, and she fell back a step, her heart racing. "My God, are you *mad*? I might have shot you!"

"You *did* shoot, madam. It seems I was wrong about that, after all." He eyed her calmly, smiling as if a young lady fired upon him every day, and he found it all terribly amusing. "Fortunately, you're a dreadful shot. Still, you've got more nerve than I gave you credit for."

This close, she could see his gray eyes were as cold as the ocean during a northern winter. He might smile as charmingly as he pleased with that handsome mouth, but his eyes told the story of who he was. "I do indeed, Your Grace. Enough nerve to fire a second time."

"Very well, madam. You've made yourself perfectly clear. I'll be on my way." He ambled toward the door, his body loose and his stride careless, for all the world as if he didn't have a pistol aimed at the back of his head.

But when he reached the door, he turned. "Until we meet again, madam." He offered her an elegant bow, but this time, there was no humor in those frigid gray depths. "You can be certain it will be soon."

Then he turned and vanished through the door and up the stairs, the thud of his expensive Hessians against the floor fading as he neared the entryway. The front door creaked open, and a few moments later a carriage door slammed shut.

Once he was gone, and the clop of the horses' hooves had faded to silence, she slid down the wall at her back until she was sitting on the floor, her legs splayed out in front of her, her knuckles white around Ambrose's pistol.

Her head fell against the wall behind her with a soft thud, her entire body shaking.

The hole she'd blasted in the floor was nearly as big as her closed fist. It would be the devil to patch it up, but at this point, what was one more hole?

That was the least of her worries, now.

CHAPTER 4

She'd *shot* at Maxwell Burke. Fired upon a peer of the realm. Not a baron, or a viscount, or even an earl. An earl would have been bad enough, but *no*, nothing would do for her but to fire upon a duke.

Indeed, he'd made it impossible *not* to shoot at him, and it wasn't as if she'd hit him. Surely, that counted for something?

But then he wasn't just any duke, either, but the Duke of Grantham. The Duke of Grantham, a man who'd ruined more aristocrats than Hammond Court had spiders, and goodness knew one couldn't stir a step in this house without one of the crawly, eight-legged creatures scampering over one's toes.

Even the Prince Regent himself was said to be terrified of the Duke of Grantham.

If one must shoot at a duke, Grantham was the very last one in England one should choose. But it was too late now. She'd nearly blasted a hole through the toe of that glossy boot of his, to say nothing of the foot underneath.

She'd made an enemy of him. A tidy morning's work, that.

She gripped the edge of the table and heaved herself to her feet, but what had once been her perfectly sturdy skeletal system had abandoned her, and her entire body was now wobbling like a blancmange. Her knees were the first to give up the ghost, deserting her with such suddenness she toppled into one of the chairs with an undignified squeak.

Her heart was battering like a wild thing against her ribs, her stomach was turning somersaults, and her head was dizzy with delayed shock, but there was no time to waste. Abby would have heard the pistol shot, and she'd be in a panic by now.

Rose's breath wheezed in and out of her lungs as she scrambled up the back staircase to the third floor, either from the exertion, or the shock of nearly shooting a duke—she couldn't have said which.

She couldn't have said much of anything at that moment, but she regained her tongue quickly enough when she burst onto the third-floor landing and nearly ran straight into Abby, who was creeping toward the stairs with a hairbrush in one hand, and a pillow clutched to her chest with the other. "A shot. I h-heard a pistol shot."

"I know, I know." Rose held out her hands in a calming gesture. "But it's all right, Abby, I promise you."

"All right? How can it be all right?" Abby brandished the hairbrush in her fist. "Is he still downstairs? I'll teach him not to darken our doorstep again, I will!"

"With a hairbrush? What do you intend to do, groom him to death?" Rose glanced at the pillow, and a hysterical laugh leaped unbidden from her throat. "Then tuck him into bed?"

"Knock him about the head, then smother him, more like."

"I wouldn't advise it. He's quite large, and quicker than he looks." It was rather unfair that a man of that size should have such distressingly speedy reflexes.

"God above, Rose." Abby sagged against the wall, the pillow sliding from her slack fingers. "I thought you'd been *shot*."

"No. I, ah, I was the one doing the shooting." Was that better, or worse?

Worse, because Abby went such a strange gray color Rose rushed toward her and caught her before she fell into a swoon. "Here, perhaps you'd better sit down." She steered Abby from the corridor into the bedchamber, and across the room to the bed.

"Who did you shoot?" Abby grabbed her hand. "Please tell me there's not a dead body downstairs that needs burying."

"Not a single one." Though it had admittedly been a near thing. If the duke had shifted even a scant half foot to the right . . . well, it had been a remarkably foolish thing for him to do, attempting to seize the pistol as he had, and it would have served him right if he had ended up dead. Still, it was a blessing she hadn't shot him, as no one wanted to start their day with a dead duke in their kitchen. "I didn't shoot *at* him, just, er, *near* him."

"Him? Who?" Abby was still clutching at Rose's

hand, her knuckles white. "Don't tell me you've shot at Mr. Turnbull?"

Mr. Turnbull was one of the shopkeepers in town. They'd run up quite a debt with him over the past year, and the man hadn't been patient about collecting it. Not that patience would have done him any good. One couldn't squeeze blood from a stone.

"It wasn't Mr. Turnbull." Which was rather a pity, as it would have been a great deal simpler if it had been.

"Who, then?"

"Er, well . . ." Rose bit her lip. She didn't want Abby involved in this mess, but how did one hide having nearly shot a duke? The entire village would know of it soon enough, and the duke would no doubt have the magistrate upon them before they'd even had their morning tea. "Well, as I said, I didn't actually shoot—"

"*Who*, Rose? Who was it?"

"I gave him a dozen chances to leave before I fired, but he—"

"Rosamund Elizabeth St. Claire, you will tell me the truth at once! Who did you nearly murder in our kitchen?"

Rose squeezed her eyes closed. "The Duke of Grantham."

Silence. She opened one eye, then wished she hadn't.

Abby was staring at her in horror. "The Duke of Grantham! Oh, dear God, Rose."

"What else was I to do? He broke into the house! I ordered him to leave ever so many times, but he refused! And he attacked our door!"

"Do calm down, Rose—"

"It's not as if I *intended* to shoot at him, Abby! He tried to snatch my pistol out of my hand, and it went off, completely of its own accord! I assure you, he left in full possession of all of his bits and pieces, and with the same arrogant swagger with which he entered."

Oddly, the shot hadn't appeared to frighten or humble him in the least. It was as if he thought a pistol ball wouldn't dare to strike the Duke of Grantham.

Perhaps he was right. It was astonishing that ball hadn't hit him.

Or *her*, come to that.

Dash it, there went her knees, wobbling again. "He's going to come back, Abby. He said as much before he left." He wouldn't come alone, either. No doubt he had dozens of burly footmen awaiting his orders at Grantham Lodge, all of them prepared to knock down doors and shatter windows on the duke's command.

"He'll be sorry if he does!" Abby brandished the hairbrush and waved it about threateningly as if daring the Duke of Grantham to come anywhere near her horsehair bristles. "But why should be come back? What does the Duke of Grantham want with us?"

With them? Not a thing. The duke hadn't come to Fairford for *them*.

He'd come for Hammond Court. She and Abby were no more important to him than the spiderwebs dangling from the cornices in the drawing room. Something to be dealt with, to be swept aside, and never again given a second thought. "He wants Hammond Court, Abby."

Which was rather a problem, considering they had no place else to go.

Indeed, their problems were piling up faster than she could solve them. It wasn't enough that Hammond Court was tumbling down around their ears. Every day dawned with another new crack in a window, a new leak in the roof, or a new rut in the front drive, and that was to say nothing of the battered front door and the sizable hole in the kitchen floor.

If that hadn't been enough to drive her to despair, now they also had an angry, vindictive duke who appeared to have come all the way from London for the pleasure of seeing them tossed out into the snow.

Banished, from the only home she'd ever known.

Worse, he might just have the means to do it.

That note he'd shown her was no counterfeit. She'd know Ambrose's hand anywhere. If he'd sent that note—and it appeared as if he had—the twisted game Ambrose and the Duke of Grantham had been playing for the past two decades might not yet be over.

If it had only been the note, she might have been able to convince herself nothing would come of the duke's threats, but there was something else, as well.

In the hours before he died, Ambrose had made a desperate effort to tell her something—something about Hammond Court, and the Duke of Grantham. He'd been so weak by then, all she'd been able to gather from his frantic mutterings was that the duke would come here once Ambrose was dead and that he'd try to . . .

Well, she hadn't any idea what he'd try to do. Ambrose had tried to tell her, but he'd been too incoherent for her to make sense of his ramblings. She'd understood only that the duke would try to do something, or take something, and that she must do everything in her power to stop him.

Then, before she could say a word, Ambrose had lapsed into unconsciousness, and he'd never woken again. There'd been no time to ask him anything—no time even to squeeze his hand.

He'd taken one last gasping breath, and then he was gone.

Now here was the Duke of Grantham not even a week later, note in hand, strolling about the house as if it already belonged to him.

"Hammond Court? But that's absurd, Rose! I'm sure the Duke of Grantham fancies himself an important personage indeed, but even he can't simply appear on the doorstep and order people from their homes."

No, not under ordinary circumstances, but when had Ambrose ever done anything in the ordinary way? He'd always been a gamester, a magician, a man who delighted in sleight of hand. He might yet have one final card up his sleeve. Was it so difficult to imagine he intended to play it from beyond the grave?

"Rose?"

"Of course, he can't, Abby." Rose patted Abby's hand, but a thousand misgivings were crowding into her head at once. There was something amiss here. She could feel it. "Still, I think it might be wise of us to send for Sir Richard and see if he can provide some illumination on the subject."

Sir Richard Mildmay was Ambrose's oldest and dearest friend and the executor of his will. He'd urged her more than once this past week to sit down with him to go over Ambrose's papers—but the weather had turned foul, and between the leaking roof and damp floorboards, she hadn't had a spare moment.

So, she'd put it off. Now it was beginning to look as if that had been a mistake.

A grave one.

"Yes, that makes sense." Abby straightened her shoulders. "Very well, then, we'll summon Sir Richard, and see if he can make sense of it, but you must promise me something first, Rose."

"Of course, Abby. Anything."

"If the Duke of Grantham does come back here, promise me you won't shoot him."

Rose snorted and squeezed Abby's hand. "Not a single shot. I swear it."

Goodness knew they were in enough trouble already without her firing upon the Duke of Grantham.

Again.

No matter how tempting it might be.

CHAPTER 5

A sound night's sleep was meant to reassert one's nobler nature, to push back into place whatever higher principles had been knocked askew the day before. Max was meant to wake in the morning refreshed, the cobwebs cleared from his mind, a better man than he'd been the day before.

Or some such bollocks as that.

He was as wicked today as he'd been yesterday, his heart as black and shriveled as it had ever been. He hadn't forgiven that fair-haired chit—whose bloody name he *still* didn't know—for nearly blowing his foot to bits, nor was he any less determined to have his way in the end.

So, when he called Townsend, his land steward, into his study after he'd breakfasted, he was in no mood for prevarication. "Some murderous vixen has tucked herself into Hammond Court tighter than a mouse in a hole. It's *my* house, and I want her out, Townsend, as quickly as the thing can be managed."

Townsend blinked. "Murderous vixen? Does this, er, murderous vixen have a name, Your Grace?"

"I presume so, Townsend. Most people do." Max cast the man a withering look over the top edge of his spectacles. "Damned if I know what it is, though, and neither do I care."

"Of course not. Only this vixen, Your Grace. Is she a young lady, with fair hair, and green eyes?"

Yes, that was her. He'd thought he was dreaming when that delicate, sylphlike creature had emerged from the shadows with an enormous dueling pistol clutched in her slender fingers. It had been the strangest moment, so incongruous he'd had a wild urge to laugh.

Of course, that was before she'd shot at him. Or shot near him, at least. Far too near for comfort. The hearing in his right ear might be permanently damaged.

It all became a great deal less amusing, then.

"Is she about this tall, Your Grace?" Townsend held a hand up to his shoulder.

"For God's sake, Townsend, I didn't measure her, nor did I sketch her likeness, but yes, that sounds like her."

"Yes, Your Grace. The trouble, Your Grace, is that she's not a murderous vixen at all, but rather—"

"Ambrose's *chère amie* if I don't miss my mark."

Townsend gasped. "Oh, no, Your Grace! That's not—"

"The lady has dreadful taste in lovers if you ask me. Get rid of her, Townsend."

As far as Ambrose's paramour was concerned, he was only interested in one thing, and that was how to expel her from his house, but God only knew how many other guns she had hidden on the premises. He refused to get drawn into an armed standoff with a young lady who looked like a bit of dandelion fluff.

He was a duke, damn it. It wasn't dignified.

"Well, you see, Your Grace, it might prove to be a trifle more difficult to toss her out than you anticipate." Townsend turned his hat in his hands. "The young lady you describe sounds very much like—"

"I don't see what's so difficult about it. If she gives you any trouble—and I warn you, Townsend, she *is* armed—then a discreet application of funds should solve the matter. I'll leave it to you to decide how best to go about it, but make it quick, man. I expect you to report back to me this afternoon to confirm she's gone." Max bent over the papers scattered across his desk, waving his hand in a vague dismissal.

Townsend said nothing, only stood in front of the desk shuffling his feet until at last Max looked up. "For God's sake, Townsend, why are you still here? Get on with it, will you?"

"Yes, Your Grace, but the vixen . . . that is, the young lady, Your Grace. She's not Ambrose St. Claire's paramour. She's his daughter."

Max froze, his fingers going slack around his quill. "That's impossible. Ambrose doesn't have a daughter."

Townsend gave him a pained look. "I beg your pardon, Your Grace, but I'm quite sure the young lady you saw at Hammond Court is Miss Rose St. Claire, Mr. St. Claire's adopted daughter."

"*Adopted* daughter?" He didn't like the sound of this. Not at all. "What the devil are you on about, Townsend?"

Townsend lowered his voice, the tips of his ears turning pink. "As to that, Your Grace, it seems . . . well, I don't like to talk out of turn, but if the gossips are to be believed, Miss St. Claire is the illegitimate daughter of Mr. St. Claire's former cook. The woman passed away some nine years ago, but Miss St. Claire has remained at Hammond Court ever since, in a sort of, er . . . daughterly capacity."

Max stared up at Townsend, speechless. Ambrose had taken in some brat born on the wrong side of the blanket? How the devil had the man managed to keep *that* little morsel out of the gossips' mouths? He prided himself on knowing everything there was to know about his enemies, but he'd never heard a soul breathe a single word about this Miss St. Claire before.

Then again, Ambrose had always been a cagey devil. He'd had dozens of secrets, and he knew how to keep them. "So, what you're telling me, Townsend, is that Miss St. Claire does in fact have a right to be at Hammond Court?"

Townsend nodded, his Adam's apple bobbing miserably in his throat.

That spastically bobbing Adam's apple didn't bode well. Not well at all.

"She's, ah, well, I don't like to be the bearer of bad news, Your Grace—"

"Come, Townsend." Max dropped his pen onto the desk and leaned back in his chair, gesturing to Townsend to continue. "Let's have it out, shall we?"

"Yes, Your Grace." Townsend cleared his throat. "Miss St. Claire is the beneficiary of Mr. St. Claire's fortune. Not that there's much of a fortune to speak of, you understand, Your Grace, but I'm afraid there's rather a strong chance Hammond Court belongs to her now."

Belonged to *her*? Hammond Court, his family's legacy, his mother's childhood home belonged to that tiny menace of a chit who'd tried to shoot him yesterday? No, it was impossible. Ambrose himself had summoned him to Fairford, and there'd been nothing ambiguous about that note.

Except . . . *claim your treasure*. There'd been no mention of what treasure that might be, or how he was meant to claim it.

Damn it, it *was* bloody ambiguous, wasn't it?

But what could Ambrose have meant by *treasure*, if not Hammond Court? God knew there wasn't a single thing Max wanted in Fairford, aside from that house. Was this just another of Ambrose's pranks, then? A final move in the game they'd been playing for years, the last twist of the blade?

He tore off his spectacles, his fingers tightening around them until he nearly snapped them in half.

Damn. This was a disaster.

He tossed the bent spectacles on his desk, pinching the bridge of his nose between his fingers. "You're quite sure about this, Townsend?"

"Reasonably sure, Your Grace. All of Fairford has been talking about it. It's just gossip, of course, but gossip in Fairford generally turns out to be true." Townsend sighed. "That grand house, Your Grace, and poor Miss St. Claire all alone in it."

Ah, so it was poor, lonely Miss St. Claire, was it?

Max rolled his eyes. "I can assure you, Townsend, that Miss St. Claire is perfectly capable of taking care of herself."

"Yes, Your Grace, but that house is quite a burden for such a young lady." Townsend shook his head. "The whole thing is likely to collapse around her ears before the winter's out."

Yes, that was true, wasn't it? The house was a catastrophe waiting to happen. It wasn't surprising, really, given it had been in Ambrose's possession for nearly two decades. He'd always been careless with his things.

Houses, windows, gardens, doorknobs.

Friendships.

And now his daughter, as well.

It would cost a fortune to make Hammond Court habitable again—a fortune Miss St. Claire didn't possess—and that was to say nothing of the upkeep required.

Far better just to tear the thing down and be done with it.

Even if it had been in proper condition, what was a young, unmarried lady like Miss St. Claire going to do with such an enormous house? She couldn't hope to make proper use of it.

Perhaps all wasn't lost, after all. The girl likely only wanted money, and he had plenty of that. A flash of guineas, and the house would be his. Once he had it in his possession, he'd see her sent on her way quickly enough.

"Your Grace?" There was a knock on his study door,

and his housekeeper poked her head inside. "I beg your pardon, Your Grace, but I have a note here for you."

"A note? From who, Mrs. Watson?" No one in Fairford knew he was here, and even if they had, they were likely to keep well away from him, unscrupulous London dukes not being quite the thing in a rustic little village like Fairford.

"The boy didn't say." Mrs. Watson approached the desk and handed him the note. "Will that be all, Your Grace?"

"Hmm? Oh, yes." He waved Mrs. Watson away, his attention already on the paper in his hand. His name was written on the front in an elegant, flowing script, quite pretty, and certainly feminine.

There was only one lady in Fairford who knew he was here.

No, surely not.

But if not her, then who? He ripped open the note with an odd twist of . . . something in his chest. Not anticipation. Certainly not *that*. Irritation, perhaps. Yes, that was what that twinge under his breastbone was.

Irritation.

The note was one line only, an invitation for him to call on her at Hammond Court at his earliest convenience. He stared down at it for a moment, then folded it, slipped it into his pocket, and rose from his chair.

There was no sense in putting it off. He'd wasted two decades on this business already, and he was ready to be done with it. Done with Ambrose, with Fairford, and with Hammond Court and all the memories lurking inside those crumbling walls. "Come along, Townsend."

"Yes, Your Grace. Er, where are we going, Your Grace?"

Max grabbed the coat he'd draped over the back of his chair. "Miss St. Claire has summoned us to Hammond Court."

"Has she, indeed? I would have thought you'd be the last person she—" Townsend broke off, clearing his throat. "I mean, that's a bit curious, is it not, Your Grace?"

"Rather, yes." The note had appeared innocent enough, but then so did Miss St. Claire with those big green eyes of hers, and she'd nearly shot him in the foot yesterday.

What was the chit up to this time? Nothing good, that much was certain. He unlocked the bottom drawer of his desk and retrieved the pistol he kept there.

Townsend's eyes widened. "Your Grace?"

"You can never be too careful, Townsend." He didn't intend to shoot the chit, of course, but Miss St. Claire had proved herself a worthy opponent yesterday. An unmanageable bit of baggage as well, of course, but worthy, all the same.

The lady needed to be made to understand that he wasn't trifling with her.

Hammond Court was *his*, and he would have it, even if it meant crushing a bit of dandelion fluff under his boot on his way through the door.

By the time they arrived at Hammond Court, it was snowing again. Not the light, fluffy flakes from this morning, but a wet, heavy snow layered on top of the morning's ice. Max trudged up the drive, Townsend at his heels, icy water dampening the toes of his boots as he made his way over the ruts that led to the front door.

He'd need a new pair of Hessians after this. His tassels would never recover from such a dousing, and that was to say nothing of what had once been a perfectly serviceable beaver hat.

Townsend paused partway up the drive, staring up at the house. "Goodness, it's in a state, is it not, Your Grace? It's rather a lot to manage, and poor Miss St. Claire without any servants now."

"No servants?" Surely Miss St. Claire wasn't living here alone, without a single servant to protect her? Not that it mattered a whit to him, of course, except the pistol made a great deal more sense now. He must have frightened the wits out of her when he battered his way inside yesterday.

"None but her old nursemaid, Abigail Hinde, but poor Abby is well on in years, Your Grace, and a trifle lame now. One of the village lads, Billy Lucas, pops around here now and again, as well. He's a good lad, is Billy, but he's young yet. I doubt either of them is much help to Miss St. Claire." Townsend frowned up at the silent façade. "Such a pretty house as it once was, too. Now it looks as if it's been abandoned."

Yes, he'd thought the same when he'd come yesterday and found the house all dark and silent, and without a flicker of movement behind the windows. But the next thing he knew, he'd been staring at the deadly end of a pistol.

No doubt Miss St. Claire was watching them at this very moment, plotting her next move. He peered up at the windows, shielding his eyes from the snowflakes, but the windows stared back at him like a row of glassy blank eyes, revealing nothing.

"What's happened here?" Townsend pointed at the door Max had assaulted yesterday morning. The knob he'd kicked loose was nowhere to be seen, and in its place, a rather feeble-looking rope had been strung through the gaping hole, and presumably fastened to something inside to hold the door closed. "This is a disgrace, this is."

Good Lord. Perhaps he might have been a trifle less aggressive.

"This isn't right, Your Grace." Townsend picked at a bit of shredded wood where the knob had once been, his face darkening. "Why, any scoundrel or thief who happened by here could be inside her house with one quick slice of a blade through that rope there."

An unpleasant emotion uncurled in Max's stomach. Regret? No, it was something more, something worse, something closer to shame, or one of those other useless emotions, the sort he didn't generally indulge.

Nor would he do so now, only . . . well, he'd never broken into a house. Perhaps kicking down a young lady's door was a bit much even for his neglected conscience.

What had become of the doorknob? If Miss St. Claire had fetched it, why hadn't she repaired the door? It had been left that way overnight, for God's sake. Townsend was right. Any scoundrel in Fairford might have strode right in while she slept.

He wandered around the top of the drive, kicking at the snow until he spotted the rusted corner of the door plate, then the knob itself a short distance away. He leaned down, snatched them up, and slipped them into his greatcoat pocket.

Townsend raised an eyebrow. "Your Grace?"

"I'll send one of the footmen to see to it." Miss St. Claire was a troublesome chit, but she didn't deserve to die in her bed at the whim of some villain.

He raised his hand to knock on what was left of the door, but before his fist met the wood there was a muted shuffle of footsteps, and a moment later the rope loosened. He peered around the side of the door, and there, the piece of rope dangling from her hand and a tranquil smile on her face, stood Miss St. Claire.

CHAPTER 6

The wild sprite Max had encountered yesterday morning had disappeared.

The young lady who answered the door today was wearing a somber, dark green day dress. Her fair hair had been pulled back into a severe bun, but a handful of wayward locks had escaped their prison and were waving about her head in an untamed profusion of golden fluff, rather like a halo.

At least, he *might* have thought so, if she hadn't nearly shot him less than twenty-four hours ago. There was, thankfully, no sign of the pistol today, but Miss St. Claire was no angel. He'd do well to remember that when she was smiling at him as she was right now, with those long, dark eyelashes, and rosebud pink lips.

"Good afternoon, Your Grace, Mr. Townsend."

"How do you do, Miss St. Claire?" Townsend smiled and offered her a bow.

"I'm a trifle the worse for wear today, Mr. Townsend, but I daresay I'll survive. It's good of you to come so quickly, Your Grace." She stood back from the doorway, gesturing them inside. "Do come in, won't you?"

"So gracious, Miss St. Claire." Max made his way over the threshold, Townsend on his heels. "I'd hardly know you as the same lady who nearly put a pistol ball in my foot yesterday morning."

"You entered my home without an invitation yesterday morning, Your Grace, and as you can see, my door is rather the worse for wear for it." She didn't look at him, but busied herself with the rope, looping it back through the hole and tying the other end around the banister. "I'd just as soon keep it from suffering the same fate again today. One needs one's door during the winters in Fairford. It's rather cold out, you see."

Townsend cast him a horrified look. "*You* broke down Miss St. Claire's door?"

Heat rushed into Max's cheeks. Damn it, he'd been hoping that wouldn't come up. "I didn't intend to cause any . . . I thought the house was abandoned."

Townsend stared at him for an instant, mouth agape, then quickly schooled his features into bland expressionlessness. "Of course, Your Grace. I'm certain anyone else would have smashed the door to bits, had they been in your place."

For all Townsend's deference, the man had rather a knack for making him look a proper arse, didn't he? "I beg your pardon for my unexpected appearance here yesterday morning, Miss St. Claire. I assure you I don't make a habit of breaking down strangers' doors. I truly didn't think the house was occupied."

Miss St. Claire had not, it seemed, expected an apology from him. Her eyebrows rose, and she blinked up at him with those clear, green eyes. The chit had the most damnably innocent face he'd ever seen. No doubt more than one gentleman had been taken in by that face, that winsome smile.

Not *him*, of course, but other, less cautious gentlemen.

"Your apology is accepted, Your Grace. Perhaps the less said about yesterday's unfortunate incident, the better." She led them from the entryway down the hallway, still strangely familiar to him, even after all these years. If one discounted the peeling wallpaper and threadbare carpets, that is.

"The drawing room is rather chilly in the mornings, I'm afraid." She turned from the hallway into a drafty drawing room with worn draperies at the windows. "I believe you're acquainted with Sir Richard, Mr. Townsend."

A diminutive gentleman with a kind face and neatly brushed brown hair rose from a seat near the fireplace. "It's a pleasure to see you again, Mr. Townsend."

Townsend nodded. "Good day, Sir Richard."

"Your Grace, this is Sir Richard Mildmay. Sir Richard, this is the Duke of Grantham." Miss St. Claire settled into a chair beside a table where a tea tray had been set out. "Sir Richard is the executor of my father's— that is, Mr. St. Claire's will, Your Grace."

Max had been about to seat himself on a rather dusty-looking settee, but he froze halfway down, his arse hovering over the cushions. "Executor?"

Sir Richard nodded. "Yes, indeed. How do you do, Your Grace?"

How did he *do*? Well, that depended on what Sir Richard had to say, didn't it? "I wasn't aware Mr. St.

Claire had left a will. I was given to understand his death was rather sudden. A fall down the stairs, I believe?"

"The fall precipitated his untimely end, yes." Sir Richard took a sip of his tea, then set the cup aside with a sigh. "Dreadfully unfortunate, as anyone who had the pleasure of Mr. St. Claire's acquaintance must agree."

Not everyone, but Max kept that thought to himself.

"It was a lung complaint that took him off in the end," Sir Richard went on. "It's not uncommon, Your Grace, for patients who suffer paralysis to struggle with subsequent infections of the lungs, or so the doctor informed us."

Paralysis? Dear God. He was no friend of Ambrose St. Claire's—he'd wanted him dead for decades if the truth were known—yet he wouldn't wish such an awful death on anyone. Not even, as it turned out, his worst enemy. "He lost the use of his limbs?"

Oddly, Max found himself addressing this question to Miss St. Claire, but she was intent on rearranging the tea tray, and it was Sir Richard who answered him. "I'm afraid so, yes."

"I see." Did he really, though? Could anyone who hadn't experienced it truly understand what it was like to lose someone in the blink of an eye? His mother had suffered a long illness before her death, and his father's death had hardly been a surprise. He'd died long before his body had expired.

For an instant, it was as if something heavy had fallen on his chest, but he took a deep breath and shook it off. It was a tragic tale, certainly, but there were some who might insist Ambrose had reaped what he'd sown, in the end.

"There's no money to speak of, Your Grace," Sir Richard went on. "Mr. St. Claire's will addresses the matter of the house and property only."

Max didn't give a damn about the money. Whatever coins Ambrose had managed to scrape together were sure to be no more than the merest pittance to him. Miss St. Claire was welcome to all of it. Hammond Court was the only thing that mattered to him.

"As for the estate, as you can see, Your Grace, it's sadly diminished." Sir Richard waved a hand around the drawing room, indicating the meager fire and the tattered furnishings. "Mr. St. Claire's business sustained some unfortunate losses over the past few years. What little money there was disappeared rather quickly, and most of the servants along with it."

That was hardly surprising. Ambrose had been a gamester by profession, and he'd never made the sort of fortune necessary to maintain a house like Hammond Court. Even if he hadn't been injured in a fall, the house likely would have gone to ruin. It had been the height of foolishness for him to wager against Max's father for it in the first place.

But Max didn't say so. He may not care much for Rose St. Claire, but he could at least pay her the courtesy of not abusing her dead, er . . . father-ish figure to her face.

"I daresay you don't realize this, Your Grace, but Mr. St. Claire greatly lamented the rift between your families. His intentions in procuring Hammond Court were pure, but—"

"Pure!" The exclamation burst from Max's lips before he had a chance to bite it back. "Do you call cheating a dearest friend out of his home *pure*, Sir Richard?"

Sir Richard stilled, his gaze resting on Max's face. "Ambrose St. Claire was no cheat, Your Grace. I'd be happy to provide you with the facts of that transaction someday when you're ready to hear them, but perhaps now isn't the best time to go into the details of the misunderstanding between him and your father."

Not now, and not ever. Miss St. Claire and Sir Richard may ascribe some selfless motive to Ambrose's actions, but he knew better. He'd known who Ambrose St. Claire was for years, since those cold, starless nights he'd spent in the dark outside Hammond Court, watching the celebrations he'd once been a part of carry on without him.

Year after year, every bloody Christmas.

There was no word to describe how he'd felt on those nights, no word that could capture such profound loneliness.

And, as the years dragged by, one after the next, such profound hatred.

"Suffice it to say, Your Grace," Sir Richard went on, "that Mr. St. Claire had his share of regrets, and wished to make amends."

Ah, now that did sound promising. Max slid to the edge of the settee, shooting a glance at Miss St. Claire.

She was no longer fussing with the tea tray. No, she was looking right at him, her face carefully blank.

But her eyes . . .

The sun had chosen that moment to struggle through the heavy clouds, and a stream of weak light found its way past the worn draperies. It fell upon her, illuminating the fine, white skin of her brow, the riot of golden curls that framed her face, and her eyes, that deep, fathomless green gone dark with some turbulent emotion he couldn't read.

Anger, perhaps, or was it grief? Before he could decipher it, the light receded, ducking back behind the clouds, and the shadows once again hid her expression.

". . . obviously cared deeply for Miss St. Claire. Blood ties notwithstanding, no one could ever have been more of a daughter to Mr. St. Claire than she was, and of course, he knew very well how much she loves this house." Sir Richard smiled sadly. "He was the one who taught her to love it."

For God's sake, at this rate they'd be here all afternoon. "Forgive me, Sir Richard, but if we might get on with it? Did Ambrose leave the house to me, or to Miss St. Claire?"

"Well, that's the issue at hand, Your Grace." Sir Richard didn't elaborate right away, instead choosing that moment to help himself to more tea, fussing about with the spoon and sugar bowl until Max was ready to explode with impatience. "It's a rather unusual division of assets. I confess I've never seen anything quite like—"

"For God's sake, man, will you just *say* it?" Except . . .

had Sir Richard said division of assets? *Division*. That seemed rather an odd word in this context, unless—

No. Dear God, no. He hadn't, had he? He *wouldn't*, would he? Without realizing it, Max had shot to his feet. "You can't possibly mean he—"

"Has left the house to you both? That's precisely what I mean, Your Grace."

Sir Richard settled back against his chair, his teacup balanced on his knee, as if he hadn't just shattered Max's world into a million tiny pieces with one sentence.

He dropped back down onto the settee, stunned, unable to utter a single word.

Nor was he the only one. The drawing room was silent. Sir Richard had returned his attention to his tea, Townsend was glancing between Max and Miss St. Claire, wringing his hands, and Miss St. Claire . . .

Was she *smiling*?

By God, she was, the corners of those pink, rosebud lips curled ever so slightly upward. Before he knew what he was about, he was on his feet again and across the room, standing over her chair. "Do you find this *amusing*, Miss St. Claire?"

She glanced up at him, surprised. "I hardly know *how* I find it, Your Grace."

"You mean to make me believe you didn't already know about this?" She was such a pretty little liar, wasn't she? "Ambrose died more than a week ago, Miss St. Claire. Do you expect me to believe you hadn't read his will before today?"

"I daresay you'll find this difficult to believe, Your Grace, but it wasn't a task I was anticipating with any pleasure, and in any case, I don't enjoy the sort of leisure afforded to an aristocrat such as yourself. I've been busy, you see, what with the recent cold snap and the snowfall, and now the broken front door. It takes rather a lot of one's time, surviving."

Sir Richard spoke up then. "I can assure you, Your Grace, that Miss St. Claire is only just now hearing the terms of the will, the same as you are. After she saw the note Mr. St. Claire sent you, she thought it only fair you both hear it at the same time."

"Oh, yes, she's every inch the fair-minded and devoted daughter, isn't she? So good, so virtuous she's contrived to steal half my house from me!"

"Your Grace!" Sir Richard gaped at him, aghast. "I'll thank you to keep a civil tongue in your head and sit down if you please. I won't have you looming over Miss St. Claire in that threatening manner."

"*Me*, threaten *her*? I'll have you know she nearly blew my foot to bits yesterday morn—"

Before he could get another word out, Miss St. Claire made a choked sound, and then, without warning, she covered her face with her hands.

"Oh, dear." Townsend jumped to his feet and hurried across the room. "There, there, Miss St. Claire," he murmured, patting her awkwardly on the shoulder. "I'm sure His Grace didn't mean—"

"Yes, I bloody did. I meant every word of it." He *had* meant it, too, but . . .

Well, perhaps he hadn't needed to shout it quite so forcefully, because now Miss St. Claire was making soft, whimpering noises, and her shoulders were shaking. Soon enough, she'd commence wailing, and that wouldn't do.

A young lady's tears were diabolical things, and enough to unman even a heartless duke like himself. "I, ah, I spoke too hastily. I beg your pardon, Miss St. Claire. I shouldn't have—"

That was as far as he got, because she dropped her hands then, and threw her head back, the oddest sound emanating from her lips. It wasn't wailing—that is, it *was* loud, and her face was as red as a peony, her pretty features distorted and tears leaking from the corners of her eyes, but it was higher in pitch, a light, joyful sound, almost like—

"Dear God, are you *laughing*?" Had the chit gone mad? "What the devil are you laughing about?"

"It's just, it's . . . it's so *Ambrose*, isn't it?" She slapped a hand over her mouth, gasping, but there was no stifling the merriment. "Why, if he could have found a way to do it, he would have divided Hammond Court right down the middle!"

Sir Richard let out a chuckle. "Ambrose never much troubled himself with convention, did he? He didn't do things the way most people do, that much is certain, and he did love a prank, did Ambrose."

"A *prank*? Is that what you call this?" For God's sake, couldn't they see this was a disaster? What the devil was he meant to do with half a house?

"Come now, Your Grace." Miss St. Claire peered up at him, her green eyes twinkling. "You must admit it's a novel solution. Ambrose was nothing if not creative."

He stared at her, flummoxed. She was part owner

of a ramshackle house that was one stiff wind away from collapsing entirely—a house she couldn't afford to repair, much less maintain, and she'd be obliged to share it with a duke who didn't find her nearly as charming as everyone else did.

Given her circumstances, Miss St. Claire didn't have much reason to be twinkling.

Then again, now he considered it, what had she really lost? She might remain at Hammond Court as long as she liked now. There wasn't a damn thing he could do about it, and now he bore partial responsibility for the burden and expenses of the place.

A neat trick, that.

Unless, of course, he decided to tear his half of the house down and leave her with the carcass. God knew it would serve Ambrose right, for putting him in this ridiculous situation.

"I'm certain you and His Grace have quite a lot to discuss. I'll take my leave now, Miss St. Claire." Sir Richard reached for her hand. "Permit me to express once again, my dear young friend, my deepest sympathies for your loss. I'll miss Ambrose dreadfully. He was a wonderful friend to me, and truly one of a kind."

Max smothered a snort. One of a kind, yes. A liar and thief in a class of his own.

"If there's anything I can do for you, Miss St. Claire, please don't hesitate to call upon me." Sir Richard gulped down the last of his tea and rose to his feet, but he paused on his way to the door to turn a stern eye on Max. "One last thing, Your Grace. The will stipulates that neither owner may threaten or coerce the other into forfeiting their share in the house."

Was tearing down half the house considered coercion?

"If either of you attempts to take the house by any nefarious means," Sir Richard added, "you will forfeit your share, and the entirety of the house will revert to the other."

"And how, Sir Richard, does one define nefarious in this context? Who decides whether an action is nefarious?" Mightn't there be a little room to bend the rules, after all?

Sir Richard plopped his hat onto his head. "I do, Your Grace."

No, no room. Not even the thinnest margin, the merest sliver of room.

Damn Ambrose. The scoundrel was likely looking up at him from his place in hell and laughing his head off.

"Good day, Miss St. Claire, Mr. Townsend." Sir Richard gave Max a grim smile. "Your Grace."

Then he was gone, and Max, Townsend, and Miss St. Claire were left gaping silently at each other, frozen in place like a trio of waxed figures, until finally, Max cleared his throat. "I wish to have a word with Miss St. Claire in private, Townsend. Wait for me in the drive."

"Yes, Your Grace." Townsend jumped to his feet with the alacrity of a man who'd slipped a noose and vanished through the drawing room door.

But once Max and Miss St. Claire were alone, he found himself at a loss for words. He knew how to order people about—his servants, the scores of gentlemen who owed him money, or were otherwise indebted to him to some degree or other, his mistresses—but when was the last time he'd *asked* someone for something?

Years. No, decades.

He'd do well to tread carefully. That pistol could make a reappearance at any time. "Perhaps it would be best if we simply got down to the business at hand, Miss St. Claire."

"Of course, Your Grace." She folded her hands in her lap, her face giving nothing away. "I'm listening."

CHAPTER 7

"Hammond Court has been in my mother's family for nearly a century, Miss St. Claire. My maternal great-great-grandfather built it, and it was my mother's childhood home. I spent the early part of my boyhood here, and I have a strong, er . . . emotional attachment to it."

Miss St. Claire said nothing. She simply waited, those clear green eyes fixed on his face, eyebrows aloft.

She might twitch those judgmental eyebrows at him all she liked, but he'd told her the truth. He *did* have a powerful emotional attachment to Hammond Court. There was no need for her to know that emotion was hatred. "I wish to have it back. *All* of it. I'm prepared to pay you handsomely for your share of it."

For a long, fraught moment she gazed at him, but then she shook her head. "I'm afraid my share of Hammond Court is not for sale, Your Grace."

"Nonsense, Miss St. Claire. Everything is for sale."

"Not this house."

"Of course, this house. It's merely a matter of agreeing on the price."

"How unsurprising you are, Your Grace. Ambrose

warned me you'd try and make this all about money, and here we are."

Money? How absurd. He didn't give a damn about the money. No, this was about something far more important than money.

It was about *revenge*.

"There are some things that can't be bought," she added.

Bollocks. Everything could be bought, including revenge. He'd bought it himself, dozens of times over. All those boys at Eton who used to sneer at him? Their bloated fathers, who'd ridiculed his father, and spat upon the Grantham name? He owned them now, both the fathers and the sons. If he ordered them to crawl across England on their knees, they'd do it. "So provincial, Miss St. Claire. I'm not sure whether to find your naïveté charming, or pitiful."

Once again, she didn't reply, and after a moment of silence, he went on. "Did Ambrose also tell you he stole this house out from under my father when he wasn't in his right mind?"

"No. He told me he saved it."

"*Saved* it?" He jerked back, stung. That was . . . well, damned if there wasn't an uncomfortable grain of truth to that interpretation. The better part of his father's mind had completely given way to the ravages of the bottle at the time of the wager. There was no telling what might have become of Hammond Court if Ambrose hadn't taken it.

But there'd been nothing noble about it. Ambrose had simply seen a golden opportunity to snatch up a valuable piece of property for himself, and he'd seized it. "You can't mean to say you believed such nonsense?"

"Why shouldn't I have believed it? He saved me and my mother, after all." She gave him a look that was almost pitying. "That's what Ambrose *did*, Your Grace. He saved the people and things he loved."

"So, Ambrose was the great hero, saving my father from himself? You're aware Ambrose was a gamester, are you not, Miss St. Claire? A professional wagerer."

She inclined her head. "Of course, I'm aware. He didn't keep secrets from me, Your Grace."

"I see. Then you must also be aware that several years ago, the Earl of Renard accused Ambrose of cheating him out of a substantial sum of money?" There. Perhaps that would shatter her damnable calm.

But Miss St. Claire didn't so much as twitch. "Those accusations were the rantings of a gentleman unhappy over losing his fortune. Nothing ever came of it."

He leaned forward, bitterness flooding his mouth like venom, choking him. "I hate to disillusion you, Miss St. Claire, but Ambrose was no knight in shining armor. He was no hero. He was a *thief*."

"He was nothing of the sort, but I suppose it's easier for you to imagine it thus." She cocked her head, her gaze never leaving his face. "Let's be frank with each other, shall we, Your Grace?"

At last, they were getting somewhere. "By all means, Miss St. Claire."

"Your father agreed to wager for Hammond Court. It seems quite a foolish thing to me, to wager on something so substantial as a house and several hundred acres of property, but they wagered, and your father lost. Is that your understanding as well, Your Grace, or have I missed something?"

Ambrose had taught her well, hadn't he? It was a perfectly accurate summary of the circumstances, but as with most things, the facts alone didn't paint the full picture. "My father was incapacitated at the time, half out of his mind with grief over my mother's death."

"Out of his mind with drink, too, I believe, and Hammond Court wasn't the first property he'd lost."

He stiffened. It was true, devil take her. "If you mean he wasn't in a fit state to wager a bloody thing, then yes."

"Yet he wagered nonetheless." She lifted her shoulder in a shrug. "And just like so many gentlemen before him who engage in an ill-considered wager, he lost."

"Ambrose was my father's *friend*, Miss St. Claire. My father *trusted* him, only to find himself maneuvered out of his deceased wife's childhood home—a home she loved, and that he loved for her sake."

Her gaze wandered past him, to the window. When she spoke again, her voice was quiet. "What of you, Your Grace? Did you love it, as well?"

"I did once." A long time ago, when he'd still known how to love something.

"And now?"

"Come, Miss St. Claire. For all your innocence, even you must realize love can turn to hate in the space of a single heartbeat. They're but different sides of the same coin."

"No, Your Grace, they're not. A flip of a coin is a matter of chance. Neither love nor hate happens by chance—they're things one *chooses*. They're nothing at all like the flip of a coin."

"Is that so? Very well, Miss St. Claire. What are they, then, if not a coin? Astonish me."

She thought for a moment, then, "A pendulum, I suppose, or something like it, where each side exists in balance with the other."

He laughed, but it was as if the sound had been wrenched from his chest, torn out from under his breastbone. "How fanciful, but I prefer my analogy. Tell me, though. If they are a pendulum, what lies in the middle, and keeps the balance between them?"

Her eyes held his. "Forgiveness."

"Is that your way of saying I should forgive Ambrose? It would be the proper thing to do, I suppose, with him dead and buried now, but I beg you will excuse me. Ambrose *ruined* my father—ruined my family. Nothing was ever the same after he stole Hammond Court from us." *He'd* never been the same. "I'll never forgive him for what he did."

If she had even a trace of proper feeling, such a declaration should have brought her to tears, but her face remained expressionless, the only sign of agitation a few rapid blinks of those pretty green eyes. "Let me understand you, Your Grace. Because your father was in his cups at the time of the wager, you feel as if you're entitled to my share of Hammond Court?"

"Entitled? Hardly. I'd pay you handsomely for your—"

"It's not that surprising, really," she went on as if he hadn't spoken. "Feeling entitled to things that don't belong to them is, I believe, a common malady among the aristocracy."

He stared at her, speechless. That was . . . she was . . . by God, it had been years—no, *decades*—since anyone had spoken so insolently to him. He was the Duke of bloody Grantham, for God's sake, one of the wealthiest peers in England, known for his ruthlessness, and this little speck of a blond-haired chit that resembled nothing so much as a woodland sprite *dared* to insult him?

God above, who was this girl?

He already knew the answer to that question, didn't he? She may not be of Ambrose's flesh, but she was *his*, every inch of her. She was just like him, cold down to her marrow.

But even Ambrose's daughter was no match for him. He'd crushed dozens of wealthy, influential noblemen under his boot heel, and he'd made quick work of her, too. "You may call it whatever you like, Miss St. Claire, but I *will* have this house back, one way or another."

"Is that a threat, Your Grace?"

It was, yes. A subtle one, but a threat nevertheless, and if she had any sense at all, it would have been enough to send her scurrying up the stairs to pack her bags, but she remained where she was, a picture of unruffled, ladylike calm. "It wouldn't be at all gentlemanly of me to threaten a young lady, would it, Miss St. Claire?"

"That's not a denial, Your Grace. Still, I appreciate your frankness. Permit me to be equally frank. You may do as you will, but I warn you." Her green eyes had gone dark, a storm brewing in their depths. "I haven't the least intention of turning Hammond Court over to you simply because you demand it."

No, no doubt she wouldn't, but the girl had no idea the sort of resources he had at his disposal, nor did she understand how relentless he could be. "Since half of Hammond Court is now mine, perhaps I'll move in." He settled back against the settee, crossing one booted foot over the other knee. "Unless, of course, you have an objection, Miss St. Claire?"

She would object, of course, and rather strenuously. Proper young ladies didn't put themselves in the clutches of unmarried gentlemen, particularly not those with his reputation for ruthlessness.

But she only gave him a bland smile. "None whatsoever, Your Grace. I'll see to it Ambrose's bedchamber is made ready for you. It's a nice one, you see, the finest in the house, and all the windows are intact."

"No concern for your reputation, then?" He studied the tip of his boot, frowning at the damp stains. "I daresay the village of Fairford will have a good deal to say about the two of us living alone together in this house."

She shrugged. "It's kind of you to be concerned for me, Your Grace, but I've never troubled myself much over village gossip. Let them talk, if they must."

Good Lord. She had an answer for everything, didn't she? "Come, Miss St. Claire, enough of this nonsense. Since you appreciate frankness, allow me to point out the obvious."

"Of course, Your Grace." She gave him an encouraging nod. "Please do."

"This house is tumbling down around your ears." He

waved a hand around the drawing room, indicating the bare windows and shabby furniture, the fire stuttering in the grate. "You haven't got the funds to repair it."

She stiffened, her hands clenching in her lap. "You don't know a thing about my—"

"Your financial situation? Of course, I do, Miss St. Claire. Do you suppose I would come all the way to Fairford before I had possession of all the facts? I was well aware Ambrose had died without a penny to his name, even before Sir Richard confirmed it."

"How dare you pry into our—"

"I think you'd be shocked at what I'd dare, Miss St. Claire. You may argue all you like, but we both know you can neither afford to repair the house, nor continue to live in it as it is."

"I don't see why not. I'm living in it now, am I not?"

"Three of the bedchamber windows on the third floor are cracked, Miss St. Claire. The front door is, er . . . compromised, the roof looks as if it's a stiff wind from caving in, and I can feel the damp seeping into my bones after an hour in your drawing room. It's only a matter of time before you'll be forced to leave, and then what do you intend to do? Where will you go, without any money?"

A frigid smile rose to her lips. "You'll forgive me, Your Grace, if I don't choose to confide in you."

"Very well, but be aware I'm prepared to offer you enough money to enable you to live quite comfortably wherever you wish. I daresay you'd find plenty of diversions to amuse you in London. Or the Continent, perhaps?"

She'd likely never set foot outside of Fairford before, but Miss St. Claire didn't look in the least tempted by his offer. "Tell me, Your Grace. If you do take possession of Hammond Court, what do you intend to do with it? You already have Grantham Lodge. What do you need with another estate in the same neighborhood?"

"Forgive me if I don't choose to confide in you, Miss St. Claire."

She studied him for a moment, then gave a sharp nod, as if he'd somehow confirmed precisely what she'd expected, without his having said a word. "You intend to tear it down, despite your purportedly deep sentimental attachment to it."

He did, indeed, if it didn't collapse first. He wanted to be free of it—for it to be gone, so he never had to think of it again. But he didn't say so. Instead, he gave her his haughtiest look. "What I intend to do with it is no concern of yours, Miss St. Claire."

"It might not be if this were merely a house to me, but it isn't." Her voice was quiet. "It's my home."

Those three words, so softly spoken, struck him in the center of his chest, but he pushed the swell of emotion away. Hammond Court had been his mother's home once, and his own home, too, but in the end, that had meant precisely nothing. "There are other houses, Miss St. Claire. Ones with proper fireplaces, and without cracked windows."

She shook her head, but she didn't bother arguing, and instead rose to her feet. "I thank you for your visit, Your Grace. I trust I won't be the recipient of any further surprise calls from you."

"Is it a call, Miss St. Claire, if I'm half owner of the house?"

She didn't answer, and there was nothing more for him to do then but follow her into the entryway and take his leave. But if she thought she'd be rid of him so easily, she was very much mistaken.

He'd only just begun.

He offered Miss St. Claire a curt bow and made his way toward the entrance hall and out the door. It was snowing still, harder than it had been earlier, the flurries so thick he could only just make out Townsend huddled under the eaves, waiting for him. "I don't think Miss St. Claire much cares for me, Townsend."

"No. Not much, Your Grace."

They picked their way over the ice, Max's boots slipping with every step. "She seems to find you tolerable enough, however."

"Yes, Your Grace," Townsend agreed dutifully, skidding along behind him.

"Do you fancy marrying her, Townsend? It would be one way for me to get my hands on Hammond Court." Max paused, straddling a particularly deep, icy puddle. That wasn't a bad idea, now he thought of it. It was diabolical, yes, but then the best ideas generally were.

If Miss St. Claire married, the house would become her husband's property. No man of any sense would refuse to sell to him, particularly not at the sum he'd offer.

The skidding behind him stopped, and Townsend cleared his throat nervously. "Er, I don't think Mrs. Townsend would like that, Your Grace."

"There's a Mrs. Townsend?"

"Yes, Your Grace, for nearly ten years now."

"Well, how exceedingly inconvenient of you, Townsend."

"Yes, Your Grace. I do beg your pardon, Your Grace, as does Mrs. Townsend."

Max grunted. Townsend's begging didn't solve the problem at hand, did it? Miss St. Claire still owned half his house.

No matter. He'd find a way to take it from her.

He always had his way, in the end.

As soon as the duke was gone, Rose flew up the stairs and into Abby's bedchamber, where Abby was waiting for her.

Abby leaped up from the bed. "What happened? What did Sir Richard say?"

"It's . . . well, it's a trifle concerning, Abby." That was one way of putting it. Another way was that it was an utter catastrophe.

"I thought as much, what with that slack-jawed look of yours. Go on, then." Abby waved a hand. "Let's have the worst of it."

"Ambrose has left Hammond Court to the Duke of Grantham."

Abby's jaw dropped open. "You mean to say Ambrose has left you *homeless*? No, I don't believe a word of it. There must be some mistake. We must fetch Sir Richard back this instant, and—"

"No, no. Ambrose hasn't abandoned me, Abby. He

wouldn't do such a thing. No, it seems that Ambrose has left Hammond Court to me, *and* to the Duke of Grantham."

Abby's eyes went so wide they nearly dropped out of her head. "I—what? I don't understand."

"He's, ah . . . well, in essence, he's left Hammond Court to both of us. *Together*," Rose added, in case the ghastliness of it wasn't entirely clear.

She'd expected wailing, rending of clothing, and perhaps another brandishing of the hairbrush upon delivery of this news, but the explosion never came. Abby regarded her in silence for a moment, then she marched across the room and began snatching armfuls of clothing from the clothes press. "Go to your bedchamber and gather your things, Rose, while I run and fetch Billy, and tell him to ready the wagon for us."

"The wagon? Whatever for?"

"Why, we're going to stay with Mrs. Sullivan in Cirencester, of course."

"Cirencester! You know I can't leave Hammond Court, Abby."

Abby crossed her arms over her chest, her chin jutting out. "I don't know any such thing."

Dash it. She knew the stubborn thrust of that chin. "The instant I set a toe outside the door, he'll find a way to make certain I never return."

Perhaps the Duke of Grantham wasn't the ruthless scoundrel everyone claimed he was. Perhaps even he could be made to see reason, but the expression on his face when he'd told her he'd do whatever it took to have

Hammond Court . . . there hadn't been even a sliver of warmth in those frigid gray eyes.

She shuddered, chills darting down her spine. She didn't trust the man any more than she would a rabid dog. "But there's no reason for *you* to stay here, Abby. Indeed, I think it would be for the best if you went to Mrs. Sullivan's."

Her heart gave a panicked throb at the thought of losing Abby, who'd been by her side for all but the first four of her twenty-one years, but there was no help for it. This battle with the Duke of Grantham was bound to become a great deal uglier before it was over, and she didn't want Abby caught up in it. Abby would be better off in Cirencester with Maggie Sullivan, well out of the Duke of Grantham's reach, just in case he took it into his head to use the people she loved as pawns in his quest to have his way.

"I'm not going anywhere without you." Abby dumped the armful of clothes onto the bed, then turned a shrewd eye on Rose. "You ought to think about letting the duke have his way, Rose. He's likely to have it in the end anyway, no matter what you do."

"*What?* You expect me to just give up, and let him have the house? I can't do that! He'll tear it down if he gets his hands on it." Hammond Court, with its cracked windows, rutted drive, shattered front door, and hundreds of spiders, was her *home*.

She wasn't going anywhere.

"I love Hammond Court as much as you do, but you can't afford this place, Rose. It was all well and good when Ambrose was alive, but this house . . ." She shook her head. "It's a weight around your neck, now. You'll wear yourself to a thread, trying to keep up with it."

"How can you say that, Abby? Why, it would break Ambrose's heart if I abandoned Hammond Court!" It would break *her* heart, as well.

"Ambrose is gone, Rose, and you're a young lady, with your whole life ahead of you. I don't pretend to know what Ambrose was thinking when he died, but I can't believe he'd want to see you tied to this house forever."

"Then why would he leave me half of it?" She couldn't answer that question herself—not yet—but one thing was certain. Ambrose had his reasons. He always did.

It was up to her to figure out what those reasons were.

"Listen to me, pet." Abby took her hand in a gentle grasp. "The duke will pay to be rid of you. Imagine what you could do with that money, Rose! Would it be so terrible, having your freedom?"

"I don't . . . I can't talk about this now, Abby. Just please, do as I say, and gather your things."

"No! I won't just up and leave you here alone, at the mercy of that wicked duke! I'm staying right here with you."

"Abby, please." Rose clung to Abby's hand. "I don't want you caught up in this mess. Please just go, and I promise I'll join you as soon as I can. Why, I daresay it won't take more than a few days to come to some agreement with the Duke of Grantham."

A few days, or a few decades.

But Abby shook her head. "He doesn't look like the sort who makes agreements, Rose. He looks like the sort who takes what he wants, no matter if he's got a right to it or not. He's cold as ice, that one, through and through."

"Well, he hasn't much choice but to negotiate with me, has he? Come, Abby, it won't be for long. Just until I . . ." She trailed off, unsure how to finish that sentence. A hysterical laugh was crowding into her throat, but she choked it back because if she gave into it, she might never stop.

For all her bluster, she didn't fancy tangling with the Duke of Grantham. But neither could she just stand by and let him take Hammond Court from them. "He can't do a thing to me."

"He's a *duke*, Rose. They do as they please, and no one dares breathe a word against them."

"Well, what do you imagine he's going to do? Murder me in my bed?"

Abby paled. "Rose!"

Oh, dear. Perhaps that might have better gone unsaid. "That is, what I meant to say is that I'll be perfectly fine, but I need to know you're safe with Mrs. Sullivan first. Please, Abby."

Long, quiet moments ticked by until at last Abby let out a heavy sigh. "All right, but if you don't appear at Mrs. Sullivan's in two days, I'm coming back for you."

"Thank you." Rose pressed a quick kiss to Abby's cheek. "Now quickly, gather your things while I go and find Billy."

It should have taken a much longer time to disappear a person, but in the end, it was all arranged rather quickly. Billy had the wagon readied and waiting on the drive within a half hour.

A half hour after that, Abby climbed in next to him, her valise in her hand, bundled from head to toe in one of Ambrose's old cloaks to keep her warm. "You be careful. You hear me, Rose?" She grasped Rose's hand. "If anything goes wrong, you promise you'll come to me at once?"

Something *would* go wrong—it was merely a question of to what degree—but Rose dredged up a comforting lie. "Of course, but nothing will go wrong, Abby. I'll be just fine."

Abby knew better than to believe the lie, of course, but both of them were now committed to this charade that all might still be well, so she only gave Rose's hand another squeeze. "You'll think about what I said about the house?"

There was nothing to think about. Even if she'd wanted to leave, she couldn't abandon Ambrose's tenants. They were thriving, and it was by no means certain they'd continue to do so with the Duke of Grantham as their landlord. Goodness knew he'd made no secret of the fact that he despised Fairford. As soon as he'd torn Hammond Court down, he'd scurry off back to London, and let another two decades elapse before he returned.

If then.

But in the interest of getting Abby on her way, she nodded. "Yes, I will."

Abby didn't look convinced, but she released Rose's hand and turned to face forward. "Right, then. Let's go, Billy."

Then they were gone, the ancient wagon bumping and swaying its way down the icy drive. Rose waited until they'd passed through the trees and out of sight, then turned back toward the house.

She paused to stare up at the façade, at the cracked windows and sagging roof. She'd only been four years old when she and her mother came here, and her recollections of that time had grown hazy over the years, but the first day they'd arrived would be forever burned into her memory. She'd gazed up at the façade just as she was doing now, and had thought the house was like a fairy castle, with its diamond-paned windows and the stone weathered to a pale gold.

One glance and her chest had burst with hope.

Anything had felt possible, then, and as it turned out, it *was*.

But that was before, when Ambrose had held court here, and laughter had spilled out of every window. More than anything, Ambrose had delighted in people. He'd collected them, especially the cast-offs and dregs the rest of the world had given up on.

Like her, and her mother.

He'd gathered them all together and made them his family. Oh, they'd been a mismatched, ragged-edge family to be sure, made up of the odds and ends of families no one else had wanted, but a family, nonetheless.

But those days were gone, buried in the cold ground along with Ambrose. Without him, the house was a ghost, a pale imitation of what it once had been. Yet she'd hold on to it still, for all that—hold on to it until her fingernails were bloody, and her heart gave out.

No one, not even the almighty Duke of Grantham, would take it from her.

CHAPTER 8

"Here ye are, Miss Rose." Billy dumped the heavy armload of wood he'd carried into her bedchamber into the bin beside the stone hearth, a frown puckering his brow. "Yer not going to get much of a blaze from those."

Rose glanced down at the pathetic pile of damp logs, some with a thin layer of ice still clinging to them, and hid her grimace. "Nonsense, Billy. I'll be fine. Go on, now. Your grandmother will worry if you're not home soon, what with the snow."

"Ye should come home with me, Miss Rose. The wind's howling, and it's going to be a wild night. My grandmam would be happy to have ye."

She pictured the cottage Billy shared with his grandmother, and a pang of longing sharp enough to squeeze a gasp out of her pierced her chest. She could see the glow of the cheerful fire in the grate, hear the snap and hiss of the wood, and smell the tantalizing scent of stew simmering atop the blaze, his tiny, white-haired grandmother fussing over it, a spoon in her hand.

Oh, how she'd dearly love to go! So much she ached

for the warmth and company, but leaving Hammond Court, even for a single night, was out of the question. The moment she stepped foot outside the front door, the Duke of Grantham would pounce.

As for what that pouncing would entail, well . . . she couldn't say, precisely, not being overly familiar with wicked dukes, but he'd made it clear he'd stop at nothing to get this house. He likely had a half dozen servants lurking in the shadows outside her door even now, despite the snow and wind.

Hammond Court wasn't just another possession to him, any more than it was to her. For him, this was about avenging his father and punishing Ambrose. It was about retaliating for perceived wrongs, and goodness knew there were few emotions as powerful as hate and vengeance.

If she'd been in her right mind, she might have understood it. Empathized even, if not with the duke, at least with the small boy he'd once been. It must have been nightmarish, to have to watch helplessly as his mother, his father, and his home all slipped away, one by one.

But she *wasn't* in her right mind. Her mind and her heart were teeming with so much fear and anger, there was no space left inside her for empathy.

She hadn't been prepared for the menacing tightness in the duke's jaw this afternoon, and the shadow of fury in his gray eyes when she'd refused his money.

Like tarnished silver, those eyes.

If ever there was a man who couldn't abide being told no, it was the Duke of Grantham.

"I'll be fine. I promise it, Billy." She pasted a smile

on lips already trembling with the chill. "Go on home, now. I'll see you in the morning."

"Ye might move into Mr. St. Claire's room, least-ways." Billy waved a hand at the cracked window, the whorls of ice shimmering on the panes. "It's warmer in the back of the house."

"Perhaps I will." She wouldn't, because she needed to keep an eye on the drive, and this bedchamber was the only one left facing the front of the house that didn't have a shattered window. A broken one, yes, but not shattered.

At least, not yet, but if the wind had its way, it may well be shattered by morning.

Billy didn't appear convinced, but he only shook his head and made his way to the door, leaving a trail of wet footprints in his wake. "I'll come back before day-break, miss."

Then he was gone, leaving her alone in the encroaching darkness, the furious howling of the wind making the house shudder and creak around her. She knelt by the hearth, and after a good deal of trouble managed to coax a weak blaze from the damp logs.

Then, there was nothing to do but wait. It seemed to be all she ever did these days.

Wait for the night to pass, the storm to cease, for daylight to come. Wait for the next window to crack, the next leak in the roof to make itself known, the next creditor to appear on the doorstep, demanding money she didn't have.

Wait for Ambrose to die, and the Duke of Grantham

to come, his far-too-handsome mouth full of threats, accusations, and lies.

Dash it, she was wallowing again, wasn't she?

She shook the dark thoughts from her head, snatched up the thick coverlet and wrapped it around her shoulders, then took up a handful of the bedding and tucked herself into the chair nearest the window, the fire at her back. Hammond Court had long since given up any claim to grandeur, but it was still well supplied with blankets, and she built a tiny nest for herself, tucking her legs underneath her and cocooning herself inside it.

Yes, this would do. It wasn't warm, exactly, but it would see her through the night. As for tomorrow . . . well, things always looked more promising in the morning, didn't they? Goodness knew, between the dreadful weather, the crumbling house, and the enmity of a powerful, ruthless, infuriated duke, anything that could go wrong had already done so.

She settled back in her chair, gazing into the gloom. The window in front of her turned deep indigo and then faded to black as night descended, bringing with it the loneliness she'd come to dread. How strange, that it could feel as if the silence were pressing in on her from every side, even as the wind wailed with growing ferocity, rattling the glass in the panes.

This hardly seemed the same house that had once been filled with so much laughter.

She stared at the black windows until they began to blur in front of her eyes. Her thoughts ran together, one flowing into the next as her head grew heavy, her eyelashes brushing her cheeks, until she was sleepy enough that there was no distinction between one thought and the next, but just a series of shifting images flickering behind her eyelids. The snowflakes drifting through the crack in the window yesterday morning, the weak sunlight illuminating them as they fell. A black carriage with a crest emblazoned on the door, and a tall, dark-haired man with gold-tasseled boots making his way up the drive. The crack of splintering wood as his foot slammed into the door, the imprint of her pistol against her palm, and a pair of cold, gray eyes.

It would get better. Surely, it would? It must, because it couldn't get any worse.

But hadn't she told herself the same thing, after Ambrose's accident? Then, a mere week later, Ambrose was dead, the coverlet pulled up to his chin, his face so peaceful she might have believed he'd only slipped into a delightful nap if he hadn't been so still and white.

It *could* get worse—it *had* done so, and so quickly she hardly recognized the life she was living now as hers. One would think she'd have learned her lesson by now, learned never to believe it couldn't get worse, because it could, and it was tempting the wrath of fate to think otherwise.

Take it back, quickly, before—

But it was already too late. In the blink of an eye, it got worse.

So much worse.

It started with a strange snapping sound. Her eyes flew open, all vestiges of sleep dissolving in an instant. The house was forever creaking and moaning around her, the walls shuddering as it eased into its foundations like an old man inhaling and then releasing a deep breath, before settling his aching limbs around him as he fell into bed for the night.

But this was different. It wasn't one of the usual creaks or cracks, but a pop, like a twig snapping in half. She stilled, listening, and yes, there it was again! A sharp, tight snap coming from . . . everywhere, it seemed, or—

No. It was coming from the corner of her bedchamber, near the one window that remained intact. Was the glass coming loose from the frame, or was the windowsill cracking? She leaped up from the chair and flew across the bedchamber toward the window, her blankets falling away.

The window was rattling, the wind making it tremble in its frame, but that wasn't the source of the snapping sound. It was—

She stilled, her heart rushing into her throat.

It was coming from *above* her.

She looked up, and a drop of icy water splashed onto her cheek, then another onto her nose, her chin, the droplets falling quickly now, catching in her eyelashes. She gasped, her muscles pulling tight as she willed it to stop, willed the house she loved to still, but she could hear it clearly now, a low, ominous rush above her, like a river overflowing its banks, and the cursed Duke of Grantham's words echoed inside her head.

This house is tumbling down around your ears . . .

No, it wasn't. It *wasn't*. It was just another leak, much like the leaks in the drawing room and the study. Nothing a pail and a handful of rags wouldn't solve.

She peered up at the ceiling. It was as dark as Hades

outside, and the bedchamber was lost in shadows, but it looked as if . . . oh. Oh, no. She squeezed her eyes closed, sucked in a breath, then opened them again, blinking away another drop of icy water, a muttered prayer on her lips.

But prayers hadn't done her any good before, and they didn't now, because even in the gloom of the bedchamber there was no mistaking the peril about to rain down upon her from above.

What had once been a perfectly serviceable ceiling now resembled nothing so much as a hot air balloon. The white plaster was swollen into a bubble that covered an entire corner of the room, the whole of it juddering and quivering like a jelly, a steady stream of water dripping from the distended belly of it.

It was going to collapse, and soon.

No, not soon. *Now*—

Her only warning was a series of ominous popping sounds, one pop after another, like bones snapping, but she managed to leap out of the way before the balloon burst with a deafening whoosh, and a wave of water gushed forth, flooding the bedchamber.

Oh, God. Oh, dear God.

She fled to the bedchamber door, away from the deluge, but she skidded to a halt when she reached the safety of the hallway and peeked back into the bedchamber. Perhaps it wasn't as bad as it had sounded, or looked, or . . . felt. Perhaps she might yet be able to salvage it.

But it *was* as bad. No, it was worse, and it didn't take more than a glance to see it.

The force of the water had turned her chair over. The blankets she'd wrapped around herself were lying in a sopping mass in the middle of the floor. The fire she'd labored over was a wreck of smoking logs, the flames extinguished, and a thin stream of water was still dripping from the gaping hole where the ceiling used to be.

There was nothing to salvage, nothing to do but turn and drag herself into the hallway, her heart like a stone in her chest. How much longer could she keep on like this, when every day brought another struggle, another disaster?

She stumbled down the corridor towards Abby's bedchamber but paused beside the closed door of Ambrose's room. She'd set it to rights after he'd passed away, changing all the linens and scrubbing every inch of it until it sparkled, but she hadn't set foot in it since then, because she hadn't wanted . . .

She hadn't wanted to see how empty it was.

But she was so *tired*, so unutterably weary, and she missed him so dreadfully, her chest aching with it, and all she wanted, the only thing she wanted in the world right now was to be as close to him as she could be.

The hinges creaked as she opened the door, the floorboards squeaking under her feet. She didn't pause in the sitting room that adjoined the bedchamber, but made her way directly to the bed and crawled into it, pulling the coverlet over her head.

But as exhausted as she was, sleep refused to come.

Perhaps she should take Abby's advice and leave Fairford, while her memories of this place were still happy ones. Because she couldn't keep on like this, dodging Ambrose's creditors at every turn, and struggling to hold off the steady deterioration of Hammond Court at the same time.

She couldn't win a battle against the Duke of Grantham. She'd been a fool to believe for an instant that she could. Surely, Ambrose hadn't intended for her to do so. He knew how ruthless Grantham was, and how pointless it would be for her to attempt to fight him.

She was nothing, a nobody, a by-blow with no money, no family, and few friends. The Duke of Grantham would crush her under his boot heel without a second thought, and nary a backward glance. He'd have his way, no matter what she did, so what was the use in struggling? It would be much better for her to give up now before things became truly ugly.

Yes, of course that was what Ambrose would want her to do. That was likely what he'd been trying to tell her, on that last day, right before he'd died.

Only that wasn't what he'd *said*.

If he'd wanted her to leave Hammond Court, he could have told her so easily enough, but he hadn't. Instead, with the last few breaths he'd had left in him, he'd spoken of the Duke of Grantham.

A lost soul . . .

He'd said it over and over again, his hand clutching weakly at hers.

If he truly believed the duke would harm her, then why had he thrown her into the man's path by setting up this battle between them? If he'd intended for her to leave Fairford behind, why had he gone to such pains to make certain she could remain at Hammond Court, no matter how much the duke might wish to be rid of her? He might have left the house to one or the other of them easily enough.

But he hadn't. He'd left it to them both.

Was it simply a ploy, to get the duke to pay her for her share of the house, and thus ensure she wasn't left penniless? It was possible, but if that was the case, why not just leave the house solely to her? Why leave it to both of them?

Ambrose had been an unpredictable man, but for all that he'd been maddeningly opaque at times, he hadn't been the sort who did things on a whim. He'd set it up this way purposely because he'd wanted her to do something for him, something he'd run out of time to do for himself.

But what? She flipped onto her back and threw her arm over her eyes, her head a whirl of confusing contradictions. It was almost as if Ambrose had intended to *force* her and the duke together . . .

She bolted upright, her eyes snapping open. Of course! It was so obvious, it was a wonder she hadn't realized it at once! Ambrose's one sorrow, his one regret, was that he'd run out of time to make his peace with the Duke of Grantham.

So, he wanted her to do it for him.

That was what he'd been trying to ask of her, the day he'd died! What else could it be?

Ambrose had loved this house, and he'd taught her to love it as well, just as Sir Richard had said. It had never been only a house to him, but a haven of love and hope and togetherness, a place of precious memories. It would have broken his heart to see it torn down.

But the house wasn't the only thing he wanted to save.

He wanted to save the Duke of Grantham, too.

But how on earth was she meant to heal a wound that had been festering for two decades? Who was *she*, to try and reconcile a bitter, vengeful duke to the events of a past neither of them understood? How was she even meant to go about it? Why, it could take weeks, months—an entire lifetime, even—for the duke to make peace with his past, and that was assuming the thing could be done at all.

But then, Ambrose had always had such faith in her. Why, the silly man had insisted she'd hung the moon and the stars in the sky, and she . . .

Well, she'd thought the same of him, hadn't she?

She dashed a tear from her cheek. Everything she had, and everything she was, was because of Ambrose. He'd done everything for her, had given her everything. If it hadn't been for him, God only knew what would have become of her.

He'd never asked for anything in return. Not once, in all these years, had he ever asked a single thing of her.

Until now.

She rolled onto her stomach and buried her face in Ambrose's pillow. It still smelled faintly of him, the mingled scents of mint and clove from the snuff he'd favored tickling her nose and making her heart ache.

In the end, she would leave Hammond Court. She'd never been meant to stay here forever.

But it wouldn't be today, nor would it be tomorrow. The entire house might tumble down around her, just as the duke had warned it would, but she wasn't leaving until she'd fulfilled her final promise to Ambrose.

CHAPTER 9

Proper gentlemen didn't sneak up on young ladies.

A wise gentleman—and Max did like to think of himself as wise, if not always proper—didn't attempt to sneak up upon a young lady like Rose St. Claire. The girl knew how to wield a pistol, by God, and she hadn't any qualms about using it.

It was early yet, though not as dark as it had been when he'd left Grantham Lodge, and the worst of the storm had loosened its grip on Fairford. Still, it was bloody unpleasant enough this morning—cold, with a light fall of snow creeping under the collar of his greatcoat. But he lingered in the shadows nonetheless, staring up at the house, much as he'd done when he was a boy and used to sneak from Grantham Lodge through the woods to Hammond Court.

There was no light spilling from the windows this time, no Christmas carols drifting on the wind, and no glowing moon or magical silver starlight gilding the house as if it were something out of a fairy tale.

But the same loneliness he'd felt as a boy, that same hopeless sense of being nothing, of mattering to no one, of being so insignificant he was invisible, was waiting here for him still, lurking in the muted morning light, just as it always had. It didn't matter that he was a duke now—a wealthy, formidable duke, with England's most powerful aristocrats cowering before him.

Here, standing alone outside Hammond Court, he was the same tiny, isolated speck he'd been back then, a pinpoint surrounded by a vast blackness. He stood there for some time, lost in memories he'd sooner forget. When he came to himself again, the flurry of snowflakes had piled up in feathery drifts around his boots.

The gloom of the morning would help obscure his approach from anyone who happened to be peering from one of the upper windows, but he muttered a quick prayer that Miss St. Claire wasn't up there with her pert little nose pressed to the glass, her pistol cocked and ready.

It was damned risky, sneaking about like this, but if ever there was an errand he'd rather keep private, it was this one, so he took care to keep close to the trees lining the drive, darting amongst their shadows, and managed to gain the front door without being fired upon.

The flimsy bit of rope Miss St. Claire had woven through the hole where the knob used to be was still there, but just as Townsend had predicted, one slice with the knife in his pocket put an end to it quickly enough.

What had the girl been thinking, imagining such a pitiful apparatus would be enough to keep her safe? Hadn't Ambrose taught her anything? She was as naïve as a country milkmaid and as trusting as a newborn

kitten. Not that it mattered to *him*, of course, but someone had to look after the girl, didn't they?

He tore off his gloves and reached into his pocket for
his tools, but his fingers were clumsy with the cold, and
no sooner did he have the screws in his hand than he
dropped one.

"Damn." He crouched down and pawed through the
snow until at last he found the screw, but that wasn't all
he found. There was a scattering of curious bits of gray
stone, as well.

What the devil? They looked like . . . he snatched up
a piece and held it up to the meager light, squinting at
it. It *was*. A broken piece of slate tile. One of the edges
was jagged, but the other three were smooth and
straight.

He got to his feet and stepped back, craning his neck
to get a better look, and yes, there it was—a patchwork
of empty spaces on the roof. Last night's wind had torn
a dozen or more tiles loose from the eastern corner of
the roof and hurled them onto the drive below.

The eastern corner . . . wasn't that where the bedchambers were? And the window—it had been cracked
before, but now the glass was gone entirely, and a
rivulet of water was running from the outer sill down
the side of the house.

His heart—no, not his *heart*, but some other, less,
er . . . loverlike organ rushed into his throat. He leaped
through the door and rushed up the staircase, two stairs
at a time.

"Who the devil are *you*?"

Max jerked to a halt on the third-floor landing. A

boy with tousled dark hair stood in the middle of the corridor, his arms thrust out and his fists clenched as if he were prepared to dive upon anyone who dared to try and get past him.

"The Duke of Grantham." Max peered down into the fierce little face. "Who the devil are *you*?"

"I'm Billy Lucas, an' you weren't invited here, so's you may as well turn around and go back out the way you came in." Billy Lucas pointed an imperious finger at the front door.

"Did you hear what I said, boy? I'm the *Duke of Grantham*." Didn't the dull-witted lad know what a duke was?

The boy sniffed. "Don't care if you're Prinny himself. Miss St. Claire isn't seeing people, least of all some high and mighty duke. Get out, and leave Miss St. Claire alone."

Good Lord, was there a single man—or boy, come to that—in Fairford who *wouldn't* defend Miss St. Claire? The chit had them all hypnotized. "Now see here, you impertinent little imp—"

"Billy? I'm going to need another pail." Miss St. Claire's voice drifted down the hallway from one of the bedchambers. "Will you fetch the one from the stillroom for me?"

"Well? You heard the lady, Billy." Max crossed his arms over his chest and smirked down at the boy. "Do as you're told, and fetch the pail."

Billy's freckled face darkened. "Go to the devil."

The *devil*? Had the little demon truly just told him to go to the devil? A wild laugh threatened, but he choked it back and gave the boy his most fearsome glower. "Now you see here, Billy Lucas—"

"Oh! Oh, *no*!"

The cry came from the bedchamber, Miss St. Claire's voice breathless with alarm, and an instant later there was a crash that made Max's blood freeze to ice in his veins. Billy's eyes widened, his mouth rounding in horror, and without another word the two of them flew down the corridor, each tripping over the other's feet in their rush to get to her.

Billy got there first. Max came to a careening halt behind him, peering over the lad's head, and what he saw . . . well, between her panicked cry, and that crash, he hadn't expected it to be good, but nor was he prepared for the sight that met his eyes.

Miss St. Claire was sprawled on the floor on her backside, one of the chairs from the kitchen below lying on top of her. That alone was bad enough, but the bedchamber . . .

It was flooded with water, a steady stream of it still dripping from the gaping hole in the ceiling. Several full buckets stood nearby, as well as a mass of sodden, dark red silk that looked as if it had once been a bed hanging. Bits of plaster and rotted wood were scattered across the floor, and shards of broken glass were floating atop the water.

"Miss St. Claire!" Max shot forward, tearing the chair off her and tossing it aside before reaching for her, and hauling her to her feet. "Can you stand? Damnation, you're soaked to the skin!"

"I—I'm all right. I can stand. It was just a bit of a tumble, that's all."

"A *tumble*? You might have broken your neck! What were you thinking, standing upon a chair in a flooded room?" Didn't the girl have any sense at all?

"I thought if I could see what had happened, I might be able to . . ." She trailed off with a shudder. Her entire body was trembling, and her hands, which had somehow found their way into his, were like two blocks of ice.

"Billy!" He glanced over his shoulder. "Quickly, fetch some dry blankets."

Billy didn't argue this time but fled down the hallway. Max turned back to Miss St. Claire, whose despairing gaze was darting from the broken window to the hole in the ceiling, to the pond that had once been her bedchamber floor. "There's nothing to be done, is there?" she murmured, more to herself than to him. "It's utterly lost."

"Look at me, Miss St. Claire." He grasped her shoulders and gave her a gentle shake until her gaze found his. "There, that's better. You're coming back to Grantham Lodge with me, so you can—"

"No, I—I can't leave! It's out of the question." She waved an unsteady hand around the room, her mouth twisting. "Look at this mess!"

He caught her chin between his fingers and turned her face back to his. "I see it, and it will be dealt with, but not now, and not by you. You're exhausted, and half-frozen, and you're going to need a great deal more than a foul-mouthed boy and a kitchen chair to rectify this problem."

"But I can't just—"

"You can, and you will." God above, had there ever been a more stubborn woman than this one? Or a more maddening one? She was dead on her feet, her face as pale as death aside from the dark rings under her eyes, and she thought he'd simply walk away and leave her here?

She glanced around the bedchamber, biting her lip. "I think it would be best if I—"

"May I remind you, Miss St. Claire, that I am a part owner of Hammond Court? You can't do a single thing in this house without my approval. Now, not another word, if you please. You're coming back to Grantham Lodge, where you will have a hot bath and a rest, and then we'll decide what's best to be done."

Billy came scrambling back into the bedchamber then, blankets piled high in his arms. "Here you go, Miss St. Claire!"

"Thank you, Billy." She took a blanket from the top of the pile and wrapped it around her shoulders. "You've been a great help to me today." She patted the boy's shoulder. "I'm going with His Grace to Grantham Lodge, Billy, so go on home to your grandmother now."

Billy cast a suspicious look at Max, then turned back to Miss St. Claire. "You're sure you want to go with *him*?"

Max huffed out a breath. Bloody little demon.

Miss St. Claire choked back a laugh. "Yes, quite sure, but you may come by later, if you like, Billy. I'll be back at Hammond Court by this afternoon."

Max said nothing, only took her arm and led her

down the stairs to the carriage he'd left at the bottom of the drive, but if he had anything to say about it, she wouldn't be returning to Hammond Court.

Not this afternoon, or any other.

"Your Grace!" Townsend burst through Max's study door like a whirlwind, his red hair standing on end in a most disgraceful manner, his face pale and sweaty.

Max, who'd perfected the art of putting people in their places with an imperious quirk of one eyebrow, employed the tactic now, and predictably, Townsend came to a halt in front of his desk, his cheeks flushing. "Oh, dear. I do beg your pardon for bursting in upon you without knocking, Your Grace, but I've just had the most distressing news. It's Hammond Court. It's tumbled down to the ground!"

"Tumbled down to the ground?" Is that what everyone was saying? "Hardly, Townsend."

Townsend blinked. "It *hasn't* tumbled to the ground?"

"No, though I confess I would have been singularly unsurprised if it had." Max raised the eyebrow another notch to emphasize his point.

"But something's happened! Something dreadful, indeed!" Townsend wrung his hands. "Miss St. Claire is missing!"

Missing? Good Lord, were all small villages as prone to hysteria as Fairford? He tugged his spectacles off and dropped them onto his desk with a sigh. "She isn't missing, Townsend. At this very moment, Miss St. Claire is tucked into a bedchamber two floors above us, with the estimable Mrs. Watson clucking and fawning over her like a mother hen with a baby chick."

Townsend collapsed into the chair in front of Max's desk—again, without so much as a by-your-leave, and let his head drop into his hands. "Thank goodness, Your Grace! I own I was quite distressed on her behalf. One doesn't like to think of a young lady buried under piles of—" He broke off, his head jerking up. "Did you say she's *here*? At Grantham Lodge?"

"I did, yes." Those were the words that had come from his lips, at any rate. Even now, he had a difficult time believing they were the truth. Of all the places he'd have predicted Miss St. Claire would end up, he would have put Grantham Lodge at dead last. But here they were, and he had no one to blame for it but himself, as he'd been the one who'd brought her here.

What a bit of madness that had been, but damned if he'd had any idea what else to do with her. She'd been ready to collapse. He may not care much for Miss St. Claire—she was a tiresome, interfering little chit with airs way above her station—but even he wasn't coldhearted enough to leave a young lady on her backside in her flooded bedchamber with chunks of plaster and broken glass floating around her.

Rather too bad, that, but it was too late now.

Townsend was staring at him, his mouth wide open. "Close your mouth, for God's sake, Townsend. You look like a half-wit, and the sight of your gaping maw is putting me off my tea."

"Yes, Your Grace, but, er . . . begging your pardon,

Your Grace, how did Miss St. Claire happen to end up *here*?"

It was an excellent question, by God. What a great pity he didn't have a correspondingly excellent explanation for her presence in his house. Her scandalously inappropriate presence. As soon as the good citizens of Fairford learned she'd spent most of the morning cozily tucked into one of his bedchambers, there'd be no quelling the storm of gossip. "It's nothing so shocking, Townsend. I, ah . . . I happened to be in the, er, general vicinity of Hammond Court only hours after the ceiling expired."

Townsend blinked. "But Mr. Turnbull told me it happened last night, during the storm."

"Yes, that's right, Townsend." Damn it, why had he said anything at all? He could already see the wheels turning in Townsend's head.

"You, ah, you mean to say, Your Grace, that you were in the vicinity of Hammond Court *last night*?"

"No. I was there this morning."

Townsend wrestled with himself for a moment, but in the end he could no more hold his tongue than anyone else in Fairford. "Forgive me, Your Grace, but you must have been at Hammond Court quite early this morning, before it stopped snowing. That is to say, you were there mere hours after the *worst storm* Fairford's seen this decade."

He wasn't about to explain himself to Townsend, particularly when he couldn't even explain to himself why he'd rushed off to Hammond Court before the sun had even crested the horizon, when his errand could easily have waited until a more civilized time of day. So, he said only, "That's right, Townsend."

If Townsend was wise, he'd let it go at that, just as Mrs. Watson had when he'd appeared in his entryway this morning, soaked to the skin, with a nearly unconscious young lady leaning on his arm.

But Townsend had only been employed by Max for a little over a year, and he wasn't anywhere near as wise as Mrs. Watson, who'd been Max's father's housekeeper before his, and knew better than to pry into the ducal affairs.

Townsend was gaping at him, his eyes nearly popping out of his head. "Of course, that makes perfect sense, Your Grace. That you'd be lurking outside Hammond Court before sunrise, directly after a blizzard. Very right and proper, indeed."

Lurking? What an ugly word, and unfair, too. He'd never lurked in his life. "For pity's sake, Townsend, if you must know, I only went because I was concerned about Miss St. Claire's doorknob."

He hadn't *meant* to tear the doorknob off the other day. It had just happened.

When he'd tugged and kicked at it, that is.

Oh, very well, so he *had* meant to tear it off. One didn't accidentally kick a doorknob off a door, after all, but he'd been so focused on getting inside, he hadn't considered the thing properly.

"Her doorknob, Your Grace?"

"Yes, damn it. You were the one who told me she was in the house alone, and I . . ." He trailed off, fury and shame writhing like a serpent in his belly. This was all Townsend's fault, with his talk of knife-wielding scoundrels.

His assault on Miss St. Claire's door hadn't troubled him at first. Indeed, he hadn't given it a second thought until he'd gotten a better look at the damage he'd done. He'd gone to his bed that night only to find he couldn't stop thinking about Miss St. Claire and her missing doorknob, and that absurd length of rope she'd used to tie the door closed.

Did the girl think that rope would be enough to keep anyone out? It had taken only a moment for him to slice through it with his knife. What was to stop any other villain from doing the same? What was to keep him from strolling into her house, as cool as he pleased?

And once this nameless, faceless villain was inside, well . . . it didn't bear thinking about, did it?

Except he *had* thought about it last night, and once the idea caught hold he hadn't been able to *stop* thinking about it, and the longer he'd lain there, the worse it had gotten. Eventually, he'd been so tormented with visions of a gang of murderous villains overcoming Miss St. Claire, it had driven him from his bed and into the coldest, windiest morning he'd ever had the misfortune of experiencing, with a bloody doorknob stuffed in his pocket.

A gang of villains, in Fairford. Bloody ridiculous.

Still, if he hadn't appeared at Hammond Court when he had, Miss St. Claire would likely still be balanced on that blasted kitchen chair, peering up at the ceiling with her wet skirts clinging to her legs, courting a nasty lung infection. And while in the abstract he might wish for her to be made uncomfortable—it would, after all, hasten her departure from Hammond Court—the reality of the thing was rather distasteful, like crushing a butter-fly in his fist.

She was a thorn in his side, yes, but he didn't want her to become ill, or worse yet, suffer an injury. He wasn't such a blackguard as that. He merely wanted her out of his house, and preferably far, far away from him.

Farther than one of his guest bedchambers, certainly.

Townsend had gone quiet, and when Max looked up, he found the man beaming at him. "Stop that this instant, Townsend."

"Yes, Your Grace." Townsend made a halfhearted attempt to school his expression, but he couldn't quite hide the glimmer of approval in his eyes. "But it *was* good of you, Your Grace, to see to Miss St. Claire's door."

"Not another word, Townsend." For God's sake. This was the very reason he despised heroics. "I should have left the chit where I found her."

Townsend's grin vanished. "Surely not, Your Grace."

"Well, no, but what am I meant to do with her now? I can hardly send her back to Hammond Court while her bedchamber is underwater." But she couldn't stay at Grantham Lodge, either. It wasn't proper. He was an unmarried gentleman, and unmarried gentlemen didn't install innocent young ladies in their homes.

Not even if the young lady in question had been installed well out of the way of his own bedchamber, and even when said unmarried gentleman didn't find the lady in question at all alluring.

Distracting, yes. Infuriating, certainly. But alluring? No.

At least, not much so. Not so much he couldn't keep his hands to himself.

That is, there was no denying Miss St. Claire was . . . satisfactory. No doubt there were scores of gentlemen who'd find her unobjectionable enough. Attractive, even, with those green eyes, and that wild cloud of golden hair.

Perhaps even enticing.

Not *him*, of course, but other, less particular gentlemen. "It *isn't* proper for her to stay here, is it, Townsend? I'm quite right about that, am I not?"

Because now he thought of it, it would be convenient if Miss St. Claire *did* remain at Grantham Lodge. He wanted her gone from Hammond Court, and now she was, albeit temporarily. Still, a temporary absence could become a permanent one quickly enough, if he managed the thing properly.

"It's, ah, a trifle unconventional, Your Grace."

Unconventional, yes. That was the word for it. Not scandalous, or shocking—nothing so terrible as that, but merely a trifle unconventional. "Then again, it wouldn't be at all gentlemanly to toss poor Miss St. Claire out into the cold, would it, Townsend? She's a defenseless young lady, after all, and recently bereaved."

Recently bereaved, and recently made an heiress, too. Or half an heiress, at any rate, and thus vulnerable to any unscrupulous fortune hunters who happened to be lurking around Fairford. No doubt there were dozens of them. Why, it was practically his duty to take her in.

"Yes, that's so, Your Grace," Townsend allowed, but his tone was wary, and he looked suspicious.

"You needn't look at me like that, Townsend. I'm merely concerned about what's best for Miss St. Claire, just as you are."

Townsend's brows lowered. "Of course, Your Grace."

As for what was best for Miss St. Claire, well, that was obvious, wasn't it? The chit should be married off at once, before she got herself into any more trouble. But to whom? If any of the young men in Fairford wanted to marry Miss St. Claire, presumably they would have done so by now.

He eyed Townsend. "You're quite sure you're already married, Townsend?"

"Yes, Your Grace, reasonably certain. My five children were rather a mistake, otherwise."

Five children? Good Lord. "Perhaps a trifle more self-control might be in order, Townsend."

"Yes, Your Grace."

Max drummed his fingers on the top of his desk, thinking. There was no denying Miss St. Claire would be far better off if she were safely married. The lady was very young, far too pretty for her own good, and left friendless and destitute in a cruel, wicked world.

Of course, it *would* make it much easier for him to get his hands on Hammond Court if she did happen to marry a gentleman who was amenable to his influence. But wouldn't an advantageous marriage benefit her, as well?

It was a good idea, by God. A marriage, between Miss St. Claire and . . . well, someone. Anyone would do, really. Not Townsend, but another gentleman, one who would do as he was told, and turn Hammond Court over to Max as soon as the wedding vows had been spoken.

Yes, what he needed to do was to keep Miss St. Claire here at Grantham Lodge until he could find some stray gentleman or other to marry her. But what were the chances a tiny village like Fairford would yield up a suitable bridegroom?

Unlikely, at best.

London, however, was another matter. God knew there was no shortage of gentlemen in London who'd be thrilled to discharge their debt to him so easily. A nice baron would do, or perhaps a viscount. Miss St. Claire could hardly complain about becoming a viscountess, could she? Yes, a handsome, fashionable viscount would come in quite handy, one who owed him a favor, and would do his bidding without complaint, someone like—

He jerked upright. By God, he had just the viscount in mind! "I think, Townsend, that it would be best if Miss St. Claire remained at Grantham Lodge, after all."

Best for him, certainly, which was all he cared about.

"But what of the young lady's reputation, Your Grace? Fairford is a small village, and people do talk."

"Mrs. Watson is here. She'll make certain the girl's virtue remains unsullied." That should be enough to satisfy even the most prudish of Fairford's citizens, and anyway, it wouldn't matter, once she was married.

It was a clever scheme. Diabolical, yes, but clever. One of his best. And if he *did* feel just a tiny twinge of conscience at so ruthlessly manipulating the situation, it would pass soon enough.

It always did.

CHAPTER 10

"Ah, there we are. Those pretty eyelashes are fluttering, at last."

Something was touching Rose's face. Fingertips? Yes, fingertips were tapping gently at her cheek, and there was a voice murmuring something, but she couldn't quite make sense of it through the cotton wool in her head.

"Can you hear me, Miss St. Claire?"

Rose opened her mouth to reply to the kind voice, but only an incoherent stream of garbled sounds emerged as if her tongue were wrapped in velvet.

"That's it, lass. Time to come around."

She shifted, her brow furrowing at the soft warmth wrapped around her, but her eyes refused to open. Why was she so tired? Something had happened, but prod as she might, her sluggish brain could only provide a few messy bits and pieces of it. Trying to make sense of them was like groping her way through a darkened room.

She'd fallen asleep in the chair in her bedchamber last night, burrowed under a nest of blankets, her eyelids growing heavy as the sky beyond the window turned indigo, then a deep, penetrating black, without a single star visible in the sky.

But this wasn't her chair. No, it was far too cozy and comfortable. Something smooth and lavender-scented was draped on top of her, the satiny edge of it tickling her chin. It was like being wrapped in feathers, or . . . silken sheets?

She twisted in her scented cocoon, a question on her lips, but when she tried once again to give it voice, nothing came out but a weary croak.

"There, there." A cool, soft hand touched her forehead. "Just take your time, now."

With great effort, she lifted her heavy eyelids to find a face hovering above her, the pale brown eyebrows drawn with concern. It was a kind face, with a dimpled smile and laugh lines fanning out from the corners of a pair of twinkling blue eyes.

A familiar face, but she couldn't quite place—

"You look confused, and I don't wonder at it, you poor thing, with what you've been through." The face came closer. "Well, we might have known it would come to this. It's not right, for a young lady to be left all alone in a rambling old place like that."

Rose struggled up onto her elbows, her head spinning, and the lady pressed a cup into her hand. "Here, drink this. It's a soothing ginger tea, with just a touch of peppermint. I make it myself, you know."

Rose sipped obediently. Something warm and sweet slid down her throat, and she swallowed eagerly.

"That's a good girl," the lady murmured approvingly

as she set the empty cup on the table beside the bed. She was a grandmotherly sort, with graying brown hair and a generous bosom that made one want to lay their head upon it and sob out their troubles.

Rose collapsed back against the pillows. Her shoulders ached, and it felt as if someone had kicked her in the backside. "What happened?"

The lady sighed. "I'm afraid you lost a bit of your roof in last night's storm. I imagine it was the wind that did it."

"The *roof*?" No, surely not. That is, the roof hadn't been entirely sturdy, and last night's storm had been a powerful one, but surely it hadn't been so violent it had torn the roof off the house?

"Oh." Slowly, the fog in her brain cleared, and memory came rushing back. "Oh, *no*."

There'd been an odd cracking sound, so strange, unlike anything she'd ever heard before, as if wooden beams that had held fast for centuries were snapping like kindling, the swollen ceiling, and the rush of water above her head . . .

"The ceiling." The balloon had burst, and the ceiling had crashed down upon her, bringing a deluge of icy water with it. "The ceiling in my bedchamber collapsed."

"Aye, and it might have been much worse." The lady clucked her tongue. "It's a blessing the duke arrived when he did."

The duke. Of Grantham. It was all coming back to her now, like a nightmare in reverse.

"I don't say I approve of everything the duke does."

The lady fussed with the coverlet, smoothing it under Rose's chin. "Or most things even, come to that—but he did the right thing, bringing you here."

Here. The room was too dim for her to properly assess her surroundings, but the fire was roaring in the grate, the pillows cradling her head were as fluffy as a cloud, and the delicate teacup from which she'd just drank was made of very fine porcelain, indeed.

There was only one place in Fairford that could boast such luxuries.

Grantham Lodge. Where else? How could she have forgotten? The duke had appeared at Hammond Court just after dawn, taken one look at the destruction of her bedchamber, and in typical ducal fashion had begun issuing orders. Why, she'd hardly had a chance to say a word before he'd bundled her into his carriage and . . . and *absconded* with her back to Grantham Lodge.

"I'm Mrs. Watson, Miss St. Claire," the lady was saying. "I'm the housekeeper here at Grantham Lodge."

Mrs. Watson. Of course. She recognized her now. "It's kind of you to take such good care of me, Mrs. Watson."

"Oh, I'm happy to do it, Miss St. Claire." Mrs. Watson beamed at her. "You're the first guest we've ever had at Grantham Lodge, you know."

"Am I? How delightful."

"It's a shame, for such a big house as this to always be empty." Mrs. Watson tutted. "Why, such a grand house is meant to be filled with children. Don't you think so, Miss St. Claire?"

"I, ah, yes, of course." Though one couldn't quite

picture the Duke of Grantham as a doting father. "Might I trouble you for a bit more of your ginger and peppermint tea, Mrs. Watson? It's quite soothing."

"Of course, dear." Mrs. Watson patted her hand, then rose and reached for the teacup. "I'll just nip out and fetch you some more, shall I? I'll see to it a bath is brought up, as well."

"Oh, there's no need, Mrs. Watson. I don't like to put you to any trouble." Though she couldn't deny a bath did sound heavenly.

"Nonsense, Miss St. Claire. You rest now, and I'll be back before you know it."

"All right. Thank you, Mrs. Watson."

Rose waited until the housekeeper had bustled out the door before sinking lower in the bed and pulling the coverlet over her face. How easy it would be to hide here, to burrow into this dream of a bed until her heart no longer ached, and all her troubles vanished.

But it was out of the question. Now that fate had done her worst, what was to prevent the duke from finishing the job, and tearing what remained of Hammond Court to the ground?

Not a blessed thing, aside from her continued presence there.

Oh, fate was a wicked, vengeful creature, and must even now be chortling with glee over the trouble she'd caused!

But there was nothing to be done about it now except scurry home at once before the duke seized on this little mishap with the roof as an excuse to do what he'd been longing to do all along. Otherwise, all her plans and dreams to save Hammond Court—to persuade the Duke of Grantham to fall in love with it and keep her promise to Ambrose—were in utter ruins.

She'd stay for the bath, but that was *it*. No more ginger tea, or blazing fire, or soft, fluffy bedding, no matter how seductive it was. She already owed the duke her thanks. The longer she remained, the greater her debt to him would be.

The sooner she left Grantham Lodge and the Duke of Grantham behind her, the better.

"How does Miss St. Claire do?" Townsend, who'd managed to hold his tongue for the better part of the afternoon, looked up from the stack of letters he'd been answering. "Is there any news of her yet, Your Grace?"

Max had been writing his own letter, but his hand stilled at the question, and black ink spilled from the nib, spoiling the page. "Damn it, Townsend. You've made me blot my letter."

"Oh, dear. I beg your pardon, Your Grace."

Max glared down at the dripping end of his pen, then tossed it aside with a sigh. There was no sense in blaming poor Townsend. He was just out of sorts today, for no particular reason.

It certainly wasn't because he hadn't heard a single word from Mrs. Watson, or because Miss St. Claire had yet to venture out of her bedchamber. Or, more accurately, *his* bedchamber—his, that is, in the sense that all the bedchambers at Grantham Lodge belonged to him.

Not in any salacious, improper sense. Of course not.

But it was just as well if Miss St. Claire kept out of his way. The last thing he needed was the troublesome chit underfoot, distracting him with her nonsense.

Unless . . .

Was it possible she'd fallen ill? She'd been soaked to the skin when he'd come upon her this morning, and the bedchamber was positively arctic, what with that broken window. If she hadn't developed a lung complaint, it would be a blessed miracle.

Mrs. Watson hadn't asked his permission to send for a doctor, but perhaps he'd better check with her, just the same. He was reaching for the bell to summon her when there was a light tap on his study door. "Yes? Come."

"Your Grace?" Miss St. Claire's fair head appeared around the side of the door. "I beg your pardon for interrupting you. Good afternoon, Mr. Townsend."

Townsend leaped up from his chair, his cheeks going as red as his hair. "Miss St. Claire! How do you do? I'm afraid you must be done in, after such a frightening experience."

"You're kind to enquire, Mr. Townsend, but I assure you I'm quite well. Only a little tired."

"You don't *look* well." Max rose belatedly to his feet. "Though better, admittedly, than the last time I saw you."

She was wearing a pale yellow dress, the thick mass of her fair hair scraped into a prim knot at the back of her head, secured with what must be dozens of invisible pins, as there wasn't a single wayward strand to be seen.

She'd obviously borrowed the gown, as it was so large it might have fit two Miss St. Claires, with fabric to spare. She was a wee bit of a thing. It was a wonder she hadn't been killed, her dainty limbs crushed under the weight of the collapsed ceiling.

Everything about her was dainty, aside from her hair.

What business did such a small scrap of a young lady have with such a superfluous quantity of hair as that? How was it she managed not to topple over from the weight of all those wild golden curls?

He sank back into his chair, unaccountably nettled by that extravagant hair. "I don't know what you're doing out of bed, Miss St. Claire. You look perfectly dreadful."

Townsend grimaced. "Er, Your Grace, I don't think—"

"Never mind, Mr. Townsend." Miss St. Claire choked back a laugh. "At this point, I'd find His Grace's flattery much more distressing than his admittedly brutal honesty."

"Is that so, Miss St. Claire?" Max made a show of tidying the papers on his desk, but from under his eyelashes he gave her a slow, thorough perusal. "Then you won't mind my saying you look as if you've been dragged backward through a knothole."

Townsend gasped. "I beg your pardon, Your Grace, but I really must insist that you—"

"It's all right, Mr. Townsend. I don't deny I've had more peaceful weeks than this one, and I suppose it shows." Miss St. Claire smiled at Townsend, then turned her attention back to Max. "I wondered if I might have a word with you, Your Grace?"

"Of course. Townsend, if you would?"

Townsend cast him a reproachful glance, then left the room, leaving the door half-open behind him.

"Sit down, Miss St. Claire." He waved her toward one of the chairs in front of his desk.

"Thank you, Your Grace."

Max drew in a sharp breath as she settled into the chair on the other side of his desk. The heavy snowfall had dwindled to an occasional burst of snow flurries, but it was clear now, and a ray of pale sunlight fell across her face.

Her eyes were ringed with dark circles, her lips were tight as if she were in pain, and her cheeks were as pale as death. Some emotion flickered to life in his chest and swelled, mushrooming inside him until his ribs ached with it, his heart pressing against his sternum, threatening to tear it in two.

Damn the girl, what was she thinking, staying in that decrepit old house? Didn't she have any sense at all? Why, anyone could see it was merely a matter of time before another part of that house collapsed on top of her. "I can plainly see, Miss St. Claire, that you're not well at all. I insist you return to bed at once."

His voice was clipped, his tone cold, but if she resented it, one couldn't tell from the angelic smile she gave him. "I'm perfectly well, Your Grace, only a bit sore."

"That's hardly surprising, Miss St. Claire, given I found you sprawled on the floor with a chair on top of you. I can only assume you fell off it."

"I did, yes." She waved a hand as if a fall from a chair into a hip bath's worth of half-frozen water were a mere trifle. "But I didn't come to see you to—"

"Is that all you have to say? For God's sake, you

might have cracked your head open. If the beams in your bedchamber had given way, you might even now be buried under a mountain of rubble with broken fragments of your skull scattered on the floor around you!"

She stared at him, clearly taken aback by his vehemence, but she couldn't have been more shocked at it than he was. Good Lord, what was wrong with him? There was a reason the *ton* called him the Duke of Ice behind his back. He wasn't given to fits of temper, but here he was scolding Miss St. Claire like a hysterical grandmother.

How the devil had this tiny slip of a girl managed to burrow under his skin?

Then again, perhaps it wasn't all that surprising. She *was* Ambrose's daughter.

"That's, ah, wonderfully descriptive of you, Your Grace. But as you can see, my skull remains intact. Indeed, that's why I've come to see you. We didn't begin on the most cordial terms, but—"

"Cordial? You tried to *shoot* me, Miss St. Claire."

"Nonsense. If I'd intended to shoot you, Your Grace, you'd be dead. But that's neither here nor there. We didn't begin on the most cordial terms, as I said, and thus I had no reason to expect any kindness from you, but you did me a good turn today, and I'm grateful to you for it."

"You might return the favor if you had a mind to, Miss St. Claire." He leaned back in his chair, assessing her. "As you know, you possess something I want very much."

"You mean Hammond Court, of course." She shook

her head. "As much as it pains me, I'm afraid I must disappoint you, Your Grace."

"I did you a good turn, Miss St. Claire. You said so yourself. I might even have saved your life. Your life, in exchange for a ramshackle house? It seems a fair trade to me, but of course, I'd pay you handsomely, nevertheless."

"Perhaps it would be a fair trade *if* you had saved my life, and *if* Hammond Court were just a house, but it's not, Your Grace. Not to me."

No, not to him, either. It was a piece of his history, a part shadowed by loss, anger, and grief, yet he wanted it back, just the same. Ironically, Miss St. Claire might be the only person in England who could understand what Hammond Court meant to him.

"I came to thank you, Your Grace," she murmured when he didn't reply. "I don't know how you happened to be there at such an early hour, but I'm grateful you were."

He glanced down at his blotted letter, his dripping pen, the uncapped bottle of ink on his desk—anywhere but at *her*, into those green eyes shining with gratitude. "Yes, well, despite our differences, Miss St. Claire, I've no wish to see a young lady injured, or worse." He cleared his throat. "Even if such a tragedy might easily have been prevented and was a result of her extreme foolishness."

He deployed the eyebrow then, which conveyed better than words ever could how unwise it was of her to remain at Hammond Court in the first place.

But the eyebrow didn't appear to have any effect on

Miss St. Claire, who only raised her own eyebrow in return. "Yes, well, it was good of you, Your Grace." She cocked her head to the side, considering him. "I'm rather glad I didn't shoot you, after all."

A wild laugh swelled in his throat—really, the chit was half-mad—but he swallowed it back before his lips could so much as twitch. It wouldn't do for her to think he found her ridiculous antics amusing.

"I didn't wish to leave today without expressing my thanks," she went on. "And to assure you I'm sensible of the kindness you've done me."

"Leaving?" He leaped up. "You can't mean you're returning to Hammond Court?"

She blinked. "But of course, I am. Where else would I go?"

She rose to her feet, but she was a trifle unsteady. He hurried around the desk, taking her arm. "Sit down, Miss St. Claire, before you fall over."

"Nonsense. I'm perfectly well, and I must be going. Billy will be wondering where I am."

"You're *not* going back to Hammond Court." For God's sake, was the girl *trying* to put an end to her existence? "It isn't safe. One would think you'd have come to that conclusion on your own after the roof toppled down upon your head."

"Nonsense. It did no such thing. It was merely the ceiling, and only a small part of it, at that."

She tugged at her arm, but he held her fast. "It will be awkward, indeed, Miss St. Claire, if I'm forced to lock you in the guest bedchamber to prevent you from returning to Hammond Court."

She glared at him, her cheeks flushing. "Yes, it would make it a great deal easier for you if I gave up, wouldn't it? Unfortunately for you, Your Grace, I don't intend to make it easy for you to tear Hammond Court to the ground!"

God above, the girl was driving him mad. "These theatrics are hardly necessary. It does not, alas, make you any less a half owner of the house if you're not living there. Here or there, you are, I assure you, still very much in my way."

"Be that as it may, I prefer to be in your way from *there*." She glanced pointedly at his hand, which was still on her arm. "Unhand me, if you please, Your Grace."

Damn it, he couldn't let her go now, not when he was so close to putting his plan into action. But how the devil was he going to persuade her to remain at Grantham Lodge long enough for his chosen viscount to come to Fairford, court, and marry her?

How long did a courtship take? No more than a fortnight, surely, or, if she could be persuaded to fall in love with Viscount Dunwitty, the entire tedious business shouldn't take more than a couple of hours, at most.

Love was—if he could judge by his friends Basingstoke's and Montford's recent marriages—a thing one could fall into with astonishing rapidity, and Miss St. Claire was a young lady, and thus susceptible to the sorts of romantic notions that plagued all young ladies.

Why, it should be the easiest thing in the world for her to fall in love. "I must insist, Miss St. Claire, that you remain here at Grantham Lodge through to Twelfth Night. Indeed, I demand it."

"Twelfth Night!" She stared at him. "Are you mad? I can't stay in this house alone with you for weeks on end!"

"We'd hardly be alone, Miss St. Claire, with two dozen servants wandering about."

She drew herself up, her lips in a prim line. "You know servants aren't considered proper chaperones, Your Grace."

"Mrs. Watson would be highly offended to hear you say so, Miss St. Claire, but of course, I didn't mean *only* the servants. There will be, er, some others here, as well."

"Oh? Who?"

A good question, that. Think, man, think!

She raised an eyebrow as the silence stretched between them. "Your Grace?"

"I'm, er, er . . . well, the thing is, I'm . . ." *What?* Speak, damn it! But his brain, usually so reliably diabolical, failed to produce a single convincing lie with the weight of those green eyes upon him.

"I beg your pardon, Your Grace, but I really must be getting back to—"

"I'm hosting a Christmas house party, here at Grantham Lodge!"

CHAPTER 11

"A Christmas house party?" The Duke of Grantham was hosting a fortnight of jolly festivities to celebrate the wonders of the season? "*You're* hosting a Christmas house party?"

"I believe I just said so. But you look surprised, Miss St. Claire. Is there some reason, in your estimable opinion, why I should *not* host a Christmas house party?"

Under the cover of her lashes, Rose gazed at the man perched on the edge of the desk. His shoulders were stiff, his lips turned down in a stern frown, his gray eyes as frosty as winter clouds shrouding the sun. "Why, no. No, of course not, Your Grace. It's just that . . ."

Well, he wasn't precisely bursting with merriment, was he? In fact, of all the gentlemen she was acquainted with, he was the very last one she would have imagined would host a grand holiday celebration.

Indeed, it would perhaps be best if he didn't attempt it, for it was bound to be a grim, cheerless affair. "It's just that I was under the impression you detested Fairford, and couldn't wait to return to London."

He blinked. "Whatever gave you that idea? You have

a most fertile imagination, Miss St. Claire. If I ever *did* imply such a thing, I can assure you, that was before."

She waited, but he didn't continue, just stared at her with those molten eyes. "Yes, Your Grace?" Before he realized how charming Fairford was? Before he was taken with a sudden and all-consuming passion for the holiday season? Neither seemed likely. "Before *what*?"

"Before I . . . that is, before my . . ."

She cocked her head, studying him. It was a simple question, but the duke appeared uncharacteristically flummoxed. "Yes?"

"Before I . . . before I made up my mind to marry! Yes, that's it. I wish for my, er . . . my future duchess to spend a Christmas at Grantham Lodge."

He folded his arms over his chest, looking pleased with himself.

"You're *betrothed*, Your Grace?" It was the last thing she'd expected him to say. He didn't behave as if he was betrothed. Not that she had the least idea how a betrothed gentleman was meant to behave, and, of course, the duke might do as he pleased.

It was nothing to her.

Still, it was curious that little morsel of gossip hadn't reached them here in Fairford, even considering their distance from London. The good citizens of Fairford tended to keep alert for rumors regarding the Duke of Grantham, and rumors of a soon-to-be-installed duchess were important news, particularly for his tenants.

"Er, well, not betrothed, exactly, but I may be so, very soon."

"I see." She didn't, though. This betrothal seemed to

have come on quite suddenly, rather like an attack of the vapors, much like the Christmas house party itself had done. Indeed, there was something strange about this entire thing, not the least of which was the duke's shifty expression.

But in the end, did it matter? He might wed whomever he pleased. He might host the merriest Christmas party Fairford had ever seen to impress his future betrothed. He might festoon every corner of Grantham Lodge with greenery, sing Christmas carols until his lungs gave out, then drown himself in a bowl of wassail—

Ahem.

The point was, the duke's Christmas party made no difference to *her*. She couldn't possibly remain at Grantham Lodge for it. Indeed, there were a dozen reasons to be wary of his invitation, not the least of which was his reputation for ruthlessness. If she agreed to remain under his roof, she would be putting herself directly in his power.

Then again, if she wanted to fulfill her promise to Ambrose, what choice did she have? If she was going to persuade the duke to make peace with his past, she needed access to him, and it wasn't as if he were likely to bring his fine London friends to visit Hammond Court, was it? It was hardly fit for guests, with its broken windows and collapsed roof.

Even she couldn't remain there for much longer. It wasn't safe. It had only been the ceiling of her bedchamber last night, but tomorrow it could be the roof itself.

She was running out of time.

As for this Christmas party, well . . . she didn't know quite what to make of it, but if His Grace truly was on the verge of marrying, and the lady was to come here to Grantham Lodge, it would certainly be best for Fairford if she approved of the place and wished to spend time here.

It was not in his tenants' interest for the duke to remain an absentee landlord, and given Ambrose's tenants would soon become the Duke of Grantham's tenants, it was welcome news that the duke was considering marrying.

Yes, indeed. Very welcome news.

But what were the chances a lady accustomed to all the delights Town had to offer would find anything to please her in tiny Fairford? That is, it was a pleasing town, of course—why, there wasn't a lovelier place in all of England—but a lady as elegant as a future duchess must be, might find it too small and rustic to be of much interest.

Now, if Grantham Lodge had been at all welcoming, perhaps it might have been different, but as it was . . . she glanced around the study. It was an elegant room, the furnishings in the height of fashion, as one would expect of a duke. The settee was done in a rich, dark blue silk, and the desk was a massive rosewood affair, every inch of it polished to a high gloss.

The same could be said of the other rooms in the house, as well, or at least the few she'd peeked into on her way to the study. There seemed to be an endless number of sitting rooms and parlors, each more lavish than the last, with costly silk wallpapers and massive, carved stone fireplaces.

Yet somehow, for all its grandness, Grantham Lodge wasn't a welcoming place.

The beautiful silk settees looked as if they'd never been graced by a single backside. There wasn't as much as a speck of soot to be seen in any of the grand fireplaces, as if nary a fire had ever been lit in any of them. The elegant brass doorknobs didn't bear a single fingerprint. It was as if every trace of a human hand had been erased.

Everything was spotless, still, and cold.

It wasn't a *home*. For all its spiders, leaky ceilings, and smoking fireplaces, Hammond Court was alive with the memories of the dozens of lives that had unfolded there. It had been lived in, loved, whereas Grantham Lodge . . . well, if she were the Duke of Grantham's future duchess, she'd take one look at this house and flee for her very life.

"You look dismayed, Miss St. Claire."

She startled. Goodness, she'd almost forgotten he was there. "I beg your pardon?"

"Your expression." His cool, gray gaze was fixed on her, his eyebrows lowered in a frown. "What are you thinking about?"

"Thinking? Why, nothing at all." She straightened her spine and tugged her skirts into place. "Though it does occur to me, Your Grace, that if you *are* to have house guests, there might be one or two ladies among them who would agree to act as a chaperone for me."

He raised an eyebrow. "If there were any such ladies, Miss St. Claire? What then?"

She sucked in a breath, forced a smile to her lips, and sent up a quick prayer to the heavens that she wasn't making a dreadful mistake. "Then it would be entirely appropriate for me to remain at Grantham Lodge through the holidays. There can be nothing shocking about my being one among many guests, surely."

"Certainly not. Nothing shocking at all."

"But I must have your permission to send for my former nursemaid, Abby Hinde, to join me here." She couldn't make do without Abby. She needed her dear old friend, now more than ever.

"You haven't left her at Hammond Court, I hope?"

"Of course not, Your Grace. She's staying with a Mrs. Sullivan, in Cirencester."

"Very well. I'll send a footman to fetch her this afternoon. Any other demands, Miss St. Claire?"

"Well, since you ask, Your Grace, I'd be pleased to help your servants with your Christmas house party." She'd planned the holiday fete at Hammond Court for the past eight years, and they'd had some lovely celebrations.

"Yes, yes." He waved a careless hand at her. "If you like."

"Wonderful." Perhaps she could weave some of her magic here at Grantham Lodge. "I have some truly inspired ideas regarding Christmas garlands."

He blinked. "Garlands?"

"Of course. You have heard of garlands, have you not, Your Grace? Pine boughs, and kissing balls, and

the like? Garlands at Christmastime are tradition."
Goodness, he did need her help, didn't he?

Because as it was . . . she glanced around the room
again, smothering a grimace. If ever there was a place
meant to stifle any attempt at merriment, it was this one.

As for the Duke of Grantham himself . . .

She took him in, so stern and austere, clad from head
to toe in somber shades of gray and black, aside from
his cravat. It was a proper snowy white, but so rigid it
looked as if it were strangling him, and the points of his
collar were as sharp as blades.

Such ruthless elegance was off-putting. Alas, there
wasn't much she could do about his collar points, but
she could see to it his house was made inviting, and . . .
dare she hope it?

Merry.

"Then we agree, Miss St. Claire? You will remain as
my guest at Grantham Lodge until Twelfth Night?"

"If there is a proper chaperone amongst your guests,
then yes, Your Grace. I can't think of any reason why I
should not." She offered him as cheerful a smile as she
could muster. "It's kind of you to have me."

He frowned as if he hadn't the first idea what to do
with her smile or thanks. "Both the Duchess of Basingstoke and the Duchess of Montford will attend the
house party. Can you make do with one or the other of
them as your chaperone?"

Duchesses? Goodness. "I daresay I can manage,
Your Grace."

"It's settled, then." He rubbed his hands together,

looking far too pleased with himself. "Now, if you'll excuse me, Miss St. Claire, I have some letters to write."

"Of course." She rose from her chair. "Might I have your permission to have a word with Mrs. Watson and your cook, Your Grace?"

"Whatever for?"

"Why, because it's already December the fourteenth."

He frowned at her. "Yes? What of it?"

"The Christmas pudding, Your Grace. Stir-up Sunday is November twenty-first. We're already weeks behind. If you want a proper Christmas pudding, it must be prepared today. Surely, you don't intend to host a Christmas house party without a proper Christmas pudding?"

He gave her a flat look. "I wouldn't dream of it, Miss St. Claire."

"Then I do have your permission to speak to Mrs. Watson, Your Grace?"

"Yes, yes. Go on." He waved a careless hand toward the door.

"Thank you, Your Grace." She left him alone at his desk, the frown still on his lips, and skipped out into the corridor, her heart lifting. She and Abby had always made the Christmas pudding together on Stir-up Sunday. It was a tradition at Hammond Court, and every year Ambrose pronounced it the best Christmas pudding he'd ever tasted.

It wouldn't be the same this year, without him. How could it be?

But it was something.

* * *

Christmas pudding, of all the ridiculous things.

Miss St. Claire's only home was a crumbling estate, the ceiling of which had collapsed on top of her mere hours ago. She was as destitute as the poor creatures who begged for coins in Covent Garden, and she'd just willingly placed herself in the clutches of a merciless duke who was determined to tear her house to the ground.

One would think a young lady with no money, no connections, and few friends would have enough to worry about without fretting over a Christmas pudding.

Still, fussing about with the pudding was as good a way as any to keep her busy, and thus out of his way. He rose from his desk to close the study door behind her, but a low, sweet sound made him pause with his ear pressed to the gap.

Miss St. Claire was making her way down the hallway, and she was . . .

Humming? By God, she was.

"God Rest Ye, Merry Gentlemen." Comfort, joy, and all that nonsense.

He waited until the humming faded, the soft thud of her footsteps receding, then pushed the door closed, returned to his desk, and threw himself into his chair. Why must she be so bloody cheerful all the time? It was most tedious of her, and it made him feel like a perfect villain to take advantage of a lady who took such obvious delight in Christmas puddings and Christmas carols.

If he could so callously manipulate Miss St. Claire, what was next? Drowning kittens? Kicking puppies? Pulling a child's hair?

Still, he'd solved his most pressing problem. Miss

St. Claire would remain at Grantham Lodge until Twelfth Night, just as he wished.

Now, onto the next problem, and a daunting one it was. Not quite as daunting as managing a termagant like Rose St. Claire, but daunting enough.

The house party. Somehow, he'd have to lure a dozen or two of London's most fashionable people away from their warm firesides on shockingly short notice, and persuade them to spend Christmas in the cold, muddy countryside.

Which would be quite a trick, given even *he* didn't want to be here.

It was a damned good thing he wasn't anyone less than the Duke of Grantham, or he never could have managed it. As it was, he'd need Basingstoke and Montford to see the thing done.

The *ton* wasn't going to fancy the long hours of travel to Fairford, but they'd hurry off to hell itself if three dukes and two duchesses awaited them at the end of their journey.

He jerked open the drawer of his desk, snatched up a handful of paper and a new quill, and dipped the nib into the bottle of ink. He stared down at the blank page for a long moment, considering, then scrawled,

Basingstoke,
I've urgent need of you and your duchess in
Fairford. Come at once, and bring Montford and
the Duchess of Montford with you. Grantham.

There. It was a bit brusque, but they'd come, if only to satisfy their curiosity. He never spent any time at

Grantham Lodge, and he'd certainly never invited any of his friends here.

Neither Basingstoke nor Montford could resist a mystery, especially Montford.

He read the note over once again. Yes, it would do. It was just cryptic enough to lure his friends here.

Now, as far as his mythical future duchess was concerned . . .

Damn it, why the devil had he told Miss St. Claire he was thinking of marrying, of all things? He wasn't—not seriously, at any rate. Before he'd left London it had crossed his mind that Lady Emily Bolland might make a proper wife, but he'd hardly spared her a thought since he'd arrived in Fairford.

God knew the house party alone was bad enough without throwing a fictional betrothed into it, but she'd caught him off guard, and then she'd been gazing at him with those green eyes, and . . . well, he'd panicked.

It was too late to fix it now.

He'd have to invite Lady Emily. She'd come to Fairford at once if he beckoned her, if only because she fancied herself the future mistress of Grantham Lodge.

That might prove to be a problem.

He'd told Miss St. Claire he was courting this lady, so he'd have to play the part of the besotted swain, and Lady Emily was a touch too eager to be courted, and she could become a trifle irritable if she was thwarted in any way.

She was a renowned London beauty, but she was one of those sulky, petulant ladies that were so fashionable these days. There was no denying she had a lovely face, but he wasn't much enamored of her sullenness. Why, he even preferred Miss St. Claire, who was an impertinent, cheeky bit of baggage, to a peevish, bad-tempered bird of paradise.

For all her other *many* flaws, Miss St. Claire did have a pretty smile.

She smiled with her whole mouth. Hers was a country girl's smile, not the simpering half smirk so common amongst the fashionable ladies of London.

No, he didn't fancy a fortnight of Lady Emily's company, but if not her, then who?

There was no one. He didn't have many friends in London. Aside from Basingstoke and Montford and their wives, there was no one he wished to invite to his home. He had no friends at all here in Fairford, which was . . .

Perfectly fine. Just the way he wanted it.

He reached for another piece of paper, and scrawled a terse note to Lady Emily, bidding her to come to Fairford. Then he set it aside and took up another piece of paper. Within the hour, he had several dozen briefly worded invitations, each sealed with the Grantham crest, and resting in a pile at the corner of his desk.

He sat for a while, staring at them.

He had one final invitation to write, but did he dare?

It was devious, to be sure. Underhanded, and unworthy of a gentleman. Breaking Miss St. Claire's door down hadn't been his finest moment, but this would be much worse. If he did proceed, and the scheme worked—and his schemes generally did—then the ramifications of it would be far-reaching.

But not necessarily bad. Indeed, when one considered how bleak Miss St. Claire's current situation was, one could argue he was doing her a good turn. Didn't every young lady want to marry a peer? It wasn't as if Miss St. Claire had a prayer of making such a match without his interference—er, his help, that is.

Yes, his help. That was more accurate. She'd be made a viscountess, after all.

All it would cost her was half of a house.

His house. Perhaps not legally—not yet—but his all the same, and a part of the Grantham family property since his mother had wed his father. It had taken him years, decades, to retrieve each piece of the legacy his father had lost—years of watching, waiting, and meticulous planning—but bit by bit he'd gathered up the pieces of his past, like a boy collecting seashells on the sand—and put them back together again.

All but Hammond Court. Year after year, it had eluded him, the last piece of a puzzle that would make him whole again.

That it was his mother's house, the house where he'd last known joy, the house that came closer to any other to being his home—mattered not a whit. In the end, it was merely another part of his past now, a piece of his history, one as shadowed by loss, anger, and grief as every other memory he had of the lonely years he'd spent in Fairford.

He'd tear it down, and once it was gone, the memories would no longer haunt him.

Slowly, he reached for another piece of paper, dipped his pen, and began to write.

Dunwitty. I require your nephew's presence at a house party at Grantham Lodge, my country seat in Fairford. Send him at once. Grantham.

That was all, but Lord Dunwitty would know it for what it was. Not an invitation, but a summons, and one he wouldn't dream of disobeying. No, he'd count himself fortunate to have the chance to discharge his debt with a favor instead of money he didn't have, and he'd pack his nephew off to Fairford.

Just like that, it was done.

Some claimed he was ruthless, merciless—even cruel. Perhaps it was true, but it wasn't as if he were dooming Miss St. Claire to a nightmare of a marriage. Viscount Dunwitty was handsome, fashionable, and wealthy, and by all accounts a decent fellow, if a trifle dull-witted.

He'd make the girl a tolerable husband.

He held the candle to the end of the stick of wax and watched it drip until a blood-red puddle formed on the seam of the cream-colored paper, then he stamped it with his seal.

The Grantham crest. *Qui suffert, vincit.*

He who endures, conquers.

CHAPTER 12

"I can't find the lemon peel." Rose rummaged through the spice chest in the corner of the kitchen, pulling open the little drawers and examining the contents within. "There's parsley, marjoram, dill, mustard, and so on, but none of the spices used in sweets."

What would become of the Christmas pudding? One couldn't have Christmas pudding without lemon peel, or . . . no, there was no orange or candied citron, either, and no almonds or cinnamon. Perhaps she could make do without the citron, though it wouldn't be the same without it, but for pity's sake, what was a Christmas pudding without cinnamon?

She turned to the housekeeper, who was fussing with the duke's tea tray. "Is there no cinnamon, Mrs. Watson?"

"Oh, dear. There may not be, I'm afraid. We eat rather simply here at Grantham Lodge, Miss St. Claire."

Simply? How odd. Grantham Lodge was many things, but simple wasn't one of them. Why, she'd imagined the kitchen in such a grand estate would be stuffed to the brim with the finest of everything a cook could desire, from the most delicate mace to the sweetest vanilla.

Really, it was excessively disappointing, but then Grantham Lodge was a strange place, wasn't it? Both luxurious and empty at once. "Does the duke's cook not bake, Mrs. Watson?" Perhaps the duke didn't care for sweets. Perhaps even sacks full of the finest white sugar couldn't turn that sour tongue sweet.

"Well, as to that, we don't have a cook. Not a formal one, leastways."

"No *cook*?" An estate this size, with no cook? Why, such a thing was unheard of. She must have misunderstood. "You mean to say the Duke of Grantham doesn't keep a cook?"

"There's Mrs. Cowles who comes in on weekdays to prepare meals, but otherwise, no, and she's no baker, is Mrs. Cowles. Oh, she does the bread and the odd scone here or there, but no sweets to speak of."

"But, this kitchen, Mrs. Watson!" Rose glanced around the spacious, light-filled space. For a man who didn't employ a cook, the duke had the loveliest kitchen she'd ever seen, with every convenience one could imagine, as if it had been designed for one of those uppity French chefs the aristocrats were so fond of these days. She'd nearly swooned when she walked through the door. "Why, it's criminal, that such a kitchen as this should have no cook!"

It was like a horse with no rider, or a barn with no cats. A Christmas pudding with no cinnamon, or . . . or . . . a duke, with no duchess.

Now, where had that thought come from?

She pushed it aside and turned her attention back to Mrs. Watson, who'd taken the kettle off the stove and was pouring the boiling water over the tea leaves. "We haven't had any need of a cook, Miss St. Claire, what with the duke keeping away from Grantham Lodge as he has. There's not much call for fancy meals without a duke to feed, is there?"

"I suppose not, but that will have to change now." Rose nodded at the tea tray, where Mrs. Watson was arranging two withered-looking tea cakes.

"Aye, I suppose it will, at least as long as he remains in Fairford. Mrs. Clancy, His Grace's London house-keeper, is sending their chef, Monsieur Blanchard, to us for the duration of the house party, and thank goodness for it. I do hope he arrives before the guests." She cast a disconsolate glance at the two pitiful tea cakes. "Oh, dear. They don't look particularly appetizing, do they?"

"I'm afraid not, but never mind. I'll make up a fresh batch for the duke's tea." Rose took the plate with the tea cakes off the tray and set it aside. "I daresay you have flour, eggs, and milk? Is it too much to hope that you have currants?"

"Why, how kind of you, Miss St. Claire. But you must be done in after your ordeal at Hammond Court. I can't ask you to—"

"You didn't ask, Mrs. Watson. I offered, and I'm pleased to do it. I love to putter about in the kitchen, especially one as pretty as this one. I'm quite a compe-tent baker if I do say it myself. Not a cook, mind you, but I can be trusted with sweets."

"Well, if you insist on it, I won't naysay you." Mrs.

Watson stood back, watching as Rose moved about the kitchen, gathering her ingredients. "I daresay the duke will appreciate it, after enduring Mrs. Cowles's confectionary efforts these past few days."

The duke, appreciative? Rose held back an unladylike snort. She doubted there was anything she could do that would please the Duke of Grantham, but she kept this petty observation to herself and went ahead with her work, busily mixing her ingredients with the ease of years of practice.

"My goodness, child, you have a quick hand with the business, don't you? Where did you learn to bake?"

"My mother taught me. You recall she was Mr. St. Claire's cook for years before she passed away? I used to spend hours with her in the kitchen when I was a child. Everything I know, I learned at her knee."

"Of course, dear. How could I have forgotten?" Mrs. Watson patted her arm. "She was a fine lady, your mother. I daresay Mr. St. Claire must have missed her terribly after she passed away. It's been some years now, has it not?"

"Nine years," Rose murmured, her throat too thick to venture another word. Ambrose *had* missed her mother, and not just as his cook, but as his friend, and no friend could have been more loyal to them than Ambrose had been. He'd been the only one of her mother's childhood friends who'd stood by her in her hour of need.

Their hour of need. She hardly remembered it, of course, having just turned four years old when she and her mother came to Hammond Court. But her mother had reminded her over and over throughout the years that Ambrose had taken them in when all their other friends had turned their backs—that a true friend like Ambrose was rare indeed, and that they owed him everything.

Not that her reminders had been necessary. Rose had loved Ambrose almost on sight, because who could resist such a kind man? To see Ambrose's face, to bask in the warmth of the sunshine of his smile was to love him.

She cleared her throat. "My mother was a wonderful cook, but she wasn't fond of baking. I never took much of a liking to cooking, so once I was old enough I took over the baking for her, and I've been doing it ever since." She smiled at Mrs. Watson. "Did you happen to find any currants?"

"No, I'm afraid not." Mrs. Watson sighed, shaking her head. "It's a pity, because I do love currants in my tea cakes. Sarah's doing the marketing today. I'll have her fetch some, shall I? Is there anything else you need?"

Rose hesitated. The kitchen was not well provisioned, but she was a guest here, and in no position to demand currants, or anything else. Still, there was the Christmas pudding to consider.

"It's all right, Miss St. Claire," Mrs. Watson said, guessing at the reason for her hesitation. "His Grace doesn't concern himself with the doings in the kitchen. We market as we please, and I daresay it will please everyone to have currants in their tea cake, and whatever other culinary delights you can dream up."

"Well, if you're certain it's all right, we really should make up the Christmas pudding today, so there's a chance it will set up properly in time for Christmas dinner. Each of the servants must have a turn to stir, so they might make their Christmas wishes."

"What a lovely idea!" Mrs. Watson beamed. "I can't recall the last time I made a wish over the Christmas pudding. You'll have us all in the holiday spirit yet, Miss St. Claire."

Rose smiled, but in truth, she hadn't been feeling very merry this season. She always felt her mother's absence more keenly at Christmas. Now Ambrose was gone as well, and most of the servants from Hammond Court had been forced to find new places after the financial hardships of last year.

In truth, she felt more alone than she ever had.

The Christmases she'd spent at Hammond Court would soon be only memories, fading to ghosts of themselves as the years passed. How naïve she'd been, to think those Christmases would never end. How silly, to imagine time wouldn't take them from her, one beloved person after the next.

But it wasn't quite over yet. That is, it was the case that she'd be spending this Christmas with a dour duke who, despite having done her a marked kindness this morning, still clearly despised her. But Mrs. Watson was a kind soul, and it was difficult not to be cheered by her enthusiasm.

If she could bring just a bit of Hammond Court's Christmas cheer to Grantham Lodge, she'd consider her time well spent. And if it *did* soften the duke's heart just a touch, all the better. "We must have brandy, too,

Mrs. Watson, and plenty of it, as we'll need to add more to the pudding as it dries."

"Yes, of course. Now, what have I done with my paper and pencil?" Mrs. Watson rummaged in her apron pockets with a frown. "Dear me, I'd forget my head if it wasn't attached. I'll just go find it, and we'll make a list, and send Sarah off to the market at once."

By the time Max finished his last letter it was snowing again, the flakes like tiny white stars falling from a steely sky. Long shadows had gathered in the corners of his study, and without the scratch of his pen against the paper, it was utterly silent.

Too silent.

"Where the devil has everyone gone?" He tugged the cord with a bit more force than necessary, but none of his servants appeared. He pulled his pocket watch out, flipped open the lid, and checked the time.

It was half past four. Well past his teatime.

He threw down his pen, rose from behind his desk, and poked his head into the corridor outside his study door. "Townsend?"

Silence. Even Townsend, who seemed always to be hovering within shouting distance, was nowhere to be found.

He marched out into the hallway, and from there into the library, the music room, and the drawing room, but they were all equally deserted, and none of the seemingly endless number of housemaids he employed were anywhere about, their polishing cloths in hand, ducking their heads like frightened rabbits when he appeared.

For God's sake, where was Mrs. Watson? He wandered back into the entryway, the thud of his boots echoing in the emptiness. Where was Monk? Wasn't his butler meant to be guarding the entryway at all times? His entire household was missing, vanished into thin air.

He paused near the staircase, and that was when the most heavenly scent found his nose. Cloves, oranges, and cinnamon, with another, richer scent layered underneath it. He couldn't quite place it, but it smelled like . . . he drew in a deep breath, his nose twitching.

Dark sugar, sticky and sweet, and warmed brandy.

He'd never smelled anything more delightful in his life. Even Monsieur Blanchard, his chef in London, had never produced such a tempting scent as that.

It was coming from *his* kitchen, wafting up the back stairway, beckoning like a crooked finger. He opened the door and made his way down the narrow staircase, the delectable scent leading him by his nose into the kitchen and tugging an irritable whine from his stomach.

Was this where all the servants were, then? Sitting about in his kitchen, drinking warmed brandy? As if in answer, there was a burst of raucous laughter and the sound of excited voices coming from the other side of the door.

He jerked it open, then stood there gaping, amazed.

Every servant in his household was squeezed into the kitchen, which was quite a trick, really, despite the size of the room, as he employed a great many servants. Damned if he knew all their names, or any of their names, come to that, but here were half a dozen footmen, all the missing housemaids, Mrs. Watson, and Monk, and, yes, there was Townsend, a ridiculous grin on his face as he peered into the iron kettle hanging over the fire.

They were all so preoccupied with whatever they were doing, they didn't even notice he'd entered the kitchen. Why, he might have sat in his study all bloody night, perishing from hunger and cold, and not a single one of them would have been any the wiser.

He opened his mouth to let out a proper ducal howl, but then snapped it closed again when he saw who was presiding over the kettle.

Well, he might have bloody known, mightn't he?

There, right in the middle of the melee was Miss St. Claire, a spoon in her hand, peering down into the contents of the kettle, as if waiting for something. Locks of her fair hair had escaped the ribbon at the back of her neck and were flying about her face in a wild profusion of corkscrew curls from the steam rising from the kettle.

The apron she wore was at least two sizes too large for her and had been wrapped twice around her petite frame. The front of it was stained with some sticky substance that looked like beaten eggs. There were breadcrumbs in her hair, and a daub of flour dusted one of her cheeks.

It was *not* charming. No, there was nothing at all charming about this chit taking over his kitchen and kidnapping his servants. Still, he froze for an instant, a strange sensation in his chest that felt a bit like longing.

Which was utterly ridiculous, of course, as there

wasn't a single thing here he wanted. He crossed his arms tightly over his chest to keep any unwanted emotions from sneaking back in, and barked, "Having a pleasant time, are you?"

His voice rang out through the kitchen, cutting through all the chatter. Dozens of heads all jerked toward him at once, and one by one, the big smiles on his servants' faces faded, replaced with looks of horror.

Every face, that is, but one.

Miss St. Claire turned toward him, her cheeks rosy from the heat, and her face wreathed in smiles. "Oh, Your Grace! You've come just in time!"

"Just in time, Miss St. Claire?" He marched across the kitchen toward her, the servants stepping back to allow him to pass, parting for him as if he were Moses, or, well . . . admittedly, something less miraculous. "I'd sooner say far too late."

If she noticed the servants' uneasy shuffling, she paid no mind to it. "Not at all, Your Grace. You're just in time to have the first stir of the Christmas pudding."

"I'm referring to my tea, Miss St. Claire. It's *late*." He pulled his pocket watch from his waistcoat and made a show of studying the face. "Forty minutes late, to be precise," he added, with a cool glance at Mrs. Watson. "I might have perished from hunger, with none of you any the wiser."

Mrs. Watson darted forward, wringing her hands. "Oh, dear. I do beg your pardon, Your Grace. We were just—"

"Perish, from a late tea? Why, what nonsense." Miss

St. Claire laughed and offered him the spoon. "Come, Your Grace, have a stir, and make your wish."

"What I wish for, Miss St. Claire, is my tea." He eyed the spoon in her hand. "I don't recall expressing a desire for Christmas pudding, or authorizing the making of one at the expense of my tea."

Her brows drew together. On a less open face, that expression of innocent confusion might have looked like a ploy, but she appeared genuinely baffled. "But it's well past Stir-up Sunday already, Your Grace. The Christmas pudding is meant to be prepared on Stir-up Sunday. No one in the household has had a chance to make their Christmas wish."

"I despise Christmas pudding. Mrs. Watson, my tea, if you would be so kind. As for the rest of you, I daresay you have something else to do?"

He turned to go, but he only made it a few steps before Miss St. Claire stopped him with a word. "No!"

"*No*?" He whirled around to face her, not so much angry as stunned. "Did you just say *no* to me, Miss St. Claire?" No one said no to him. Ever.

Given the way everyone else blanched, she should have realized her mistake at once and slunk away in shame, but instead, her chin shot up, and she met his gaze without flinching. "I did, indeed. You might not care for it, Your Grace, but I daresay the others would like to make their wishes."

"Wishes, Miss St. Claire, are for children."

That stubborn chin rose a notch higher. "Stir-up Sunday is a tradition, Your Grace."

Tradition be damned. He didn't care one whit for it,

and he nearly said so aloud, but the words stilled on his tongue when he noticed the expressions on his servants' faces, the way they shuffled their feet, and averted their gazes.

Very well, perhaps the chit had a point. As foolish— no, as *useless* as Christmas wishes were, his servants did appear to want theirs, and . . . well, as much as he scorned such sentimentality, he found he couldn't quite deprive them of it.

Not with Miss St. Claire's accusing green eyes fixed on him.

"Very well. Have your wishes. *Then* may I have my tea?"

"Oh, yes, Your Grace. I'll bring it up at once. You see your tray is right here, all ready to go, and Miss St. Claire made some lovely tea cakes for you."

He glanced at the tray, where a pot of tea was steeping, and beside it a plateful of what looked to be very nice tea cakes.

Very nice, indeed.

He edged closer to the tea tray, his mouth flooding with saliva, reached for one of the perfectly browned cakes, and took a cautious bite.

His eyes dropped closed, an involuntary groan escaping his lips. God, they were perfect. Fluffy, as light as air, and bursting with sweet currants, just as a tea cake was meant to be. He devoured the rest of the cake in one bite, manners be damned, savoring the treat until the last bit of the cake had melted on his tongue.

When he opened his eyes again, Miss St. Claire was

watching him, her face unexpectedly soft, and a half smile curving her lips. "Do the cakes suit, Your Grace?"

He held her gaze for a long beat, then another, a strange fluttering in his chest. He couldn't have said what expression he wore just then, but as they gazed at each other, her eyes went a dark, unfathomable green, like a forest hidden under a canopy of leaves, the warm, gold flecks in their depths like dappled sunshine.

They stared at each other, the moment going on and on, heavy with the crackling tension between them. He was dimly aware of the room falling silent, of his servants' curious glances, but he couldn't tear his gaze away from the curve of her parted lips. Heat thrummed through his veins, unfurling in his belly. He flexed his fingers, digging his nails into his palms to keep from reaching for her, and dragging the back of his knuckles across the soft, warm skin of her cheek.

What would her lips taste like?

Cinnamon and sugar, sweet, dark treacle—

"Your Grace?" She swallowed, her slender throat rippling. "The t-tea cakes?"

He stepped back and dropped his gaze. "They'll do, I suppose."

He didn't wait for her reply, but turned on his heel and left the kitchen, shaken, her green-eyed gaze heavy on his back.

CHAPTER 13

That night, Rose dreamed of tea cakes stuffed with currants, the rich scents of brandy and cinnamon, and dark, heavy eyelashes hiding a pair of smoky gray eyes.

Why were the best dreams always so fleeting? She would happily have lingered in the warm, scented silence of that dream for hours, but she woke with a thousand worries rushing through her mind at once, and the dream dissolved like sugar on her tongue.

Had another window cracked? Had a blizzard overtaken her bedchamber while she slept? Was Mr. Turnbull at the door, shaking his fist and demanding payment? Was the roof leaking?

But no, the customary chill was absent. She was surrounded by warmth, suspended in softness as if cradled in a cloud. She opened her eyes. Above her, the pale green silk bed hangings shimmered in the morning light pouring through the window.

Ah, yes. She was at Grantham Lodge. Grantham Lodge, which, as cheerless as it was, could at least boast roaring fires and snug beds.

She permitted herself a luxurious stretch, reaching

her arms above her head and curling her toes against the fine linens before she tossed the coverlet aside and hurried to the window. A riot of snowflakes had been whirling about when she went to her bed last night, but now the sun was shining as bright as a gold sovereign, illuminating a beautiful blue sky.

It was an ideal winter morning. The sort of morning when Ambrose would have rousted them early from their beds, so they might go skating on the pond at the bottom of the hill behind Hammond Court.

She traced a fingertip over the lacy patterns of frost on the glass, the ice sparkling like diamonds in the sun. How lovely it would be to skate this morning! To twirl about on the ice, her head back and her arms raised to the sky.

A pang of loss pierced her chest, and she might have given way to the tears hovering on her eyelashes, but before they could fall, a soft knock on her bedchamber door made her turn.

"Rose?" Abby peeked around the edge of the door, her tentative smile vanishing when she caught sight of Rose's face. "Oh, my poor lamb. Come here."

She opened her arms, and Rose dashed across the room and threw herself into them, burying her face in Abby's soft bosom.

"What's this, now? I thought to find you all smiles this morning, as pretty a day as it is. What's happened now?"

"It's nothing, really. I was just thinking it's the perfect day to go skating, and wishing . . ."

Wishing for things that could never be.

It wasn't much of an explanation, but Abby understood at once, just as she always did. "There, there," she murmured, stroking Rose's hair.

They stood silently for a while, Rose sniffling into Abby's shoulder while Abby soothed her, but she didn't indulge her tears for long, if only because Ambrose would have disapproved of spending such a lovely day as this weeping.

"There now, that's better." Abby dried Rose's cheeks with the corner of her apron. "Just a bout of the megrims, eh? Well, that's to be expected. I thought perhaps that wicked duke had said something to upset you."

"No. He's been . . ." She trailed off, uncertain how to finish that sentence.

That scene over the Christmas pudding yesterday had been both predictable and surprising at the same time. Predictable in that the duke had behaved precisely as she imagined a spoiled aristocrat would when he'd been made to wait a few extra minutes to be served his tea.

That is, like a child denied a sweet.

He'd been as close to throwing a tantrum as she'd ever seen a grown man come, though he'd done it with the sort of withering arrogance one would expect from a fashionable duke.

Still, a tantrum was a tantrum, no matter how elegantly it was thrown.

But then, against her every expectation, he'd yielded to her demand that he permit his servants to have their Christmas wishes. Despite his fury—and he *had* been furious, if that vein pulsing in his temple could be trusted—instead of tossing her out into the snow, his gray eyes had met and held hers, and she'd seen something in those shadowy depths, something that had surprised her.

She couldn't say what it had been, but it was like a closed door opening a tiny crack, just enough so one might get a glimpse of what lay on the other side.

For all his professed loathing of Christmas wishes, he'd permitted his servants to have theirs. Oh, he'd acquiesced with bad grace, of course, yet that fleeting moment when he'd yielded had struck right at the tenderest part of her chest.

He hadn't stayed to make a wish for himself, which was a great pity, because if ever there was a man who needed to believe in wishes, it was the Duke of Grantham.

A lost soul . . .

She glanced back out the window, gazing at the sun sparkling on the spirals of frost painting the glass, and at the pure blue of the sky above, turning an idea over in her mind. "I wonder, Abby, if I might go skating today, after all."

"Oh? And how's that? Bit of a walk to Hammond Court, and in this cold? Your fingers and toes will be frostbitten before you're even halfway there."

There was no arguing that point. Even as warm as the bedchamber was, there was a distinct chill near the window, with the wind sneaking past the duke's costly glazing.

She turned away from the view, her chest swelling

with anticipation as the idea took shape in her mind. It wouldn't be easy—goodness, no—but if she could manage it, perhaps that crack she'd seen in the duke's façade yesterday might open again, only this time wide enough for her to slip through.

"Perhaps I can persuade the duke to take me. I might even coax him to skate himself."

Abby stared at her, her hands braced on her hips. "Just how do you suppose you'll manage that, eh? He doesn't look much like the fun-loving sort to me."

No, he didn't, but surely that was even more reason to go ahead with her plan? Why, it would do the duke a world of good to do something solely for the pure pleasure of it, and what could be more pleasurable than spinning on the ice?

Then again, a gentleman who was so ill-tempered as to find fault with Christmas pudding wasn't likely to be tempted by blue skies and smooth ice and spinning, was he?

For pity's sake, what sort of person didn't love Christmas pudding? She'd never heard of such a thing.

Well then, she'd have to come up with something else, wouldn't she? Some other reason to lure him out of that grim, dark study of his and into the fresh air and sunshine. "If I could persuade him that his house party guests might wish to skate, perhaps he'd agree to come and see the pond, at least." As for getting him out onto the ice, well, she'd worry about that once she'd gotten him there.

"Well, I suppose he's got to do something with them, doesn't he? Those high and mighty sorts are used to being entertained at every moment." Abby gave her a doubtful look. "But I'm afraid you've got your work ahead of you, convincing him. I've never seen a man less inclined to merry frolics than the Duke of Grantham."

Neither had she, but Ambrose must have had some faith in the duke, or else he wouldn't have lured him to Fairford, and right to her doorstep. She couldn't be certain he'd meant for her to undertake a quest to help the duke find joy where before there'd been only shadows, but it was a worthy cause, regardless.

The duke had done her a favor yesterday, after all, by bringing her to Grantham Lodge. Surely, she could do this much for him? "Help me dress, won't you, Abby?" Rose hurried to the clothes press to fetch her green woolen day dress, her mind made up.

She'd made Ambrose a promise, one she wouldn't go back on, even if it meant enduring an afternoon of the duke's sharp tongue, and that infuriatingly arrogant scowl.

"Ice skating?" Max gazed over the top of his spectacles at Miss St. Claire, who was standing in front of his desk, her green eyes wide with a hopefulness that was utterly absurd, given the request she'd just made. "Forgive me, Miss St. Claire, but did you just say you want me to take you *ice skating*?"

"Yes, Your Grace. That's what I said." She folded her hands in front of her, a perfect picture of innocence. "The pond at the bottom of the hill behind Hammond

Court will almost certainly be frozen by now. It's quite a large one, and lovely for skating."

The girl had lost her mind. "Allow me to congratulate you, Miss St. Claire."

A pucker appeared in that smooth white brow, one that should have marred that angelic face, yet somehow made her look adorably confused, and only enhanced her appeal.

"Congratulate me? Whatever for?"

"You, Miss St. Claire, have managed to hit upon the one activity I detest above all others. I commend you on your fertile imagination. Now, run along, and find something useful to occupy yourself." He waved a dismissive hand toward the door. "More of those tea cakes wouldn't go amiss."

Miss St. Claire was without a doubt the most troublesome lady alive, but there was no denying she made delicious tea cakes.

But of course, she *didn't* run along, but crossed her arms stubbornly over her chest, because she was incapable of doing a single thing asked of her without an argument.

"What can you possibly have against ice skating, Your Grace? It's lovely, especially on such a sunny day as this."

"It's cold and wet, and the skates pinch." At least, he assumed they did. It had been so long since he'd gone ice skating, he couldn't remember.

She scoffed. "Oh, what nonsense."

Nonsense? The gall of the chit.

"You do realize, Your Grace, that you'll need to

provide some sort of entertainment for your house party guests."

What the devil? "You mean to tell me, Miss St. Claire, that in addition to feeding them, housing them, and permitting them to drink all my best port, I'm meant to entertain them, as well?" No, surely not. That couldn't be right. Why would anyone ever host a house party, if that were the case?

She stared at him for a moment, as if trying to determine whether or not he was jesting, then threw back her head in a laugh. "Why, of course, Your Grace! Have you never hosted a party before? An ice-skating outing would be just the thing. I believe ice skating is quite popular among the fashionable set, and the Hammond Court pond is ever so much nicer than the Thames."

He tore his spectacles off and rubbed the bridge of his nose. She'd been in his study for fewer than ten minutes, and a headache was already pulsing behind his eyes. "There will be no ice skating, Miss St. Claire. I assure you, any further argument on this matter is a waste of your breath."

"Very well. I'll go by myself, then."

She turned with a flounce of her skirts, and the next thing he knew, he was on his feet. "No. You're not going alone. It's out of the question."

"I don't see why it should be."

"What if the ice is unsound? You could crash through, and there won't be a soul there to fish you back out again."

She shrugged. "The pond isn't terribly deep, Your

Grace. Besides, I've skated on it by myself dozens of times before. I know how to check the ice for soundness. I'll be perfectly safe."

"You'll be frozen through before you ever get to the pond, and if you do fall through, it'll be a long walk home with wet clothing." Not but that a dousing in an icy pond might do her a world of good by cooling some of the heat from that saucy tongue of hers.

"You could send me in your carriage."

"No. I can't spare the driver, or the carriage today." It was a bald-faced lie, of course. He had nowhere to go, and even if he had, he owned several carriages and employed an under coachman.

"No matter." She turned toward the door with a toss of her head. "The walk will keep me warm enough."

Damned if she didn't have an answer for everything.

She had a hand on the doorknob before he managed to dredge up another objection. "You don't have any skates!" Good Lord, he sounded half-hysterical.

"Not to worry, Your Grace. There are dozens of pairs of skates at Hammond Court."

"Hammond Court!" He was around the desk in an instant and at the door, looming over her. "Has it escaped your memory, Miss St. Claire, that Hammond Court's roof caved in? Do you not recall nearly being crushed under a pile of rubble only yesterday?"

"A pile of rubble! Why, it was only a few bits of wood and flakes of plaster, for goodness—"

"Don't forget the slate tiles I found littering the

grounds in front of the house. Those jagged edges are sharp, and could leave a nasty—"

"And it wasn't the roof, Your Grace," she went on, as if he hadn't spoken. "It was the ceiling, and only a part of it, at that. The rest of the house is safe enough, and as it happens, the ice skates are in the stillroom, far away from my bedchamber. I'll just pop through the door in the back courtyard and fetch them. I'll be back out again in a trice." She gave him a sunny smile. "See? There's nothing at all to worry about."

Worry? Who was worried? Not him.

She marched to the door and would have left the study, as cool as you please, if he hadn't stopped her with a hand on her arm. "One hour, Miss St. Claire. One hour, and not a moment longer. Do you understand me?"

She grinned, and his gaze caught and held on the sweet curve of those pink rosebud lips. She had the most damnably distracting mouth.

"You'll come, then? How wonderful!" She clapped her hands together, gleeful. "You won't regret it, Your Grace."

"On the contrary, Miss St. Claire. I already regret it."

"Nonsense! It's the most pleasurable thing ever, gliding about the ice."

"I won't be going anywhere near the ice, I assure you."

Disappointment flickered in her eyes, but the irrepressible smile was soon back. "When you said an hour, you meant an hour of *skating*, of course, didn't you, Your Grace? Because it will take us at least half that time to get there, and that would hardly be fair, you know."

She was still talking as she made her way into the hallway, but he paid her no mind as he trailed along after her, letting her prattle on as he ordered Monk to have the carriage made ready. What was the use in arguing, when every day that passed showed more plainly than the one before it that Miss St. Claire would have her way, no matter what he said?

He'd thought *he* was stubborn.

He hadn't had the faintest idea what he was getting himself into when he'd brought her here. She was too cheerful, too tempting, with that wide smile of hers, and that glint of mischief in her lovely green eyes. She was too skilled at wrapping people around her little finger, just as Ambrose had been.

He'd do well to remember that.

CHAPTER 14

The Duke of Grantham wasn't pleased. No, he was most decidedly displeased, so much so one would think he were on his way to witness a hanging, rather than to enjoy a lovely afternoon of ice skating on a sunny winter's day.

"It's fortunate it's been so cold lately, is it not, Your Grace? The pond is certain to be frozen all the way through, even in the middle, where it's deepest. It'll be ever so spacious for your guests."

Silence.

Rose turned to him, a determined smile on her lips, but it faded at the sight of the duke's dark glower. Oh, dear. His grim frown was enough to frighten the sun itself behind a cloud.

"We'll have to fetch the rest of the skates from Hammond Court on our way back, so everyone might skate together if they wish," she went on, with determined cheerfulness. "Why, it'll be like the frost fair on the Thames five years ago, with all of us out on the ice together. Perhaps we might even have warm cider."

No response. If the duke had any opinions about the frost fair, he didn't share them.

"I daresay you must have seen the frost fair, Your Grace?" He would have been in Town at that time, and nearly all of London was meant to have turned out for it. "From what I heard of it, there was skating and dancing, hot apples and gingerbread, and even nine-pin bowling on the ice. Oh, how I would have loved to have seen it myself! Do you suppose we might attempt to recreate it? I daresay your guests would be delight—"

"Do you *ever* cease talking, Miss St. Claire?"

She glanced at him from the corner of her eye. His dark brows were drawn together in a frown, his lips were tight, and the hint of warmth she'd thought she'd glimpsed in his eyes last night was nowhere to be seen today. Those gray depths were as frozen as the thick layer of ice over the pond.

Perhaps she'd imagined it.

His words, and the quelling tone in which he said them would most certainly have silenced many a young lady, but she'd never been one to hold her tongue, no matter if it was a duke who'd hushed her.

In any case, he'd likely had enough silence to last him a lifetime.

"Not often, no," she replied cheerfully, as they made their way down to the pond below Hammond Court, the skates she'd thrown over her shoulder bouncing against her back as she walked. "Have you any ice skates of your own at Grantham Lodge, Your Grace?"

Somehow, she doubted it. They didn't even have citron for the Christmas pudding at Grantham Lodge.

It seemed wildly optimistic to imagine he kept a pair of ice skates.

"Humph."

She waited, but that solitary grunt was the duke's only reply.

Well, it was something, anyway. Better than the ominous silence he'd maintained since they'd climbed into the carriage at Grantham Lodge. Still, she was obliged to smother a sigh as they reached the pond's edge.

Goodness, this was quite a task Ambrose had given her, wasn't it? She wasn't sure she was equal to it. She'd never come across anyone more determined to be displeased with everyone and everything than the Duke of Grantham. It was stealing her own joy in the beautiful day, like a cloud obliterating the sun.

What must it be like to be a young, handsome, powerful duke—a man with the world at his fingertips—yet still unable to find a single moment's pleasure in anything? To see the sun's rays upon the ice, setting it alight like a sea of glittering gems, and to feel nothing but discontent?

She seated herself on one of the large, flat rocks that surrounded the pond, tugged her gloves off, and bent to fasten the leather straps of her skate to the ankle and toe of her boot, but it was dreadfully cold, and she was obliged to keep stopping to blow on her hands.

Beside her, the duke let out an irritable sigh. "For God's sake, Miss St. Claire. We'll be out here all night at this rate."

"I do beg your pardon, Your Grace, but my fingers are a trifle stiff."

"Move over." He waved an impatient hand at her when she merely gaped up at him. She slid across the rock, stifling her gasp when he plopped down beside her and held out his hands. "Give me your foot."

Did he mean to . . . ? No, surely not.

He huffed out a breath. "Your foot, if you please, Miss St. Claire. I'd rather not spend the afternoon in the freezing cold while you fuss with your skates, if it's all the same to you."

Well, then. This was unexpected. But she offered her foot as commanded, biting off another gasp when the duke's warm, gloved fingers wrapped around her ankle. He rested her foot on his thigh and began to wrestle with the straps of her skates.

She stared, mesmerized, as those long, clever fingers maneuvered the buckles, his knuckles brushing the hem of her skirts as he worked. He had wonderful hands, strong and confident, and as for his . . . well, she hadn't anything to compare it to, not being accustomed to touching gentlemen's thighs, but his seemed exceptionally sturdy.

He made quick work of fastening both skates onto her feet. "All right then, Miss St. Claire. Get on with it," he muttered, jerking his head toward the pond.

Goodness, her knees were a trifle wobbly now, but once she'd made her way across the snowy bank and onto the ice, she regained her balance and was soon gliding about with the ease of long practice. She circled the edge of the pond a few times, admiring the bare branches of the trees surrounding the banks, their dark bark frosted with an icy crust of snow.

But soon enough she struck out for the smoother ice near the center of the pond, the soothing hiss of the blades rolling over the blue-tinged ice whispering in her ears, until she forgot where she was and drifted along, one foot chasing the other, and her skirts floating out behind her.

It was just as it had always been. Ambrose was gone, and her beloved Hammond Court was soon to follow, slipping from her fingers even now, but somehow, this moment felt as it ought to feel, as it had always felt.

It was just as she remembered it.

Perhaps that was what came of doing it year after year. No matter how much time passed between one skate and the next—those long summer months when skating seemed an impossible thing, a mere fantasy— once winter came and the pond iced over again, it was like coming home.

It was another Christmas tradition, one of Ambrose's favorites. He'd given her this moment, and every other moment before it.

A lifetime of memories.

"Take care, Miss St. Claire."

The duke's voice rang out across the pond, echoing around her. She slowed, dragging her heel across the ice to stop, and turned to face him.

She'd gone farther than she realized, far enough so he was only an outline now, a lone figure standing at the edge of the pond, his hair rustling in the breeze, his dark coat stark against the landscape of white surrounding him.

He looked terribly alone.

Slowly, she went back the way she'd come, toward him, her heart heavier than it had been when she'd set out across the ice, though if someone had demanded she put words to the strange weight of emotions in her chest, she couldn't have done so.

Something about him standing there, more alone than any man she'd ever seen—

"For God's sake, Miss St. Claire, are you daft, skating so far away from the bank?"

She blinked at him. Goodness, he seemed unaccountably angry. "It's perfectly safe, Your Grace."

"You can't be certain of that, especially farther out. Who did you imagine was going to fish you out, if you fell through? By the time I reached you, you'd be lost under the ice."

She stared at him. Had he actually been concerned for her welfare? "I beg your pardon for worrying you, Your Grace, but—"

"Don't be absurd. I wasn't *worried*," he snapped. "If anything, I'm annoyed with your carelessness. I don't fancy a dunking in an icy pond, Miss St. Claire. This coat is a Weston."

Annoyed. Yes, that was an easier emotion than worry, wasn't it? "Your coat is safe, Your Grace. As I said before, I've been skating on this pond dozens of times. I know this ice as well as I know the back of my hand."

"Dozens of times? How tedious." He crossed his arms over his chest. "I can't imagine why you'd want to subject yourself to it over and over again."

"Tradition, Your Grace. Do you not have any Christmas traditions of your own?"

But perhaps not. Ambrose had told her that after the duke's mother passed away, he was sent off to Eton, and he only ever returned to Fairford for school breaks after that. By then his father, the Ninth Duke of Grantham, had become something of a hermit, and rarely permitted his son to leave his sight.

What had happened to him, during those years? Had he had any friends? Had his father cared for him, as Ambrose had done for her? Or had he been alone, the Christmas traditions he'd once cherished becoming hopelessly entangled with darker, lonelier memories?

She waited, but he didn't answer—rather a habit of his—but just as she was about to give up, he spoke. "Ginger."

That was all—just that one word, but she leaped upon it like a thief on a golden guinea. "Ginger? Do you mean gingerbread?"

"No. Ginger biscuits."

He wasn't looking at her, his gaze fixed on some point above her head, as if ginger biscuits were something scandalous to wish for, something to be ashamed of wanting. "I've made dozens of batches of ginger biscuits, Your Grace. I'd be happy to make some for you, if you like."

He let out a short, hard laugh. "You can't, not like these. It's an old recipe, long since lost. My maternal grandmother used to make them for me when I was a boy, and my mother after her. They're made with treacle, I believe."

Ginger biscuits, made with treacle? Years ago, she'd found a loose clutch of old, handwritten recipes in the stillroom, the paper brittle and yellowed with age. Mightn't she find the recipe there? "Well, they sound lovely."

He didn't reply, and this time she waited to no avail. His lips remained sealed. She let out a quiet sigh and turned back toward the ice, taking care to remain closer to the bank this time, so as not to annoy him again.

Ginger biscuits, of all things. Such a foolish thing to wish for, such a ridiculous memory to have held on to for all these years, but they'd been lovely, those ginger biscuits. Or perhaps they were called ginger nuts? The memory was hazy, but hadn't his grandmother referred to them as ginger nuts?

Of all the things Max had managed to forget about Christmases at Hammond Court, he'd never quite been able to forget those blasted biscuits, no matter how hard he'd tried. They'd been delicious, yes—light, and sweet with treacle, but with a tiny bite from the molasses.

But it was their scent that made them linger in his memory.

It was strange, the small details the mind held on to. The warm, spicy scent of them had permeated the entire house, from the kitchen all the way to his bedchamber. No other scent spoke of Christmas to him as powerfully as the scent of ginger. Even years later, the merest whiff of it made him ache with longing.

But he didn't want to think of it—not here, and not now, with Miss St. Claire's inquisitive green eyes upon him.

Not anywhere, come to that. Not after he'd done his best to forget everything about those early years at Hammond Court. What good did it do, to remember? Any warm, safe feelings he'd ever had about those years had long since disintegrated into anger and resentment.

It was far easier not to take the chance—far easier not to remember. He shouldn't have even mentioned it to Miss St. Claire at all. He wasn't sure why he had, except she'd looked so earnest when she'd asked about his Christmas traditions.

Perhaps he'd had other traditions at one time, but the only one he could recall with perfect clarity was lingering on the drive outside Hammond Court, his toes and fingers numb with the cold, watching through the windows as the Christmases he recalled from his childhood had gone on without him.

It was rather a far cry from Miss St. Claire's tradition of ice skating.

He watched her twirling in a circle, her arms outstretched to the sky, the sun catching on the golden hair that had escaped her hat, lovingly caressing the sunny locks, as if they were long-lost kin. It was a clumsy enough maneuver, that twirling, her skates threatening to skid out from underneath her with every turn, but the awkwardness didn't make it any less fascinating to watch her.

Perhaps it made it more so.

She spun as if she hadn't a care in the world, a picture of pure, perfect joy. Even now, with all her troubles, she could still spin on the ice, such a brilliant smile lighting her face he couldn't tear his gaze away from it.

She'd learned that smile from Ambrose. He may have been a scoundrel, a cheat, and a liar, but one couldn't say of him that he'd squandered his life. The man knew how to seize a moment, and he'd taught his daughter to do the same. He'd always been good at that—at plucking beauty out of thin air and shaping it, stretching it, making the most of moments everyone else saw as ordinary.

A pain pierced him at the thought, sharp enough to make him catch his breath. It wasn't grief—no, not that. Never that, not for Ambrose. No, the emotion swelling in his chest, pressing against his ribs and flooding his mouth with bitterness wasn't grief.

It was *fury*.

This was what Ambrose had been doing, while he'd been moldering away at Grantham Lodge with his drunken father during the holidays? Ambrose had been *here*, watching his beautiful daughter spin on the ice. Perhaps he'd even taken her hands in his and spun with her.

He took a step forward, his feet sliding against the snowy bank, damp seeping into his boots. Another step, then another, until he was right on the edge, close enough to see the wind tossing her hair about, strangely incredulous at the sight of her, her arms still open wide, as if gathering the sun to her chest, and—

"Oh!" The hard scrape of a blade against the ice snapped him out of the trance he'd fallen into, just in time to see her stumble over the hem of her skirts. Her arms pinwheeled, and then she was falling, her backside slamming into the ice with a hard thud.

"Rose!" Somehow, it was her given name that burst from his lips, despite his never having thought of her as anything other than Miss St. Claire. He darted forward, the ice slipping beneath his feet as he stumbled over to her and caught her hands in his. "Are you all right?"

She said nothing, but her slender body trembled against him as he eased her up onto her feet, keeping her upright with his hands wrapped around her waist. "Are you hurt?"

Her shoulders were shaking, her breath coming in great, gasping pants. Good God, had she broken an arm? A leg? "Miss St. Claire! Are you injured?"

She tipped her face up to his, still gasping, her pretty, pink lips split wide in a grin. "No, Your Grace. I'm fine."

She was laughing. *Laughing*.

All at once, the ugliness inside him, the hatred and fury and bitterness, dissipated, drifting away on the wind.

What must it be like, to have such reserves of joy inside you? To have a smile always hovering on your lips, a laugh always waiting to burst forth, as she did? She was motherless, fatherless, penniless—a young lady of no consequence, tainted with the stain of illegitimacy, and utterly alone in the world, yet here she was, smiling and laughing and spinning on the ice as if she held every-thing she could ever want right in the palm of her hand.

Was it any wonder the sun sought her out?

He gazed down at her, his heart pounding, mesmer-ized by those laughing pink lips. If he touched her, dragged his fingertips across her cheek, or grazed her bottom lip with his thumb, could he touch the happiness that lived inside her? Absorb it, through the layers of their skin?

Slowly, he reached for her and caught a lock of her hair in his hand. It was soft, sun warmed, the silky strands glinting like threads of gold between his fingers.

"Y-your Grace?" She was no longer laughing, but she didn't pull away, only stared up at him, eyes wide, her shallow breaths trembling on her lips.

"I don't understand," he murmured, only half-aware of what he was saying. "How can you be so . . . how can you have so much joy inside you?"

A soft sigh left her lips, and for a moment, one wild, heart-stopping moment, she turned her face toward his hand, her soft cheek nestling against his palm. "Joy is a choice, Your Grace."

Was it? Or was it a gift given to some, and denied to others?

He released her hair and took a step back. "We've stayed too long, Miss St. Claire. It's time to return to Grantham Lodge."

CHAPTER 15

The ride from Hammond Court back to Grantham Lodge was silent. When the carriage stopped in the drive, the duke politely handed Rose down, but he avoided her gaze and vanished into his study as soon as they were through the front door.

Monk raised an eyebrow at her, but she could only give him a helpless shrug.

Something had happened at the pond, something she hadn't expected. That he'd touched her at all was shocking enough, but the gentleness of his fingers in her hair, and his expression when he'd gazed down at her had been . . .

She hardly knew what. She didn't have the words to explain it, but it had made her belly quiver.

She climbed the stairs slowly, made her way to her bedchamber, and perched on the edge of her bed, her fingers tight around the bundle of papers she'd folded and secreted in her pocket when they'd passed through Hammond Court's stillroom on their way back to the carriage.

She couldn't say whether or not the duke's grandmother's gingernut recipe was among the fragile pages, but she'd taken a moment to gather some of her own stores of preserved ginger and lemon peel from the kitchen, just in case. They were far superior to anything that could be had at the shops.

If she was going to make the duke ginger biscuits, then she was going to do it the way it was meant to be done. As for whether or not she was going to make them at all, well . . . she hadn't decided yet, which was rather ridiculous, on the face of it. She'd made dozens of biscuits in her lifetime. Why should she be hesitating over making these?

They were just biscuits, for heaven's sake.

Except, of course, that they *weren't*. She had only to recall the expression on the duke's face when he'd spoken of them to know that. There would be no going back again once she'd plucked on this thread, and the duke might not thank her for dragging his painful past into the light.

But she'd never been good at minding her own concerns. Perhaps that was why Ambrose had assigned her this task—because he'd known once she got the barest glimpse behind the duke's grim façade, she'd poke and pry at it until she'd wrenched it loose.

Of course, she may not have the recipe at all. She withdrew the thin bundle of papers from her pocket and leafed through them one by one, unsure if the quivery feeling in the depths of her belly was a hope she'd find what she sought, or a hope that she wouldn't.

She took up the first paper, smoothed it carefully against her knee, and leaned over, squinting at the faded ink. Marrow pudding. Marrow pudding? Dear God, that sounded dreadful.

She rifled through the pages one by one, the brittle paper crackling in her fingers, struggling to decipher the spidery handwriting. Venison pasty. Fish sauce with lobster. Oxford pudding. Yorkshire pudding. Boiled plum pudding.

The Grantham family, it seemed, was fond of puddings.

This could be a bundle of Christmas recipes—any one of these dishes might well grace a Christmas table—but they were main dishes only. She neared the bottom of the pile without finding a single recipe for sweets or confections until only a few scattered papers remained. She took up the second to last page, but her heart was already sinking. Well, then, it seemed she *did* want to make the duke's ginger biscuits, after all, fool that she was.

Gooseberry Fool. Wait. Gooseberry Fool? That was a sweet, surely?

She reached for the final paper, her hand shaking, and there, written across the top of the page, she found what she was looking for.

Max's Ginger Nut Biscuits. She scanned the paper, breath held. Flour, sugar, butter, three ounces of bruised caraway seeds, four ounces of pounded ginger, and . . .

Three and a half pounds of treacle.

She stared down at the paper, her heart slamming against her ribs. Somehow, this tiny scrap of paper had survived three generations of Granthams, only for her to find it, against all odds, tucked into an old weather-beaten wooden box on a forgotten shelf in the stillroom.

It couldn't possibly be a coincidence.

It must be a sign, surely? Surely, she was *meant* to find it?

She leaped up from the bed, the scrap of paper still clutched between her fingers, and rushed across her bedchamber, ready to dash down to the kitchen and begin pounding ginger at once, but she paused at the door.

No. Not yet.

After yesterday's fanfare over the Christmas pudding, she'd have the attention of every servant who wandered through the kitchen door before she'd even laid her ingredients out, and soon enough they'd all be clamoring for ginger nut biscuits.

It wouldn't do.

These were for the duke, and the duke alone. It even said so at the top of the recipe.

Max's Ginger Nut Biscuits.

Perhaps it was silly of her, but some instinct inside her recognized that he wouldn't wish for the others to know anything about this.

These weren't just biscuits to him.

They were a memory, and memories were private.

So, she waited, sitting quite still at the edge of her bed. At some point, Abby bustled in and clucked disapprovingly at Rose's damp hems, and helped her change into a dry gown before bustling off to fetch her a dinner tray.

It remained untouched on the table beside the bed.

The sun sank lower, the hard, bright blue of the afternoon sky giving way to a gold-streaked sunset, then a deep lavender twilight, and still she waited until the sound of voices and footsteps faded, and the household settled down to rest with a creak and a groan.

Only then did she creep out of her bedchamber and steal down the staircase into the entryway below. It was deserted. She peered down the hallway that led to the duke's study, but all was dark and quiet.

Yes. This was what she wanted. Silence, and privacy.

Her skirts swished against the marble floors as she turned and made her way down the servants' staircase to the kitchen below.

Mrs. Watson had banked the fire and placed the covers over the stove, but it was lovely and warm still, with every surface scrubbed clean. She lit several lanterns to work by, placing them on the long, wide table in the center of the kitchen, then dragging the heavy sacks of flour and sugar from the larder, and the butter and cream from the cook's pantry.

The gentle lantern light cast a soft glow over the kitchen, and it wasn't long before she'd lost herself in the scent of the spices, and the give of the dough between her fingers. She hummed under her breath as she worked—"The First Noel," one of Ambrose's favorites—and the biscuits took shape under her hand, as if by magic.

Max hadn't bothered to light the lanterns.

He hadn't, in fact, moved from the chair he'd thrown himself into when he'd retired to his study after he and Miss St. Claire had returned from Hammond Court.

Rose. The name suited her. One couldn't look at her face, her lips, without thinking of rose petals.

It had been hours, but he sat here still, a half-empty glass of brandy cradled between his fingers, surrounded by darkness, aside from the flickering light of the fireplace in front of him.

Sitting alone in the dark had become a habit of his since he'd returned to Grantham Lodge. Sitting in the dark, and thinking of . . . nothing. He stared at the flames, reassuring himself that his mind was indeed blank—not a single thought in his head—until gradually he became aware it wasn't true.

There *was* something in his head. A lady with green eyes and laughing pink lips.

Laughing. Even now, hours later, he couldn't puzzle it out. What had there been for her to laugh about? It didn't make sense.

She didn't make sense.

It had been a mistake to allow her to persuade him to take her to Hammond Court today. A mistake to watch her as she twirled about on the ice in the sunshine, a mistake to tell her about . . . well, anything at all.

Even now, he wasn't sure why he'd done it, except that she had the most disturbing way of prying into his head, of casting a narrow band of bright light into the darkness, sending all the ugly thoughts hiding there scattering. She hardly needed to say a word, and he was flayed open like a split oyster, black pearls exposed, and no chance of returning them to their safe, tight shell.

No, they were out now, rolling about causing mayhem, and he had no bloody idea what to do with them.

But he knew what he wouldn't do—remain in the dark a moment longer, staring into his fire and daydreaming about a lady he didn't understand, and didn't even *like*.

He raised the glass to his lips, drained the last dregs of his brandy, and rose to his feet. He'd go to his bed and hope that tomorrow would bring Basingstoke and Montford to Grantham Lodge, and put an end to all this wretched *thinking*.

God knew, he needed the distraction.

He wandered from the study into the darkened hallway, then down the corridor to the staircase, but paused with his foot on the bottom step.

Something was amiss.

He stilled, listening, but the only sound was the soft ticking of the grandfather clock on the first-floor landing. There was no one about, not a stray servant to be seen, yet there was some disturbance, one he could sense more than anything, and without thinking he turned from the stairs and made his way around the corner to the back staircase that led to the kitchens.

The door at the bottom of the steps was closed, but there were faint stirrings coming from the other side of it—the drag of a bowl across the wooden surface of the table, the soft rustle of a burlap flour sack.

He knew what he'd find before he opened the door, yet at the same time, he wasn't prepared for the sight that met him once he did.

The light was low, just the barest, soft glow centered around the flour-dusted table. A few bowls and a rolling pin were set to one side, and several small piles of what looked like crushed spices were mounded in a corner.

Presiding over this fetching domestic scene was Miss St. Claire, her head bent over her work, a thick length of dark golden dough spread beneath her fingertips. The heavy scents of treacle and ginger hung in the air, and above that, the rich, dark sugar scent of his grandmother's ginger biscuits baking.

The scent struck his chest, nearly sending him to his knees.

It was so achingly familiar, that scent. How could it be so familiar still, after so many years? He sucked in a silent breath, his head swimming with the peppery, citrus scent of the ginger, and for an instant it was as if he were a boy again, running into the kitchen, his cheeks red from the cold and his belly growling, straight into his mother's waiting arms.

It smelled the same as he remembered, sharp but still sweet, and so very much like home, before everything fell apart.

"Ginger nut biscuits." He drew closer, his voice sounding strange even to his own ears. Too hushed, almost reverential.

Miss St. Claire froze, not looking up, her busy hands stilling on the dough. "Yes."

"How?"

She looked up then, an uncertain smile on her lips. "Ginger biscuits are a common enough sweet, Your Grace."

"No." He shook his head. "Not those. Those are my grandmother's biscuits."

She reached for a cloth and took her time wiping her hands clean of the dough, taking care to avoid his gaze.

"When you mentioned them today, I recalled I'd seen a small cache of recipes tucked into a wooden box in Hammond Court's stillroom. I thought I might find the biscuit recipe among them, and I did."

"Is that why you insisted we go into the house? So you could fetch the recipes?"

"Yes."

He stared at her, unfamiliar heat rising in his cheeks. Even his fiercest grumbling hadn't deterred her from returning to the house. He'd made an almighty fuss, but she'd held firm, and all the while, she'd been hoping to do something kind for him. "May I see the recipe?"

"Of course." She reached into her apron pocket, took out a brittle bit of paper, and held it out to him. He drew closer, his fingers brushing her softer ones, still slightly sticky from the dough.

He took the paper, and yes, there it was, so faded now it was nearly unreadable, but he knew his grand-mother's handwriting, and if there'd been any doubt, his name was scrawled right across the top.

There was no mistaking it, this little piece of his grandmother, and his mother as well, right in the palm of his hand. For an instant, he had a profound urge to clutch the scrap of paper to his chest, but he held it back out to Miss St. Claire, clearing his throat. "You, ah, you made the biscuits for me, then?"

It was a foolish question, perhaps, yet it seemed in-credible she should have done him such a kindness when he'd been anything but kind to her.

But she merely shrugged, the small smile still play-ing about her lips. "It's nothing so marvelous, Your

Grace. Once I found the recipe it was a simple enough matter to make them, and so I did. Anyone else would have done the same."

Would they? No, he didn't think so. No one had ever done anything like this for him before. He stared at her without speaking, because not a single word came to his lips. He might have thanked her—yes, that would have done nicely—but it didn't seem adequate, somehow.

But she didn't seem to expect a thank-you, or anything else. "I have a batch of biscuits in the oven nearly ready to come out. Will you stay and have some?"

"I—yes, of course." How could he not?

He seated himself on the bench to one side of the table. She returned to her dough and a silence that should have been awkward stretched out between them. He didn't speak—he'd never been one for idle chatter, and there was a strangely tenacious lump in his throat—but sat quietly, the warm, rich scent of treacle and ginger wrapping around him as he watched her work the dough, her small, dainty hands a blur of motion.

She laid out another tray with tidy rows of biscuits, and walked them to the stove, fetching the first tray out before sliding the new one in. When she returned to the table, she bore a plate with biscuits piled high in the center, a mouthwatering curl of steam rising from them.

"Here we are, Your Grace." She set the plate in the center of the table, then returned to the stove and fetched a tray holding two silver cups and a silver chocolate pot. She put the tray next to the biscuits, then slid into the chair across from his.

"Ginger biscuits, *and* chocolate?" His grandmother

had always served her ginger biscuits with chocolate, as well, and his mother had continued the tradition. The two treats were inextricably linked in his memories, but he hadn't mentioned chocolate at the pond today. Unless Miss St. Claire was some sort of sorceress, she couldn't possibly have known it.

Though looking at her now, with the glow of the lamplight framing her face and gilding her hair, he could almost believe she *was* a sorceress. She was certainly not like any other young lady he'd ever known.

But she only shrugged. "They go together quite nicely, do they not?"

"They do." He nodded at the silver pot. "I didn't realize I owned a chocolate pot."

"I don't believe it's ever been used before. Rather a pity, really, as it's a pretty one." She cocked her head, considering the pot for a moment, then nudged the plate of ginger biscuits closer to him. "Biscuit, Your Grace?"

He reached for one. They were still warm, thick, and dense, but soft enough that he might leave his thumbprint in them, as he'd done as a child. They were just as they should be, the butter slick under his fingertips, the scent teasing his nose.

And, dear God, the *taste*.

The snap of the ginger, the dark sweetness of the treacle . . . he closed his eyes, and for an instant he was a little boy again, sitting at the table with his mother and grandmother, his fingers and toes still numb from his play outdoors, the spicy taste of ginger nipping at his tongue.

Neither of them spoke. He kept his eyes closed,

living inside the memory while it lasted. Across from him, Miss St. Claire didn't speak either, only munched quietly on her own biscuit.

But when he opened his eyes again, she was watching him, a faint line between her brows and her lower lip caught between her teeth. "Are they as you remembered them, Your Grace?"

He gazed at her through the gloom. "They're perfect."

And they were. Not just their scent, or the flavor of them melting against his tongue, but perfect in the way a thing could only be if it was done utterly unselfishly.

"I'm glad." She nodded and rose to her feet, picking up the tray and taking it with her.

There was nothing for him to do then but rise as well, and make his way to the kitchen door. But he paused halfway there and turned back to her, and the next thing he knew, he'd taken her hand in his. "Thank you, Miss St. Claire, for . . ." He searched for the proper words, but they didn't come. How did you thank someone for giving you back a piece of yourself you'd thought was gone forever? "Thank you."

She smiled. "You're most welcome, Your Grace."

He raised her hand to his mouth. It was fleeting, not a kiss so much as a brush of his lips across her knuckles, but he lingered long enough to inhale her, to feel the silky glide of her skin against his lips.

It was long enough to snatch a shuddering breath from his lungs, to weaken his knees. Long enough to make him do something exceedingly foolish—something he never would have done if he'd been in his right mind, but with the soft glow of the lamplight on her face, the sweetness lingering on his tongue, and the scent of ginger swirling in his head, it was as if he'd stepped into another world, one she'd weaved around him with an act of pure kindness.

He eased her closer, her skirts brushing his pantaloons, ducked his head, and let his lips touch hers. She let out a soft gasp, her hands flying to his chest. "I . . . Your Grace . . ."

He waited, a shuddering breath on his lips, expecting her to jerk back, to push him away, but the seconds ticked by, and she only gazed up at him, her eyes a dark, stormy green, her fingers pressed against her lips as if holding his kiss there.

He didn't think anymore then, but caught her hand in his and pressed a kiss to the fingertips that had rested on her lips only moments before. Then he cupped her cheek in his palm, and teased his mouth against hers again, pausing to suckle lightly on her plump lower lip.

She made a low, needy sound, her warm breath drifting over his lips, and God, that sound, the hunger in it—a rush of desire flooded through him, heat settling low in his belly, and there was nothing he could do then but sweep his tongue against the seam of her lips, seeking entry.

Did she know that was what he wanted? Had she ever kissed a man before? Her lips remained closed, but she rose to her tiptoes and wound her arms around his neck, her slender body pressing against his, and all at once he was drowning in heat, his head swimming with desire for her.

This was the moment to stop—to set her gently away from him and bid her good night before his desire overwhelmed his reason, but that wasn't what he did. Instead, he teased her lips open, desperate to surge into her welcoming heat and tangle his tongue with hers.

"Open for me," he murmured against her mouth, licking gently at the seam of her lips, coaxing her to let him inside. He nibbled at her, pressing soft kisses on one corner of her mouth, then the other, the spark of his desire swelling hotter in his belly until it flared into a conflagration.

A low groan tore from his chest as he dragged his tongue over her luscious bottom lip, so tender and plump. His hands fell to her hips, cupping her slender curves as he traced his tongue over the perfect, tiny bow of her upper lip. "I want to taste you," he whispered against her trembling mouth.

She let out a breathless little moan. "Yes."

It was the softest whisper against his mouth, and then, so slowly he thought he might go mad, she parted her lips for him. He froze for an instant, afraid the slightest twitch on his part would frighten her away, but she let out a breath, and melted against him.

"*Yes.*" He locked his arms around her, pressing his palm into the arch of her back. She tasted like cinnamon and ginger, sweet, dark treacle, and seductive heat. He stroked her tongue with his, urging her to open wider for him, a low growl rising from his chest as she obeyed, her lips parting further, her tongue seeking his.

There was no going back, then.

He was mad for her, drowning in the taste of her, catching her breathy sighs and moans on his lips, the scent of sugar and spices whirling in his head, dizzying him.

She kissed him back hesitantly at first, her tongue grazing his shyly, but she was holding him tightly, her fingers curled into fists against his chest, gripping handfuls of his waistcoat, and a low, pained groan tore from his throat.

God, what was happening to him? He'd kissed women before—dozens of women—but it had never been like this, with the blood roaring through him like a raging current, sweeping everything before it.

Logic, reason, cautiousness—they all fled with the sweet stroke of her tongue against his, and for one breathless instant he was in danger of crushing her against him and taking her mouth roughly, all the pent-up desire from . . . when? The first moment he'd seen her, pistol in hand, ordering him from her house?

Or had it been after that? Had it been today, when he'd watched her spinning on the ice, her arms out and the sun illuminating her, turning her into a blur of light and motion?

He didn't know—God, he didn't *know*—he knew only that he wanted to kiss her forever, to crush his lips to hers and swallow her soft whimpers, but he held himself back, letting just the tip of his tongue tease hers before sucking her bottom lip into his mouth.

He slid his fingers under her chin, keeping her face tilted up to his as his tongue twined once again with hers, deepening the kiss, the pads of his fingers stroking the soft skin of her jaw as he took her mouth deeply, searching every secret corner for the taste of her.

She met him, every slide and stroke and thrust, her breathless pants matching his, their lips clinging together, and God, how was it so good? It was just a kiss, yet he was on fire for her. He cupped her cheek to urge her closer and dragged his lips down the front of her neck, his fingers tracing the smooth, warm skin of her throat, lingering over her pulse point, a dangerous surge of desire swelling in his belly when he felt it racing against his fingertips.

Did she want him? Was that what the wild beating of her heart meant?

The thought that she might desire him maddened him, and before he knew what he was about he'd grasped her hips, and was lifting her onto the table, his hand fisting her skirts, desperate to . . .

To *what*?

To take her? She was innocent and under his protection.

He wasn't a good man, and hadn't been, not for years—no, decades. He ruined men as easily as snapping his fingers and rarely felt an instant's regret over it.

But *this* . . .

Would he steal the virtue of a young lady grieving the only father she'd ever known? A young lady who had nothing, and not a single soul aside from her elderly nursemaid to protect her?

Would he *ruin* her?

No. That was too heartless, even for the Duke of Ice. He released his grip on her skirts and smoothed them down over her legs before backing away from her. "I . . . this is . . . I beg your pardon, Miss St. Claire. This wasn't well done of me."

"Your Grace, I . . ." She trailed off, biting her lip.

"Go up to your bedchamber, Rose." He dragged a hand through his hair, his gaze averted, because if he looked at her, he'd take her into his arms again, and God help them both then. "Go." He jerked his head toward the kitchen door, his voice harsher than it needed to be. "*Now.*"

She didn't move, and for an instant, he thought she might argue, but for the first time since he'd laid eyes on her, she didn't say a word. She remained still, and he could feel her gaze on him, but when he didn't look up, she did as he'd bid her, her footsteps quiet against the stone floor of the kitchen.

The door opened, then closed again.

Only then, did he look up. The plate of ginger biscuits was on the sideboard, right where she'd left it, the tray with the chocolate pot and cups beside it.

But she was gone.

CHAPTER 16

It was the ginger biscuits that did it.

Max had risen early, and spent all morning in his study, sprawled in the chair behind his desk, unanswered letters in a pile before him, and the ink drying on the nib of his pen. Instead of working, he'd been staring out the window like a proper half-wit, the remembered scent of ginger twining around him like wispy clouds of fog.

In the end, there was no other explanation. The ginger biscuits had been his downfall.

Not the gleam of firelight on Miss St. Claire's hair, or the seductive parting of those rosebud lips, or the sweet pink flush that had colored her cheeks when she caught his gaze on her.

Not the kiss.

Certainly, not the kiss. He'd kissed dozens of ladies and never lost his head before. No, it must have been the ginger biscuits.

There, then. That was settled. Now he could return his attention to his work.

He seized his pen and dipped it in the ink, but paused

with it poised above the page. The trouble was, he couldn't deny even to himself that he'd been caught in her spell from the moment he'd wandered into the kitchen last night. Like every other unwary fly before him, he'd only realized he was tangled in her silken web until it was too late to free himself.

Though to be fair, she was an exceedingly kind-hearted spider.

It wasn't that she was the only one who'd ever done him a good turn. He was often the recipient of his acquaintances' generosity, but with the exception of Basingstoke and Montford, such favors weren't motivated by kindness. They were bribes, manipulations, and transparent attempts to ingratiate themselves with him. He was accustomed to such machinations, and on his guard against them.

Why, then, should he suppose Miss St. Claire's ginger biscuits were anything other than another shameless attempt to curry his favor? God knew she had a powerful incentive to attempt to wriggle her way into his good graces.

That was the rub, wasn't it? He had every reason in the world to question her motives, but damned if he didn't think her entirely innocent, regardless, because . . . well, because he was a great fool, evidently.

He never gave anyone the benefit of the doubt. *Never*. He'd seen too much ugliness to trust in the goodness of human nature.

But there wasn't a single ugly thing about Rose St. Claire.

It was the green eyes, damn her. One glimpse into

those guileless green eyes, and it was impossible to suspect her. Either she was in possession of the purest heart he'd ever had the misfortune to encounter, or else she was a spectacular actress.

Those green eyes, taken in conjunction with the ginger biscuits was a fatal combination. Was it any wonder he'd lost his mind? Was it any wonder he was sitting here mooning over Miss St. Claire, like some ridiculous, starry-eyed schoolboy?

He needed to see her, that was all, but she'd been hiding from him all morning. He'd been waiting for hours for her to venture downstairs, so he might . . .

Might *what*? Tell her that he regretted kissing her last night? He *didn't* regret it. There wasn't a man alive who could regret such a kiss. Was he to become a liar now, along with all his other sins?

Very well, then. He'd beg her pardon and promise that such a thing would never happen again. Yes, that would be the proper thing to do.

But how could he be sure it *wouldn't* happen again?

It shouldn't have happened the first time, but it had, and after such a thing as a kiss like that happened once, it would take almost nothing for it to happen again. A sidelong glance from the corner of those lovely green eyes, a flutter of dark eyelashes, a curve of those rosebud lips, the accidental brush of fingertips . . .

He'd been over that kiss a thousand times since last night—had run through the moments leading up to it over and over as he'd tossed in his bed. The soft glow of the lamplight on her face, in her hair, illuminating her smile. Yes, that was how it had begun. The lighting was to blame for this entire debacle.

Then, as soon as he'd touched her, it had spun dangerously out of control.

He'd spun out of control, in a way he never had before.

Touching Miss St. Claire was forbidden, for one, but also the height of foolishness, not to mention unforgivably selfish. As innocent as that kiss had been, if anyone had happened to witness it, it would be more than enough to ruin her.

For all his other wicked sins, he wasn't in the habit of ruining innocent young ladies.

But even so, he couldn't quite make himself promise he wouldn't do it again, if given the chance. So, he'd simply have to make sure he didn't *ever* get the chance.

He'd stay away from her, that was all. He simply hadn't been himself last night. No, he'd been mesmerized by a pair of green eyes, and seduced by the scent of ginger, the flavor of dark sugar on his tongue. Of course! He'd only kissed her last night because he'd been . . . confused.

As soon as he saw her this morning, he'd find she was just an ordinary young lady, much like every other, and not the green-eyed goddess he'd dreamed about last night. Whatever madness had him in its grip would dissolve then, and he might get back to the business at hand.

Revenge. Revenge against her *father*, no less.

He tossed his pen aside and snatched his pocket watch up from the corner of his desk. It was nearly eleven o'clock in the morning, and she had yet to make her appearance downstairs.

Where the devil was she?

He rose, pushing his chair back with more force than necessary, and marched to the doorway, ignoring Townsend's startled look. He wandered into the corridor, peering into the entryway beyond.

He *wasn't* waiting for her. It was important he keep reminding himself of that, particularly given the curious glances Monk kept casting him every time he poked his head out of his study.

Yes, he'd risen earlier than usual, and it was true that once he entered his study of a morning, he rarely emerged for the rest of the day. Nor did he have a habit of pacing about up and down the corridor like a caged animal, but none of that had anything to do with the fact that the entryway had the best vantage point from which to monitor the staircase.

And yes, while it was also the case that Miss St. Claire couldn't reach the ground floor without descending that particular staircase, that didn't mean he was *waiting* for her. He was just a touch restless this morning, for no particular reason.

"Is there anything I may assist you with, Your Grace?" Monk edged closer, his gray brows drawn together. Monk had been observing him with increasing puzzlement as the morning waned.

Really, couldn't a man linger in his own entryway without every servant in the house looking askance at him? It was his house, for God's sake. "No, Monk. I'm merely, er . . . looking for Mrs. Watson."

"Of course, Your Grace. I believe she's in the linen closet with several of the downstairs maids. Shall I fetch her for you?"

"No, I—no, thank you, Monk." Max sidled back down the corridor to escape Monk's curious gaze, but not before he saw the man's lips twitch.

Impertinent scoundrel.

Townsend looked up when he came back into the study, his forehead puckered with a frown. "All right, Your Grace?"

"Of course, I'm all right. Why do you ask, Townsend? Don't I *look* all right?" Good Lord, was his idiocy visible on his face?

"Oh, yes, Your Grace. Very well, indeed. It's just that you're rather restless this morning."

Max threw himself into his chair with a sigh. "I've no idea what you're on about, Townsend. I'm not *restless*. I'm just a trifle agitated."

Townsend bit back a grin. "Yes, Your Grace."

"What the devil are you grinning at, Townsend?" First Monk, and now Townsend. He was surrounded by impertinent scoundrels. Couldn't a man get any peace?

"Nothing at all, Your Grace. Is there anything I can do to assist you?"

"No." Nothing short of rousting Miss St. Claire from her bed and dragging her downstairs so he could be done mooning over her, that is.

"Very well, Your Grace, if you're quite sure."

He wasn't sure of a single, bloody thing anymore. "Actually, Townsend, now I think of it, there is one thing."

"Of course, Your Grace. How can I help?"

"Miss St. Claire's bedchamber ceiling. Hire some villagers from Fairford to go to Hammond Court and repair it, will you?" Good Lord, what was he doing? He'd well and truly lost his wits.

Townsend blinked. "*Repair* it, Your Grace?"

Max huffed. "Are you going deaf, Townsend?"

"Not that I'm aware of, Your Grace, but just to make certain, you want me to see to it the damage to Miss St. Claire's ceiling is repaired?"

"You seem to have forgotten that it's *my* ceiling as well, Townsend." Max gave Townsend as withering a look as he could muster. "See to the roof, as well. Whatever tiles are missing or broken must be replaced, and any others that were loosened in the storm must be secured. While they're at it, they may as well see to replacing the damaged windows."

A wide smile lit Townsend's face. "Of course. Right away, Your Grace."

"Cease that absurd grinning at once, Townsend."

"Yes, Your Grace." Townsend pressed his lips together and bowed his head over his work.

Max rolled his eyes. For God's sake, he might have known Townsend would make far more of this than the situation warranted. Did no good deed go unpunished?

Pursuing repairs was ridiculous, of course, given he intended to reduce the whole bloody place to a pile of rubble as soon as he got the chance. But odds were Miss St. Claire would end up back at Hammond Court after the house party ended, and he wasn't so hard-hearted he'd banish her to a flooded bedchamber and let her freeze.

She *had* gone to quite a lot of trouble with those ginger biscuits, after all, and he wasn't a man who liked to let a debt go unpaid.

Silence fell over the study as he and Townsend turned their attention back to their work, but he couldn't set his mind to the tasks at hand—not with Townsend stealing glances at him every few minutes—nauseatingly approving glances. More than once, Townsend opened his mouth to speak, then snapped it closed again.

But God knew the man couldn't hold his tongue for long. It was only a matter of time.

Three, two, one . . .

"If I might just say, Your Grace," Townsend finally burst out. "How commendable I think it is that you—"

"You may *not* say, Townsend. Not a single, blessed word."

"Yes, Your Grace." Townsend gave him a meek nod, but damned if he couldn't feel the man vibrating with suppressed admiration for the rest of the morning.

Rose wasn't avoiding the Duke of Grantham.

To be fair, it might appear that way to someone who didn't realize how terribly busy she was this morning. She'd woken some hours ago, but it had taken her a disgraceful amount of time to emerge from the comforting nest of her blankets.

She'd washed and dressed quickly enough, but alas, just as she was on her way out her bedchamber door she spotted a tiny tear in a sleeve of the violet dress she'd chosen to wear, and there was nothing for it but to sit and mend it. She would have gone down once she'd completed that chore—certainly, she would have—but her hair chose that moment to stage a mutiny. No matter how long she sat in front of the looking glass, attempting to wrestle it into submission with her hairbrush, it refused to behave itself.

She *wasn't* hiding. It was just that with one thing and another, it had edged past noon and she had yet to make her way downstairs. But that wasn't the same thing as *hiding*. The Duke of Grantham had kissed her, yes, but that was neither here nor there. Certainly, it was no reason for her to cower in her bedchamber as if she were a naughty schoolgirl.

Of course, it wasn't. Why, the very idea was absurd.

It was true she'd never been kissed by a gentleman before, so she had been a bit surprised at the shivers that had darted down her spine when he'd dragged his warm fingertips across her cheek, and the, er, the sounds that had found their way out of her mouth when he'd teased his tongue between her lips had been something of a revelation.

His *tongue*. Goodness.

Was that a thing aristocrats did? She'd never heard of such a thing before, but there was no denying it had been distracting. So distracting, in fact, that she hadn't done a single thing to stop him.

So distracting, she'd, ah, kissed him back. Whoever could have imagined such a prickly man could have such soft, gentle lips? And his hair—she'd only touched it for a moment, sifting her fingers through the strands at the back of his neck, but it had been shockingly soft, like threads of silk between her fingertips.

Oh, dear. This was rather bad, wasn't it? How was she ever going to look at him again without recalling how gentle his lips were, how soft his hair was?

She met her reflection's gaze in the looking glass. A hot flush was rushing up her neck and into her cheeks, turning them scarlet. "Dash it!" She tossed the hairbrush onto the dressing table and pressed her palms to her burning cheeks.

She'd *kissed* the Duke of Grantham. What had she been thinking, kissing a duke? Especially that particular duke? Why, he was the closest she'd ever had to an actual enemy, and what had she done?

Kissed him. Or, to be fair, she'd kissed him *back*.

Surely, the first thing wasn't nearly as bad as the second.

"Rose?" The bedchamber door opened behind her, and Abby entered, her furrowed brow clearing when she saw Rose seated at the vanity. "There you are. Have you not been downstairs yet?"

"No, I—I've been trying to tame my hair. It's a fright this morning." It wasn't a lie. Her hair *was* a fright, but no more so than any other morning, and it wasn't the reason she was lingering in her bedchamber.

Lingering, but *not* hiding.

"Why, you silly thing, why didn't you ring?" Abby joined her in front of the glass, taking up the hairbrush. "You seemed fatigued this morning when I brought your tray, so I thought I'd let you sleep, but I confess I expected you to come down before this."

"I was just on my way."

Rose darted a glance at Abby in the mirror, then looked quickly away, but not before she saw Abby's brow wrinkle. "Whatever is the matter with you, Rose? You're dreadfully flushed. Are you ill?"

"There's not a thing the matter with me, I promise you." Rose toyed with the hairpins scattered across the top of the vanity, avoiding Abby's gaze. "Is, ah . . . has the Duke of Grantham appeared downstairs yet?"

He had, of course, likely hours ago. Why wouldn't he? It wasn't as if she was the first young lady he'd ever kissed. Why, a handsome gentleman like the Duke of Grantham must have kissed dozens of young ladies. Hundreds, even. He likely hadn't given her a second thought since she left the kitchen last night.

"The Duke of Grantham!" Abby had been running the hairbrush through Rose's curls in long, soothing strokes, but now her hand froze. "I might have known *he* had something to do with it!"

"To do with what? I haven't the faintest idea what you're talking about." But the treacherous blush was deepening to a telltale magenta, the heat scalding her cheeks.

"Is that so? Then why are you turning as red as a summer strawberry?" Abby's furious gaze met hers in the glass. "What's that wicked duke done this time?"

Oh, dear. This had all the makings of a catastrophe. "Nothing at all, Abby, I promise you."

Abby didn't reply, but she assessed Rose's reflection in the mirror with unrelenting intensity, her mouth pulled into a stern line. Rose gulped, but by some miracle, she managed to hold Abby's gaze without squirming.

Whatever else might come of it, Abby could *not* find out the Duke of Grantham had kissed her last night, because if she did, Abby would see to it she removed Rose from Grantham Lodge before she could squeak out a word of protest, and then all of her plans would fall to ruins.

What did it matter if the duke had kissed her? It had been a single, isolated moment. If they hadn't been alone in a dark kitchen, and she hadn't done him a good turn with the ginger biscuits, it never would have happened at all.

It wasn't as if the duke had any particular affection for her. Quite the opposite.

Perhaps he wasn't accustomed to receiving unexpected kindness from people. Considering how snarly he was, that would hardly be surprising. He might just have been overwhelmed with gratitude, or . . . well, he'd been overwhelmed with *something*, certainly.

Either that, or he'd merely been toying with her. He was *betrothed*, for pity's sake, or nearly so. Betrothed dukes didn't kiss inconsequential young ladies like her for any reason other than mere diversion.

In the end, it didn't matter why he'd kissed her, as long as it didn't happen again.

But surely, there was no danger of that?

"I don't like it, Rose." Abby began working the brush through Rose's hair again, her strokes considerably less soothing this time. "I don't trust that man—or any duke, come to that—and it isn't proper for you to be under the same roof with him."

"At least his roof is intact." Rose's eyes watered as Abby gave a particularly vicious tug. "If you keep on that way, Abby, I won't have a hair left on my head for you to brush."

Abby set the brush aside with a sigh. "Look at me, dearest."

Rose met Abby's gaze in the glass. "I know what you're going to say—"

"You don't have to remain here, Rose. We have another choice, and you know it just as well as I do." Abby laid her hands on Rose's shoulders. "Give the Duke of Grantham Hammond Court, Rose. Take the money he's offered you, and start a new life somewhere else."

"I can't do that, Abby." Not yet, that is. "It's not what Ambrose wanted."

"Do you suppose he wanted *this* for you?" Abby waved a hand around the elegant bedchamber. "He loved you, child. He never would have wanted you to put yourself at the mercy of a scoundrel like the Duke of Grantham."

Rose sighed. It was true that Ambrose couldn't have foreseen how things would play out with the duke. How could he have done so? Yet he'd asked her anyway—no, begged her to see his last wishes carried out, and she wouldn't fail him. Not after everything he'd done for her.

She shook her head. "And leave the tenants at the duke's mercy? No, Abby."

"There's not a single one of them that would begrudge you your freedom, Rose." But there was a note of resignation in Abby's voice, and a moment later she took up the brush again. She ran it through Rose's hair until it shone, then tied the curls back with a violet-colored ribbon.

"There." Abby took in her reflection, a proud smile curving her lips. "You look as pretty as a spring flower. Go on down, now, and find Mrs. Watson. She was looking for you earlier."

"I will." Rose got to her feet and kissed Abby on the cheek. "Thank you, Abby."

"You stay away from that wicked duke, you hear?" Abby called out just as Rose closed the bedchamber door behind her.

"I daresay he'll take care to stay away from *me*," she muttered as she made her way down the corridor, dragging her feet with every step.

There would be no avoiding the duke entirely. This was his house, after all. But perhaps a day apart wouldn't go amiss, and she could easily keep herself occupied in the kitchens for most of the day. The duke wouldn't come looking for her there—not after what had happened between them last night.

But perhaps the less she dwelled on *that*, the better.

She'd nearly reached the landing when she heard it.

A cacophony of voices chattering excitedly. She tiptoed closer to the staircase, her breath catching as the unmistakably deep timbre of the Duke of Grantham's voice rose above the others, welcoming them all to Grantham Lodge.

She stilled, nerves fluttering against her breastbone. They were here.

The duke's guests had arrived from London, and it sounded—goodness, it sounded as if there were dozens of them, all talking at once. A tinkle of high-pitched laughter, decidedly feminine, reached her ears, and then a low, rich laugh in response.

It was *him*. She couldn't say how she knew, as she'd never heard him laugh before. The man hadn't ventured even as much as a smile since he'd arrived in Fairford, but somehow, she recognized it at once as *his* laugh.

It was a quiet laugh, yet somehow it echoed inside her, swelling into every dark, empty corner. Who was making him laugh like that? She edged closer to the landing and into the entryway below.

A soft gasp rose to her lips.

It was filled with ladies and gentlemen, all of them dressed in elegant cloaks and hats, and all of them chattering to each other as if they were the best of friends. Monk and two of his upper footmen were scrambling about, collecting hats, gloves, and cloaks, and through the open door she could see a half dozen or so carriages in the drive, the coachmen at the horses' heads.

Why, it looked as if all of London had come to Fairford.

In the midst of the melee stood the Duke of Grantham, and beside him one of the most stunning ladies she'd ever seen. She was dressed in a deep, midnight-blue cloak, and even from this distance, Rose could see the color matched a pair of wide eyes as blue as sapphires. A smart hat set rakishly atop a thick mass of dark, lustrous curls, and her crimson lips were curved in a coquettish smile.

The duke was holding her hands, and she was smiling up at him, and suddenly the very last thing Rose wanted to do was to venture downstairs and face all those elegant people.

She wasn't one of them. They'd know it at once, and from what she knew of aristocrats, they wouldn't hesitate to make her feel it. But there was no help for it. Either she went down, her head held high, or she hid in her bedchamber until Twelfth Night.

As tempting as it was, she wouldn't get anywhere hiding in her bedchamber.

So, she gripped the railing, the wood slippery under her sweating palm, and placed her foot on the step below her. One step, two, another . . .

For better or worse, the house party had begun.

CHAPTER 17

Grantham Lodge—so still, so silent, so reassuringly tomblike on the best of days—had descended into chaos in the blink of an eye.

Max stood in the midst of the melee doing his best to hide a scowl, but it was there at the corners of his lips, threatening to spread to the rest of his mouth. How in the world could he ever have thought a house party was a good idea?

Alas, short of tossing his guests out the door and cursing them all to the devil, there wasn't much he could do to stop them coming. No, there was nothing for it but to paste a charming smile to his mouth as they descended upon him, barreling right over poor Monk, who was doing his best to welcome them and stay upright under the stampede at the same time.

And the carriages were still coming. Soon enough, the drive was crowded with them. Harnesses jingled, and horses snorted as the coachmen darted about, lobbying for space. Carriage doors opened, and then slammed closed again after disgorging their passengers, all of whom were shrieking, gossiping, and creating unholy mayhem.

Good God, what a commotion. How many people had he invited? It looked as if all of London had just appeared at his front door. The walls were shaking from the tumult.

If he could have escaped, he would have fled in an instant, hospitality be damned, but it was too late for a dignified retreat. Monk, curse him, had opened the door the instant the first carriage appeared at the top of the drive, and now aristocrats were crowding into Max's entryway like a swarm of fashionable bees.

Or a plague of buzzing locusts.

Lady Emily was the first through the front door. She spied him at once, swept forward like an advancing army of one, and promptly took possession of his arm. "Grantham! My goodness, I thought we'd never arrive, but here we are, at last!"

"So, I see." He bowed and skimmed his lips over the knuckles of her glove. "How do you do, Lady Emily?"

"Well, much better, *now*." She beamed up at him, a coquettish smile playing on her lips. "But I'm afraid it was a dreadfully tiring journey. Gloucestershire is ever so far away. Why, I almost imagined we'd left England entirely. I never conceived it could be such a distance!"

"How d'ye do, Grantham." Montford appeared at Lady Emily's elbow. "It's about time you invited us to your country seat. Rather rude of you to wait two decades, eh?"

"London is as dull as a tomb without you, Grantham,"

Lady Emily gushed. "Hasn't London been a deadly bore without Grantham, Montford?"

"Has Grantham been away?" Montford smirked at Max. "I hadn't noticed."

Lady Emily let out a tinkling laugh. "Shame on you, Your Grace!"

"I'm only jesting, Grantham. London has been as tiresome as a long Sunday sermon since you deserted us. I don't know how I endured it." Montford grinned. "What's prompted this uncharacteristic burst of holiday spirit? After such a lordly summons, I expect to be wildly entertained."

"What will you have, Montford? Pantomimes, Mummers, and Christmas pudding?" It all sounded damned unpleasant to Max, particularly the pantomimes, but he couldn't help grinning back at Montford. He, Montford, and Basingstoke had been friends since his first year at Eton, and they were among the few people with whom he felt utterly at ease.

"Why, all of it, of course. We didn't come all the way from London to sit on our hands, did we, Lady Emily? Now, where has my duchess got to?" Montford turned and scanned the entryway. "Ah, there she is, talking to . . . by God, that looks like Dunwitty."

Well, that hadn't taken long. "It *is* Dunwitty."

Montford turned back to Max, his eyes narrowing. "I didn't realize you and the viscount were such close friends, Grantham."

Max glanced over Montford's head. Yes, there was Dunwitty, just as his uncle had promised he would be. He was chatting with the Duchess of Montford, who was dusting the snow from her cloak. Just behind them was Basingstoke, handing his hat and stick to Monk, his duchess's arm linked with his, her cheeks pink from the cold.

Everyone was here, then. Everyone, that is, except Rose St. Claire.

Where was she? He pulled his pocket watch from his coat and glanced down at the face. It was half past noon. Had she somehow slipped down the stairs without his noticing? Perhaps he should check the kitchens—

"—confess I find myself quite curious about Grantham Lodge, Your Grace."

He jerked his attention back to Lady Emily, who was simpering up at him, eyelashes fluttering, her lips pursed in a pretty little pout. "I beg your pardon?"

"Grantham Lodge. I don't mind saying I didn't know quite what to expect, as you've kept it such a deep, dark secret, you naughty man." She let out a throaty laugh. "But it's ever so lovely! Such a perfect place for a fortnight of Christmas festivities! Really, Your Grace, I can't think why you haven't hosted a house party before now."

Because he detested Fairford? Because he detested Grantham Lodge? Because he detested Christmas? No, none of those replies would do, would they? Pity, as they were all the truth.

But somehow he managed to dredge up a charming smile for Lady Emily. "I prefer London to the country, my lady, but when business called me to Gloucestershire, I couldn't pass up the opportunity to make the most of a winter's visit to Fairford."

There. That was an acceptable lie.

"Well, I'm overjoyed that you did, Your Grace." She cast him a smoldering glance from under her thick, dark lashes, her blue eyes gleaming under her heavy lids. "What's Christmas, after all, without a house party?"

"You're very good to come all this way, my lady, especially given the suddenness of the invitation. I had thought we might . . ." He trailed off as a movement to his left caught his eye, and he whirled toward the staircase, his pulse thumping.

Even before he turned and his gaze landed on her face, he knew who he'd find.

And there she was, outside her bedchamber at last. Today Miss St. Claire was wearing a simple, violet-colored day dress that, for all that it was an ordinary enough garment, appeared to his fevered gaze to cling most scandalously to her curves, emphasizing every graceful arch and hollow of her slender frame.

She hesitated on the first-floor landing, her green eyes wide as she took in the crowd of people milling about the entryway.

"You were saying, Your Grace?" Lady Emily laid a proprietary hand on his arm.

He didn't answer, because he couldn't tear his gaze away from Miss St. Claire. Her gown wasn't fashionable or elegant. Indeed, it was rather worn, the cuffs and collar a bit threadbare, but it skimmed her curves in a way that was both innocent and seductive at once.

Look away, man! For God's sake, look—

"Who is that young woman, Grantham?" Lady Emily

turned toward the staircase, her gaze following his. "Is she one of your maidservants?"

His *maidservant*? She might not be dressed in the height of fashion, but there was no mistaking Rose St. Claire for a servant. "Hardly, Lady Emily."

His voice was a touch louder than it needed to be, and abruptly the chatter around them faded to silence as every head turned toward him. He wasn't the center of attention for long, however. Once they caught sight of Miss St. Claire, many of them turned to watch her as she made her way down the last few steps.

What was it about her that held his gaze? She was lovely, yes—he'd long since stopped pretending otherwise—but there were a half dozen lovely ladies in the entryway, and he wasn't mesmerized by the sight of any of *them*.

She paused on the final step, her cheeks flushing scarlet as she noticed she'd become the center of attention. She glanced behind her as if she were considering scurrying back up the stairs and vanishing into her bedchamber.

That wouldn't do. He needed her downstairs, with him.

No, not with *him*, but with Dunwitty, of course.

He stepped forward and held out a hand to her. "Ah, here you are, Miss St. Claire."

She cast an apprehensive glance at his hand, but she could hardly refuse to accept it, and after a moment she placed the tips of her fingers in his palm. "Your Grace."

His fingers closed around hers, and he drew her into

the entryway. By then, the guests had converged near the bottom of the staircase, and all of them were regarding her with varying degrees of curiosity. It was the oddest moment, with their excited chatter all quieting at once. It was as if they knew her appearance among them must be significant, somehow.

It made no sense. There was no way they could possibly know he—

What? That he *what*? The only reason Rose St. Claire was here was because she was in his *way*, and he wanted her out of it. That was all. Otherwise, she was of no importance to him whatsoever.

He released her hand and took a step back. "This is Miss St. Claire. She's, er . . . an old acquaintance of my family who has graciously agreed to attend the house party."

"You mean to say she's your *guest*, Grantham?" Lady Emily glanced at Rose and a smirk lifted one corner of her lip. "How curious."

No one seemed to know what to say to that, and a brief, uncomfortable silence fell. A hot flash of anger heated Max's blood, but before he could say a word, Francesca, the Duchess of Basingstoke, and Prue, the Duchess of Montford hurried toward Rose with warm smiles. "This must be the young lady we're to chaperone these next few weeks. How do you do, Miss St. Claire? I'm the Duchess of Basingstoke, and this lady here is the Duchess of Montford."

"It's lovely to make your acquaintance, Miss St. Claire." Prue took Rose's hand. "You must promise to show us around Fairford. I hear it's a charming village, and I believe you grew up here?"

"Yes, Your Grace." Rose gave her a shy smile. "Though I'm afraid it will be rather a quick visit, and I daresay you'll find it terribly dull. Fairford is tiny."

"No matter." Prue waved away the objection. "I grew up in the Wiltshire countryside, in a little burg very much like Fairford, and Francesca spent a good part of her childhood in a small village in Herefordshire. I daresay we'll be endlessly diverted, will we not, Francesca?"

"Indeed." Francesca nodded, smiling.

Rose's shoulders eased at their warmth. "I'd be pleased to show you Fairford, Your Graces."

Max let out a silent breath. It had been a stroke of genius, asking Prue and Franny to chaperone Rose. They'd take good care of her, leaving him free to get on with the business at hand. All he needed was a private word with Dunwitty to set the scheme in motion.

"Mrs. Watson." He nodded to his housekeeper, who was waiting by the doorway with Monk. "If you'd be so kind as to show my guests to their bedchambers?"

"Of course, Your Grace." Mrs. Watson bustled forward, a small army of housemaids following behind her. "Why, you all must be frozen half-solid after such a journey! I daresay you're anxious to be out of your damp things."

Mrs. Watson took charge of the two duchesses and assigned a housemaid to each of the other guests. Within minutes the entire swarm was clambering up the staircase.

Peace, at last!

But before he could take Dunwitty aside, Montford and Basingstoke descended on him, their eyebrows raised.

"What is it? Why are you two gaping at me?" Max waved a hand at the staircase. "Go with your wives."

Basingstoke glanced at Montford, who let out a heavy sigh. "Forgive me, Grantham, but I would have sworn you said that young lady's surname is St. Claire."

Damn it. What had he been thinking, inviting Montford and Basingstoke? They were far too adept at ferreting out his secrets. "Yes. What of it? I don't see why it should concern—"

"St. Claire, as in *Ambrose* St. Claire, the gentleman you've been vowing revenge upon since we were all together at Eton? Your nemesis, your sworn enemy, your—"

"I know what a nemesis is, Montford." God above, had there ever been two nosier dukes than these? Still, there was no sense putting it off, as neither of them would rest until they got his confession. "Miss St. Claire is, ah . . . Ambrose St. Claire's . . ."

"Yes?" Basingstoke's eyebrow inched up another notch. "His *what*, Grantham?"

Max huffed. "His adopted daughter."

"His *daughter*?" Basingstoke's face darkened. "What the devil are you up to, Grantham?"

"Not a blessed thing, I assure you." Nothing that wasn't for the girl's own good, at any rate. "Miss St.

Claire's house is in disarray, so I invited her to stay at Grantham Lodge. I'm merely doing her a favor."

Montford crossed his arms over his chest. "And what house would that be, Grantham?"

Max sighed. Only a duke would dare to question another duke, which was why it was exceedingly unfortunate that Montford and Basingstoke were his best friends. Nothing good ever came of three dukes in one house. "Hammond Court."

Silence. Finally, Basingstoke cleared his throat. "I repeat, Grantham. What the devil are you up to?"

"Nothing you need worry yourselves about."

Basingstoke's eyes narrowed. "Grantham—"

"Might we delay this discussion until a later time? I've some business to attend to." It wasn't a lie. He did have business—rather important business—and Dunwitty had already vanished up the stairs.

His friends glanced at each other, then Montford gave a curt nod, his lips tight. "Very well, Grantham, but I warn you. We'll have it out of you one way or another."

With one last threatening scowl, his friends marched up the stairs after their wives.

Max retreated to the study, seated himself behind his desk, and rang the bell. A few minutes later, Monk appeared. "Your Grace?"

"Fetch Lord Dunwitty to my study, Monk. I need to have a word with him."

"Of course, Your Grace. Right away."

* * *

There was really only one place where a lady who was determined to hide from a houseful of aristocrats could go.

The kitchens. Aristocrats weren't known for frequenting the kitchens.

So, while Mrs. Watson and the housemaids were occupied with herding the guests up the stairs, Rose took the opportunity to slip through the crowd. Fortunately, the duke was busy with the Dukes of Basingstoke and Montford and didn't see her disappear down the back staircase.

Imposing gentlemen, those dukes. Very, er . . . ducal, and both of them extraordinarily handsome. Neither were as striking as the Duke of Grantham, but there was no denying they were pleasing to look at. It hardly seemed fair. Didn't dukes have enough advantages without being handsome, as well?

The kitchen was deserted. That was rare enough, but everyone was occupied with the guests, and the kitchen boy had likely slipped outside so he might see all the grand horses and carriages.

She had it all to herself, so she may as well do something useful. She'd already furnished Mrs. Watson with some very nice iced tea cakes for afternoon tea, but perhaps a baked custard for supper wouldn't go amiss.

She'd laid out her ingredients, and the pretty etched-glass custard cups, and was just fetching the eggs from the cook's pantry when a deep voice startled her. "Miss St. Claire?"

She jumped, and one of the eggs she was transferring

to a bowl slipped from her fingers and landed on the floor. The shell cracked, and yellow yolk oozed out. "Drat."

"I do beg your pardon." A fair-haired young man was peeking around the edge of the pantry door. "I didn't mean to startle you."

She glanced up from the mess and into a pair of velvety brown eyes. He was one of the duke's guests—she'd caught a glimpse of him when she'd come down the stairs—but they hadn't been properly introduced, and she didn't know his name.

He'd remembered hers, though, which was surprising.

"I . . . it's quite all right." She took up a cloth from the table and quickly wiped up the mess, dropping the broken shells into the bowl. "Have you lost your way?"

What in the world was he doing down here, otherwise?

"Oh, no. I came in search of James, the footman who showed me to my bedchamber. He dropped this."

He held up a gold button, and she recognized it as one from the footmen's livery.

"I thought I might return it to him." He sauntered closer, his brown eyes fixed on her face with a look she couldn't quite read, but that nonetheless made heat flood her cheeks.

"I haven't seen James, but I'll make certain to return it to him." She held out her hand, and he dropped the gold button into her palm. She expected him to turn and leave at once—aristocrats and kitchens, after all—but he remained where he was, his gaze lingering on her face.

"Is there anything else I can do for you, er . . . my

lord?" Was he a lord? She hadn't the vaguest idea, but it seemed a safe guess, given that the house was teeming with London's upper ten thousand.

"I do beg your pardon—again. Lord Dunwitty. It's a pleasure to make your acquaintance, Miss St. Claire."

"I—thank you." Goodness, how strange. What could he want with her? And now she thought of it, what sort of lord came all the way down to the kitchen to return a button to one of the footmen?

No sort of lord she'd ever heard of.

"That's a great many eggs you have there, Miss St. Claire." He peered over the edge of the bowl. "What are you making?"

"I thought I'd make a baked custard for pudding this evening."

"Lovely! I do adore a baked custard."

He grinned at her—a sweet, boyish grin. Very charming, indeed, and she did like the way his fair hair flopped into those playful brown eyes. He was handsome—all of the duke's gentlemen friends were handsome, it seemed—but as pretty as he was, he didn't make her heart thrum in her chest like—

Well. Like no one at all.

It was just as well, too, as the Duke of Grantham's breathtakingly beautiful future betrothed was now here, and rather possessive, if the jealous grasp she'd had on his arm was any indication.

But then she *was* his betrothed. Surely, she had the right to grasp him wherever she—

No. No, that wouldn't do. The duke's romantic affairs weren't her concern, and she wouldn't think on it. It wasn't as if the duke was likely to initiate a second kiss with *her*. No, there would be no more pounding hearts, heated flushes, or breathlessness.

No more kissing. Certainly, no more kissing.

"May I stay and help?"

Lord Dunwitty fluttered his eyelashes at her. He was shameless, yet she couldn't prevent her laugh. "Have you made many custards, my lord?"

"Not a one," he admitted cheerfully. "But if you'll permit me to stay, Miss St. Claire, I promise to make myself as useful as possible."

"How do you propose to do that, then?" She cast him as stern a look as she could manage, but the twitch of her lips rather spoiled the effect.

"I could measure your ingredients for you. If I acquit myself well enough, then perhaps you'll permit me to stir the custard. Will that do?"

She let out a heavy sigh. "I suppose it will have to, won't it?"

"Wonderful!" He pulled one of the kitchen stools free of the table and sat down, giving her a grin that had no doubt charmed every young lady in London. "Perhaps later, you'll consent to a walk through the grounds. You may show me all the secret nooks in Grantham's gardens."

"Certainly not, my lord." She gave a haughty sniff. "I can't wander about the grounds alone with you. We haven't been introduced."

"Of course, we have. Don't you recall it? I am Viscount Dunwitty, and you are Miss St. Claire."

"*Properly* introduced, my lord."

"Oh, dear. That *is* a problem, isn't it? Well then, once we've finished the custard, perhaps we might go in search of the Duchesses of Basingstoke and Montford. I'll politely request a proper introduction to the lovely Miss St. Claire, and we'll invite them to accompany us on our walk. I daresay they'll agree, after such a long drive in the carriage. Will that do?"

There could be no objection to that, surely? "Very well, my lord. If Their Graces agree to join us, then I can't see any reason why I should object."

"Wonderful! Now, where shall we begin with the custard? This French brandy seems as promising a start as any." He nodded appreciatively at the bottle. "I do adore a pudding made with French brandy."

"We begin with boiling the water, my lord," she replied primly.

"Oh." He let out a glum sigh, cradling his chin in his hands. "That's rather less exciting."

She couldn't help the laugh that bubbled from her lips. He was perfectly ridiculous, of course, but between the two friendly duchesses and lively Lord Dunwitty, perhaps this house party wouldn't be as dreadful as she'd feared. "Don't despair, my lord. If you're very good, I'll let you grate the nutmeg."

"Well, that's something, at least. I'll endeavor to acquit myself with—"

"Miss St. Claire? What are you doing down here?"

Rose had just set the kettle to boil and gathered a handful of nutmegs, but at the sound of the abrupt voice, they slipped from her fingers and rolled under the worktable. "Oh, dear. I—"

"Not to worry, Miss St. Claire." Lord Dunwitty stood. "I'll fetch them for you."

"Thank you, my lord." But she hardly spared Lord Dunwitty a glance, because standing in the kitchen doorway was the Duke of Grantham, his gaze flicking between her and the viscount, the strangest expression on his face. Beside him stood a small, dark-haired gentleman with pinched lips and a Gallic nose. "I beg your pardon, Your Grace. I was just making a baked custard for—"

"Baked custard!" The little gentleman beside the duke gave a disdainful sniff. "My dear madam, if His Grace requires a custard, I will prepare *cannelés de Bordeaux*."

Was that a pudding? She'd never heard of it.

The haughty little man peered at Rose, the tip of his nose twitching like an outraged mouse. "I am not accustomed to sharing my kitchen, Your Grace. Custard, indeed! *C'est intolérable!*"

His kitchen? Ah, this must be Monsieur Blanchard, the duke's French cook from London. Why, what a thoroughly unpleasant little man! He might have his kitchen all to himself, and welcome.

But the duke didn't reply to Monsieur Blanchard. He didn't give any indication he'd even heard him but continued to stare at Rose, his dark brows drawn together in a scowl.

Goodness, what in the world was the matter with him? Was he angry at her for making use of the kitchen? He never had been so before, but—

"Here you are, Miss St. Claire." Lord Dunwitty

emerged from under the worktable and offered her the nutmegs. She took them in trembling fingers.

"I see you're making productive use of your time, Dunwitty." The duke's voice was perfectly civil, but the look in his eyes . . . dear God. He looked as if he could happily wring someone's neck.

No, not *someone's*. Lord Dunwitty's.

But if the viscount noticed, it didn't seem to trouble him in the least. He leaned a hip against the worktable and offered the duke a bland smile. "Always, Your Grace."

"Pardon me, Your Grace," Monsieur Blanchard interrupted in a petulant tone. "I must insist that your servants stay out of my kitchens. I can't have *les filles idiotes* running about, distracting me with their custards. I must have quiet when I am working on *mes créations*—"

"Miss St. Claire isn't my servant." The duke's gaze slid from the viscount to Rose, and his hard expression softened ever so slightly. "And she may do as she pleases in the kitchens, whenever she pleases. Are we clear, Blanchard?"

Monsieur Blanchard shot Rose a resentful look, but he muttered, "*Oui*, Your Grace."

"Good." The duke didn't linger. After one last narrow glance at Dunwitty, he turned on his heel and disappeared through the kitchen door without another word, leaving Rose with an outraged French cook, a flirtatious viscount, and a handful of nutmegs.

CHAPTER 18

"My goodness, Grantham, what's put you in such a temper this evening?" The Duchess of Basingstoke, who'd agreed to act as Max's hostess for the evening, studied him over the top edge of her wineglass. "You're positively glowering."

Glowering? Nonsense. What did he have to glower about? "I've no idea what you mean, Francesca. I'm perfectly content."

She snorted. "As content as a hunting dog who's lost the fox, perhaps. That scowl of yours has put poor Lady Dowd off her baked custard. Rather a pity, really, as it's delicious."

Max pushed his custard cup aside. "It has too much nutmeg."

Dunwitty's fault, no doubt. What did a viscount know about custard? Miss St. Claire would have been better off keeping her custard out of reach of Dunwitty's clumsy hands.

Not that it mattered to *him* what she did, of course. She might crack eggs and grate nuts all day long with

Dunwitty, and he wouldn't bat an eye. No, if he *was* out of temper, it had nothing to do with Rose St. Claire.

His plan was proceeding precisely as he'd intended.

The more perfectly conceived a scheme was, the greater the chances of a flawless execution, and that was what he was seeing at the dinner table this evening—the flawless execution of his wicked, deceitful scheme to see Miss St. Claire safely wed to Viscount Dunwitty.

He couldn't be any happier about it. He was downright jubilant. So overjoyed, in fact, that if Dunwitty's hand brushed Miss St. Claire's shoulder one more time, he might just explode with . . . bliss.

"Take care with that glass, Grantham." Francesca nodded at the wineglass clutched in his fist. "It's one white knuckle away from shattering in your hand. It's not quite the thing, bleeding at the dinner table, is it?"

"White knuckle?" He glanced down at his hand. Damn it. His knuckles *had* gone white.

He loosened his grip. He should have seated Francesca at the other end of the table, and not directly at his right, where she could witness his every frown and twitch.

She was far too perceptive, and there was little doubt she'd report everything back to Basingstoke, who'd be eager enough to listen. Both he and Montford had grown more frustrated with him with every day that passed, but they'd yet to pin him down for an interrogation.

Still, two nosier devils than Montford and Basingstoke never existed. It was only a matter of time before they cornered him, and once they did . . .

What then? Perhaps he'd tell them the truth about his schemes. He wasn't a good man, but he'd always drawn the line at lying to his friends. Still, it would be best if the plan was a bit further along before he was called to account.

Not that he had anything to be ashamed of. Not in the least.

He'd arranged for Miss St. Claire to marry a viscount, for God's sake. Surely, there was nothing he need reproach himself for in that? Most people would say he'd done her a good turn, putting Dunwitty in her way.

Indeed, by the looks of things, both Dunwitty and Miss St. Claire were vastly pleased with each other's company. Dunwitty had hardly ceased talking for the entire meal. For his part, Max always found the man to be a bit on the dull side, but Dunwitty was unusually animated this evening, and if Miss St. Claire's smiles were any indication, she found his conversation utterly charming.

Perhaps it would even turn out to be a love match.

"There's that glower again," Francesca murmured, raising an eyebrow. "Is it the viscount who offends you, Grantham, or is it Miss St. Claire?"

"Neither of them offend me." Unless they were together.

Which was ridiculous, given he was the one who'd been so reckless as to throw them into each other's way. But then, no good deed went unpunished. Or had it been a bad deed? He was no longer sure, but it did feel as if he were being punished for . . . well, something.

Francesca followed his gaze. "I can't see how Miss

St. Claire could offend you. She's a lovely young lady, is she not?"

She was. Far too lovely. That was the very reason she offended him, damn her. If she'd been a trifle less appealing, his head wouldn't be so muddled. None of this made any sense. He'd brought Dunwitty here so he could rid himself of Rose St. Claire, but now . . .

He'd found the idea of a marriage between them palatable enough at one time, hadn't he? But somehow the reality of seeing them together every day was far less agreeable than he'd anticipated. And they were together constantly. Every bloody time he turned around, there was Dunwitty on Miss St. Claire's heels, flirting with her, and making her laugh.

"As for Dunwitty, he's harmless enough, and he seems quite captivated by Miss St. Claire." Francesca turned narrowed, dark blue eyes on him. "It would be a wonderful thing for her if he fell in love with her. Don't you think so, Grantham?"

He had done, once, but somewhere in the midst of his perfect scheme, he'd changed his—

No, damn it, he hadn't. It was too late for that, and in any case, it was nonsense. He was as determined as he'd ever been. "I don't like to disappoint you, Francesca, but I have no opinion whatsoever concerning Miss St. Claire's romantic affairs. I couldn't be less interested, I assure you."

"Of course not, Grantham." A sly smile curved Francesca's lips, and her eyes danced as she plucked his wineglass from his hand. "We'll just leave this on the table, shall we?"

He hardly heard her, because just then a bright laugh echoed down the table, and he turned just in time to see Miss St. Claire throw her head back, her cheeks flushed, and her pink lips parted in that laugh that struck him directly in the center of his chest.

When had her laugh become so familiar to him, so necessary? He'd only heard it half a dozen times, but it wasn't the sort of laugh one forgot, once they'd heard it the first time.

So joyous a laugh as that could never be forgotten.

He'd never found Dunwitty at all amusing, but apparently, Miss St. Claire didn't share his opinion. She was smiling as Dunwitty whispered some nonsense in her ear. Their heads were bent close together, and Dunwitty's hand rested next to hers atop the table, so close he could have covered her fingers with his.

"It's time the ladies retired, Your Grace." He tore his gaze from Rose—that is, Miss St. Claire—and turned to Francesca. "If you'd do me the favor of taking them out."

Francesca paused for an instant, far too much understanding in those clever blue eyes of hers, but then she nodded. "Very well, Your Grace." She rose, and the chatter died away as heads turned toward her. "Ladies, I believe it's time we left the gentlemen to their vices."

The ladies rose from the table in a swish of silk skirts, but they may as well have been invisible, for all the attention he paid to them. Only one lady mattered, and she was the only one he could see.

Miss St. Claire offered Dunwitty a warm smile, but she didn't linger.

Max's gaze followed her as she passed out of the dining room, and a tangle of emotions swelled in her wake, twisting inside his chest like a nest of writhing snakes. They were so intertwined he could hardly tell one from the next, but as his gaze returned to Dunwitty at the other end of the table, one slithered loose and reared up, head weaving, tongue flickering, hissing its displeasure.

Jealousy. He was *jealous* of Dunwitty.

Jealous, and frustrated, and underneath it all lay a baffling regret. This was what he'd wanted, yet at the same time, he couldn't shake the feeling that commanding Viscount Dunwitty to court Rose St. Claire may have been the worst mistake of his life.

"Miss St. Claire! Will you join us?" The Duchess of Montford patted the empty space beside her on a plump, green silk settee near the fireplace.

"Yes, do come, won't you, Miss St. Claire?" The Duchess of Basingstoke, who was seated on the other end of the settee, beckoned her forward with a curl of her gloved fingers.

Goodness. Summoned not just by one duchess, but two? Given the cool reception the other ladies had given her, Rose had reconciled herself to a long evening of solitary reading. She'd brought a copy of Miss Burney's *The Wanderer* to keep herself occupied, but it seemed the duchesses took their chaperone duties quite seriously.

And one didn't naysay a duchess, did one? Certainly not *two* duchesses.

She set the book she'd been reading aside and hurried across the drawing room, the hair on her neck rising at the sensation of other ladies' eyes upon her, but both duchesses greeted her with friendly smiles.

"Now, Miss St. Claire," the Duchess of Montford began. "Do sit down and tell us all about yourself. How long have you lived at Hammond Court?"

All about herself? Oh, dear. This charming tête-à-tête was destined to end as quickly as it had begun, then, as duchesses did not generally waste their graciousness on the daughters of servants, particularly those daughters who were born on the wrong side of the blanket.

But she'd never been ashamed of who she was, and she wouldn't hang her head now. "I was four years old when I came to Hammond Court with my mother, so nearly seventeen years now. She—my mother—was Mr. St. Claire's cook."

They'd shove her off the end of the settee now, or worse, get up and leave themselves, abandoning her in the middle of the drawing room with every eye upon her—

"Yes, I believe Mrs. Watson told me as much. She had a great deal of admiration for your mother," the Duchess of Basingstoke said. "As I understand it, she was a treasured friend of Mr. St. Claire's."

Rose blinked. She hadn't expected such kindness, and for one horrifying moment she felt tears press behind her eyes. "She was indeed, Your Grace."

"Oh, you must call me Francesca. All of my friends do."

"I'm Prudence, or preferably Prue, as Prudence is a

bit too antiquated for me," the Duchess of Montford added.

"Prue, and Francesca," Rose repeated dutifully. "I'm afraid I haven't ventured far from Fairford since then. I've never even been outside of Gloucestershire. Sadly provincial of me, I'm afraid."

Prue patted her hand. "I think I mentioned before that Franny and I were both raised primarily in the English countryside. Franny spent part of her childhood in London, but I only visited for the first time the year before last."

The Duchess of Basingstoke—Francesca—leaned closer, a mischievous smile on her lips. "Not all duchesses are as perfectly pedigreed as the aristocracy would have you believe, Miss St. Claire."

"No? Well, I . . . that's . . ." No. It was no use. She couldn't think of a single thing to say in reply to that.

Prue laughed. "Oh, dear. We've stunned her speechless, Franny. However does that keep happening, do you suppose?"

"It does happen with astonishing regularity, does it not? Too much forthrightness, I imagine, but no matter. Come, Miss St. Claire, you may be at your ease with us, as we're all certain to become the greatest of friends."

Friends? For the duration of the house party, perhaps. After that, she'd likely never see either lady again, as they hardly moved in the same social circles. Still, they seemed in earnest, and she didn't have many friends. Or any friends, really, and she'd quite like to, if only for a fortnight. "Thank you. I'd like that very much. You're both too kind."

"Well, now that's settled, do tell us about yourself." Prue gave her another smile. "I understand you and Mr. St. Claire were extremely close—as close as a father and daughter, Mrs. Watson said."

"Very close, yes. I—I miss him dreadfully, I'm afraid." Dash it, there were the tears again, pressing more insistently this time.

"You poor thing." Francesca seized her other hand and gave it a reassuring squeeze. "It's dreadfully difficult, isn't it? I lost my own father at quite a young age, and it felt as if my heart had been torn still beating from my chest."

Rose cast her a grateful glance. "It does. I hadn't been able to put words to it, but that's exactly how it feels—as if you've lost some vital part of yourself."

"Oh, my dear." Francesca's fingers tightened around Rose's hand. "I'm afraid so, but the pain does ease after a time, and you'll always have your memories of him. No one can take those away from you."

No, they couldn't. She wouldn't let them.

The three of them were quiet after that, but both Prue and Francesca kept her hands in theirs, and after a time the tears receded, and her heart resumed its steady beat.

"How do you and Grantham get on?" Prue asked, breaking the comfortable silence. "He was no friend of Mr. St. Claire's. I imagine that must make it rather awkward between you."

"Yes, it . . ." She'd been about to say it *had* been awkward, but the truth was, since the day Sir Richard had revealed the terms of Ambrose's will to them, and the bitter argument between them that had followed, the

Duke of Grantham had been, well . . . perhaps one couldn't say *gallant*, precisely, but in his own way, he'd been quite . . .

Indulgent? Was that the proper word to use?

He'd rescued her from the flood at Hammond Court, brought her to Grantham Lodge, and turned her over to the tender ministrations of Mrs. Watson. He'd permitted her to muck about in his kitchens, complimented her tea cakes, albeit begrudgingly, and had even taken her ice skating, though anyone could see he didn't enjoy it.

"You were saying, Miss St. Claire?" Prue prompted.

"Please, you must call me Rose. I was about to say that it has been awkward, but while it is the case that the duke has never made any secret of his enmity for my father, and neither can he and I agree upon what's to be done about Hammond Court—"

"Hammond Court!" Francesca glanced at Prue, her blue eyes wide. "Forgive me, Rose, but do you have a say in what happens to the house, then?"

"I do, yes. My father left Hammond Court to both the duke and me . . . together." Now why should her voice have cracked on that last word?

"Together!" Francesca and Prue exclaimed, both of them at once.

Rose glanced around the drawing room, her cheeks going hot. If every eye in the room hadn't already been upon them, they were *now*.

"Forgive us, Rose," Prue whispered. "That was expressed a bit too enthusiastically. But goodness, how strange, that Mr. St. Claire has left the property to you both! What do you suppose he was thinking, doing such a thing?"

That Maxwell Burke, the Duke of Grantham needed saving, and that she was the one to do it, that's what.

A lost soul . . .

She didn't say so, however. Those few last precious moments she'd spent with Ambrose were between the two of them and no one else. So, she only shrugged. "I can't be certain, but the duke wasn't at all pleased."

"No, I imagine not." Francesca sat back against the settee, tapping her lips with a finger. "What had you been about to say, before we interrupted you? About it being awkward with the duke?"

"Oh, yes. Of course, it was awkward at first, but now the initial shock has passed, the duke has been rather good to me, all told."

Francesca and Prue glanced at each other again, some sort of silent communication passing between them. "Has he? Well, Grantham *is* a gentleman, although a reluctant one at times."

A reluctant gentleman. Yes, that was a good description of the Duke of Grantham. "He brought me here to Grantham Lodge after my bedchamber at Hammond Court flooded, and—"

"Flooded!" both ladies exclaimed, once again with perhaps a touch too much enthusiasm, but it hardly mattered now, as the other ladies in the room were already whispering among themselves, having given up pretending they weren't eavesdropping.

"Yes, I'm afraid so. The house is in sad disrepair." It would likely stay that way, too, unless she could somehow work a miracle on the Duke of Grantham. "But the duke was kind enough to invite me to his house party, and he took me ice skating when I asked."

"Ice skating," Francesca repeated as if she'd misheard. "The Duke of Grantham went *ice skating*?"

"Goodness, no! I did everything I could think of to coax him onto the ice, but he defied me at every turn. It's rather a shame, really, because if ever there was a gentleman who needed a bit of fun, it's the Duke of Grantham."

This time, Francesca and Prue didn't even attempt to hide the glance between them, or the wide smiles that rose to their lips. "I couldn't agree more, Rose," Prue said with a laugh. "Dear me, how I would have enjoyed seeing you attempt to lure him onto the ice."

"Yes, well, I'm not very alluring, it seems, as he had no trouble at all resisting me."

"Resist *you*, Miss St. Claire? Nonsense."

The teasing voice came from behind them, and all three of them turned to see that the gentlemen had finished their port and were wandering into the drawing room. Lord Dunwitty came straight toward them and swept into an elegant bow. "I daresay there isn't a gentleman alive who could resist *you*."

"My goodness, Lord Dunwitty," Francesca scolded, patting her chest. "What can you mean, sneaking up on us like that?"

"I beg your pardon, Your Grace." Lord Dunwitty paused by the settee and offered Francesca a charming smile. "Have I interrupted you at your secrets?"

"There's not a single secret to be had here, my lord."

Franny waved a dismissive hand at him, but her lips were twitching. "Go on about your business, you wicked man."

"Of course, there are secrets. All ladies have secrets. Come now, you can tell me." Lord Dunwitty pressed a finger to his lips. "I won't tell a soul. I promise it."

Prue snorted. "Not a single secret shall pass our lips. You're an inveterate liar, my lord, and a shameless flirt."

Lord Dunwitty pressed a hand to his chest. "You wound me, Your Grace. As punishment for your cruelty, you must forfeit Miss St. Claire to me this instant." He turned his attention to Rose. "Do you play chess, Miss St. Claire?"

"I do, but very ill, indeed."

"Ah, even better, as I hate to lose." He held out his hand to her. "Come, and favor me with a game, won't you?"

She hesitated, taking in his outstretched hand. His brown eyes were twinkling, and his lips were curved in a mischievous grin. Prue had the right of it—he *was* a shameless flirt—but he was great fun, and surely there could be no impropriety in a game of chess in the middle of a crowded drawing room?

"Very well, my lord." She took his hand and let him assist her to her feet, but the Duke of Grantham appeared in the drawing room doorway just then, and the look on his face when he saw her hand on Lord Dunwitty's arm . . .

Dear God, he looked positively murderous, his brows lowered over icy gray eyes, his lips pressed into a tight, grim line.

She paused, confused. "Your Grace?"

His gaze darted to her face, and God above, she'd never in her life seen eyes as cold as his were in that moment, like a tempestuous winter sea. If a look could have frozen her where she stood, she'd have turned into a block of ice in an instant.

"Going somewhere, Miss St. Claire?"

"I—I . . ." But it was no use. That icy gray gaze made the words tangle on her tongue, and she fell silent.

Lord Dunwitty came to her rescue, saying smoothly, "Miss St. Claire and I are having a game of chess, Grantham. With your approval, of course."

A moment passed, then another. Rose held her breath. Surely, he wouldn't forbid them a harmless game of chess?

But the duke seemed to shake off the displeasure that had seized him and waved a careless hand toward the games table in the corner of the drawing room. "By all means, Dunwitty. Miss St. Claire may do as she pleases."

He swept past them without a backward glance and joined Lady Emily in a distant corner of the drawing room.

"Shall we, Miss St. Claire?"

Rose's gaze had followed the duke, but now she turned back to Lord Dunwitty with a smile. "Yes, indeed."

Lord Dunwitty led her to the games table, but only half of her attention was on the chessboard as he laid out the pieces. Her attention insisted on wandering back to the duke, who was seated rather closer than necessary to Lady Emily, an inviting smile on his lips.

Inviting, or was it more seductive? Was that what one would call the suggestive curve of those handsome lips? But then Lady Emily *was* his betrothed, or nearly so, and he might bestow as many lascivious smiles on her as he pleased.

For her part, Lady Emily was basking in his attentions, her cheeks aglow, and her air as she glanced around the drawing room decidedly triumphant. Rose could hardly blame her. It was no small victory, catching the eye of a gentleman like the Duke of Grantham.

But it was nothing to do with *her*. She jerked her attention back to Lord Dunwitty, who was making himself as agreeable as any gentleman ever could. Really, he was quite the most agreeable man she'd ever encountered. One couldn't help but be charmed by him.

Indeed, she was *excessively* charmed.

Why, then, did her attention keep wandering to the opposite side of the room? Goodness knew there was nothing of any interest to her unfolding over there, though she couldn't help but notice that for all of the duke's protestations that it didn't matter a whit to him what she did, he spent quite a lot of time glowering at her, his dark eyebrows lowered over those smoldering silver eyes.

"White or black, Miss St. Claire?"

"I beg your—oh. White, I suppose." She dragged her attention back to the chess board and pushed one of her pawns forward two squares.

Smoldering. Yes, smoldering, drat him, all the ice from earlier melting in that smoky heat, hotter with every moment that passed, until that dark gaze was positively singeing her skin, until bit by bit, moment by moment, she could think of nothing else, her concentration, her calm, and her very wits deserting her. She was dizzy with heat, fire unfurling in her belly until she could hardly keep her seat—

"Pawn to E4, Miss St. Claire."

"Er, yes. Pawn to . . . to . . ." She closed her fingers around her own pawn, but it was no use.

In an unguarded instant, her eyes locked with the duke's, and there was no escaping him, no looking away. Flames engulfed her, scorching heat rising higher and higher, his eyes tracking her flush as it surged into her cheeks, and flooded her chest and throat.

"Take care, Miss St. Claire. You're about to lose one of your rooks."

Her what? Her . . . oh, her rook. Chess. She was playing chess with Lord Dunwitty. "Yes, of course. Pawn to . . . to . . ." Her breath was short, and the board was swimming before her eyes. "Forgive me, Lord Dunwitty, but I'm afraid I have rather a bad headache."

He looked up from the chessboard with a frown. "You do look a bit flushed."

"Yes. I think it's best if I retire." She rose, her knees shaking.

He shot to his feet. "You're unwell, Miss St. Claire. Please take my arm."

"No, no, it's quite all right, my lord. I—it's only a bit of fatigue. Perhaps we might finish our game tomorrow?"

He opened his mouth to answer, but she didn't wait for a reply.

She fled the drawing room like a perfect coward before her wobbly legs gave out on her. A blur of startled faces turned to follow her—Francesca's and Prue's, their mouths falling open as she darted past them without a word. Lady Emily, her pretty lips turned up in a smirk, and poor Lord Dunwitty, who was no doubt wondering what it was he'd said or done wrong.

As for the Duke of Grantham—she took great care not to glance at him as she hurried past, but she could feel that blistering gaze on her, as palpable as fingertips drifting down her spine, the touch searing her like a brand.

CHAPTER 19

Shame scalded Rose's cheeks as she ran down the corridor to the entryway.

How dreadfully rude she was, to not even pause to bid good night to the company, particularly Francesca and Prue, who'd been so kind to her! How ridiculous, as well, scampering off like a child fleeing a punishment!

Yet she couldn't make herself stop, her slippers sliding across the marble floor of the entryway, her skirts clutched in her fist as she scurried up the stairs toward the safety of her bedchamber.

Up, up, up she fled, past the first-floor landing, the grandfather clock striking eleven, then up another flight—dear God, so many stairs—to the second-floor landing where her bedchamber lay—nearly there now, just three more doors! Abby would be there, waiting for her, and all would be well.

"Wait, Miss St. Claire!" A hand caught her wrist, halting her in her tracks.

Dash it, she'd been so close!

For an instant, she thought it must be Lord Dunwitty

who'd caught her, but when she turned to face her captor, it wasn't the viscount's brown eyes that met hers, but a pair of intense gray eyes, some emotion she couldn't define swirling in their depths. Instead of fair hair falling boyishly over a handsome forehead she found a mass of riotous dark waves, as if he'd been dragging his hands through the thick curls.

So impossibly soft, that hair, softer than any man's hair should be, like a secret for her fingers alone.

"What just happened down there?" The duke—for of course, it was he—stared down at her, that fearsome frown that had chased her from the drawing room still puckering his forehead. "What happened? What did Dunwitty say to you?"

Say? Did he imagine it was Lord Dunwitty who'd sent her careening toward her bedchamber? She stared up at him, transfixed by those eyes that seemed to change color with his moods. They weren't gray so much as a dark, molten silver now. They tended to become so when he was agitated.

She fell back a step, stunned. When—dear God, *when*—had she come to know that about him? When had she begun watching him so closely that she could read his moods in his eyes?

"Answer me, Miss St. Claire." He released her wrist, his hands closing over her shoulders.

"Lord Dunwitty?" she repeated, dazed. What did Lord Dunwitty have to do with it?

"Yes. Viscount Dunwitty. That gentleman you were just playing chess with? You do remember him? Did he say something to upset you?"

"Upset me? No! No, of course not." What could Lord Dunwitty have said to upset her? "He's behaved like a perfect gentleman."

He regarded her for a long, silent moment, searching her face, but at last, his hold on her shoulders eased, and he blew out a breath. "Good, that's . . . good. But why then did you flee the drawing room? You bolted like a frightened horse."

"I . . ." But what could she say? That it had been *him* she'd been running from? That a mere glance from his turbulent gray eyes could overset her in a way a thousand longing glances from Lord Dunwitty never could? That every time she felt his attention on her, she trembled? "It's nothing so dramatic as you imagine, Your Grace. I'm just fatigued, that's all."

"*Is* that all?" A muscle ticked in his jaw. "Forgive me, Miss St. Claire, but young ladies don't flee the drawing room because they're fatigued. It appeared to be a great deal more than that to me."

"It wasn't." But of course, it was. It was the plunging sensation in her chest when he'd strolled into the drawing room this evening and gone straight to sit beside Lady Emily. The way he'd bent his dark head toward hers, and the smile on his face when he'd whispered in her ear.

All of which, of course, meant she was a great fool.

But she'd sooner die than reveal such a humiliating truth to him. So, she lifted her chin and forced herself to meet his eyes. "I don't see what's so surprising about it. House parties are terribly fatiguing, Your Grace."

"Are they, indeed? But you didn't appear to be

fatigued at dinner. Quite the contrary." Slowly, gently, he eased her backward, until her spine was pressed against the wall. "I don't believe you are fatigued. I think there's another reason you fled, Rose."

Rose. Dear God, the aching sweetness of her name, when it slipped from the tip of his tongue. Such a plain, simple name, but when he spoke it, it became seductive and infuriating, tempting and tormenting at once, because what she wanted more than anything in that moment was to taste her name on his lips.

Even as his future duchess waited for him two floors below.

All at once, she was furious, both at him for tempting her, and at herself for longing for something she could never have. "You may think what you like, Your Grace. It's nothing to me what you believe. Now, please let me pass. I have a headache, and I'd like to go to my bed now."

"No, I don't think so." His gaze held hers, something she couldn't define shimmering in the silver depths. "Not just yet."

She forced herself to hold his gaze, but her body was trembling, her heart pounding. She might have ducked away—for all that he didn't seem to want to let her go, he wasn't preventing her from marching past him—and been safely tucked into her bedchamber in an instant, a locked door between the two of them.

But that wasn't what she did.

No, she remained where she was, her blood racing through her veins, some ancient feminine instinct that had been slumbering inside her—slumbering while it waited, apparently for *him*—urging her to stay, to wait, to see what would become of his hot, silver eyes roving over her, heating every inch of skin they touched. "What do you want from me, Your Grace?"

He let out a soft laugh. "Ah, but you see, that's the problem, Rose. Ever since the first day we met, when you threatened to put a pistol ball between my eyes, I don't know what I want anymore."

Something unfurled inside her then—an ache only *he* seemed able to call forth, sweet and dark and insistent, tugging low in her belly, and setting off a cascade of hot sparks down her spine. "How unfortunate. I'm sorry for you, Your Grace, but I don't see that it has anything to do with me."

"But it *does* have to do with you, Rose." He reached for her, dragging his knuckles down her cheek. "It has everything to do with you, and those damnable green eyes."

She sucked in a breath. "Me? You can't be blaming *me* for—"

"Oh, but I do blame you, Rose." He leaned closer, his breath warm against her neck. "This whole debacle is entirely your fault."

Debacle? What debacle? "How is it *my* fault? Because I have green eyes? Why, how dare you insinuate—"

"It has nothing to do with their color." He reached for a loose lock of her hair, rubbing the strands between his fingers. "As lovely as you are, it's not your beauty I'm referring to. I can assure you, there is no shortage of young ladies with fair hair and green eyes in London, but not a single one of them drives me as mad as you do."

She was driving him mad? "I don't understand. Why—"

"*Why?* Damned if I can explain it." He drew her closer, wrapping her in the warmth of his body. "Perhaps whoever said the eyes are the windows to the soul had the right of it. Romantic nonsense, if you ask me." His gaze held hers as he pressed the lock of her hair to his lips. "Or I used to think so, until I met you."

"M-me?" But why? There was nothing special about *her*. There wasn't one man in a hundred who'd even spare her a glance while a ravishing creature like Lady Emily was in the room.

"Yes, you, Rose. My God, how can you have no idea?" He touched the pad of his thumb to her lower lip. "Did it escape your attention that I couldn't take my eyes off you tonight?"

"B-but you spent the entire evening glowering at me!" Such a glower he had, too. She was no coward, but even she'd fled that penetrating gray gaze tonight because it made her feel . . . well, things she'd much better not.

"I did, indeed. As I said, you're driving me mad." His eyes softened, the hard gray melting to a cloudy silver. "No man wishes to be driven mad by a lady, Rose, especially such a termagant as you."

"Well, I . . ." What was she meant to say to that? Was it a compliment, or an insult? "I beg your pardon, then. It wasn't as if I've been *trying* to drive you mad."

"No?" He laughed, low and seductive, and nuzzled his face against her neck. "You must have a natural talent for it, then."

He traced the tip of his tongue over the shell of her ear, pausing to nip at her earlobe. Heat flared in her belly, but instead of pulling away, as a proper lady should do, she swayed toward him, her fingers curling into his evening coat. "For driving gentlemen mad?"

Surely, that wasn't a good thing?

"Not *gentlemen*, Rose." He slid his palm down her throat, caressing the hollow at the base with light, teasing fingers. "Just *me*."

"Oh." Her eyes dropped closed, a helpless moan falling from her lips. "That's . . . that feels . . ." But she didn't have a single word that did it justice. How could anything feel so delightful?

"Maddening?" he asked, dropping a kiss in the arch between her neck and shoulder.

Maddening, delicious, intoxicating.

But there was no time for her to answer him—no time for her to do anything at all, because Max took her mouth then, his wicked tongue slipping between her lips, stealing her breath, her words, and her reason.

This. Ever since that first heated kiss between them in the kitchen, *this* was what she'd been waiting for.

He gave it to her. He gave her everything. Hot, slick, sweet . . . a raw moan rose in her throat at his taste, his heat. He kissed her and kissed her, and she took every slide of his tongue, every stroke, lick, and nip, all while straining toward his lips, greedy for more.

He teased and tormented, tracing his tongue over her lips again and again, until at last he gave in to her broken pleas for more. Then he took her mouth harder, tugging her lower lip between his own and sucking on it until she was panting for him.

He was insatiable, low groans breaking from his lips as he ravaged her mouth, but his hands were gentle—the long, slow slide of his palm down her spine, the light stroke of his fingertips against her jaw. He touched her with infinite care, with tenderness, and when he raised his hands to cup her cheeks, she saw they were shaking.

Something inside her gave way, then, some tiny but significant piece of her heart.

Yet this was madness, all the same. Any of his guests could wander into the corridor and see them. At any moment, Abby could open the bedchamber door and catch them in each other's arms.

But she didn't pull away. She waited, her body trembling as he drew her closer, his eyes as black as midnight as he lowered his head to kiss her again, tugging her lower lip into his mouth to suck on it. A low, needy whimper rose from her chest, shocking her.

Not once, in all her twenty-one years, had she ever made a sound like that before.

She wrapped her fingers around his forearms and held on as his tongue darted between her lips. He slid his fingers lightly down her throat, then lower, testing her collarbones with his fingertips, then swept his hands over the quivering skin of her shoulders, left bare by the gown she wore.

"Beautiful," he murmured as his lips followed the path his hands had taken, his mouth lingering at the curve of her neck and shoulder. "Even more so than I imagined."

"Y-you imagined this?" Muscles twitched against her palms as she reached up to trace the contours of his chest, then let her fingers slide lower, grazing the hard plane of his stomach.

He smiled against her throat. "Every single day since you forced me to go ice skating." He skimmed his lips over her ear, his breath stirring the wispy hair at her temples. "I couldn't take my eyes off you that day." He chuckled, low and seductive. "I've never seen a lady spin that way before."

"Or fall so clumsily, I daresay." She twined her arms around his neck, pressing closer, and she might have remained there all night, gathered against his broad chest, her fingers sifting through the soft hair at the nape of his neck, if they hadn't heard a footstep on the landing.

They both froze, but it must have been a servant, because they continued up the stairs to the attics.

He tore his mouth away, but rested his forehead against hers. They were both breathless. He touched his thumb to her lower lip, opening her mouth for him, then leaned over and placed a sweet kiss there before stepping back, away from her.

"I beg your pardon, Rose. We can't . . . you should go to your bedchamber." He sucked in an unsteady breath, brushed the loose locks of hair that had tumbled from her chignon back from her face, and pressed a quick, soft kiss to her forehead. "Quickly, before I forget myself."

Rose pressed a shaking hand to her trembling lips. She should do as he said at once, fly into her bedchamber and put an end to this madness.

Because he wasn't for her.

Never for her. How could she have forgotten that? He was a duke. A *duke*, and soon to be betrothed to another lady, and she . . .

She was no one.

"Yes, I think that would be best." She ducked her head, avoiding his gaze as she made her way down the corridor to her bedchamber. She opened the door, slipped inside, and closed it behind her, then fell back against it, her heart still hammering.

She'd kissed the Duke of Grantham. *Again.*

"Rose?" Abby bustled in from the tiny sitting room that was attached to the bedchamber. "I've been waiting for ages for you, pet. Where have you . . ." She trailed off when she caught sight of Rose, all the color draining from her cheeks. "Rose?"

Rose huddled against the door, but even if she could have escaped that keen gaze, she never kept secrets from Abby. A hot flush scalded her cheeks as Abby took her in from head to toe.

Disheveled hair, flushed skin, swollen lips . . .

"Oh, Rose." Abby let out a low cry and brought a shaking hand to her mouth. "What have you done?"

The sun hadn't yet risen when Max rose from his bed, dressed hurriedly, and made his way from his bedchamber down the stairs. The house was silent, the entryway deserted, so early the servants were still asleep in their beds.

No one saw him slip out the door and into the dark, silent grounds of Grantham Park.

He'd been pleased enough when he'd gone to his bed with Rose's kiss still lingering on his lips, but he'd woken sometime in the night to find her sweet taste had vanished, leaving the leaden flavor of regret behind in its wake.

There'd been no hope of sleep again, after that.

He wandered through the gardens, his boots crunching over the icy pathways, heedless of his direction. It didn't matter where he went. He simply couldn't bear to be inside any longer with his thoughts haunting him, swirling about him like invisible ghosts.

But of course, his thoughts followed him as he wound from one end of the gardens to the other, as thoughts tended to do.

No answers, though. No, those were elusive, no matter where he was.

When had everything become so complicated? Until he'd arrived in Fairford, he'd known precisely who he was, and precisely what he wanted.

Vengeance, plain and simple. What was so bloody complicated about that?

He'd go to Fairford, make certain Ambrose St. Claire was good and dead, seize Hammond Court, and finally put to rest the bitterness and anger that had been plaguing him for two decades.

But there was no rest here. No, only more plague.

House parties, and ice skating. Ginger biscuits, and Christmas pudding.

Those things might be harmless enough if he'd been another sort of man, but he was the Duke of Grantham. Ruthless, cruel, and cold down to the depths of his shriveled black heart.

The Duke of Ice. What was the wicked Duke of Ice meant to do with a Christmas pudding?

Taken together with Hammond Court's crumbling walls, Monsieur Blanchard's temper tantrums, Lady Emily's petulant pout, and—worst of all—Viscount Dunwitty's handsome face and charming manners, what should have been a straightforward case of revenge had become tangled, indeed.

Then there were the green eyes. Lovely green eyes, and a joyful laugh that made him want things he'd never wanted before. That made him wonder, for the first time in two decades, what would be left for him *after* he'd enacted his revenge.

Or even if he wanted to enact it at all.

Come to Fairford, and claim your treasure . . .

What had Ambrose even meant by that? Because with every day that passed, Max became more convinced that he hadn't been referring to Hammond—

"I might have known you'd do this the hard way, Grantham."

Max whirled around to find a pair of tall figures advancing toward him down the pathway, their faces lost in the early morning shadows.

"Six days, Grantham." Montford emerged from the gloom, his hands thrust deep into his greatcoat pockets.

"Rather an admirable game of cat and mouse, but we've caught you out, at last. I can't say I approve of the location. You couldn't have chosen someplace warmer for your theatrics?"

"What theatrics? I'm not—"

"You might have waited until sunrise, at least," Basingstoke grumbled, joining them on the pathway. "Who has theatrics before sunrise? It's not very gentlemanly of you, Grantham."

Good Lord, but he had the most interfering friends imaginable. "I told you, I'm not—"

"Of course, you are." Montford sighed as if Max were a tiresome child. "You just don't realize it yet. That's why we're here."

"Indeed. So, what's the trouble, Grantham? I do hope you haven't torn Hammond Court to the ground while Miss St. Claire is otherwise occupied. Because such underhanded behavior would be beneath you as both a gentleman and a duke."

Perhaps so, but at least such machinations on his part would make *sense*. "If you must know, I've asked Townsend to undertake some of the more urgent repairs at Hammond Court."

Basingstoke glanced at Montford, eyebrows raised. "I'm pleased to hear it, Grantham. May we assume all of your intentions toward Miss St. Claire are as honorable?"

That depended on how one defined the term "honorable." There were those who'd argue his plan to secure a viscount for Miss St. Claire was as honorable and selfless a deed as one could perform for an otherwise unmarriageable lady.

Except, of course, once they dug a little deeper, they'd find it wasn't honorable at all.

Montford frowned when he didn't answer. "Let's back up a bit, shall we, Grantham? Did you, or did you not leave London and sneak off to Fairford without so much as a word to anyone, so you might seize Hammond Court for yourself, now Ambrose St. Claire is dead at last?"

"Seize it? What an ugly word, Montford. I merely came to investigate the circumstances and see if I could purchase it, and I'll have you know Ambrose St. Claire himself summoned me here."

"From beyond the grave? Forgive me, Grantham, but I find that a bit difficult to believe."

Max rolled his eyes. "Don't be absurd, Montford. He sent me a note before he died, of course, bidding me to come to Fairford and seize my treasure, or something equally as dramatic and ridiculous as that."

"Ah. But instead of an empty house, you found Miss St. Claire? Rather a nice surprise, I would think. She's a pretty little bit of a thing."

"A pretty little bit of a thing, is she, Montford? I'll have you know that pretty little bit of a thing nearly put a ball between my eyes when I appeared on her doorstep." After he'd broken into her house, that is, but the less his friends knew about that business with the doorknob, the better.

"Did she, really?" Basingstoke chuckled. "Well, it's

not at all surprising that Ambrose's daughter is a young lady of spirit."

Spirit? Is that what they were calling it?

"Miss St. Claire is, er . . ." Montford cleared his throat. "She's Ambrose's *natural* daughter, I take it?"

The circumstances of Rose's birth weren't their concern, but she'd never made any secret of it, and God knew neither Basingstoke nor Montford would let this business rest until they had every bloody detail. "She's the natural daughter of Ambrose's cook. The lady passed away some nine years or so ago, but Miss St. Claire remained at Hammond Court after she died."

"Miss St. Claire is the illegitimate daughter of St. Claire's late *cook*?" Basingstoke shook his head. "Good God. That's rather a difficult position for the young lady to be in."

Exceedingly difficult, yes, but he'd never heard her bemoan her fate. She seemed to think herself the luckiest young lady in the world, to have been known and loved by Ambrose. "By all accounts, Ambrose was fond of the girl. So fond, he left her half of Hammond Court."

"*What?*" Montford halted in the middle of the pathway. "Ambrose St. Claire left half of Hammond Court to Miss St. Claire?"

"Yes." Max gritted his teeth. "I might have known he'd remain a thorn in my side, even after he died."

When he'd first come to Fairford, he'd thought it ludicrous Ambrose was so devoted to his cook's daughter that he'd made her an heiress, but that was before he knew Rose. Now, however . . . well, if ever there was a young lady who could burrow under one's skin, wriggle under one's breastbone, and insinuate herself into the tender tissue underneath, it was Rose.

"Her presence here at Grantham Lodge certainly makes a great deal more sense now," Montford muttered. "I assume you're after her half of Hammond Court?"

Was he? It had begun that way, certainly, but now . . .

Everything had changed. After decades of negotiations, Hammond Court was finally in his grasp, merely waiting for him to reach out and pluck it like a ripe bit of fruit, and instead, he was seriously considering letting it slip through his fingers, all because of a young lady with pretty green eyes. "It's hardly a secret that I've been trying to get my hands on Hammond Court for years. It was my father's house, and it rightfully belongs to me."

"You intend to purchase Miss St. Claire's half, then?" The glint in Basingstoke's eyes belied his casual tone.

"Precisely. So, you see, it's nothing so nefarious as what you two are imagining." At least, not on the surface.

"If it's as simple as you say, Grantham," Montford asked, "then why is Miss St. Claire here at Grantham Lodge? Why haven't you made the lady an offer, and taken possession of the house?"

"I did make her an offer, but the lady is, ah, reluctant to sell." To put it mildly. "She insists that Hammond Court isn't merely a house to her, but her home, or some such nonsense."

But the inflection in her voice when she said the word "home," the softness in her face . . . it made him want outlandish things. On one or two occasions, he'd even caught himself longing with everything inside of him for Hammond Court to be hers.

"That doesn't sound like nonsense to—" Montford broke off, his eyes narrowing. "Wait a moment, Grantham. Is this business with Rose St. Claire what prompted your sudden house party?"

"Dunwitty!" Basingstoke groaned. "Don't tell me you invited Dunwitty here to—"

"What?" Montford jerked his head toward Basingstoke. "What's Grantham done this time?"

"Don't you see, Montford? He's brought Dunwitty here to—to—" Basingstoke turned his sharp gaze on Max. "Marry her? Christ, Grantham, I hope it's to marry her, because if you're scheming to turn that sweet young lady over to Dunwitty as his mistress—"

"No! Of course not, Basingstoke!" Had he really become such a villain that his friend would think so poorly of him? "What do you take me for?"

Basingstoke searched his face, then blew out a breath. "Thank God. I beg your pardon, Grantham, but this business with Ambrose St. Claire and Hammond Court brings out the worst in you."

Max couldn't deny it, and yet it stung, that Basingstoke had thought for even a moment that he'd do such a thing. He would never . . .

Or would he? If Miss St. Claire had been another sort of young lady—a bit less endearing, a trifle less angelic, might he have done the unthinkable? Had he strayed so far from the man he'd once been, as to do something so ruthless as that?

Montford shook his head. "Christ, Grantham."

He glanced from Montford to Basingstoke and threw up his hands in disgust. Now they'd gotten this much out of him, he may as well confess the whole bloody thing. "I don't deny I brought Dunwitty here with the intention of his marrying Miss St. Claire. After they married, he was meant to turn over her portion of Hammond Court to me."

Basingstoke shook his head. "This is beneath you, Grantham."

"Is it truly so terrible, Basingstoke, for me to arrange for Miss St. Claire to be made a viscountess? She's a penniless, friendless young lady, born on the wrong side of the blanket. What other prospects does she have?"

"Perhaps it wouldn't be so terrible if you were doing it to help her, but you're not. You're doing it for yourself." Basingstoke's expression was grim. "It's not the marriage itself, but the subterfuge behind it, Grantham."

"Miss St. Claire and Lord Dunwitty aren't pieces on a chessboard you may move about as you please," Montford added.

"I'm not . . ." But he was, wasn't he? Wasn't that precisely what he'd been doing?

"I advise you to think carefully before you take this any further, Grantham," Montford went on. "Is it really so important for you to have Hammond Court? After all these years, what does it matter any longer?"

It *did* matter. Or it had, once. It had mattered more than anything.

But did it still? Did it matter more than Rose? Was he so determined to have Hammond Court it didn't matter that he'd have to hurt her to get it? She wouldn't have any smiles to spare for him once he took her home away from her.

She'd despise him then, and he'd deserve it.

Ambrose had taken something precious from him, yes. He'd made a laughingstock of the Grantham name. He was the reason behind all those lonely years at Eton, with the other boys snickering behind his back. Ambrose had been at least partially responsible for his father's deterioration, and his shameful death.

Max had carried that bitterness with him for decades. It had given him a purpose, but it had changed him, too. It hadn't brought any happiness. Instead, it had made him harder, colder, and more ruthless.

Yet, who was he, without it?

"No serious harm has been done yet. It's not too late to change your mind. You're a better man than this, Grantham." Montford laid a hand on his shoulder, then turned to follow Basingstoke down the pathway, back toward the house.

The shadows in the garden grew shorter as the sun inched over the horizon, but Max remained where he was, heedless of the passing time and the guests requiring his attention, turning one question over and over in his mind.

Was he a better man than this?

He didn't have an answer.

CHAPTER 20

Max paced from one end of the entrance hall to the other, taking care to avoid Monk's curious gaze, the thump of his boots against the marble floor seeming far louder than they ever had before.

Thump, thump, thump . . .

God above, what an unholy commotion. Couldn't a man pace his own entryway without every guest in the entire house overhearing it? He felt like a fool. He'd be better off retreating into his study just as he did every morning, and forgetting this nonsense entirely.

"Good morning, Your Grace."

He whirled around at the sound of that light, musical voice, and there, on the second-floor landing stood the lady he'd been waiting for. He'd thought of nothing else but *her* since he'd abandoned his bed before sunrise.

She was wearing a woolen day dress this morning, of some indeterminate shade of green that turned her eyes the color of a winter sea.

"You're up rather earlier than usual, I think?" Her pretty pink lips curved in a sweet smile and damned if his knees didn't go weak, and his tongue tie in knots.

"Good morning, Monk." She reached the last step and turned her dimpled smile on the butler. "How does Mrs. Monk do? Is she over her cold yet?"

There was a Mrs. Monk?

"She's much improved this morning, thank you, Miss St. Claire. Nearly herself again. I'll be certain to tell her you enquired after her."

"Yes, please do, and don't forget to bring home the almond cake I made for her yesterday. Perhaps it will tempt her appetite. You did say she was fond of almond cake?"

Monk beamed. "I did, indeed. It's kind of you to think of her, Miss St. Claire."

Max glanced at Monk, then back at Rose, lingering on the smile that had won her the never-ending adoration of every servant at Grantham Lodge. How had he ever imagined he could steal Hammond Court from her?

As of this morning, he'd abandoned his diabolical scheme, and a good thing, too, because one of his servants likely would have bludgeoned him in his bed for daring to hurt Miss St. Claire.

But this wasn't a day to dwell on bludgeoning, or wicked deeds that would never come to pass. No, today was about something else entirely. "Have you breakfasted yet, Miss St. Claire?"

"I have, Your Grace. I'm afraid I was quite lazy this morning. Abby was kind enough to bring me a tray in my bedchamber."

He shuffled his feet. "I see. Then you're at leisure today?"

"Indeed, I am. It did occur to me that some more

Christmas baking might be in order. Do you care for plum pudding, Your Grace?"

"Plum pudding? Yes, plum pudding is very well, but I, ah, I thought I might . . . that is, it occurred to me you might enjoy . . ." He glanced down at his feet, the tips of his ears heating.

She ducked her head, trying to catch his eye. "Yes, Your Grace? Is something amiss?"

"No, nothing. I just wished to enquire whether you might like to . . ." He paused to swallow. Why was his throat so dry?

"Yes? Might like to what, Your Grace?"

"Perhaps you don't recall, but before the house party commenced, you mentioned the need for Christmas greenery."

Monk made a faint choking sound, then hastily cleared his throat to cover it, but it sounded suspiciously like a smothered laugh.

Rose glanced at Monk, her brows pulling down in a puzzled frown. "Yes. It's tradition to decorate on Christmas Eve."

"Right. Just so." Good Lord, this was torture. Just *say* it, man.

He took her arm and led her to the opposite end of the entryway, out of Monk's hearing. "It occurs to me, Miss St. Claire, that perhaps you have a point about the Christmas decorations."

"I do?"

She sounded so shocked his lips twitched, in spite of himself. "Oh, I assure you I still find it tiresome in the extreme, and a great waste of time. I fail to understand why anyone would find hanging prickly garlands to be an enjoyable activity, but I suppose you're correct in thinking my house party guests might find it pleasurable."

"Such a generous acknowledgment, Your Grace. You quite stun me." She bit her bottom lip, but there was no stifling the quirk at the corners of that sweet, pink mouth.

Good Lord, that smile. Had he actually managed to persuade himself it *wasn't* charming?

"Shall we walk the grounds a bit then, Your Grace?" She glanced over his shoulder toward the entryway door. A cheerful stream of morning sunshine poured through the glass, illuminating the spotless white marble floor with a blinding glow. "We're certain to find any number of trees that will lend their boughs to our cause, and it is a lovely day for a stroll."

"Well, I thought perhaps we might go out in the sleigh, instead." He'd never fancied sleigh riding himself. As recently as just a few weeks ago he could hardly have conceived of a more tedious activity than being dragged about the snow while crowded into a narrow sleigh.

But if he were crowded into a sleigh with Rose St. Claire, well . . . the narrower, the better, and what else were they meant to do with such egregious piles of snow everywhere? As for decorating for Christmas, that did seem the sort of thing that might keep a pack of bored aristocrats amused for an afternoon.

A proper host would have invited the entire party, of course, but in this case, the entire party happened to include Dunwitty, and he didn't fancy the idea of sharing Rose with the viscount. It wasn't that he was stealing her away. Of course not. Nothing so dramatic as that—

"Sleigh riding!" She let out a squeal, and his gaze shot back to her.

Did she approve of his suggestion? Was she pleased? He could hardly tell, what with her gaping at him as she was, and an unpleasant pang of uncertainty seized him. He'd hoped to please her with the suggestion. Had he made a mess of it? God knew he wasn't at all in the habit of pleasing anyone other than himself.

"If you like the idea, I thought we might go out this morning, and see which trees have the lushest greenery to offer," he added, awkwardly enough.

"I like it very much, and we're just in time, as tomorrow is Christmas Eve."

"We'll bring the entire party out tomorrow morning to cut the garlands, along with the wagon to haul them." No doubt she saw right through his rather flimsy ploy to get her to himself. Monk certainly did, if the restrained snort from the other side of the entryway was any indication. "But if you'd prefer to wait and go with the others tomorrow—"

"No! No, I—I'd be delighted to go sleigh riding with you." The smile he'd become obsessed with found her lips then. "Why, it's just the thing, Your Grace! I wonder I didn't think of it myself."

Just like that, the tightness in his chest eased. "Very well. Go and fetch a wrap, Miss St. Claire, the warmest you have. The wind is brisk, and it's rather cold, despite the sunshine."

"Yes, of course!" She turned without another word and flew up the stairs, her skirts billowing out behind her. He watched her go, then resumed his pacing, marching from one end of the entryway to the other. Halfway through his third turn, he caught Monk's eye.

His normally taciturn butler was smiling. *Smiling*, like an utter fool.

Max rolled his eyes and turned and marched back in the other direction.

It wasn't until he'd completed another full rotation through the entryway that he realized he was smiling, too.

The Grantham Lodge sleigh was, like everything else at Grantham Lodge, a particularly fine one, but unlike the stiff settees and spotless fireplaces, Rose couldn't find fault with it.

Who could possibly find fault with *anything*, on such a day as today, least of all the snug little two-seater sleigh, a handsome, lacquered green affair with gold striping outlining the panels. The doors were embellished with the prettiest gold-leaf pattern as well, and the interior was a rich, red velvet.

It was like something out of a fairy tale. Joy curled inside her like a sleeping cat, warming her as they skimmed over the snow.

"Are you warm enough, Miss St. Claire?"

He'd frowned when she'd reappeared in the entry-way in the same coat she'd worn to the skating pond last week. It was a bedraggled-looking garment, to be sure, and worn rather thin, its best days behind it, but instead of scolding, he'd merely ordered more rugs to be piled into the sleigh.

"Yes, very cozy, Your Grace." She drew one of the soft, fleecy rugs to her chin and tucked her feet closer to the hot bricks one of the footmen had placed on the floor.

But the warmth at her feet paled in comparison to the warmth of his body pressed so closely against hers, a muscular column of heat running the length of her leg from her ankle bone, and all the way up her thigh to her hip. It was quite distracting, really, but even if she'd wanted to move away—and she wasn't at all sure she *did*—there wasn't a sliver of spare space to be had.

She was at the mercy of the hard thigh pressing so close to hers.

Cozy, indeed.

The duke had a second sleigh, a much larger one that could seat eight people comfortably. She'd noticed it tucked into a corner of the carriage house, but he'd chosen this much smaller one for today, along with a pair of beautifully matched black horses to pull it.

Perhaps this smaller sleigh was faster. Perhaps he wanted to have their outing over with as quickly as possible, but it didn't seem so. If he wished to avoid her, as she'd half expected he would after their kiss last night, he wouldn't have suggested this sleigh ride in the first place. It would have been the easiest thing in the world for him to hide away in his study, as he usually did.

He was a confusing gentleman, the Duke of Grantham.

Maxwell. *Max*. The name suited him.

She pressed her fingers to her mouth, her lips tingling at the memory of their kiss. Such a revelation, that kiss! As it turned out, passionate kisses like the one they'd shared weren't confined only to the lips.

She'd felt that kiss *everywhere*.

But after the abruptness with which he'd pulled away from her and sent her off to her bedchamber, she'd expected he'd put as much distance between them as possible today.

Instead, it appeared as if he'd been *waiting* for her this morning.

Abby wasn't going to be pleased when she found out about this sleigh ride, especially not after the two hours she'd spent last night lecturing Rose about the dangers of trifling with aristocratic gentlemen.

Especially dukes. According to Abby, dukes in general—and the Duke of Grantham, in particular—were horrible, wicked creatures who'd think nothing of ruining a young lady like her, then hurrying off to London without a backward glance.

She peeked at him from the corner of her eye. He didn't look wicked *now*, with his thick, dark curls blowing in the wind and one of his rare smiles softening the corners of his lips.

But she wouldn't puzzle over it now. She would simply enjoy the cheerful crunch of the runners as they whooshed over the snow, the wind whipping through her hair and biting color into her cheeks. "Look, Your Grace! See how the sun sparkles on the snow? It's as if we're flying through a field of diamonds!"

He turned to her, that grin still playing about his lips. "What a fanciful description, Miss St. Claire. Are you a poet?"

Hardly. Ambrose had had a knack for turning a phrase, though. Perhaps some of it had rubbed off on her. She didn't say so, however, but only laughed, the wind catching the sound in its fist and sending it whirling into the blue sky. "Not a bit, I'm afraid, but I daresay a day like today might turn even the dullest scholar poetic. But do you know, Your Grace, what would make this even more delightful?"

"I'm afraid to ask," he said dryly, shifting the reins between his gloved fingers with ease, turning the horses' heads to the right, toward a line of towering trees in the distance, their massive branches heavy with snow. "But I daresay you'll tell me anyway."

"Bells! I can't think of a single thing more festive than bells at Christmastime."

"Oh, something tells me you can, Miss St. Claire. You have a distressingly fertile imagination."

"Just imagine it, Your Grace. The sun shining down from a blue sky, the bells strung onto the horses' harnesses jingling merrily and echoing in the crisp morning air with their every prancing step."

"Very well, I'll admit that doesn't sound entirely unpleasant. Is there anything else you require?"

"Bells, and flasks of hot cocoa and cider, and caroling, and . . . oh!" Without thinking, she seized his arm. "Have you ever gone on a moonlit sleigh ride, Your Grace?"

"What, sleighing at night? That sounds dangerous, not to mention freezing cold."

"Well, it must be done on a clear night, but you'd be amazed, Your Grace, at how well you can see in the moonlight. It's quite as bright as daylight, under a full moon."

He was quiet for a moment, then. "You speak as someone who's been on a moonlit sleigh ride."

"Only once, years ago." It was before her mother had died, the Christmas before she'd turned twelve. It had been Ambrose's idea, and she'd never forgotten it. But she wouldn't speak of Ambrose now, or indeed, ever— not to the Duke of Grantham, as it was the one subject on which they would never agree.

It was strange, though. Ambrose had invariably spoken of the previous duke, Max's father, with barely concealed disdain, but whenever he spoke of Max, it had always been with a note of tenderness in his voice, even after the rift between the families had dragged on for years.

Her sympathies had always lain with Ambrose, of course. It had been easy for her to blame the Ninth Duke of Grantham for the ugliness, and to despise his entire family for it, but now . . . she cast a surreptitious glance at Max.

What must it have been like for him, to have his home taken from him by a man he'd trusted? A man he'd considered a second father? Oh, she didn't blame Ambrose. She might not know the whole story behind that ill-fated wager, but she was certain he must have been thinking of Max and his mother when he wagered for Hammond Court.

But Max had only been a child then, and too young to understand. No doubt his father had poisoned him against Ambrose, and from there, it had only gotten worse.

Within only a few years, Max's father was dead, and Max was alone.

Such a dreadful loss. Was it any wonder he hated Ambrose? His resentment was misplaced, yes, but being here with him now, in the sleigh beside him, her limbs tucked tightly against the warmth of his, her heart gave a sympathetic wrench in her chest.

Where had all his righteous anger, all his resentment gotten him? He was a wealthy, powerful duke, yes, part of the *haute ton*, with dozens of fashionable, titled friends, and yet . . .

He was alone. More alone than any man she'd ever known.

It wasn't right, that he should have lost everything.

"There's a gathering of tall pine trees just over the next rise. I thought their boughs might do for our decorations." He gave her a slight smile. "But I will, of course, defer to your superior knowledge, Miss St. Claire."

"How gentlemanly of you, Your Grace." They were nearing the tree line that had been only a distant blur before, so close now she could make out the spiraling branches of a grove of massive pine trees, the tips of the needles white with snow.

"Goodness. They're magnificent." The Cotswolds abounded with ancient trees—there were a great many large pines on Hammond Court's land, as well—but she'd never seen any as massive as these before.

"They'll do, I suppose, if the guests insist upon smothering my house in greenery on Christmas Eve."

"I daresay they *will* insist upon it. One must have garlands on Christmas Eve, Your Grace. It's tradition."

He grunted. "More trouble than it's worth if you ask me." But he brought the sleigh to a stop underneath the trees and tipped his head back to study the thick, gnarled branches. "Which ones do you like best, Miss St. Claire?"

"I hardly know. Goodness, they're enormous." Many of them were wider than her thigh.

"Indeed. No doubt some fool will insist upon climbing them tomorrow, only to fall and break his neck."

Well, wasn't that a cheerful thought? "There are plenty of low-lying branches. They'll make lovely garlands."

"I'm pleased you approve, Miss St. Claire." He paused, his gaze lingering on her face. "Perhaps we should return to Grantham Lodge before too long. I'm afraid you must be cold. Your cheeks are as rosy as winter apples," he murmured, a husky note in his voice.

"Are they?" And still redder now, if the heat surging into them was any indication. She clasped her gloved hands over her cheeks, suddenly shy. "I'm happy to return whenever you are, Your Grace." She peeked up at him from under her lashes. "But I'm not at all cold."

Quite the opposite, in fact.

He didn't move, the reins slack in his hands as he stared at her, his gaze moving from her eyes to her lips, then back again. "I, ah, I don't believe I ever thanked you, Miss St. Claire."

"Thanked me? For what?"

"The ginger biscuits. It was kind of you to make them for me." His throat moved in a rough swallow. "It reminded me that I do have some happy memories of my time at Hammond Court."

It was, of all things, the one she wished most to hear him say, and hope, bright and warm, burst inside her chest. This was what Ambrose had wanted from her—she felt sure of it. Yet somehow, between the pistol shot and the broken doorknob, the collapsed ceiling and the ginger biscuits, this business between her and the Duke of Grantham was no longer about the favor Ambrose had asked of her.

This was no longer about Ambrose at all. It had been weeks since her courtship—for lack of a better word— of the Duke of Grantham had been about fulfilling a promise to Ambrose.

Now, it was about the duke himself.

She couldn't pinpoint the moment it had happened— perhaps it had been the ice skating, or the ginger nuts, or the kisses that made her heart pound—but some- where along the way, without her realizing it was hap- pening, the duke's happiness had become what *she* wanted, too.

Even if it meant losing Hammond Court. Surely, that was what Ambrose had intended all along? This had never been about the house. It had been about Maxwell Burke from the very beginning.

Hammond Court was always meant to be Max's. It was his family's home and a part of his legacy. It would hurt her to leave it—oh, so much! It would be like tearing loose one of her limbs, but if she might see the tightness ease from the duke's jaw, the cold watchfulness fade from his eyes, and a smile touch those stern, straight lips, well . . . how could she ever regret that?

It was still far too rare, his smile, but perhaps by the time this strange interlude between them ended, she'd have that pleasure. If she had that, then perhaps she could leave Hammond Court behind without any regrets.

"If you're truly not cold, shall we go on for a bit, Miss St. Claire?" He glanced up at the sky, then back at her, the sun lighting his eyes, turning them a clear, translucent gray. "There's not a cloud to be seen. As long as the weather holds, and you're not too chilled, we might go for a bit longer if you like."

"I would like that, very much." She swallowed against the lump in her throat. "Perhaps we might go by Hammond Court, on the way back? I have a bundle of wood shavings from last year's Yule log I need to fetch."

"A bundle of wood shavings?" He stared at her. "Why would you save such a thing?"

Goodness, didn't he know anything about Christmas? "Why, so we might use them to light this year's Yule log, of course."

He groaned. "You mean to say we need a Yule log, as well?"

"Why, of course, we do, Your Grace. You can't possibly have Christmas without a Yule log. It's—"

"Tradition?"

"Just so." She gave him her most angelic smile. "It must be a very large, grand log—thick enough so that it will continue to smolder until Twelfth Night has passed."

Another groan. "Can't we just light a candle?"

"Oh, yes! We must have a Yule candle, as well. I nearly forgot!" She tucked the rug more firmly around her as he flicked the reins, and the horses bounded forward, their tails twitching. "How good of you to remind me, Your Grace."

CHAPTER 21

They approached Hammond Court from the east, in order to save the horses' hooves and the sleigh's delicate runners from the deep furrows of frozen mud cratering the front drive.

Max brought the sleigh to a stop in the courtyard behind the kitchen, but they didn't stir. They both remained in the sleigh for a long moment, staring up at the house, neither of them speaking.

Great swathes of ivy climbed up the pale, weathered stone. Rose had always loved the romantic extravagance of the ivy, with its trailing vines and thick, glossy leaves, but Ambrose hadn't been as fond of it. He claimed it damaged the stonework, and every winter he'd insisted on its being cut back. Now he was gone, it had run rampant, twining around the arched sills of the windows all the way up to the second floor.

The house looked different to her, somehow. It wasn't, of course. It was the same dilapidated house she'd left several weeks earlier—the same home she'd always known, but it looked lonelier.

For all its flaws, it had never looked lonely to her before.

Was this how it would always look, once she was gone? So dark, empty, and deserted? Her heart sank at the thought. Such a house deserved a family, with young children scampering up and down the hallways, their little fingers leaving smeared prints on the doorknobs, and smudges on the woodwork.

Could Max ever put aside his hatred of Ambrose, and learn to love Hammond Court as she had? Or was it destined for ruin, with only the thick branches of ivy holding the crumbling walls together?

"You look troubled, Miss St. Claire. I daresay you have some unpleasant memories from the last time you were here. Would you prefer we not go in, after all?"

She shrugged off the strange melancholy that had seized her and shook her head. "No, no. We must have the shavings from last year's Yule log. It's—"

"Tradition." A smile twitched at the corner of his lips.

She turned toward him, and the sight of his faint grin thawed the ice in her veins as if she were a blossom turning toward the sun. "Oh, have I mentioned that, then?"

"Once or twice, yes."

He stepped out of the sleigh and reached to hand her out, the warmth of his hand closing around the tips of her fingers sending a shower of sparks down her spine.

The hinge of the outer door protested, releasing a halfhearted squeal as she pushed it open. She crept down the darkened hallway toward the archway that led into the stillroom—yes, crept, because she felt oddly like an intruder, sneaking about a home that was no longer hers.

It was dark, and the faint smell of decay tickled her nose. Had it always been so? Could she have grown so accustomed to it over the last year that she no longer noticed it?

It was a distressing thought, and more distressing still was the hollow thump of her footsteps on the floor, the echo of it, as if it had been centuries since anyone had walked here, and the house didn't know what to make of the sound.

The door that led to the stillroom stood open, and . . . oh, dear. It looked shabbier than ever, after the luxury of Grantham Lodge.

Shabbier, and *cold*. A shiver raced through her, and she wrapped her arms around herself. "Goodness, it feels like an icehouse in here. The sooner we fetch the shavings, the better."

"Lead the way, Miss St. Claire."

She rummaged in the drawers until she found the bit of cloth she'd wrapped the shavings in. She slipped them into her pocket, then turned toward the kitchen. "Since we're here, I may as well fetch the last of my preserved ginger, in case we want more ginger biscuits."

An involuntary sigh left her lips as she passed through the door into the familiar space, the duke—*Max*—so close behind her, she could feel the warmth of him against her back.

The stove and the scrubbed kitchen table were just as she'd left them.

So familiar, this room, so much the home she remembered.

The kitchen had always been special to her—her own little place tucked under the staircase, rather like a secret. How many years had she spent here, at her mother's knees? Nearly eight years, before her mother had passed away. How could the time feel so brief now?

One blink, and it was gone.

She smothered a sigh, and made her way over to the spice cabinet, but stopped halfway across the floor, frowning down at the smooth wooden boards under her feet. "How curious. The floor has been repaired." The gaping hole left when the pistol ball had struck the floor had vanished. "Billy must have been here, and seen to it."

Except, had it been Billy? Where would he have gotten such fine boards? They were the same warm oak as the older boards, the match nearly flawless.

"Yes, I suppose he must have done." Max took her arm and led her toward the spice rack in the opposite corner of the kitchen. "It's a cozy room, isn't it? I've always thought so."

"It is, yes. It's my favorite room in the house." She paused, unsure whether or not to voice the question hovering on her lips, but Christmas was nearly upon them, and Twelfth Night soon afterward, and then Hammond Court would be his.

All she wanted, all she hoped for, was that he would allow himself to love it as she had. The house deserved it, but perhaps even more than that . . .

He did. After all these years, Max deserved to come home.

She cleared her throat. "Then you *do* have happy memories of your time here?"

He didn't answer at once, but wandered toward the window, his back to her as he looked out onto the court-yard to the stables beyond, and behind them the crest of the hill, where the sun gilded the snow with a warm, golden glow. You couldn't see it from the window, but at the bottom of the hill was the pond where they'd skated.

Well, where *she'd* skated. He'd mostly scolded. A smile rose to her lips at the memory. Strange, that it should somehow have become a happy one.

"My mother and I used to sit at that table and drink chocolate together on cold winter afternoons." He nodded at the kitchen table before turning his gaze back to the window. "I learned to ride my first pony on Hammond Court's grounds. I sat at my grandmother's side on the pianoforte bench in the drawing room while she played, more times than I can count."

He stood tall, his back straight, but there was some-thing in his voice that tore an ache into her throat. It hurt him, to remember it—she could sense it in every ragged breath he drew into his lungs. She drew closer, afraid to make a sound lest she startle him, and he reverted back to the silence he'd maintained for two long, lonely decades.

"So, to answer your question, Miss St. Claire. Yes, I do have happy memories of Hammond Court." He braced his hands on the windowsill, his broad shoulders rigid, and added softly, "Many happy memories."

She never meant to touch him. There was no distinct moment in which she made the decision to rest her hand on his back. It was as if her arm moved of its own accord, her palm landing gently between his shoulder blades, the fine wool of his greatcoat soft under her fingertips.

He went still, the muscles of his back pulling tight, but before she could step back and beg his pardon, his entire body seemed to melt under her touch. This man— the hardest man she'd ever known—calmed and stilled underneath her fingers, his head dropping between his shoulders.

She had no defense for that, no way to guard herself against such a profound act of trust.

"Rose." So quiet, the sound of her name on his lips, just a rasp, hardly a word at all.

She slid her hand up his back, her fingertips grazing the ends of his hair, then sliding down to stroke the sliver of bare skin at the back of his neck.

He turned to her then, a low groan falling from his lips.

He was going to kiss her. It was there in his hot silver gaze, the suggestion of a kiss throbbing between them, the intent of one, just waiting to be breathed into life, and she wanted his mouth on hers. Had wanted it since that night in the kitchen at Grantham Lodge, when she made him ginger biscuits and tasted the sweetness of dark sugar and ginger on his lips.

She waited, her heart beating a mad tattoo in her

chest, her body trembling. He moved closer—so close she could hear the rasp of his breath sawing in and out of his chest, and in that instant, she would have sworn she could feel his heart, beating in time with hers.

He came closer still, his warm breath drifting over the shell of her ear.

Yet still, he didn't touch her.

It might have only been a moment, but it felt as if an eternity passed as they gazed at each other, his eyes so dark, darker than she'd ever seen them before.

"What do you want, Rose?" He lowered his head, his lips hovering over hers.

"I—I—" Her murmur dissolved in a soft gasp, her eyes dropping closed as he traced a fingertip over her lips.

"No, Rose. Look at me." He dragged his knuckles down her cheek. "Open your eyes, and look at me."

Her eyelids were curiously heavy, the heat he always seemed to call forth in her unfurling in her belly. But she did as he bid her, holding his gaze, the blazing heat she saw in those depths searing her, setting her every nerve ending alight.

"Yes, like that," he whispered, before asking again. "What do you want, Rose?"

What she wanted . . . oh, it was something she shouldn't want, something that was certain to end in disaster and heartbreak, but even so, she was already leaning into him, his heat drawing her closer—so close it seemed the most natural thing in the world to rest her palms against his chest and slide her fingers into his hair. "You. I want you, Max."

It was true. He was a *duke*, a man destined to leave

her behind with nothing but memories to comfort her, but God help her, she couldn't deny the truth.

She wanted him. She'd wanted him for weeks now, it seemed.

He let out a breath then, long and deep and slow as if he'd been holding it, the soft drift of it tickling the wispy curls at her temples, and then he was reaching for her, sliding his fingers into her hair, his palms brushing the sensitive skin at the back of her neck, and this time it was she who held her breath, held it as his lips drew closer, then closer still . . .

When the kiss came at last, it was so soft, so light, she might almost have imagined she was dreaming it, the tender press of his firm lips against hers. But it was no dream, for all that he took her mouth gently, the tip of his tongue dancing against the seam of her lips, and dear God . . .

Dear God. Her eyelids fluttered, and her eyes drifted closed, all the reasons why they shouldn't be here, like this—Ambrose and Hammond Court, Lady Emily, and his imminent return to London—fading from her mind with every brush of his lips.

She could do nothing but twine her arms around his neck, sink into his kiss, and give way to the passion rushing through her blood.

She'd never known desire could be like this—so powerful it stole her reason, her logic, and snatched every thought from her head as it swept her up in its undertow, drawing her deeper and deeper until she'd gone too far, and she was drowning in it.

Drowning, with no wish to surface.

Perhaps he knew, then—perhaps he felt her surrender—because a low growl ripped from his chest. She opened her mouth to him, and he grew more ravenous, his fingers tangling in her hair as he swept his tongue into her welcoming mouth, stroking inside again and again. "So sweet, Rose," he whispered against her lips, his voice hoarse. "How can you taste so sweet?"

She tried to answer, but she had no words. A soft sound left her lips instead, a sound unlike any she'd ever made before—not a word, but a moan, or perhaps a sigh, but he didn't need words to understand what she was asking for, what she needed. He simply gave it to her, his big hands sliding lower, one settling into the arch of her back and the other cupping the curve of her hip. He eased her closer until she was pressed against him, her breasts crushed to his chest, his thighs touching hers, a thick column of heat throbbing against her belly.

She knew what it was, and what it meant. He wanted her as much as she wanted him. It was madness, a mistake, yet she found herself pressing closer, the sensitive tips of her breasts hardening.

Just one more kiss. One more . . . surely, one more little kiss wouldn't matter? One harmless little kiss, then she'd force herself to slip free of his arms.

But it was no use. She was falling deeper into him with every moment, her breath catching as his hands moved over her, unfastening the buttons of her cloak, and she was helping him, their frantic fingers tangling together as they worked them loose one by one, and this was no longer just an innocent kiss, no longer innocent at all, but she couldn't stop, didn't want to stop.

"Wrap your arms around my neck, Rose," he murmured, before taking her lips in another wild kiss.

She obeyed without protest, without thinking, because in that breathless moment, she could deny him nothing. She rose to her tiptoes and wrapped her arms around his neck, and the next thing she knew, the floor vanished from beneath her feet. "Max?"

"Shhh. I've got you." He swept her up into his arms and cradled her against the hard plane of his chest as if he couldn't bear to let her go.

As if she were precious.

He carried her to the kitchen table, set her down carefully, and stepped into the open space between her thighs. He made quick work of the buttons at the back of her dress, loosening the half dozen at the top, then pushing the fabric aside so he could touch his lips to her throat, her neck, the hot drift of his breath against the trace of dampness his lips left on her skin driving her mad.

She squeezed her eyes closed on a desperate groan, twisting the wool of his coat between her fingers to drag him closer, closer, her head thrown back to give him access, because dear God, how could anything feel as heavenly as his mouth on her neck?

"Max, I want . . ." What? What did she want? She hardly knew, but—

More. She wanted more. More of his mouth, more of his teasing lips, more of his heart thrashing against her palms, more of his whispers in her ear, and his breathless groans.

"What, Rose?" He brushed his lips over her collarbone

and nipped gently at the hollow between her neck and shoulder, making her tremble in his arms. "What do you want? Say it again."

She drew back so she could look into eyes gone a deep, smoky gray, her heart hammering, and her breath stuttering in her chest. "You. I want you, Max."

He gazed down at her with burning dark eyes, lingering on her eyes, her lips, the pale bare skin of her throat, and slowly, slowly he lowered his forehead to hers. "Then I'm yours."

Hers. For now, yes. Just for these few stolen moments.

There was no escaping that truth, but even as she knew it—knew that this could only lead to heartbreak— she touched her parted lips to his.

Because it was already too late. It had been, since the first moment his mouth touched hers.

She was already lost.

He couldn't get enough of her. The glide of her soft skin under his fingertips, her breathy little gasps and sighs, her panting breaths in his ear, and the sweetness of her lips against his.

It had never been like this for him before. Of all the ladies he'd kissed, all the sophisticated beauties he'd taken to his bed, never—not once—had he ever been consumed by such an insatiable hunger for a woman as he was by *her.*

It was a kind of madness, the depths of his desire for her.

It was dangerous. Ruinous. It made a man careless, reckless.

But she was clinging to him, kissing him, needy little pleas falling from her lips, and the thought was there and then gone again, no match for the wild passion burning between them.

He dipped his head, pressing his nose into the soft skin behind her ear and breathing deeply of the scent that clung to her—fresh air, snow, pine needles, and *her*. She made his head spin, and his cock surge desperately against his falls.

"*Rose*." His voice was a husky, guttural growl as if he'd gone feral. "I need you closer." He caught her by the hips and slid her toward the end of the table, her legs dangling off the edge, and then he pressed closer, wedging himself into the sweet vee between her legs.

He reached down to fist her skirts, tugging them up, up . . .

No. It was too much. He'd lose control, and she was an innocent.

But it was as if she'd read his mind, because in an instant she'd wrapped her legs around his waist and was urging him closer, her heat burning him through the cloth of his pantaloons. "Yes," she whispered against his ear. "Like this."

Yes. This was what he wanted. To lose himself in her.

He tugged her earlobe into his mouth and gave it a sharp nip, desire roaring through him when she let out a little cry and jerked in his arms. "I've thought of nothing but our kiss since that first night." He traced his thumb over her mouth, parting her lips. "Open for me, sweetheart."

He leaned down, drawing closer, Rose's breath rushing from her lungs as his lips brushed over hers. Her mouth was warm, her lips soft and giving, and somehow kissing her was nothing like he'd imagined it would be, yet at the same time it was familiar, too, like coming home.

"Max." She gasped as he kissed his way over her jaw, then down her neck to her throat, pausing to drop a soft, quick kiss on the dimple in her chin before taking her lips again, delving deeply into that warm cavern where she was sweetest, his body trembling with barely leashed desire.

He couldn't get enough of her. Would never get enough of her.

He wanted her. He wanted her so badly he couldn't think, couldn't *breathe*, and she wanted him. Somehow, against every odd, every law of fair play, this lovely, kind, joyful spirit wanted *him*.

He brushed a few wispy locks of hair back from her face and pressed his lips to the pulse point at the hollow of her throat, triumph roaring through him when he felt the frantic flutter of it against his tongue. "All day, and every night, your kiss has haunted me, Rose." He let his fingers drift down her neck to the secret space between her breasts. "You've bewitched me."

"I . . . oh." She dug her fingers into his shoulders when he cupped one of her breasts in his palm.

"You're so pretty here, Rose." She was tiny, her curves slight, and never—*never*—had he touched anything as perfect as her. "Look at me. I need to see your face when I touch you."

Her eyelashes fluttered against her flushed cheek-bones, but she was no coward, his Rose, and she raised her face to his, her green eyes as dark as emeralds under heavy, slumberous lids.

"Yes, that's good." He cupped her cheek in his palm to keep her from looking away, then slowly, gently dragged his thumb over one of her nipples. Once, then again, his breath turning ragged as it peaked under his caress.

"Ah." Her flush deepened, her lips parting.

"You're sensitive here." He slid the pad of his thumb over the hungry nub again, his belly tightening with want when she gasped, her hands grasping his shoulders. "Does it feel good when I touch you here, Rose?"

She nodded, her teeth catching her lower lip, still red and swollen from his kisses. He made quick work of the rest of her buttons, tearing them loose with clumsy fingers until her dress hung loosely around her neck, and he could slide it from one of her shoulders, his breath stuttering in his lungs as he revealed an expanse of silky, creamy flesh.

His gaze dropped to the tender points of her nipples, the palest blush pink visible through the thin cotton of her shift. He imagined trailing his lips over that vulnerable skin, kissing and licking it. Biting it. He swayed forward, gazing at her pouting nipples, mesmerized by them.

What would she taste like?

"Oh, I . . . *Max*." She trembled in his arms as he

ducked his head and closed his lips around her nipple, and God, she was perfect, delicious. He nipped and suckled and teased until the sensitive peak darkened to a deep, cherry red, standing out in sharp relief against the damp cotton of her shift.

"You're so lovely," he whispered, drawing back to blow softly on the hard peaks. She cried out, her fingers sliding into his hair and gripping hard, holding him against her as he devoured her, running his thumb in lazy circles around one delicious peak while he suckled the other. "Do you think about me, Rose?"

She nodded, but that wasn't enough for him. "Say it."

"I—I think about you, Max."

He caught her chin in his hand, raising her face to his, his thumb still working her swollen flesh. "What do you do when you think about me?"

She could only stare at him, her cheeks coloring.

His hand shook as he slid it over her hip, caught a handful of her skirts in his fist, and raised them, the fabric sliding up her shins and over her knees, then higher, until inch by inch, he revealed the prettiest pair of thighs he'd ever seen. "Do you touch yourself, Rose?"

She sucked in a breath, a flush racing down her neck and flooding her chest. "I . . ."

"Like this?" He dragged his palm over her belly, the tips of his fingers grazing the soft thatch of hair between her legs. "I want to make you feel good. May I touch you, Rose?"

Her tongue darted out to lick the corner of her mouth, her eyes burning. "Yes."

Slowly, carefully, he slid his hand closer to the damp curls between her legs, groaning when he found her wet for him. Her eyelids fluttered closed again, but her hips shifted, straining toward his touch. "Please."

"Open your eyes. I want to see your eyes." She obeyed at once, the green eyes that had so mesmerized him fluttering, and her legs sliding open, welcoming him inside.

He made a low, crooning noise in his throat. "Yes, like that. So good, Rose."

Her hips jerked forward when he touched a fingertip to her core, her entire body shuddering as he drew lazy circles around her slick center.

"Oh, *please*, Max."

"God, yes. You're so wet for me, Rose." He grazed his thumb over that tight, slick knot of flesh that was straining for his touch.

"*Ah.*" Her neck arched and her hips jerked as he stroked her again, and then again, his chest rising and falling with each of her quickened breaths, his cock surging against his falls. He was ready to explode just from the sight of her, the way she writhed against him, her mouth slack with pleasure, whimpers and broken pleas falling from her lips.

He eased closer, one hand on her thigh to keep her open to him, stroking and teasing her with the other until she was panting for him, then he sank one long finger inside her and thrust gently. "That's it, love. Find your pleasure. I want you to fall apart for me."

Her hips were moving faster with his every stroke, rising to meet his caresses, then all at once she tensed.

"*Max*." Her body went rigid against his, and an instant later she fell over the edge with a breathless cry, her back bowing. He stayed with her until the spasms subsided and she went limp, her head falling onto his shoulder.

He was painfully hard still, his cock twitching insistently, but he made no move to satisfy it. He simply held her as her small body trembled against his.

"Don't let go, Max." She nuzzled her face into his neck, her breathing gradually calming. "Not yet, please."

Something stirred to life inside his chest then, the ache of it both painful and sweet at once. "Never."

Neither of them spoke again, but he cradled her against his chest, his fingers tracing up and down the delicate line of her spine, a half smile on his lips.

CHAPTER 22

"What the devil do you want *now*, Grantham?"

Max glanced up from the papers strewn across his desk to find Lord Dunwitty looming in his study doorway, his lips pinched together, and his brows lowered in a fierce scowl.

"Dunwitty." Max waved toward the chair across from his desk. "Do sit down. It's good of you to come."

"I wasn't aware I had a choice." Dunwitty strode across the room, dropped into the chair, and fixed him with a baleful glare. "In any case, I'm here, just as you commanded, so I repeat, Grantham. What is it you want *this* time?"

"You look a trifle grim this morning, Dunwitty." Tonight was the Christmas Eve ball, but the viscount didn't appear to be anticipating it with any pleasure. He looked as if he were facing the gibbet, rather than an evening of merry holiday frolics. "Are you not enjoying your stay at Grantham Lodge?"

"I wouldn't say that, Grantham. While I don't care for being summoned to Fairford as if I were one of your servants—"

Ah. Not so much grim, then, as angry.

"—it hasn't been quite the chore I anticipated. There have been certain diversions that have kept me entertained, some of them quite pleasing, indeed."

Pleasing diversions. There was no mistaking the *diversion* Dunwitty was referring to, and he didn't like it.

Still, he could hardly blame Dunwitty. The viscount was merely doing as he'd ordered. That was the trouble with these wicked schemes. If you coerced a man into marriage by threatening to ruin his uncle, he was likely to do precisely as he was told.

Which was rather awkward, now that Max intended to marry Rose himself.

But it couldn't be helped. He'd been fascinated with Rose for weeks now—since the day she'd taken him skating—but it had taken their kiss in the kitchen at Hammond Court yesterday to make him realize the truth.

He was in love with Rose St. Claire.

Madly, wildly in love, and like most besotted fools, he didn't care for the idea of another gentleman courting his beloved. So, Dunwitty would have to go, and the sooner, the better. "As loathe as I am to deprive you of your pleasing diversions, our marriage experiment is over, Dunwitty."

Dunwitty raised an eyebrow. "Over?"

"That's right. Over. I no longer wish for you to court Miss St. Claire. Or marry her. Or touch her in any way," he added, in case Dunwitty had some clever notions about absconding with Rose. "I will, of course, still release your uncle from his obligations to me."

He'd thought Dunwitty would be pleased, but his scowl intensified until his glower threatened to set the desk between them aflame. "You truly believe it's as simple as that, don't you, Grantham? It's nothing more to you than moving pieces about the chessboard."

The chessboard, again? Montford had said something similar, and it was damned insulting. Not to him, but to Rose. If Dunwitty knew her at all, he'd know she wasn't some ivory chess piece to be tossed about on a whim. Yes, he'd seen her that way at first, but now . . .

She was *everything* to him.

But he wasn't going to explain that to Dunwitty. Instead, he leaned back in his chair and gave the viscount a mocking smile. "Well, I am rather good at chess."

"I suppose you intend to marry her yourself." Dunwitty's lip curled. "You don't deserve her, Grantham."

No, he didn't, but by some miracle Rose seemed to think him worthy of her, and hers was the only opinion that mattered. "That's not your concern, Dunwitty."

Dunwitty eyed him, his arms crossed over his chest. "It would be convenient for you if I simply disappeared, but I'm not your pawn, Grantham."

"Forgive me, Dunwitty, but that's precisely what you are. Or were."

He wouldn't have been surprised if Dunwitty had leaped across the desk and grabbed him by the throat then, but the viscount only laughed. "Is that so? Tell me, Grantham, have you had any news from London recently?"

"No." Who would send him news? He hadn't any real

friends in Town aside from Basingstoke and Montford, and they were here.

"Well, I have. Rather important news. Shall I enlighten you, Grantham?"

Enlighten *him*? Arrogant pup. "No. Gossip doesn't interest me."

"This isn't gossip. It's the truth, and I think it will interest you very much. The Marquess of Oxenden died yesterday."

"So did a number of other people, I imagine. I don't see what that has to do with me, Dunwitty." What did it matter to him if some ancient marquess expired?

"Were you at all acquainted with the marquess, Grantham?"

"Not well acquainted, no." He'd met him once or twice, though not recently. The marquess was nearing eighty years, and rarely ever left his country estate in Oxfordshire.

"I see. Perhaps you don't know, then, that the Marquess of Oxenden is—or was—my maternal grandfather." Dunwitty smirked at him, looking for all the world like a cat with a bellyful of cream. "That rather changes things, does it not, Grantham?"

Oxenden, Dunwitty's grandfather? How the devil had that little detail escaped his notice? Dunwitty had inherited the viscountcy years ago when his father passed away. That meant there'd been no troublesome elder brothers standing between him and his father's title, but there could well be a dozen uncles preventing Dunwitty from taking his grandfather's marquessate—

"I'm my grandfather's sole heir, which makes me the

current Marquess of Oxenden. I daresay you're aware, Grantham, that the Oxenden title is a blessed one."

As it happened, he *was* aware, because he made it his business to be aware of aristocrats' changing fortunes. Or he *had*, before he began rusticating in Fairford.

By blessed, Dunwitty meant *wealthy*.

If he'd realized Dunwitty stood to inherit from Oxenden, he wouldn't have chosen him to court and marry Rose. It was too risky, what with these ancient aristocrats dying off at the least convenient times and leaving their massive fortunes to their arrogant grandsons.

Dunwitty—troublesome pup that he was—hadn't only traded the title of viscount for the considerably grander marquess, he'd also increased his modest fortune by tenfold, at least.

Alas, that sort of money made him far more difficult to manipulate.

"I see you understand me, Grantham. I'm more than capable of meeting my uncle's obligations to you." Dunwitty leaned over the desk, his eyes gleaming. "You have nothing to hold over me anymore—nothing left with which to blackmail my family."

How naïve the boy was. There was always *something*, some scandalous secret hidden away, like a mad aunt, or a ruined niece—something the family would prefer never saw the light of day. It was simply a matter of digging deep enough to find it.

Not that any of this mattered now. "What a happy coincidence, then, that I'd already made up my mind to put an end to the scheme."

"The scheme, yes." Dunwitty made a great show of

studying the tip of his boot, but a smirk twitched at the corners of his lips. "But not necessarily the courtship."

Courtship? What bloody courtship? There was no courtship any longer, unless . . . good God, did Dunwitty think to rival him for Rose's affections?

A silence fell as they stared at each other, each weighing the other's mettle, Max's face aching from the effort of hiding his fury. Underneath the desk, his hands clenched into fists.

At last, Dunwitty broke the silence. "You understand, Grantham, that I was a trifle put out when I was torn away from my comfortable fireside in London and banished to the wilds of Gloucestershire."

"Thankfully, your warm fireside still awaits you in London, Dunwitty." It wasn't *quite* the same as tossing him out of the house, but it was a broad enough hint.

"Gloucestershire, of all places. I've never seen so much bloody snow in my life. All this bother, to marry some chit I'd never laid eyes on." Dunwitty gave him a slow, maddening smile. "Then, of course, I laid eyes on her."

Max didn't fall into fits of temper. He didn't shout, or rage, or challenge other gentlemen to duels. He certainly didn't engage in fisticuffs with his house party guests. But now, he would have happily leaped over his desk and hurled Dunwitty to the floor.

"Of course, there are plenty of pretty young ladies in London," Dunwitty went on, heedless of the danger he was inviting. "But I've yet to come across a single one who has Miss St. Claire's sweetness. It would be pleasant, would it not, Grantham, to have such a lovely, obliging wife?"

"What makes you think Miss St. Claire would have you, Dunwitty?"

Dunwitty laughed. "You think she'd rather have *you*? Come, Grantham. Your reputation is well known. Surely, the rumors of your ruthlessness have made it as far as Fairford."

Of course, they had. Rumors always did. But he'd never been the cold, merciless Duke of Grantham when he was with Rose. That is, he'd been curt from time to time, and arrogant, and his manners had been lacking on occasion. Then, of course, there'd been that business with her doorknob, and his loathing for her father, and—

Very well, damn it. He *hadn't* always been at his best with her, but he hadn't been at his worst, either, unless one counted his plot to manipulate her into a marriage with Dunwitty, then take Hammond Court from her.

God above, but he'd been a perfect devil, hadn't he? He had to tell her, to confess the truth to her, and soon. What would she think of him, once she knew? His only saving grace was that he'd put a stop to his plans before any real harm had been done.

Except was that really true? Hadn't he harmed Rose? She didn't know it yet, but he'd betrayed her trust, lied to her, and manipulated her.

Christ, Dunwitty might be right. Why would she want *him*, after she knew the truth?

Particularly when she could have Dunwitty, with his

brown eyes, fair hair, and easy smile. He was young, fashionable, and handsome, with charming manners and an impeccable character.

If that weren't bad enough, he was also a bloody marquess now, and a wealthy one, at that. Dunwitty was everything a proper gentleman should be, what every young lady longed for.

Would it be so surprising if, given the choice between him and Dunwitty, Rose preferred Dunwitty?

But she'd kissed *him*, cried out for *him*, gazed up at him with her pink lips curved in that secret smile, and her beautiful green eyes hazy with desire. She'd touched him with such sweetness yesterday, such tenderness, and she'd fallen apart so beautifully in his arms.

Surely, that must mean something? Rose wasn't the sort of lady who'd give herself to a man she didn't care for. But would she still care for him, once she found out what he'd done?

"I see you understand me, Grantham."

Max jerked his attention back to Dunwitty. "Perfectly, yes, but I'm not entirely certain you understand *me*. As you said, my reputation for ruthlessness is well known. I'm not the sort of gentleman you want as your enemy, Dunwitty."

"It's Oxenden now. And I don't take orders from you, Grantham."

Such arrogance. Max could almost admire it.

Dunwitty rose from his chair, but he paused at the door. "I'm leaving for Oxfordshire early tomorrow, to see to my grandfather's affairs. But I will attend your ball tonight, Grantham, and I *will* dance with Miss St. Claire."

"Just dance with her?" He didn't like the sound of that. Just the thought of Rose in Dunwitty's arms made bile crawl up his throat. But he'd endure it, and the next day, Dunwitty would be gone.

Dunwitty smiled. "That's up to Miss St. Claire."

There was an entire floor between Rose's bedchamber and the ballroom, but the echo of laughter reached her as soon as she stepped into the corridor, coaxing a smile to her lips.

The Christmas Eve ball was to take place this evening. The guests were decorating the ballroom with the garlands they'd gathered on their sleigh ride this morning, and Grantham Lodge was positively shaking with the tumult.

Was there anything more pleasing than laughter at Christmastime?

Oh, dear. That was dreadfully sentimental of her, but such merriment put her in mind of the Christmases they'd had at Hammond Court.

If anyone had told her Grantham Lodge would be a scene of such an explosion of Christmas cheer, she wouldn't have believed a word of it, but this house wasn't at all the cold, joyless place she'd first thought it was.

It had been a *lonely* place, that was all. Now it wasn't any longer.

She closed her bedchamber door and made her way

down the stairs to the ballroom, pausing in the doorway to take in the scene unfolding before her, breathing deeply of the fresh, clean scent of the pine boughs.

It was every bit as chaotic as it sounded.

As far as the garlands, Max had been as good as his word. At his direction, they'd all risen early this morning and gathered in the entryway, still blinking the sleep from their eyes, to find three handsome sleighs waiting for them in the drive, the horses pawing at the ground, and the bells on their harnesses jingling.

They'd set off into a glorious morning, with blue skies above, and the sunrise gilding the new snow a pale pink. They spent all morning gathering greenery, then returned early in the afternoon to sit down to a splendid luncheon. Afterward, Rose had gone upstairs to rest before the ball, but she hadn't wanted to miss the decorating.

Everyone was here, all of them talking at once, and the ballroom was already half-smothered in greenery. It was rather a mess, to be honest, but everyone seemed to be enjoying themselves, and joyous occasions often were messy, weren't they?

No one had noticed her yet, so she allowed herself to linger in the doorway for a bit, searching for a tall, broad-shouldered figure with wavy dark hair. She found him at once, as she always seemed to do these days, as if her heart were leading her gaze directly to him.

Romantic nonsense, yes, but the truth was, there might be a wild boar running loose in the ballroom, and Max would still be the first thing she saw when she opened the door.

He was standing near the fireplace, helping a group of ladies tie bits of gold thread to the ends of what looked like dozens of kissing balls, the clumsiness of his big hands on the delicate bundles causing peals of laughter to ring out from that corner of the room.

Lady Emily was by his side, smiling coquettishly up at him, her dark eyelashes fluttering, and Rose's heart sank. Perhaps it would be best if she returned to her bedchamber and spent the rest of the afternoon contemplating her own foolishness in kissing a duke who'd made no secret of the fact that he was considering a betrothal to another lady.

But just as she was about to scurry out the door, a feminine voice called out to her. "Rose! Do come and help us with these boughs, won't you? I'm afraid we're making a mess of them."

She glanced back to find Francesca and Prue beckoning her over. They were seated on a settee, a mountain of greenery on the floor beside them, and both of them were nearly buried in pine boughs.

"Thank goodness you're here!" Prue waved a helpless hand at the pile of greenery in her lap. "However did we end up with so many boughs, Franny? For pity's sake, what am I meant to do with them all?"

"Why, make kissing balls out of them, or prepare to answer to the kissing ball committee for your negligence." Francesca nodded toward the group of ladies in the corner, her mouth twisting. "I confess I don't see why we need quite so *many* kissing balls."

"I daresay Lady Emily is plotting to steal a kiss from

Grantham." A sly smile curved Prue's lips. "A lady must make the most of her opportunities, mustn't she?"

Francesca snorted. "If she hasn't gotten one from him yet, then she isn't going to."

"I daresay you're right, and it's just as well." Prue cast a look in that direction then shrugged. "I don't think they suit, and from what I've observed, neither does Grantham."

Rose said nothing, but her cheeks were positively scorching.

"Do sit down, Rose." Francesca patted the settee.

"What do you think?" Prue asked once Rose was seated, with a rather daunting heap of pine boughs in her lap.

Rose stared down at them in dismay. "I think I haven't the faintest idea how to make a proper kissing ball."

"Oh, as to that, simply cut the branches to a proper length, then tie the ends together with the ribbon." Francesca passed her a pair of sewing scissors and a length of white silk ribbon.

"No, no." Prue waved the ribbons away. "Never mind the dratted kissing balls. I meant, what do you think about Grantham and Lady Emily, Rose?"

Rose kept her head down, because her cheeks had burst into flames, and her friends were sure to notice it. "I don't."

It was nothing but the truth. She'd gone to great— some might say even extraordinary lengths—*not* to think of Max and Lady Emily, and consequently, she had no opinion regarding them at all.

No opinion whatsoever.

There was a heavy silence, then Francesca asked, "Do you suppose he's kissed her?"

Kissed her. Max, kissing Lady Emily with those firm warm lips, his hands roving over her back, her hips, her breasts, his low voice rasping in her ear, telling her how sweet she was, how he couldn't stop thinking about her—

Dash it, this was the very reason she didn't want to think about it, but there went all her determination, scattered like leaves in the wind. "I couldn't say. I, ah, I don't know a thing about the duke's kissing habits."

Another silence, then Prue asked Francesca about . . . something. Rose couldn't hear them over the sudden roaring in her ears.

Had Max kissed Lady Emily? He must have done, mustn't he? That is, he hadn't singled her out with any particular attention, but if he hadn't kissed her since she'd come to Grantham Lodge, then surely he must have done so in London. If he *had* kissed her, then he hadn't any business at all kissing Rose. Really, it was very badly done of him!

But she'd kissed him back, hadn't she? Oh, *why* had she kissed him back? How could she have been so stupid? No proper young lady went about kissing a duke. Abby had warned her that no good would come of her permitting the Duke of Grantham to trifle with her.

But it hadn't *felt* like trifling. It had felt like . . . love.

And there was her answer before she even had a chance to draw her next breath.

She'd kissed Max because she couldn't *not* kiss him. Even before his lips had touched hers, when his mouth had still been hovering close, his breath warming her lips, she'd already been lost to him.

"What about you, Rose?" Francesca said, interrupting Rose's guilty musings. "What—"

"*Me!* Why should I have kissed the Duke of Grantham? I haven't . . . I didn't . . . I wouldn't . . ." But try as she might, she couldn't quite push the rest of the denial past her lips. She had in fact kissed Max, quite a few times, and done much more than kiss him besides, and oh, why couldn't she manage to tell one little lie without blushing? "It would certainly be very foolish of me to kiss the Duke of Grantham, wouldn't it?"

Dear God, could she have made any more of a mess of that? For pity's sake, that bumbling reply was as good as a confession.

Francesca made a faint choking noise. "Er, I asked what you intended to wear to the ball tonight."

"Oh." Oh, *no*. Rose opened her mouth but snapped it closed again without saying a word. What was there to say? And now here was that silence again, and a deafening one it was, too, teeming with unasked questions.

Rose waited, her hands clenched together, a patch of sticky pitch on her thumb and pine needles poking into her palms, for one of her friends to *say* something, anything, but she couldn't help cringing when Francesca cleared her throat.

Oh, dear. Perhaps silence was better, after all.

"I'm going to wear my dark blue silk. Basingstoke asked for it particularly, which makes me think the foolish man has gone and bought me jewels to match it." Francesca shook her head, but her voice was fond.

"You do look lovely in blue. I believe I've decided on my red velvet for tonight." Prue laid a hand over Rose's trembling one. "What about you, Rose? Have you anything in green? With your hair and eyes, I daresay you look stunning in green."

Rose sucked in a calming breath, her eyes stinging. They were tremendously kind, her friends. "I'm afraid not. That is, I have my green wool, but it's not nearly grand enough for a ball." She didn't have *anything* grand enough for a ball, which was rather a problem. Abby had promised they'd find a way to make do, but alas, one couldn't simply pull a silk ballgown from thin air, could one?

But it couldn't be helped. It might be better if she didn't go to the ball, after all.

"I have just the thing! I brought a lovely, forest-green silk with me, just in case I changed my mind about the blue. I daresay it will fit you beautifully, Rose, as it's a bit too tight for me. It's so perfect, it might have been made for you." Francesca clapped her hands together, gleeful.

Her, wearing a gown fit for a duchess? "Oh, but I couldn't wear your—"

"Nonsense, Rose. Of course, you can. It doesn't do anyone a bit of good sitting in my wardrobe, does it?"

"Franny's right, Rose, and it will give us such pleasure to dress you." Prue took her hand. "Promise you'll meet us in my bedchamber after dinner, won't you?"

How could she possibly refuse such a kind offer? "I—I promise, and thank you both. I confess I was a bit anxious about it."

Francesca pressed her hand. "What are chaperones for, if not to provide silk gowns?"

"And jewels," Prue added. "Don't forget jewels. Emeralds, I think, to match your eyes."

Emeralds? Goodness.

"But there will be no ball for us, and no dinner either if we don't finish the task assigned us." Francesca cast a dark look at the pine boughs overflowing her lap. "It's rather nonsensical, really."

"Indeed." Prue cast Rose a sidelong glance. "If a gentleman is determined to kiss a lady, he doesn't need a kissing ball to do it."

CHAPTER 23

"For a man with your aversion to all things merry, your Christmas ball appears to be a resounding success, Grantham." Montford swallowed the last of his champagne, then set his glass aside on a table so smothered with pine boughs it looked as if an entire forest had sprouted in Max's ballroom.

"Yes, well done, Grantham. I'm pleasantly surprised. I confess I don't understand this, however." Basingstoke frowned at the knot of greenery and ribbons dangling from the crystal chandelier above his head. "Where did all the bloody kissing balls come from?"

"The kissing ball committee got rather carried away, I'm afraid." If ever there was a sentence Max would have sworn he'd never utter, it was *that* one.

"Kissing ball committee?" Montford gave him a blank look. "I didn't realize there was such a thing."

"Where ladies are involved, Montford, there's a committee for everything. I overheard Lady Emily issuing orders to the other ladies regarding the proper way to decorate a ballroom, and I might easily have mistaken her for a military commander deploying his troops." Basingstoke shuddered. "It was rather terrifying, really."

"Speaking of Lady Emily, how do you and she get on, Grantham?" Montford helped himself to another flute of champagne from the tray of a passing footman. "Is she destined to become the next Duchess of Grantham?"

Basingstoke laughed. "Ah, now I understand. It's not surprising you ended up with eight dozen kissing balls, Grantham. The lady is nothing if not hopeful."

"What say you, Grantham? You'll have to find a wife soon enough, unless you intend to ignore your obligations to your title." Montford shrugged, but he turned a sharp gaze on Max. "Why not Lady Emily? She'll make you a tolerable wife."

Perhaps she would have, once, but in only a few short weeks, his life had changed so drastically he hardly recognized it as his own. He would have scoffed if either of his friends had told him one small lady could throw him into such chaos.

Then he'd kissed Rose, and nothing had been the same since.

But a ballroom stuffed to the rafters with gossiping aristocrats wasn't the time or place to go into *that*. He'd spent most of today keeping a respectful distance from her, so as to keep the *ton* from whispering about her behind her back. He wasn't going to blurt out his secrets now, where anyone might overhear him.

Of course, he'd also kept his distance from Rose to keep from kissing her again.

He'd have to take care to keep away from her until

the house party ended, and his guests returned to London. He was far too besotted with Rose to risk even the briefest of glances at her, as it would be sure to give him away.

But it was Christmas Eve, and the house party was approaching its conclusion. Soon enough, he'd have her all to himself, and then—

"You should listen to Montford, Grantham." Basingstoke sipped at his own glass of champagne, his gaze on Lady Emily, who was on the opposite side of the ballroom, smiling and flirting her fan as she talked to Lord Dowd. "I daresay Lady Emily will do for you well enough."

Max snorted. "Is that what you said when you made your proposal to your duchess, Basingstoke? 'I suppose you'll do well enough'?"

"Good Lord, no. Not a bit of it, Grantham. I told her she was an angel, and deserved much better than me, then begged her to have me anyway, because I couldn't live without her."

"Well done, Basingstoke." Montford nodded approvingly. "One thing a man in love knows how to do, Grantham, is beg. You may as well have Lady Emily, unless, of course, there's another lady you love? A lady you can't live without? A lady you'd fall to your knees for? I'd prefer to see you wed to a lady who can properly subdue you."

Max rolled his eyes. "Why is that, Montford? Because you wish to curse me with your own fate?"

Montford grinned. "No. Because it's far more amusing for me that way."

"If there is such a lady, you'd better snatch her up, before someone else does. Oh, look. There's Viscount Dunwitty, just coming into the ballroom." Basingstoke nodded toward the doorway. "What appropriate timing. He appears to be searching for someone. Now, which young lady do you suppose has caught his eye, Grantham?"

Dunwitty stood in the archway, his arrogant gaze moving over the company like a king surveying his court—or like a marquess, at the very least. He was dressed in fashionable black pantaloons and a perfectly tailored coat, looking nauseatingly . . . golden.

"Oh, I can tell you *that*, Basingstoke. Dunwitty's looking for Miss St. Claire. He seems rather enamored of her, doesn't he? But never mind him. Lady Emily is just on the other side of the ballroom." Montford gave Max a nudge. "Why not ask her to dance, Grantham?"

He didn't want to dance with Lady Emily. All he wanted, all he cared about, was Rose. It was past ten o'clock. She hadn't yet made her appearance in the ballroom, and he was growing more agitated with every moment that passed. Every time he caught a glimpse of golden hair, he jerked his head toward the doorway.

He'd done it so many times, he'd gotten a crick in his neck.

Yet still, no Rose. What was keeping her? Francesca and Prue had stolen her away directly after dinner, and he hadn't laid eyes on her since. It had only been a few hours, but it felt like an eternity.

It was driving him mad.

Since their interlude in the kitchens at Hammond Court, he hadn't stopped thinking about her for a single instant. Her fingers in his hair, her soft laughter, her passionate kisses, and her breathlessness when she'd cried out for him. God, the way she'd cried out for him. Just the memory of his name on her lips made him hard. He'd spent every minute since then with a cock as stiff as a fireplace poker.

He'd sought her out everywhere today, hungry for even the barest glimpse of her—a flash of her green eyes, a fleeting glimpse of her smile. He strained to hear her voice when they were in the same room together, ached for the sound of her laugh.

The sleigh ride this morning had been pure torture. He hadn't dared to ask her to share the two-seat sleigh with him. He'd somehow ended up with Lady Emily instead, but all the while he'd thought about how Rose had looked when they'd gone out yesterday, her cheeks pink from the cold, the golden length of her hair flying out behind her as they'd skimmed over the snow, the warm, curved length of her thigh pressed against his.

But as much as he wanted to be near her, he'd kept his distance. He couldn't bear to be near her and not touch her, and God knew he couldn't touch her. He couldn't trust himself to lay a single finger on her without the desire smoldering in his belly flaring to feverish life, and sweeping all before it.

It was the most exquisite, delicate torment, but torment was torment, no matter how exquisite, and this was torment to a degree he'd never known before. The house party couldn't end soon enough.

"Ah, there's my lovely wife at last, and wearing the gown I favor." Basingstoke was gazing at the entrance to the ballroom, his face alight with admiration. "A man can't really complain about his wife lingering so long at her looking glass when the result of her efforts is so enchanting, can he?"

"You'll not hear a single complaint from me. Prue looks ravishing, as always. She grows more beautiful every day." Montford let out a yearning sigh, his gaze locked on his wife.

There'd been a time when Max would have mocked his friend mercilessly for such a lovelorn sigh as that. He would have claimed no matter how enamored he became of a lady, he'd never permit himself to become so besotted he couldn't look at her without sighing, but now—

"There's Miss St. Claire. My, she does look fetching tonight." Montford turned to Max with a sly grin. "Don't you think so, Grantham?"

"She's a lovely young lady. Sweet tempered, as well." Basingstoke glanced at Dunwitty. "I'd wager she can have the viscount for the asking if she wants him."

Max whirled around, his heart vaulting into his throat. "Miss St. Claire? Where is she? I don't see her."

"She came in with Prue and Franny just now, but it looks as if she's lingering outside the door. The lady is a bit shy, perhaps. This is her first ball, is it not? Ah, there she is." Basingstoke let out a low whistle. "Very pretty, indeed. That shade of green suits her. Don't you think so, Grantham?"

Max didn't answer. Francesca, Prue, and Rose were

gathered near the door, surveying the company, but he only had eyes for one of them.

Rose, every inch of her perfect, resplendent.

The chandeliers had all been lit in honor of the grandness of the occasion, and the candlelight from above shone down upon her as if it had singled her out for all its attention, setting her golden hair ablaze.

Max echoed Montford's hungry sigh, albeit silently. She looked like a spring day, a cool, summer forest dappled with light, a sunrise.

She was wearing a green silk gown and a necklace with a single, tiny emerald draped around her graceful neck. The stone nestled into the hollow of her throat, dragging his attention to that tempting expanse of creamy, bare skin.

He'd kissed her there, touched his tongue to that tiny hollow, caressed her silky skin, and buried his fingers in the thick, golden mass of her hair.

She'd worn it up tonight, bound in a simple knot at the back of her neck, but a few golden curls had been left loose. They brushed her white shoulders, and he . . . good Lord, he was jealous of those curls, because they were touching her bare skin.

He flexed his hands, his fingertips aching to brush her curls aside so he could press his lips to the warm, scented place at the back of her neck. She'd sigh and gasp for him then, and twine her arms around his neck, her fingers sinking into his hair.

"Grantham? Are you all right?" Montford frowned. "You've got the oddest expression on your face."

No, he wasn't all right. He was bewitched, beguiled,

his soul burning for the only lady in England who'd somehow, when he least expected it, found her way into his heart.

It had mattered to him at first, hadn't it, that she was the daughter of his worst enemy? It seemed like a lifetime had passed since then. He no longer cared about it. Not about Ambrose, his father, or the feud between them. Not about Hammond Court or his plans of vengeance.

All the ugliness that had passed between him and the St. Claire family faded away as he gazed at Rose St. Claire.

Come to Fairford, and seize your treasure . . .

"Grantham?"

Rose was still lingering at the door with her two stalwart chaperones, her hands folded in front of her, but she was glancing about, her gaze roving the ballroom as if she were looking for someone.

Him? Could she be looking for him? He sucked in a breath and held it, waiting.

More than one head had turned when the three ladies entered the ballroom, and more than one admiring male gaze lingered on Rose, but she didn't seem aware of it. One gloved hand came up to clasp her neck as she continued her study of the ballroom, until at last, her eyes found his, and she stilled.

The other guests passed between them, laughing and chatting, all of them making their way to the floor to form the sets as the musicians struck up another song, but it didn't matter how many people stood between them.

Nothing in the world could have torn his gaze from hers.

She was *his*, and he was going to take her out onto the floor. He was going to dance his first dance of the evening with her, everyone else be damned.

"Grantham's coming this way, and . . . my goodness, Rose!" Prue squeezed her arm, a gasp on her lips. "He's staring right at you! Dear me, I've never seen Grantham look at any lady the way he's looking at you."

Rose's heart fluttered against her rib cage as Max broke away from his friends and began to make his way toward her, his gaze still holding hers. It wasn't prudent, his singling her out in this way, but she couldn't have stirred a single step. Her every limb was still, waiting for him.

Heads turned as he passed, whispers rising in his wake.

There was no mistaking his destination.

"My, he looks as if he'd like to gobble you up, does he not?" Francesca's voice was vibrating with quiet satisfaction. "I think we can safely conclude the duke admires you in green, Rose."

Without looking away from Max, Rose fingered a fold of her green silk skirts. If ever there was a gown fit for a duchess, it was this one. It was the first silk gown she'd ever worn. When Francesca and Prue had slipped it over her head, she'd thought she couldn't feel any more beautiful than she did the moment the cool, soft silk caressed her skin.

Until now, with Max's heated gaze on her, taking in every inch of her, from the top of her head to the tips of the green silk slippers peeking out from under her skirts.

It seemed to take forever for him to cross the ballroom, and she had to resist squirming under the curious gazes darting back and forth between the two of them, but she would have waited forever for him to reach her.

By the time he stopped in front of her, her entire body was quivering with . . . anticipation? Excitement? Nervousness? Yes, it was all of those at once, yet more than that, too. She *ached* for him, the fine hairs on the back of her neck rising at his nearness, clamoring for his touch.

"Miss St. Claire." He bowed and held out his hand. "May I have this dance?"

Goodness, he was so handsome, so elegant in his severe black evening dress and his elegant white cravat, his eyes more silver than gray tonight, and his dark hair brushed back from his face.

All but that one dark wave that insisted upon falling over his forehead.

She'd become obsessed with that wayward wave. It gave him away, that disobedient lock of hair. It told anyone who cared to look that Max wasn't the tightly controlled, stern gentleman they all believed him to be.

But no one else *had* cared to look, and so it had become hers alone, a precious secret only she knew, that underneath the ruthless Duke of Grantham, there was another man, a softer man—the man with a wayward curl, who touched her with so much tenderness.

"Rose?" Prue gave her a gentle nudge. "The duke has asked you to dance. Will you oblige him?"

Had she not answered him? No, he was still standing before her, his hand held out, a small, private smile on his lips as if he knew what she'd been thinking. "Yes, of course, I will." She seized his hand with a bit more eagerness than was appropriate, and a hot flush bloomed on her cheeks. "That is, I'd be delighted to dance with you, Your Grace."

"Thank you, Miss St. Claire." He gave Franny and Prue a polite nod and led Rose to the floor. Every eye in the ballroom was upon them, but she forgot the curious stares soon enough and melted into his arms.

There wasn't a single person in this ballroom whose gaze mattered more to her than his.

And his gaze . . . oh, she might have drowned in those smoky gray eyes! How had she ever imagined his eyes were cold? They were soft now whenever he looked at her, a deep, warm glow in their depths.

It was his eyes that had gotten her through the long hours since their passionate encounter at Hammond Court. They hadn't spoken much since then, just a few snatches of polite conversation here and there, but his gaze followed her everywhere, and when she spoke to any of the other guests, he turned his head to listen to her.

"You shouldn't have worn that gown tonight, Rose." His voice was quiet, his palm warm and steady against the arch of her back.

She peeked up at him from under her lashes. "Do you not like my gown, Your Grace?"

"I like it very much, indeed. Rather too much. But every gentleman in the ballroom tonight is looking at you, and now I'll be obliged to challenge them all to duels." His lips twitched. "It's not quite the thing, fighting duels on Christmas Day."

Was he . . . goodness, was he *flirting* with her? "Duels! Why should you challenge them all to duels?"

He didn't answer at once, merely gazed down at her, the smile still on his lips. They moved through the figures of the dance, his gloved fingertips grazing hers. "Don't you know?" he murmured at last. "Because you're mine, Rose."

His. It was a small word, and spoken so softly, but that single, tiny word might have been an epic romantic poem for the way it exploded inside her heart.

His. It was, above all things, what she wanted to be.

A dozen questions spun in her head. What did it mean, for her to be his? Was he hers, as well? What of Lady Emily? But not a single one of them made it past her lips.

They didn't matter. Nothing mattered, but him.

Everyone else—Francesca and Prue, Lord Dunwitty, Lady Emily, even the ballroom itself, all faded to nothing. There was just the two of them, the music swelling around them, the candlelight and curious faces blurring before her eyes as he took her through the dance, her hand tucked snugly into his, and his strong fingers resting on her waist.

She was in love with him. She'd fallen in love with the Duke of Grantham.

All she wanted was to remain in his arms—for the rest of this dance, and all the dances that came afterward. For this moment, and for all the moments yet to unfold.

But all too soon the music came to an end. The other couples in the set separated and began making their way off the dance floor. For an instant, she and Max remained still, and let the world move around them, but then his fingers tightened around hers. "Will you save another dance for me, Miss St. Claire?"

"I'll save all my dances for you, Your Grace." Dear God, had she said that *aloud*? She dropped her gaze, her cheeks burning, but his soft laugh made her glance up at him again.

"Soon, Rose. Very soon."

He placed her hand on his arm and led her from the dance floor back to Francesca and Prue. They were standing with their husbands, both of them wearing wide smiles, like two satisfied cats who'd got all the cream.

"You and Miss St. Claire look very well together, Your Grace." Prue gave Max a playful grin.

"Indeed, you must dance again tonight, so we may have the pleasure of watching you," Francesca added, with a sly wink at Rose.

"Yes, I suppose you'd better, Grantham." Montford shook his head, but his lips were twitching. "Miss St. Claire has done the impossible. She's made even *you* look gallant."

"Hush, you wicked man," Prue scolded, tapping her husband with her fan.

"Indeed, you must dance again, but until then, perhaps you should take one of the other ladies out to the floor, Grantham." Francesca gave Max a meaningful look.

Rose didn't care for the thought of relinquishing Max to another lady, but he'd caught the notice of the *ton* by dancing his first dance of the evening with her. The guests were already whispering, and Lady Emily was glaring at her as if she could quite happily wring her neck.

"Yes, of course. Thank you for the dance, Miss St. Claire." Max took her hand and skimmed his lips over her glove, then with another bow, he made his way across the ballroom to Lady Emily.

It wasn't at all pleasant, having to watch him take Lady Emily to the floor, but Rose didn't have time to think of it, because Viscount Dunwitty appeared then, and held his hand out to her with a bow. "Will you dance, Miss St. Claire?"

There wasn't another gentleman in the ballroom—in Fairford, or Gloucestershire, or even all of England who could rival Max, but she was fond of Viscount Dunwitty, all the same. He was a kind, good-humored gentleman, and he'd been unfailingly attentive to her during the house party.

The smile she gave him as she took his hand was a genuine one. "I will indeed, my lord."

CHAPTER 24

L ORD Dunwitty made a number of heroic attempts to engage Rose in conversation, but alas, love being what it was, her thoughts kept drifting back to the magical dance she'd just shared with Max. By the time they'd made it halfway through the quadrille, the viscount had given up and fallen silent.

If she'd been attending as she should have done, she might have realized sooner that he'd been easing her closer to the edge of the knot of swirling couples well before he grasped her hand and led her toward the entrance to the ballroom.

As it was, they were nearly out the door before she noticed. "Where are we going?" She stopped in the middle of the corridor and tried to tug her hand free from his grasp. "Lord Dunwitty! I insist you release me this—"

"Not just yet, Miss St. Claire. I wish to have a private word with you."

He hurried her down the corridor and into the portrait gallery at the end of the hallway. Once they were out of sight of the ballroom he loosened his grip, and she snatched her hand away. "How dare you? I believed you to be a gentleman, Lord Dunwitty. Was I mistaken?"

"No. I—I beg your pardon, Miss St. Claire. I mean you no harm, but I must have a word with you, away from the ballroom. It won't do if we're overheard."

A refusal hung on the tip of her tongue, but his tight lips and lowered brows made her pause. He'd never been anything other than cheerful and easygoing throughout the entire house party, but now he looked troubled.

"Very well, my lord, if you must." Still, she backed away from him, prepared to flee if he made another move to touch her, and crossed her arms over her chest to hide her trembling hands. "I'm listening."

He opened his mouth, then closed it again. Finally, he let out a sigh. "This is rather awkward."

"Perhaps you'd better get it over with, then." There was some chance they'd been seen leaving the ballroom together, and she couldn't linger here with him for much longer without it resulting in a storm of gossip.

"Very well. I've agonized over whether or not to tell you this, but after your dance with the Duke of Grantham, it's become apparent to me that—forgive me, Miss St. Claire—but it appears as if your heart is vulnerable to him."

She stared at him, heat mounting in her cheeks. What in the world did he *mean*, speaking to her of such a thing? "The state of my heart, Lord Dunwitty, is not your—"

"It's not my concern. Yes, I know, and I assure you, this conversation brings me no pleasure, but you're a lovely, kind young lady, Miss St. Claire, and I esteem you too much to leave Grantham Lodge without making you aware of who the Duke of Grantham is. You deserve to know the truth about his machinations."

"Machinations?" If ever there was a word to make her belly twist with dread, it was that one. "I don't understand."

"No. How could you?" Lord Dunwitty dragged a hand through his hair, then drew in a breath, and met her eyes. "I believe you and the duke share a property in Fairford? Your late father's home, if I understand correctly."

"We do, yes. Hammond Court." But what could Hammond Court have to do with this?

It was a silly question, wasn't it? Hammond Court was the only reason Max had come to Fairford in the first place. From the start, he'd vowed to take it away from her, by fair means, or foul. From the beginning, it had been the one thing that stood between them.

Was she really such a fool as to believe a few kisses, some sweet words, and one dance meant it no longer mattered? Suddenly, she wanted nothing more than to slap her hands over her ears, to shut out whatever it was Lord Dunwitty was going to tell her.

But it was already too late for that. Even now, he was opening his mouth, and the words were tumbling out. "Hammond Court, yes. The duke is eager to get his hands on the property, I believe?"

"Yes, he—yes. It belonged to his family at one time. It's part of his legacy."

Lord Dunwitty regarded her in silence for a moment,

his brown eyes filled with something that looked very much like . . .

Pity.

Dear God. Whatever he was about to tell her, it was going to be terrible.

So terrible, it would break her heart into a thousand pieces.

"The duke brought me here to Grantham Lodge for a purpose, Miss St. Claire. My uncle had some unfortunate luck with a business venture of his, and he owes the duke a large sum of money. Until a recent change in my circumstances, there was no hope of his paying it."

"Your uncle's financial difficulties aren't my concern, my lord."

"Please, Miss St. Claire, let me finish."

Could he not see that she didn't want to hear anything more? Couldn't he tell her heart was floundering, sinking? But there was little she could do now but listen, so she gave him a reluctant nod. "Very well."

"The duke summoned me to Fairford to do him a service. In exchange, he pledged to forgive my uncle's debt. I didn't hesitate at the time, but now I wish to God I had."

"A service?" It was a harmless enough word. There was no reason it should make her stomach pitch with alarm, but she was obliged to steel her spine and raise her chin before she could meet Lord Dunwitty's gaze without flinching. "What sort of service did the Duke of Grantham require from you, my lord?"

"You must understand, Miss St. Claire. This was

before I knew you. Almost as soon as I met you, I knew I could never go through—"

"It's quite all right, my lord." But it *wasn't* all right. Nothing would ever be right again, once he told her the truth. She knew it, and yet the only thing worse than knowing what he was about to say, was *not* knowing it. "I would be grateful to you if you'd simply get on with it."

"Of course. Forgive me." He blew out a breath. "I was to come to Fairford, sweep you into a whirlwind courtship, and propose marriage to you before the house party ended." A dull, red flush crept into his cheeks. "Then, once we'd married, I was to—"

"Turn over my share of Hammond Court to the Duke of Grantham."

Dear God, what a fool she was! How could she not have realized it at once? Handsome, fashionable aristocrats like Lord Dunwitty didn't single out inconsequential young ladies like her for their flattering attention.

Neither did dukes.

How easy she'd made it for them! And how they must have laughed at her.

She was going to be sick. Bile was crawling up her throat, flooding her mouth. She was going to cast up her accounts, right here in the duke's elegant portrait gallery.

"Yes." He gave her a miserable nod.

"I see. That's . . . well, it's a clever scheme, isn't it?" Clever, ruthless, and unconscionable. In short, a scheme worthy of the wicked Duke of Grantham.

If she'd been a different sort of lady—the sort of lady

who'd marry a man she didn't love in exchange for a title and money—it might have worked. But she was far from being that lady. If Max had known her at all, he would have realized from the start his scheme would never work.

But that was the point, wasn't it? He *didn't* know her, and she didn't know him, and a few seductive kisses and false promises didn't change that. No doubt they'd been part of his ploy to begin with.

"From the very start, I thought it callous, and heartless." Lord Dunwitty's tone was grim. "Yet to my everlasting shame, I agreed to it for my uncle's sake, and I don't know if I shall ever forgive myself for it. Once I came to know you, I realized I could never go through with it. You deserve a great deal better than to be the victim of such a cruel deception."

Rose nodded, but she hardly heard him.

All this time—the ice skating, the sleigh ride, those devastating kisses, and the passion that had burned so brightly between them—while she'd been sighing over Max, and weaving romantic fantasies, he'd been plotting to steal Hammond Court from her.

"I beg your pardon most sincerely, Miss St. Claire." Lord Dunwitty caught her hands in his and pressed a feverish kiss to her knuckles. "If you could forgive me—if you ever could find it in your heart to . . . to love me, I'd consider myself the most fortunate man in England."

Gently, she drew her hands away. "I do forgive you, my lord, and I hope for every happiness for you, but I'm afraid my affections are engaged elsewhere."

"It's Grantham, isn't it?"

Alas, despite everything, it was. Had ever a lady disposed of her heart as foolishly as she? "The heart is a reckless organ, is it not, my lord?"

"Alas, I'm afraid it is." He hesitated, as if unsure what to say or do, but finally, he offered her a deep bow. "I'm leaving Grantham Lodge early in the morning and am unlikely to see you again. It has been a great honor and pleasure to know you, Miss St. Claire. I will always wish you the best."

He turned to go but then paused. "I'm no admirer of the Duke of Grantham, Miss St. Claire, but there is something else you should know."

There was *more*? She'd heard quite enough already, but he looked so earnest, she couldn't refuse him. "Very well. What is it, my lord?"

"This morning, Grantham called me into his study and told me he'd changed his plans. He warned me to stay away from you for the remainder of the house party. To his credit, I believe he thought better of the scheme." He gave a helpless shrug. "I don't know if that makes any difference to you, but I thought it right you should know."

Did it make a difference? She hardly knew.

Their tryst in the kitchens at Hammond Court had taken place the afternoon before Max's chat with Lord Dunwitty. It wasn't likely the timing was coincidental, but in the end, what did it matter? After this, she could never trust Max again. For all she knew, he'd given up the scheme with Lord Dunwitty so he could seduce her himself.

Why shouldn't he? It was as good a way as any to get his hands on Hammond Court, and goodness knew she'd given him every reason to believe he'd succeed, falling into his arms as she had.

But she managed a halfhearted smile for Lord Dunwitty. "Thank you, my lord."

He nodded, and then he was gone, his footsteps echoing down the corridor. She was left alone, and as still as the portraits of Max's forbears hanging silently on the walls. If she moved, she'd shatter into a thousand pieces, so she remained as she was, taking in one shuddering breath after another until she was certain she could keep herself together, just for a little while longer.

Then, she ran.

Through the portrait gallery and down the corridor to the staircase, her heart pounding against her ribs, and up to the third floor where her bedchamber awaited, praying all the while Max wouldn't find her.

She couldn't bear to see him now, nor could she bear to stay at Grantham Lodge for another moment. As soon as she could find Abby, they were leaving here, despite the darkness and the cold. It had been a mistake—a tragic mistake—to come here in the first place.

But there'd be plenty of time to think about her mistakes, once she'd left Grantham Lodge far behind.

There'd be plenty of time to fall apart, then.

A lifetime.

* * *

Max's dance with Lady Emily dragged on for an eternity. Once he was free, he immediately went in search of Rose, but she was nowhere to be found. He paced from one end of the ballroom to the other, searching for golden hair or a green silk gown, but she seemed to have disappeared after her dance with Dunwitty.

He was waiting near the entrance when the next dance ended. Francesca, pink cheeked and smiling after a vigorous country dance with her husband, joined him there, while Basingstoke hurried off to fetch her a glass of lemonade. "You're scowling again, Grantham, but I suppose I would be, too, after a dance with such a sour-faced Lady Emily."

"I can't find Miss St. Claire."

"The last I saw of her, she was dancing with Lord Dunwitty, but that was quite some time ago." She frowned. "Now I think of it, I haven't seen him recently, either."

Damn it. How had he not noticed Dunwitty was missing, as well? "I need to find her."

"Yes, of course. I'll see if she's in the ladies' retiring room, shall I? You might check her bedchamber, Grantham. Perhaps she became fatigued and went to bed."

"Perhaps." But he didn't think so. She hadn't appeared at all fatigued when they'd danced together. She'd spun in his arms as if she could have remained there all night, gazing up at him with sparkling green eyes.

He strode from the ballroom toward the staircase, a vague sense of foreboding niggling at him. He might not care much for Dunwitty, but the man was a gentleman. He'd never take liberties with Rose, or hurt her in any way, unless . . .

He stopped, one foot on the bottom stair.

No, surely not. Dunwitty despised him heartily enough, but he wouldn't blurt out the private details of their arrangement to Rose before Max had a chance to speak to her himself.

Would he?

He darted up the stairs, but when he reached the landing, he hesitated. Rose's bedchamber was down the corridor, but he hadn't gone more than two steps up when a strange flash of intuition made him turn around, and . . .

No. No, no, no.

There, two floors below was Rose. She was hurrying through the entryway, her cloak thrown hastily over her shoulders, and Abby Hinde was with her, standing at the open door with a valise in her hand.

"Rose!"

She froze, then slowly she turned, and the look on her face . . . dear God, he'd never forget it. She was as pale as the snowflakes drifting through the open door, as pale as the marble floor they landed on, and as cold as the drops of melted snow they left behind.

His Rose, with her smiling lips, looked at him with eyes as frigid as two green chips of ice. In an instant, he was at the bottom of the stairs, his hands wrapped around her shoulders. "Rose, please wait. Come and talk to me, give me a chance to explain."

"Explain what, Your Grace?"

Your Grace. Not Max any longer, but Your Grace.

"I know Dunwitty told you, Rose." She was no dissembler. He could see the truth on her face as surely as if she'd spoken it aloud.

And there, in the green eyes he'd grown to love, was an ocean of hurt.

God, he had to make her understand—

"There's nothing to explain, Your Grace. Lord Dunwitty made it all perfectly clear. The house party, the ball, the sleigh ride . . ." She waved a hand around as if encompassing all of Grantham Lodge. "It was all an elaborate ruse to take Hammond Court from me."

Beside her, Abby gasped. "*What?* Rose, what are you saying?"

"I'll explain it all later, Abby. Wait for me in the wagon, won't you? I must have a word with the duke, but I won't be long."

"No, Rose. I'm not leaving you here with *him*." Abby turned on Max, her face as hard as stone.

"It's all right, Abby, I promise you." Rose held Max's gaze, not sparing Abby a glance. "Please, do as I ask. It will be quicker this way."

For a long moment, Abby didn't move, then, with another glance of such fiery wrath it should have felled Max where he stood, she disappeared into the darkness.

"Did you ever intend to become betrothed to Lady Emily? Or was that just another lie?"

Rose's voice was calm, but she was so white, and underneath her cloak, she was shivering. He reached for her instinctively, but she backed away, shaking her head. "I asked you a question, Your Grace."

Lady Emily, the house party, Hammond Court—

none of it mattered to him now. All that mattered was *her*. He tried to tell her—he opened his mouth to say the words and beg for her forgiveness—but he could only stare at her, the truth tangling on his tongue.

Yet he wouldn't lie to her again. Since he'd come to Fairford, he'd told enough lies to last a lifetime. "I never intended to become betrothed to her. When you asked me why I decided to remain in Fairford rather than return to London, an impending betrothal was the first excuse that came to my mind. That's all."

"I see." She nodded, but there was something oddly mechanical about the gesture. "The ice skating, and the sleigh ride, and the . . . the . . ." A spasm of pain crossed her face. "Everything else? Was that part of the scheme?"

"No! You don't understand, Rose. I don't deny I plotted and schemed to take Hammond Court from you, but that was before I—"

Before I fell in love with you.

The words were there on his tongue, waiting to be breathed into existence, but she didn't give him a chance to say them. "The house party, Your Grace. You never intended to have one, did you? You merely seized your chance after the ceiling collapsed at Hammond Court. That was quite a stroke of luck for you, wasn't it?"

He couldn't deny it. There was nothing he could say, but he tried, even as he knew it was hopeless. "Rose, please listen—"

"Once you had me here, it was simply a matter of summoning Lord Dunwitty to Fairford. Such a clever scheme, to have a house party. That way, no one would suspect he was anything other than one of your guests.

Did . . ." She looked away, clearing her throat. "Did Prue and Francesca know? Were they a part of it, too?"

"*No*. They would never . . . no one knew but Dunwitty, though Basingstoke and Montford guessed it after they arrived." They'd warned him this would happen, hadn't they? He should have listened to them, he should have . . . God, there were so many things he should have done differently.

And so many things he shouldn't have done at all.

"It was a brilliant scheme, Your Grace." Her voice was dull. "I never suspected a thing. Silly of me, after you warned me you'd have your revenge on Ambrose. Well, now you have."

"Rose, please." His hands tightened around her shoulders, his grip desperate, but she made no attempt to resist him. She didn't fight him, or try to squirm free, but only waited, her body limp, as if her spirit, her very soul, had been drained.

He'd done that to her. *Him*. She had the bravest, purest soul he'd ever known, and he'd crushed it like a butterfly in his fist, a bit of dandelion fluff under his boot heel.

"I wonder what Ambrose would make of us now?"

She laughed a little, but it was a dull, flat sound, such a mockery of her true, joyful laugh he nearly staggered with the pain of it. "Rose—"

"Do you know why he left Hammond Court to both of us, Your Grace?" She met his gaze, but it was as if she were looking right through him.

"No." Even now, after everything, that was still a mystery to him, a missing piece of the puzzle.

"I don't think he ever intended for me to have the house. After two decades, he still looked upon it as yours, as part of your legacy. He only wanted to give me the chance to make you love it as he did. As I do. All these years later, he still hoped you might make peace with your past."

"My past?" He stared at her. "Hammond Court, the circumstances of his will . . . you think he did all this for *me*?"

Come to Fairford, and seize your treasure.

"Yes. It's amusing when you think about it." She gave him a sad smile. "All this time, you've been trying to take something away from me, and all the while, I was trying to give something back to you. For Ambrose's sake. It was the last thing—no, the *only* thing—he ever asked of me."

Her words fell between them with a dull thud.

Give something back to you . . .

Was it possible he'd been wrong about Ambrose, for all these years?

He groped for the hazy memories from before those dark, lonely nights when he'd stood on the drive of Hammond Court, staring up at the house, his heart breaking in two. Before the wager, and his mother's death, before his father's collapse, before he'd lost everything.

Those memories were nearly gone now, just a handful of broken, scattered pictures flickering in his mind, but the Ambrose he'd known then . . . would he have done this for him?

Back then, Ambrose had been like a second father to

him. God, he'd tried so hard to forget that, but now . . . could Ambrose really have been waiting all these years, to give him back what he'd lost?

"Ambrose made one mistake, though." Rose let out another of those terrible laughs, but this time it trailed off into a sob. "His faith in me was dreadfully misplaced."

Is that what she thought? That she'd failed? "No! Rose, don't you see? I'm not the same man I was when I came to Fairford. I never should have . . . I made a mistake with Dunwitty, one I regret more than I've ever regretted anything in my life, but—"

"He used to call you a lost soul. Ambrose, I mean. Did you know that? He always said it with such sadness, such regret. I don't understand why he wagered for the house in the first place. That part never made sense to me. I doubt we'll ever know, now."

She turned for the door, but he caught the sleeve of her cloak. "Please don't leave, Rose. Don't go."

Gently—far more gently than he deserved—she disentangled the fold of her cloak from his fingers. "I have to, Your Grace. It's cold outside, and Billy and Abby are waiting for me in the wagon."

"The wagon! No. I won't permit you to leave here in an open wagon, Rose. At least let me send for my carriage."

"No, Your Grace. I don't want your carriage." She turned away from him, toward the door. "I don't want anything from you anymore."

Then she was gone, the light flurry of snowflakes whirling through the air in her wake.

CHAPTER 25

"I'm wearing the Duchess of Basingstoke's gown." Rose fingered the fold of the silk gown that was peeking out from under her cloak. It was such a lovely shade of green. She'd never worn anything so fine, and when she'd faced her reflection in the glass, it had felt as if anything were possible.

Had that only been hours ago? It seemed as if an eternity had passed since then.

"Francesca's gown," she said again, speaking into Abby's ear to be heard over the clatter of the wagon wheels thumping down the road between Grantham Lodge and Hammond Court. "I've stolen a duchess's silk gown."

It was rather a serious crime. The silk alone was worth far more than their wagon and the horse pulling it, and it had no doubt been made by one of London's most fashionable modistes. Thieves had been whipped for less. Hanged, even.

Even so, she couldn't work up even the dullest twinge of alarm. If the chill of the wind hadn't crept underneath her cloak to bite at the bare skin of her legs, she likely wouldn't have noticed the gown at all.

"I don't suppose Her Grace will mind, dearest." Abby gave her hand a comforting pat. "Why, I daresay she hasn't given it a thought. I'll see that the gown is sent back to her first thing tomorrow morning. No harm's been done."

Rose glanced at Billy, who was seated on her other side. He didn't appear to have an opinion on either silk gowns or duchesses. He maintained the same grim silence he'd observed since he'd fetched them at the entrance to Grantham Lodge.

The same scowl, as well.

He'd glared daggers at the house, his lip curling at the sight of the grand carriages crowding the drive, and the dozens of harried servants scurrying about. Even the Christmas greenery festooning the staircase hadn't earned his approval. But he'd reserved his most pointed ire for the duke, who'd stood frozen in the doorway as they'd climbed into the wagon, watching them go with an expression she wouldn't soon forget.

Utter desolation. She'd never seen him look so lost, and it had ripped another hole into her already bleeding heart. How could she still feel such pain on his behalf, after all he'd said and done? His lies and subterfuge?

It was a pointless question. She already knew the answer.

Even now, less than an hour after she'd discovered how thoroughly he'd betrayed her, her hurt and anger were no match for the depth of her love for him. Foolish, misguided heart! What use was it having a heart at all, if she must be cursed with such an irrational one?

But there was nothing rational about love, was there? Nothing wise. On the contrary, it was quite the stupidest emotion in existence. It made young ladies weep, yearn, and swoon like tragic heroines, and gentlemen rave and tear their hair, and forget themselves. Behind nearly every duel in London, nearly every ruination, one could find love lurking in the corner, snickering to herself.

And *this* was the emotion poets penned odes to!

If she'd had the least idea love could be so dreadful, she never would have permitted herself to fall—

"The drive," Billy said suddenly, breaking his grim silence as he turned into the narrow road that led to the entrance of Hammond Court. "What's happened to it?"

Abby turned to him, startled. "The *drive*, child? What do you mean? Nothing's happened to it."

"It has. It's different. Smooth." He slowed the horse, muttering to himself as he peered through the darkness at the length of the road illuminated by the narrow beam of light from their lantern. "Someone's seen to the ruts."

Abby snorted. "Nonsense, Billy. Who would have . . ." She trailed off, going still, and listening. "By God, the boy's right. But how? Those ruts were as deep as ditches. It must have taken loads of stone to fill them!"

Rose squinted down at the road passing underneath the wagon wheels. It was too dark to see much, but instead of the usual creak and groan of the wheels rumbling over the craters, there was only a low, steady crunching sound, as if they were driving over a deep, even layer of gravel. And while their progress up the drive wasn't precisely smooth—their old, dilapidated wagon never offered a smooth ride—she also wasn't gripping the edge of her seat in a desperate attempt to stay upright, so neither was it the bone-shattering assault to the backside it usually was.

"You don't suppose . . ." Abby began, her voice lowered. "Could it be that—"

"The Duke of Grantham had it repaired?" Of course, it had been *him*. He was the only person in all of Gloucestershire who could have gotten such an onerous job done in the few weeks since they'd left Hammond Court.

At Christmastime, no less.

But why? And when? It must have been after their sleigh ride yesterday, of course, or else she would have noticed it when they—

No. They hadn't come down the drive at all yesterday. Max had taken another route. Otherwise, she would have noticed that it had been repaired.

It had been his idea to approach from the east side, past the stables, and into the kitchen courtyard. He'd said it was to save the sleigh's runners from the rutted road, but that couldn't have been the reason, because the drive must have already been repaired by then.

Had he not wanted her to see it? But why?

Unless . . . had it been a surprise?

Her throat closed, and tears sprang to her eyes. *Why*, of all the people in the world to show her such an unexpected kindness, must it be *him*? Why must it be *now*, when she'd just made up her mind to banish him from her heart forever?

She didn't want his kindness. Not *now*. She didn't want to be beholden to the Duke of Grantham for a single thing.

Worse, it didn't even make any sense! He'd told her himself he was going to tear Hammond Court to the ground. Why had he bothered to repair the drive, then? What did it matter if it were smooth, once Hammond Court was gone?

Was it all part of his ruse? But what would he have to gain by—

"Oh, my goodness." Abby seized Rose's arm. "Rose, look!"

They'd reached the end of the drive. Billy brought the wagon to a halt, but none of them alighted. They all sat there, mouths open, staring up at the house. It was as dark as the sky above it, but Billy raised the lantern, and a soft curse fell from his lips as the light passed across the front of the house, catching on the dull glint of smooth, shiny glass.

"The broken windows." Rose covered her mouth with her hand, hardly able to believe what she was seeing.

The damaged windows that looked down upon the drive were gone. Every cracked pane, every jagged edge, every sagging casement had been removed, and a new, sturdy window put in its place.

Max hadn't just seen to the drive. He'd taken care of the windows, too.

She set the lantern carefully onto the seat of the wagon, her hands suddenly too shaky to hold it steady. For a long time, no one said a word, but finally, Abby stirred. "Come inside, Rose. You'll catch your death sitting outdoors in the cold in that thin silk gown."

Abby climbed down from the wagon and held out her hand to Rose, who took it without a word and allowed Abby to lead her to the front door.

The length of rope was gone. The old doorknob and plate were back in their accustomed places, but they'd been scraped free of rust and dirt, and polished until they gleamed a glossy black in the lantern light.

She reached out and ran her fingertip over the smooth iron plate, but she made no move to open the door, afraid of what awaited her inside.

Because he wouldn't have stopped at the door. Even after such a short acquaintance, she somehow knew that once Maxwell Burke made up his mind to do something, he wouldn't rest until it was finished.

"Standing out here in the cold isn't going to change anything, Rose." Abby gave her a gentle nudge. "Open the door."

It was an odd feeling, stepping over the threshold and slipping inside after so many weeks away. She'd never been gone from Hammond Court before—not even for a single night—and the strangest sensation seized her as she passed into the entryway.

It was as if she were trespassing. As if this were someone else's home, and she no longer had any right to be here.

But then, it *was* someone else's home, wasn't it? It belonged to Max now.

"Why, Abby?" she whispered, tears once again rushing into her eyes. She was exhausted and heartbroken, and she couldn't make sense of any of this. "Why did he do it?"

"I can't say, dearest." Abby gave her a helpless shrug. "Perhaps he doesn't intend to tear it down, after all. Perhaps he's made up his mind to keep it, and live here."

Perhaps he had. It should have lifted her spirits. It was what she'd hoped for, after all. It was good news, then. Yes, very good news, indeed. Yet, as they made their way past the staircase, and by silent mutual agreement down the corridor that led to the drawing room, it only made Hammond Court feel more distant than ever.

Nothing was the same. It didn't even smell like the same house. The faint odors of mildew and dust had vanished, and in their place was the scent of soap, lemon, and a faint whiff of wax candles.

"Light the lamps, won't you, Billy?" Abby bustled about while Rose waited in the middle of the room, and Billy fumbled with the wicks. She was afraid to sit down, or even to stir a step. The room felt so different, somehow, she couldn't quite get her bearings, and she soon saw why.

They all gasped as the flame flickered to life, and the lamp lit the darkened room.

"Oh, my goodness." Abby's eyes widened as she looked around the drawing room.

It had been utterly transformed. That is, most of the furnishings were the same—even the Duke of Grantham couldn't furnish a house the size of Hammond Court in only a few weeks' time—but the worn, moldy window hangings had been replaced with heavy, figured silk drapes in a pretty, pale shade of green, and a dozen new, richly embroidered pillows were scattered over the settees and chairs.

And everything . . . every scrap of cloth, and every pane of glass had been scrubbed clean. Every inch of wood had been polished, and the rugs looked as if they'd been beaten to within an inch of their lives. The spiderwebs were gone. Not a single silken thread dangled from the cornices. There wasn't a speck of dust to be seen or a single flake of ash in the fireplace. The pails that had stood in every corner had vanished—there was no need for them, now that the leaks had been repaired.

Rose wandered over to the fireplace and ran her hand over the marble mantel. "Do you suppose the chimneys have been swept, as well?"

But of course, they had been. Max had seen to everything, right down to the carpet fringe, which lay in perfect order, the threads as straight as a row of pins. With such attention to detail, he was hardly going to neglect the chimneys. The fires would burn properly now, instead of stuttering and smoking, and would warm the rooms, as a fire was meant to do.

She turned around in a circle, trying to take it all in, but it was too much, and she dropped onto the settee before her knees buckled from the shock of it all.

Abby settled into the space beside her. "You didn't know?"

"No, I . . . I knew the floorboards in the kitchen had been repaired. I thought Billy had seen to it, though that didn't seem right." She glanced at Billy, who shook his head. "I said as much to Max—that is, to the Duke of Grantham, and he didn't correct me. He never said a word about any of this."

"It's all so strange, is it not?" Abby glanced around the room with a puzzled frown. "I love Hammond Court as much as you do, Rose, but Grantham Lodge is a grand, elegant estate, one befitting a duke. Why should he need another house? Do you suppose he really does intend to live here?"

Rose could only shake her head. Max had never breathed a word to her about moving to Hammond Court, but if he had made up his mind to live here, it meant she'd accomplished what she'd set out to do.

She'd fulfilled her promise to Ambrose.

Only a few short weeks ago, it was all she'd hoped for, but now, the thought made her heart sink further. Persuading Max to love Hammond Court had always been akin to catching a perfect snowflake on the tip of her finger. She wanted desperately to succeed, but in the deepest, most secret recesses of her heart, she hadn't truly believed it was possible.

Or was it only that she'd wished for more?

She'd wished for him to love *her*, too.

But now, it was as if the snowflake had brushed her fingertips and hovered there for an instant in all its complex beauty, yet as soon as she'd bent her head toward it, it had melted away to nothing, leaving only a drop of water behind.

Somehow, it hurt more to *nearly* succeed, to feel that soaring hope inside her, than it did to never being close to it at all.

If only he hadn't lied to her. She might have borne it, then. She might have been able to wish him well and leave Hammond Court with a joyful heart.

She glanced around the drawing room, at the elegant new draperies, the shiny new windows. It was Hammond Court still, the way she remembered it in its best days. How happy she should have been, to see it thus restored! And perhaps she would be happy, someday, when she looked back upon it.

But now everything was overshadowed by Max's lies.

Yet even that wasn't what hurt the most.

She could have forgiven the lies, in time. What she couldn't forgive was the jagged sliver of doubt he'd planted inside her—deep inside a heart that had never been touched by any man before *him*—that he'd never really cared for her. That everything—the skating and the sleigh rides, his delicious kisses and whispered words, and the pleasure he'd given her—were all just part of his scheme.

That what she'd thought was love was nothing but another lie.

He'd denied it, yes, but how could she believe him? He was a duke. A *duke*, and she was a young lady of no name and no consequence, tucked away in an obscure little village that most London aristocrats had never even heard of.

How could *she*—plain, provincial Rose St. Claire— ever matter to a man like the Duke of Grantham? It was ludicrous.

Of course, he'd lied to her. She'd been a fool to imagine for even a moment it could be anything else.

To his credit, I believe he thought better of the scheme in the end . . .

Lord Dunwitty had done her a kindness, telling her that. It *did* matter to her that Max had abandoned his scheme. When the heartbreak had passed, and the ache of his betrayal had faded, it might provide her with some small comfort.

But it wasn't enough. How could she ever trust him again?

She didn't know. She didn't know anything anymore, and it wouldn't do the least bit of good to sit here and worry over it. It would only spin her thoughts into increasingly frantic circles, like a dog chasing its tail.

It would, alas, all still be waiting for her in the morning. "I want to go to bed, Abby."

"Yes, I think that's a good idea. Billy, will you run ahead to light the lamps?"

"Aye."

Billy went off to do Abby's bidding. She and Rose followed after him, but the stairs that had seemed manageable enough a few weeks earlier took ages to climb tonight. Her feet dragged with every step. By the time they'd made it halfway up the staircase, Billy was waiting for them at the top, and the hallways above were illuminated with a soft glow.

"Miss Rose's bedchamber as well, Billy, if you would," Abby called up to him.

He dashed off down the corridor. From below there

was the sound of the bedchamber door opening, then Billy's exclamation of surprise. "Zounds, would ye look at this!" He poked his head out the door and shouted down the stairs, "Ye won't believe it, Miss Rose!"

Oh yes, she would. At this point, she'd believe anything, and she already suspected what she would find on the other side of her bedchamber door.

But when she crossed the threshold, she couldn't prevent a gasp of surprise.

All of Hammond Court now shone like a new penny, but this was different.

Special care had been taken in this room.

The ballooning ceiling, the floods of water awash with bits of wood and flakes of plaster had vanished. The cracked beams that had led to the collapse must have been repaired, as well, because the ceiling above her head was now as smooth as a bowl of cream. If there'd been any other damage from the water, there was no sign of it now. Not a hint of damp, or even so much as a water stain.

The ceiling had been painted a soft, warm white, and—

"Oh! What a lovely color!" Abby breathed. "Like springtime."

The rest of the room was now a lovely, grassy green color. A new rug in pretty shades of cream, green, and gold had replaced the old one, which had been destroyed in the flood, and underneath the thick pile, the floorboards gleamed.

Her chair was in its usual place in front of the window, but it had been carefully repaired, and now it boasted a thick cushion embroidered with wildflowers. New draperies had been hung as well, heavy silk ones that would do wonders to keep the chilly drafts at bay.

Rose turned in a circle, her throat growing ever tighter as she took it all in. A pretty porcelain vase stood on the mantel, along with a pair of silver candlesticks, and a new coverlet was spread over the bed.

"My goodness." Abby's voice was hushed, but after a quick glance at Rose, she said no more. Not about the bedchamber, or the Duke of Grantham. Instead, she bustled over to the bed and pulled back the coverlet. "Off to bed with you now, pet."

Rose did as she was told, too confused and heartsick to protest.

"Go on home now, Billy," Abby added, nodding at the bedchamber door. "You were a good lad, to fetch us tonight. I'll come and see you and your grandmother tomorrow, and thank you properly."

Billy had drawn closer to the mantel and was peering at the silver candlesticks with interest, but now he nodded and turned to the door. "Aye, Miss Abby."

Abby closed the bedchamber door behind him, then returned to Rose, and began working on the buttons on the back of the silk gown. Soon enough, she was tugging it over Rose's head, and tucking her underneath the covers in just her shift. "Now, don't you worry about a thing, pet. I'll see to it the duchess gets her ballgown back, as good as new."

"Abby?" Rose reached out and seized Abby's hand. "I—I think you were right, about leaving Hammond Court. I should have listened to you. I'm ready to go, now. It's best if we go soon, I think." She swallowed the lump in her throat, but it nearly choked her. "As soon as we can."

"If that's what you want, dearest. We can talk about it tomorrow." Abby brushed her hair back from her face, then leaned down and dropped a kiss on Rose's forehead. "Go on to sleep, now."

Then, with a murmured *good night*, she was gone.

Rose lay still, blinking up at the freshly painted ceiling. She would have welcomed the peaceful oblivion of sleep, but no matter how tightly she squeezed her eyes closed, it wouldn't come.

Max's face swam behind her closed eyes. His expression, when she'd told him she didn't want anything from him anymore, the devastation in his eyes—it was all she could see as if it had been burned into her eyelids.

Finally, she could stand it no longer. She tossed the coverlet aside, rose from her bed, and crept toward the window. It was snowing lightly, the downy flakes falling from a starless sky, and for an instant, she thought of another snowfall, of featherlight snowflakes gleaming in the gray morning light, and a puddle of icy water in the corner of her bedchamber.

Max had come that day, in his glossy black carriage with the gold, spoked wheels, with his orderly boot tassels, and his handsome beaver hat set rakishly atop his dark waves.

And she'd nearly shot him in the foot.

Despite everything, a small smile tugged at her lips. What had he been thinking, trying to wrest that pistol from her? Foolish, arrogant, stubborn man! It was a wonder he wasn't missing a toe now.

But her smile faded again soon enough, replaced by a weight so heavy she thought it might crush her. How could her life have changed so drastically, in so short a time?

How had it come to this?

She stood at the window for a long time, staring into the night, her bare toes numb with cold, and watched the pretty snowflakes whirling through the darkness.

But her answer never came.

CHAPTER 26

After weeks of heavy snow and howling winds, the sun chose to shine with renewed brilliance on Christmas morning, illuminating an endless sky the color of a blue jay's wing. It was the sort of day Christmas *should* be—a day of beauty, hope, and promise.

But it was utterly wasted on Max.

It was as if the glorious weather were mocking him with its brightness. Inside his chest, in the space where his heart was meant to be beating, there was nothing but a dark, silent cavern of misery.

It was midmorning when Bryce brought the carriage to a stop in front of the entrance to Hammond Court. It would have been much earlier, if Basingstoke and Montford hadn't caught him rushing out the door just after sunrise and persuaded him to bathe and change before appearing on Rose's doorstep.

Was she looking down on him from her bedchamber window, even now? Or had she already run for her pistol? He blinked up at the façade, shading his eyes from the sun glittering off the new glass windows, but the house looked as deserted as it had the first day he'd arrived in Fairford.

At least the windows were now intact, and the door-knob and plate properly attached to the door again. There was still a great deal left to do to make the house truly habitable, but there was some comfort in knowing the roof wasn't about to collapse on top of Rose, and neither was she any longer at risk of freezing in her bed or midnight attacks by a roving band of scoundrels.

It was something, but not enough. Nothing he could do for her would ever be enough. If she'd let him, he'd give her everything.

He'd give her himself. All he was now, and all he hoped to become.

Whether she'd have him or not, well . . . she'd made herself painfully clear last night.

I don't want anything from you anymore.

He paused on his way to the door, a wave of dark despair crashing over him. Was there any chance at all she'd change her mind? Would she even open the door to him?

He wouldn't find out by lingering in the drive like some tragic hero. He tried to shake off his doubts, but as he strode to the door the sun ducked behind a cloud, as if to warn him he was marching toward his doom.

But before he could raise his hand to knock, the door flew open.

He caught his breath, but it wasn't Rose waiting on the other side. It was Abby, her lips tight, her eyes nar-rowed, her fisted hands planted on her hips. "I expected *you'd* turn up, sooner or later. What do you want *now*, Your Grace?"

"Rose." It wasn't a gentlemanly reply, particularly given the low rasp in his voice when he said her name, but the time for subtlety had passed. "I want Rose."

Abby sniffed. "You should have thought of that before you tried to snatch her home out from under her, shouldn't you, Your Grace?"

Of course, he should have. That was obvious, wasn't it? But he smothered the retort on his lips. Abby was standing between him and the inside of the house, so aggravating her didn't seem wise. She could slam the door in his face at any moment, and it would hardly endear him to Rose if he attacked her door again.

"I've come to tell Rose that Hammond Court belongs to her now." It wasn't the only reason he'd come, but it was the truth, all the same. "I'll see to it all the necessary repairs are carried out, and the house is maintained to a decent standard of safety and comfort."

"Is that so?" Abby swept a suspicious gaze over him. "Just why would you want to do that, Your Grace?"

Why? "Because I . . . because she . . ." For God's sake, couldn't the woman see that he was expiring for love for Rose, right in front of her eyes? Even if Rose didn't want him, he still wished for her happiness.

One glance at him, and it was all painfully obvious, as his reflection in his looking glass had plainly told him this morning. But he'd be damned if he'd confess to Abby that he was in love with Rose before he told *Rose*, so he said only, "Because Hammond Court is more hers than it ever could be mine."

Abby's eyebrows shot up. "That matters to you, does it?"

"Anything that has to do with Rose matters to me, Mrs. Hinde. Now, may I please see her?"

She stared at him for a moment, as if trying to gauge his sincerity, then shook her head. "She's not here."

"Not here?" Where else would she be, if not at Hammond Court? Damn it, he didn't like the sound of this at all. "Where is she?"

"That's not for me to say, Your Grace."

She started to close the door, but without even thinking about it, he shoved his foot into the gap to prevent her. "Wait. Is she coming back?"

Abby only shook her head. It was plain Rose had instructed her not to reveal her whereabouts to him. God, this was a nightmare. If she slipped through his fingers now, he might never see her again. "If she does come back, will you tell her I was here? That I came looking for her? Please, Mrs. Hinde."

For the first time since she'd opened the door, Abby's face softened a fraction. "I'll tell her, Your Grace, but see you don't make me sorry I did."

With that, she shut the door in his face.

There was nothing for him to do then but climb into his carriage, and return to Grantham Lodge, but what was he meant to do there? He couldn't bear to sit and stare out his window, wishing things were different. It was Christmas morning, and a new year was upon them. No gentleman worth a damn spent Christmas Day wallowing in misery, for God's sake. This was meant to be a joyful time, a time of new beginnings.

Not a time for giving up.

He stood there, staring at the closed door, until Bryce leaped down from the box and made his way over. "Your Grace?" He blanched when he got a look at Max's face. "Is something amiss, Your Grace?"

Amiss? His entire world had just collapsed around him, so yes, something was amiss, but there was no sense in taking it out on poor Bryce. "I've had better days, Bryce."

"May I help, Your Grace?"

No. No one could help him. No one but Rose.

But he could help himself. "Wait here for me for a bit, if you would, Bryce. I won't be long."

"Of course, Your Grace."

He nodded to Bryce, then wandered off, heedless of the direction he took, but perhaps it wasn't surprising that he found himself at the pond behind the house, where Rose had taken him ice skating several weeks ago.

The cold lingered, despite the warmth of the sun, but the gentle rays were making quick work of the ice-encrusted trees that surrounded the pond, crystalline drops of water falling from their branches.

The toes of his Hessians were wet, his gold tassels more bedraggled than ever now. He'd have to get new ones when he returned to London.

God, London. It felt as far away as the endless stretch of blue sky above him. Nothing there seemed to matter anymore—not his townhouse, his companions at White's, or any of the elegant trappings of his old life. In only a few short weeks, everything that mattered, everything he cared about, was here.

Whoever would have thought he'd find his salvation in Fairford, of all places?

Not him. Not anyone, except perhaps . . .

Ambrose St. Claire.

He sat down on the flat rock where he'd helped Rose with her skates, taking in the sparkling sheath of ice spread out before him, and the dripping trees that sheltered it, their low-lying branches reaching for the frozen pond like open arms.

The day they'd come here, and he'd watched her spinning on the ice, her arms raised to the sky, her face wreathed in smiles . . . he hadn't known it then, but that had been the day everything had changed for him.

How could a man look upon such joy, and not be changed by it?

Joy is a choice, Your Grace.

He'd scoffed at the idea at the time, but he'd been fascinated with her that day, so much so he couldn't stop himself from touching her.

Those fleeting moments with her had been his first taste of pure, true joy.

She'd given that to him.

Come to Fairford, and seize your treasure.

That cryptic note was so typical of Ambrose. The man had loved nothing so much as creating a bit of drama. It had infuriated Max at the time, but perhaps he understood it now.

The treasure Ambrose had referred to wasn't Hammond Court. It never had been.

It was Rose. *She* was the treasure, and only a fool walked away from such a precious treasure, a treasure of inestimable worth.

He wasn't returning to London. Not without Rose. He was going to stay here in Fairford, at Grantham Lodge, and spend every day begging her to forgive him.

Begging her to be his.

Montford was right, as it happened. A man in love does know how to beg.

Beg, he would. If it took the rest of his lifetime to persuade her, then so be it. A lifetime in pursuit of such a lady was a lifetime well spent. He rose to his feet, stomped the snow from his boots, and began to make his way up the hill, back toward his carriage.

First, he had to find her. She'd been at Grantham Lodge only last night. It was still quite early in the morning now, and it also happened to be Christmas Day.

She couldn't have gotten far. He'd find her, but first, there was something he had to do.

"Sir Richard isn't at home, Your Grace."

Max looked down his nose at Sir Richard Mildmay's butler. The man was lying, and not at all convincingly. "Not at home? How curious. You *are* aware it's Christmas Day?"

"Er, yes, Your Grace." The man's nose gave a nervous twitch. "What I meant to say, Your Grace, is that Sir Richard is not at home to visitors today."

"Ah, I see. No matter." He strolled over to an upholstered bench against a wall in the entryway and seated himself with the air of a man who was settling in for a long time. "I'll wait."

The butler blinked. "*Wait*, Your Grace? B-but it's Christmas Day!"

Max unleashed the sardonic eyebrow. "Yes, I believe we've already agreed on that. It would be a pity if I were obliged to miss my Christmas dinner, but I'm afraid my business with Sir Richard is rather urgent and can't wait."

The butler gaped at him, his mouth hanging open, but when this tactic didn't produce the desired effect—namely, Max's absence—he turned on his heel with a huff. "If you'd be so good as to remain here, Your Grace."

Oh, he'd remain, all right. He'd sleep in Sir Richard's entryway, if necessary.

Fortunately, he wasn't obliged to wait long at all. Within minutes, the butler returned, and with him was Sir Richard Mildmay, looking thunderstruck. "What in the world are *you* doing here, Grantham? It's Christmas Day, man! Don't you have a dozen guests expecting their Christmas dinner at Grantham Lodge?"

"I do, yes, and not a single patient one among them. That I'm waiting on a bench in your entryway instead of entertaining them should tell you just how urgent my business is."

Sir Richard sighed. "Is there even the smallest chance, Grantham, of your leaving here without having your way?"

"Alas, I'm afraid not." Max gave him a thin smile. "I'm a duke, Sir Richard. I'm far too accustomed to having my way to give it up now."

"For God's sake. All right then, Grantham. Let's get this over with, shall we? I've got a perfectly lovely roasted goose waiting for me."

He waved an impatient hand at Max, who rose from his place on the bench and followed Sir Richard down the hallway to a small study. Sir Richard nodded at a chair and took the seat behind his desk. "Now then, Grantham. You have my attention. What the devil do you *want*?"

Why did people keep asking him that? It was perfectly simple. He wanted Rose.

But this entire business had begun with the rift between his father and Ambrose, and that was as good a place to start as any. "Several weeks ago, when you revealed the terms of Ambrose St. Claire's will to myself and Miss St. Claire, you said something about Ambrose having only ever had the purest of intentions regarding Hammond Court."

"Yes, I did. As I recall, Your Grace, you scoffed at the idea."

"And that surprised you, Sir Richard? You know the details of my history with Ambrose. You can't reasonably have expected me to react in any other way."

Sir Richard observed him for a moment, then shook his head with a sigh. "No, perhaps not. It was an ugly business, and you got the worst of it."

Ugly, yes. So ugly that it had turned him from a tender-hearted young boy into a heartless, vengeful man. But this wasn't about him. Not this time. "You said at the time that you'd be happy to provide me with the details of the transaction between Ambrose and my father, once I was ready to hear them." Max crossed one foot over the other knee and sat back in his seat. "I'm ready."

Sir Richard rolled his eyes. "It's been two decades, Grantham, and you've made up your mind to be ready *today*? On Christmas Day?"

"I'm afraid so. I beg your pardon for the inconvenience, but after waiting two decades for the truth, I'm not inclined to wait any longer."

Sir Richard muttered something about uppity dukes, but he let out a resigned sigh and made himself comfortable in his chair. "Very well. You're aware that your mother and Ambrose were dear friends?"

"I was under the understanding that Ambrose was dear friends with *both* of my parents, Sir Richard."

"Yes, but it was Caroline who was Ambrose's childhood friend. Your father didn't come to Fairford until much later, after his father inherited the dukedom, and moved his family to Grantham Lodge." Sir Richard leaned over the desk. "Ambrose was fond of your father, Your Grace, but it was Caroline he was devoted to. Especially in the later years, after your father started drinking."

Max stiffened, but there was no denying it. He did his best to avoid thinking about those years, but he could recall more than one incident caused by his father's fondness for the bottle, starting from when he'd been a small boy.

"Your mother loved your father, Grantham, but poor Harcourt had his demons. I don't know the whole of it, but I do know those demons chased him right to the bottom of the bottle. He wasn't a bad man by any means, but he was a weak one. By the time you were out of leading strings, the liquor had already begun eating away his wits."

"I remember his rages." They were among his first memories, in fact. When it got too bad—when his father's crazed shouting could be heard echoing throughout Hammond Court, his mother would snatch him up, run to her bedchamber, and lock the door behind her.

How old had he been, then? Four years? Five?

"As bad as it was, Caroline might have held on—she loved Harcourt that much—but then she became ill. She was an intuitive lady, your mother. She knew she was dying, even before the doctors diagnosed her with consumption. Harcourt had already lost a good deal of the property that wasn't entailed by then. There was very little money left, and Grantham Lodge had already deteriorated to the point they were obliged to remove to Hammond Court. She was terrified he'd leave you with nothing. So—"

"She asked Ambrose to wager against my father for Hammond Court." He'd been too young to understand what was going on, and his memories were hazy, but he recalled some snatches of conversation that hadn't made sense at the time, and weeping.

His mother, weeping.

"Perhaps it wasn't right of her." Sir Richard gave a helpless shrug. "But she did what she felt she had to, to protect what was left of your legacy. Ambrose didn't hesitate to help her. Not just for her sake, but for yours, too."

"Mine?" But he knew. Before Sir Richard got a word out, he knew what he was going to say.

"Ambrose *adored* you, Max." Sir Richard met his eyes. "He couldn't have loved you more if you'd been his own son."

How could that be the truth? If Ambrose had cared so much for him, why had he abandoned him after he'd taken Hammond Court away? "If it's as you say, then why did he turn his back on me? All those years, and he never came to see me once. All those Christmas parties—"

He broke off, nearly choking on the lump lodged in his throat.

All those nights—years' worth of them—standing alone on the drive in the dark, with Hammond Court right there, so close he could touch it, but as far out of reach as the stars. Years of watching it all unfold without him, his heart a cold, dead weight in his chest—

"He never turned his back on you, Max. Your father could never forgive Ambrose for taking Hammond Court from him. He wanted revenge, so he took the one thing Ambrose cared for the most. He took you."

Was that how it had been? He thought back, groping for the forgotten memories. His father, raging against Ambrose, and forbidding Max ever to see him again—

"Ambrose begged your father to let him see you. He tried over and over again, up until it was no longer just your father who refused to have anything to do with him. It was *you*, as well. Ambrose never blamed you for it. He knew Harcourt was poisoning your mind against him."

All this time, years—no, decades of raging against Ambrose, of hating him, and it hadn't been Ambrose who'd taken everything from him.

It had been his own father. Knowing who his father was, having witnessed his rages, how could he not have seen it before?

Because he was my father, and I loved him. He had. Despite everything, he'd loved his father with the fierce devotion of a young boy who had no one else.

"Hammond Court was always meant to be yours again, Max. Ambrose promised your mother he'd give it back to you, but, ah . . . forgive me, but over the years you earned yourself something of a reputation for ruthlessness, and Ambrose was afraid to turn Hammond Court over to you. He feared you'd tear it down, and of course, he had Rose to think of by then."

Come to Fairford, and seize your treasure.

After all that had happened between them, in the end, Ambrose still trusted him with his most precious treasure.

Rose.

"So, he came up with the rather unusual idea of leaving the house to both of you. I tried to dissuade him at first, but he believed if anyone could bring you home to yourself, it was Rose." Sir Richard smiled. "Well, I could hardly argue with that, could I? Rose St. Claire has the kindest heart I've ever known."

She did. Her heart was a miracle. It had taken him time to realize it, but that joy he'd wondered at—the joy he'd tried to touch that day she'd spun on the ice—at long last, he understood.

She'd told him joy was a choice. Kindness was, as well.

Her joy came from her lovely, kind heart.

"Thank you, Sir Richard. You've been most helpful." Max jumped to his feet. "I'll return you to your Christmas goose."

"Wait, if you please, Your Grace. Now you're here, we may as well settle the rest of our business. It will save me a trip to Grantham Lodge tomorrow." Sir Richard rifled through his desk and pulled out a thin stack of papers.

"Might we do this another time, Sir Richard?" He had to figure out where Rose was. Find her, and tell her he—

"It won't take but a moment, Your Grace." He pushed the papers across the desk toward Max. "You now have what you've wanted all along. Hammond Court is yours."

"Mine?" Max stared down at the papers. "How can it be mine? Ambrose left it to both—"

"Rose has relinquished her share of the house to you." Sir Richard nodded at the papers. "See for yourself, Your Grace."

"Relinquished? How . . . wait, is Rose *here*?" He whirled around, lovesick fool that he was, as if he expected she'd be standing there in the doorway of Sir Richard's study, her arms open to him. "I need to see her."

"Alas, I'm afraid that's out of the question, Your Grace. She made it clear to me that she doesn't wish to see you, but she bade me give you those. Perhaps you'd better sit down and read them."

Max dropped down into the chair again, his hands shaking, and skimmed the papers. He was too agitated to read every word, but he absorbed enough of it to understand that Rose had indeed signed over her share of Hammond Court to him, and it looked as if she'd—

He froze, reading the lines over and over again, unable to believe what he was seeing. "What's this?" He pointed to a paragraph near the bottom of the page. "This bit about forgoing any remuneration."

"She doesn't want your money, Your Grace. The house is yours, free and clear. She won't accept one penny from you, despite my advice to the contrary."

"No! I don't want the bloody house, especially not this way." What was Rose thinking, giving away her share of Hammond Court? How did she intend to live, without a penny to her name? Had she gone mad?

It seemed so, because there was her signature at the bottom of the page.

Rosamund Elizabeth St. Claire, written in her fine, flowing script.

"I don't want it." He tossed the papers back down onto Sir Richard's desk. "I won't take it."

Sir Richard sighed. "I was afraid of that. I did try and warn her, but she wouldn't listen. Indeed, you've both been dreadfully troublesome."

Max's life was in perfect shambles. He'd spent Christmas Eve night on a settee in his study and hadn't slept a wink. Abby Hinde had scolded him, and Bryce had looked at him as if he'd gone mad. He had two houses—one he didn't want, and the other overrun with aristocrats, all of whom he'd abandoned without a word. It was Christmas Day, and the lady he loved refused to see him or speak to him.

He'd made an utter mess of everything, yet a small smile rose to his lips, all the same. People in love did tend to be troublesome, didn't they? He'd always thought so. He just didn't imagine he'd ever be one of them.

Now, he couldn't imagine anything else.

Sir Richard picked up the papers and returned them to his desk drawer. "Well, Your Grace, it seems we've reached an impasse. What do you intend to do now?"

There was only one thing to do, wasn't there?

Find a way to see Rose, by any means necessary.

And if it were necessary to be a trifle underhanded, then so be it.

He was the Duke of Grantham, after all. He'd have what he wanted, in the end.

And what he wanted—more than he'd ever wanted anything else in his life—was Rose St. Claire.

CHAPTER 27

The snow gathered in the corners of Mrs. Mildmay's walled garden was melting.

Rose had been sitting in the window seat for hours, watching the thin rivulets of melted snow leaking from the drifts, and running down the stone pathways. They'd shrunk quite a lot since this morning.

Nothing was ever as permanent as it seemed to be. She'd been certain the weeks of gray skies and freezing temperatures would go on forever, but this morning, the sun had returned to Fairford.

Just in time for her to leave the tiny village behind forever.

Kent was meant to be warmer than Gloucestershire. Surely, the lovely weather would endear her to her new home as soon as she arrived? Then, of course, there were the gardens. Kent could boast one of the most colorful carpets of wildflowers in all of England.

Who didn't love wildflowers? Lacy white yarrow, yellow creeping buttercup, pink knapweed, and purple wild thyme. Why, soon enough she wouldn't have a thought to spare for Hammond Court anymore.

"Come sit with me, Rose." Abby set aside her embroidery. "You've been at the window all day. You'll catch a chill if you linger there any longer."

"It's not at all chilly." But Rose dragged herself from the window seat and sat down on the edge of the bed. The urge to lay her head against the pillow and sink into a dreamless sleep was overwhelming, but she remained steadfastly upright.

It wasn't even teatime yet. She *wouldn't* take to her bed in the middle of the afternoon, or engage in any other silly dramatics.

It was just the long day catching up with her, that was all. She'd sent a note to Sir Richard only an hour after the sun had risen and had hardly had a chance to dress before his carriage was waiting for her in the drive. Abby had remained at Hammond Court to see the house was properly closed up, but only a few hours had elapsed before she'd joined Rose.

In the end, there hadn't been much for Abby to do. They'd been gone for weeks already by then. If Rose had known when she left Hammond Court the morning after her bedchamber flooded that she'd never come home again, she would have—

Well, it hardly mattered now, so there was no sense fretting over it, was there?

"You didn't eat much at dinner." Abby frowned at her. "Shall I fetch you a tray?"

She had made rather a poor showing at Sir Richard's Christmas table earlier this afternoon. She didn't have any appetite, which was rather a shame, as Sir Richard's cook had prepared a lovely roasted goose for Christmas dinner.

There'd been Christmas pudding, too, but she hadn't tasted it. It was the first time she could recall not shamelessly gorging herself on it, but she couldn't even look at it without recalling the servants at Grantham Lodge making their Christmas wishes.

Even thinking of it now made her stomach clench. "No, thank you, Abby. I'm not hungry."

But Abby rose from her chair, anyway. "Perhaps just a bit of eggnog." She didn't give Rose a chance to protest, but bustled out the bedchamber door, leaving her alone.

It was only two days until December twenty-seventh. She only had to make it until December twenty-seventh, then she'd leave Fairford for good, and undertake the three-day journey to Sir Richard's mother's house in Cranbrook.

And there, with a fresh year upon her, her life would begin anew, the past seventeen years of her old life nothing but a fading memory.

It was for the best, of course. Rather like wiping a slate clean.

She'd never imagined she'd ever become a lady's companion, but one must do something, and Sir Richard's mother was a cheerful, busy lady. It would be no hardship to serve her, and, of course, Abby was coming, as well. Really, she had no reason to complain. She'd miss Billy, and Mrs. Watson, too, but she could hardly remain in Fairford, with no place to live.

"Rose!" Abby flew through the bedchamber door, her hands fluttering about, and no eggnog in sight. "Quickly, dearest. Heavens, what have I done with your cloak?"

"Abby?" Rose stumbled to her feet. "What is it?"

"The Duchesses of Basingstoke and Montford are here. They're downstairs in the entryway, waiting for you."

"Oh." For a moment she'd thought . . . well, it didn't matter. "Francesca and Prue are *here*?" How had they known to find her at Sir Richard's? "But what do they want?"

"They say they've come to take you for a drive." Abby was scurrying about the room, searching for Rose's hat and gloves. "Here they are. Put them on, pet."

"I don't fancy a drive, Abby. I've, er . . . I've got rather a bad headache." Headache, or heartache. What difference did it make?

But Abby tutted, seeing right through this excuse. "Nonsense. If you do have a headache, it's because you've been cooped up inside all day. It's a lovely afternoon, and the fresh air will do you a world of good."

She did want to see Francesca and Prue, but what if they insisted on taking her directly to Grantham Lodge? She couldn't risk seeing Max right now, before she'd had a chance to persuade herself she was doing the right thing, leaving Fairford, and Hammond Court behind.

Leaving *him* behind.

Her determination was already wavering. It had been, since she'd woken this morning with the soft, warm coverlet under her chin, the freshly painted ceiling above her head, and the heavy silk draperies at the window holding the chill at bay.

If only she could convince herself the repairs had nothing to do with her. That he'd done it all for himself because he intended to move back into Hammond Court.

But the porcelain vase, and the silver candlesticks, and the soft green walls . . .

He hadn't chosen them for himself. He'd chosen them for *her*.

Everything he'd done had been for her.

All it would take was one glance from those gray eyes, and her resolve would scatter like petals on the wind. "I think it's best if I don't—"

"Come now, Rose. You're hardly going to refuse a pair of duchesses, are you? What's become of your cloak? Ah, here it is." Abby snatched Rose's cloak from the clothes press, and held it out to her, shaking it. "The duchesses said they're leaving Fairford tomorrow. You can't let them go without bidding them goodbye after they were so kind to you."

Rose stifled a groan. No, she couldn't allow them to leave without thanking them first. "Yes, all right." She held out her arms with a sigh, and Abby helped her into the cloak. Rose buttoned it, then went to the door, but just as she was reaching for the knob, Abby stopped her.

"Wait, Rose."

She turned. "Yes? What's the matter, Abby? You look strange."

"Oh, nothing at all, pet, just . . ." Another hesitation, then Abby blurted, "If you do happen to come across the Duke of Grantham while you're out, and he asks to speak to you, you might consider listening to what he has to say."

"*You* want me to listen to the Duke of Grantham? But you've been saying all along that he's an arrogant, heartless villain!" Rose threw up her hands. "You told me that all aristocrats are scoundrels, and you insisted the Duke of Grantham was the wickedest of the lot! My goodness, Abby. That's rather a sudden change of heart."

Abby flushed to the roots of her hair. "I never used the word *villain*."

"Scoundrel, then! Surely, that's the same thing?"

"Very well." Abby avoided her gaze. "I own I may have said he was wicked, once or twice, but he's not quite the scoundrel I—"

"He spoke to you, didn't he? When, Abby? When did you speak to him?"

"He came by Hammond Court this morning after you left. He asked to speak to you. I didn't tell him you were here," she hastened to add. "Though he's certain to find it out soon enough if he hasn't already. But he looked— that is, he seemed . . ." She sighed. "He looked as if his heart were breaking, Rose."

Oh, God. It hurt to think of it, to recall the devastation on his face when she'd left him in the doorway of Grantham Lodge last night. "He lied to me, Abby! He schemed to steal Hammond Court from me."

"Schemed, yes, but he didn't go through with it, did he? Hush now, Rose." Abby held up a hand to quiet her when Rose would have interrupted. "I'm not saying that excuses him, but—well, he did go to quite a lot of trouble to see Hammond Court set to rights, didn't he? I can't think of any reason he'd do that, but to please you."

It *had* pleased her. She was tremendously grateful to him, but had it really changed anything between them? Oh, she didn't know! So she'd done her best to banish it from her mind. If she thought too much about it, she'd begin to wonder if she was making a mistake, leaving Fairford, and her thoughts would start spinning in useless circles once again.

"All I'm saying, pet, is that a man who'd go to such lengths as that can't be all bad. Just something to keep in mind, all right?" Abby fastened the last button at the top of Rose's cloak and turned her toward the door. "Go on, now, and enjoy yourself with the duchesses. I expect you to return with some color in your cheeks."

As it turned out, when Francesca and Prue said they wanted to take Rose for a drive, that was precisely what they'd meant. Neither of them mentioned a single word about Max, and they didn't make any attempt to abscond with her to Grantham Lodge.

Instead, they insisted on riding through Fairford, so Rose might tell them all about the village, as she'd promised she would when they first arrived. It didn't take long—Fairford was mainly just the High Street.

"Well, it's lovely, isn't it, Prue?" Francesca said when they'd left the village behind.

"Yes, indeed. It puts me in mind of Wiltshire."

"Shall we drive a bit longer?" Francesca asked brightly. "It's such a lovely day."

Francesca didn't wait for a reply but ordered the coachman to take them for a short drive in the countryside. The duchesses kept up a steady stream of cheerful chatter as the carriage bumped along, and Rose did her best to match their enthusiasm, but it wasn't long before her dark thoughts caught up to her again.

It was good of her friends to try and distract her, but somehow, the drive depressed her spirits even further. Everywhere they went—every road, every building, and even every tree had a memory attached to it.

Fairford was her *home*. How could she bear to leave it behind?

But she would. She had to. She'd already signed the papers turning Hammond Court over to Max. There was no going back now. Even if she could have done it, she wouldn't. Ambrose wanted Max to have the house. She was certain of it.

But with every turn of the carriage wheels, she grew more and more despondent, until she became so lost in her misery that she lapsed into silence, keeping her listless gaze on the scenery rushing by the window, without truly seeing it.

That is, until it became so familiar she realized with a start where they were taking her. "Wait, what are we doing *here*?"

They hadn't brought her to Grantham Lodge, as she'd feared they would.

They'd brought her to Hammond Court.

"Why are we here?" She turned on Francesca and Prue, dread coiling in her stomach. It had hurt terribly to leave it behind this morning, and now she'd have to find the courage to do it all over again. "I don't want to go inside. Take me back to Sir Richard's, please."

But it was already too late. They were partway up the drive, and . . . what in the world? She pressed her nose to the window, amazed. Hammond Court didn't look precisely as it used to during Ambrose's Christmas parties, but it made her breath catch in pleasure, all the same.

It was quiet—nothing like the raucous affairs of Christmases past. Instead of the crush of carriages, the drive was deserted, and in place of the bright light spilling from every window, each was lit by the glow of a single candle only.

"My, it's a lovely house, isn't it?" Prue's voice was hushed.

"I can see why you love it so much." Francesca gave Rose a gentle smile.

"I do. I do love it." Rose's voice shook, and her eyes filled with tears.

"Oh, my dear," Prue murmured.

"Forgive me, it's just that I'm going to miss it so dreadfully." Rose dragged her arm across her cheek. "I can't think why, really. It's a terribly troublesome place, with all the dratted leaks, and the broken windows, and you can't imagine the number of spiders . . ." She trailed off, her gaze moving over the house.

There were no longer any leaks, spiders, or broken windows. Max had seen to that.

"Ah, but broken windows can be repaired, as you see. There's nothing broken that can't be repaired, Rose,"

Francesca murmured. "As hopelessly damaged as it might seem, there isn't a single thing that can't be made new again."

"Franny's right, Rose." Prue smiled. "And once it is made new, you may find it's more beautiful, more special than it ever was before."

Rose said nothing but continued to gaze at the house, strangely breathless. She had the oddest sensation in her chest. It felt almost like . . . hope.

The carriage stopped at the top of the drive. Francesca didn't wait for the coachman, but opened the door and stepped down, reaching her hand out to Rose. "Shall we have a peek inside? Come, Rose, let's have a closer look."

Rose accepted Francesca's hand, but once they were on the drive, she hesitated. The house appeared to be deserted, but someone had lit those candles, and she could think of only one person who'd spend so much time and effort just to please her.

Because, once again, this had all been done for her. It must have been, because there wasn't a single person in Fairford who could ever love this house more than she did. "Yes, I'd like to go inside."

Francesca smiled and squeezed her hand. "Wonderful. I'm so glad, Rose."

Rose dragged her feet a bit on their way to the door, a sudden shyness overtaking her, but Francesca and Prue urged her along, and soon enough they passed through the doorway and into the entryway.

"Oh!" Rose pressed a hand to her mouth.

Garlands had been woven through the spindles of

the grand staircase, and draped over the banister, all the way up to the second floor. It wasn't quite dark outside yet, but the sconces in the entryway had been lit, and a soft glow came from the direction of the drawing room.

"It's so pretty." It was lovely and warm and smelled of fresh pine, and for a moment it was as if she were a young girl again, getting her first glimpse of Hammond Court at Christmastime.

But she was no longer a child. She was a fully grown woman, and too old to run away from her problems. So, when Max stepped from the shadows of the hallway into the entryway and held out his hand to her . . .

She took it.

That was when she knew. The candlelight, the garlands, the scent of fresh pine—they all meant Hammond Court at Christmastime to her.

But it was only when she took Max's hand, and his fingers closed around hers, that she felt as if she'd truly come home.

She'd come.

It wasn't until her hand slipped into his that he realized how terrified he'd been that she wouldn't. In the hours since they'd finished preparing the house, and Montford and Basingstoke had left him here at Hammond Court alone, Max had gone from wildly soaring hope to the darkest depths of despair.

But she was here. Rose had come. Even now, he could hardly believe it, but her hand was warm inside his, her fingers wrapped tightly around his own.

And he was as tongue-tied as a schoolboy on the verge of his first kiss. "Rose, I . . ." Dozens of words rushed to his lips, but he couldn't speak a single one of them. Instead, he brought her hand to his mouth and pressed a fervent kiss to her palm.

She let out a shuddering breath. "Francesca and Prue . . ." she began, glancing over her shoulder, but the entryway was deserted.

Her friends had slipped out the door as soon as Rose accepted his hand.

"Oh." She turned back to him, biting her lip. "They said they wanted to have a peek inside, but . . ."

She fell silent, a flush rising to her cheeks, and that was when he realized she was as tongue-tied as he was. It was up to him, then. He cast about for something to say, and finally blurted, "I brought the Christmas pudding."

Christmas pudding? Dear God, of all the things he might have said to her—that he was madly in love with her, and wished to be with her always—he'd landed on Christmas pudding?

"The Christmas . . . oh, you mean the one I made at Grantham Lodge?"

"Yes." He nodded, far more vigorously than the occasion warranted. "There's a small table set up for us in the drawing room if you . . . oh, but you must already have had Christmas pudding today. Dinner was hours ago."

What had he been thinking, bringing a Christmas pudding? It was ridiculous. He was making a mess of this—

"No! I mean, no." She gave him a shy glance, her

dark lashes sweeping across her cheekbones. "I haven't had any yet."

"Oh. Would you like some?" He hesitated, then held out his arm to her, his heart pounding. He had no reason to expect her to join him, no reason to expect anything at all from her.

"I do adore Christmas pudding." She rested her fingertips lightly on his forearm.

Hope shot through him, his head spinning with it, and it was all he could do not to drop to his knees for her in the middle of the hallway. Instead, he led her into the drawing room, but she stopped on the threshold, a gasp on her lips. "Oh, my. This is so pretty, Max."

Max. Not Your Grace, but *Max*.

"I'm pleased you think so." He chuckled. "Basingstoke and Montford nearly came to blows over the proper way to arrange it all."

In the end, they'd thankfully deferred to Mrs. Watson, and a good thing, too, because the drawing room had come to life under her hands. Everything from the white linens to the sparkling silver place settings, the roaring fire to the flickering candles spoke of warmth, home, and Christmas.

All the things he wanted to give to Rose if she'd let him.

He led her to the table and urged her into the seat nearest the fire. He started for the chair on the other side, but he hadn't taken half a step before he stopped. He didn't want pudding, and he didn't want to sit across from her and chat politely as if they were strangers.

His heart was on fire for her. All that mattered, all

he wanted, was for her to know that he was *hers*, body and soul.

Rose was eyeing the silver serving plate in the middle of the table, a nervous laugh on her lips. "Oh, dear. I do hope the pudding isn't ruined. I daresay there wasn't enough time for it to set up properly, and—"

"Rose." He dropped to his knees beside her. "I'm so sorry, for my scheme with Dunwitty, and for lying to you, and for . . . well, for being the ruthless, heartless, wicked Duke of Grantham." He took her hand and pressed it to his cheek. "Please, Rose. Can you ever forgive me?"

Silence. He steeled himself for the moment when she'd turn away from him and tell him she could never forgive him.

But it didn't come.

Instead, she turned toward him and cupped his face gently in her palm. "On Christmas Eve, you said you're not the same man who came to Fairford all those weeks ago. What did you mean, Max?"

"Don't you know?" He nuzzled his cheek against her hand. "How could I—how could *anyone*—know you, and not be changed by it? You told me once that joy is a choice. That love and hate are choices. I couldn't see it at the time—I spent too many years wrapped in my revenge to see anything properly."

Now, he hardly recognized the cold, unhappy man he'd once been.

"I choose joy. I choose *you*. I love you, Rose. You're everything to me. I'm not a good man, but if you ever could . . ." He drew in a deep breath, his voice shaking.

"If you ever could love me in return, I'd spend the rest of my life endeavoring to deserve you."

His voice broke then, but she was there, her lips on his forehead, his eyes, his cheeks, and finally his lips, a kiss so tender, so sweet it brought tears to his eyes.

"I *do* love you, Max. I tried to tell myself I didn't, but you see how hopeless it is." She let out a soft laugh. "Has there ever been a more unlikely couple than the two of us? I thank the heavens for putting us together against every rule of logic and reason."

"Then you'll have me, Rose?" He searched her face, his breath held. "You'll be my duchess? We don't have to go to London if you don't like it. We can remain in Fairford, either at Grantham Lodge, or Hammond Court. Whatever you want, although we'll have to stay at Grantham Lodge at first until Hammond Court can be made habitable. Say you will, Rose. Please—"

"Shhh." She pressed her fingertips to his lips. "Of course, I will. Nothing would make me happier."

He wrapped his arms around her waist and buried his face in her lap. She stroked his hair and murmured to him, tender words of love and desire, longing and devotion. He didn't try and make sense of it all, but just clung to her, and let her voice drift over him, and into him, filling all the dark, lonely places in his heart.

EPILOGUE

"The candied ginger has disappeared again." Rose rummaged through her spices, but once again, her stores of preserved ginger were nowhere to be found. "Either someone's taking it, or it's found a way to escape the cabinet. It's the slipperiest spice I've ever encountered."

Max was lounging at the kitchen table, licking the last droplets of sweet, sticky treacle from a wooden spoon. "I'd wager Billy took it. He's a sneaky one."

"Is that so?" She gave up on the ginger, hiding her smile as she approached the table, and took the spoon out of his hand. "I've only ever caught one person pilfering my ingredients, and that's *you*, Your Grace. Shame on you, blaming poor Billy."

"Me? Nonsense." He caught her wrist and raised the spoon to his lips for one final lick. "If I have a craving for ginger, Mrs. Watson fetches it from the shop."

"Ah, but that's just it. You don't crave just *any*

ginger. It's my candied ginger you're after." She pointed a dramatic finger at the spice cabinet. "It can't be had anywhere but from *that* cabinet, and I can't help but notice my ginger stores are always curiously depleted after you've been in the kitchen."

Goodness knew, no duke ever spent as much time in the kitchen as the Duke of Grantham. Over the past year, they'd gotten into the habit of sneaking down from their bedchamber after the servants were asleep, giggling and hushing each other as they made their way through the house in the dark, and creeping into the kitchen to do some nighttime baking.

Or at least, she baked. Max spent more time sneaking tastes of the batter and watching her than anything else. It was ridiculous, of course, as they employed a most accomplished cook, but she'd always loved Hammond Court's kitchen, and she loved it even more when her handsome, smiling husband was in it.

"That's a scandalous accusation, wife." He licked the last of the treacle from the corners of his lips. "Have you any proof at all?"

"That you're a thief? One need look no farther than your lips for proof of that." She sniffed and made an entirely feigned effort to free her wrist from his grasp. "I suppose I'll have to go into the secret stores I've hidden in the stillroom. Unhand me, please, Your Grace."

"No, indeed." He slid a strong arm around her waist and drew her closer, settling her between his spread knees, his lips grazing her ear. "Tell me more about your secrets."

She caught her breath, anticipation curling down her spine. "What about the ginger biscuits? At tea this afternoon you were insisting you must have a new batch at once."

"Later." He nibbled delicately at the sensitive skin behind her ear. "Lie down with me." He patted the smooth, wide tabletop, tugging at her earlobe with his teeth.

She shivered at the caress, her fingers going slack around the spoon. "What, *here*? On the kitchen table?"

He chuckled. "It wouldn't be the first time we've, er . . . made use of the table for something other than baking. You do recall December twenty-third of last year, do you not, Your Grace? Then there was that messy incident with the raspberry fool. Why, only last week we—"

"Hush, you wicked man." She stroked her palms down his neck and over his broad shoulders to the hard muscles of his chest. A moan tore from his throat when she scraped a fingernail over his nipple, and she paused to tease the stiffening tip before moving lower, letting her fingertips drift over the delicious ridges and hollows of his stomach.

She never tired of touching him. Even after a year of marriage, his body fascinated her still. Every inch of him was hard, angular, with sleek golden skin poured over tight muscles, and then there were the intriguing sprinklings of hair . . .

She slid her hand lower until she found the thin line of dark hair under his navel, following it with her fingertips until the trail disappeared under the crumpled edge of his pantaloons.

Max growled, but he held himself still, the muscles of his abdomen twitching against her touch. "Another inch, Your Grace, and there's certain to be a ravishing."

She tutted. "Have you forgotten you asked me to teach you to make ginger biscuits? You're proving to be a most troublesome student, Max."

"Yes, but I make up for it with my exceptional skills in other areas," he murmured, brushing his lips over her neck.

She dropped her head back, baring her throat. "Don't try and tell me you no longer crave ginger biscuits, because I know—"

She broke off with a startled cry as he snatched her up into his arms and tugged her onto his lap, hiking up her skirts so she straddled him. "Ah, that's much better." He took the spoon from her, set it aside, and slid a hand under her hems, stroking his palm over her thigh. "I don't deny I have powerful cravings, but not for ginger biscuits."

"Oh? What, then?"

"I think you know." He gazed at her, reaching out to trace the lines of her face with his fingertips. "You're so beautiful, Rose, all of you. Beautiful, and *mine*. When I think of what I nearly lost—"

"Shhh. You'll never lose me." She cupped his face in her hands, her breath catching at the love, the hot desire swirling in those dark gray depths. "I'll always be with you, Max."

He smiled. "Forever?"

"Forever," she whispered, her lips hovering over his. "Now, I believe I was promised a ravishing. Take me upstairs to our bedchamber, Your Grace."

"Come, Max. You can't stand there all afternoon." Rose glided to the edge of the pond, her arms splayed out to keep her balance. "It's far too cold to be still for so long."

They'd woken later than usual after their late-night adventure in the kitchen to find a light dusting of snow glittering on the frozen ground, and a pale gray winter sky above. He would have happily lazed in bed with her all afternoon, but nothing pleased Rose so much as an afternoon of skating, and nothing pleased him so much as watching her.

It was tradition, after all, to skate at Christmastime.

He'd been watching her face as she twirled on the ice, smiling at the memory of the first time he'd seen her like this. The year had flown by in the blink of an eye, every day sweeter than the one before it.

But now he tore his gaze away and glanced down at the pair of skates dangling from his fingers. Flimsy, awkward things. "I'd much rather stay where I am and watch you."

"No, that won't do." She paused in her twirling, a grin on her lips. "You'll freeze into a statue, and then all the children from miles around will insist upon coming to Fairford to see the frozen duke."

"My skates are inadequate."

She threw her head back in a laugh, the joyful sound

echoing in the frosty air, and startling a few birds from their branches. "How do you know? You haven't even put them on yet."

"And I had much better not." He brandished the skates, giving them a shake. "Look at them! They're the most troublesome things imaginable, and that's to say nothing of the ice, which is sure to collapse underneath me as soon as I venture out."

"Oh, nonsense. It's holding me up well enough, isn't it?"

"That, my dearest wife, is because nature herself adores you, just as I do. She wouldn't dare lay a single finger on your lovely head. Well, and because you're half the weight of a hummingbird."

"I feel quite certain you'll be safe, Your Grace." She slid closer and held out her hand to him. "Help me up onto the bank, won't you?"

He caught her small hand in his and gave her a firm tug that landed her right in his arms. "Ah, now this is much better." He pressed his lips to her temple, inhaling her scent of pine and fresh winter air. "Perhaps skating isn't quite as tedious as I thought."

"Mmmm." She took a moment to rest her cheek on his chest before squirming loose and taking the skates from his hand.

"Where do you think you're going?" He caught her by the sleeve of her cloak and tried to catch her in his arms again, but she twirled out of his grip, stumbling a bit on her skates.

"Sit down here." She patted the flat rock near the edge of the pond. "I'll help you with your skates."

He sighed, but he picked his way over the snowy bank to the rock. "I won't be permitted to take you back to our bedchamber until I've skated, will I?"

She smiled up at him and patted the rock once again. "Certainly not, so you may as well do as you're told."

"Very well." He lowered himself onto the rock and stuck one foot out.

She unfastened the buckles on the leather straps, then cradled his foot in her lap, and fitted the wooden bed against the bottom of his boot. "Do you remember the first time we came here together, last year?"

He gazed down at her golden head, half-hidden under a very smart green hat that matched the dark green cloak she'd had made when they visited London in the spring. Did she imagine he could ever forget that day? It was the day he'd come alive again. "I do. It's one of my most treasured memories."

As a boy, he'd been taught to distrust love, but since he found Rose, he'd become a man who embraced it. Once he'd told her he loved her, and asked her to be his, neither of them had ever looked back.

"You helped me with my skates that day. I remember I was so surprised when you took my foot into your hands. Your fingers around my ankle made me shiver." She'd been busying herself with the buckles, her gaze on her task, but now she looked up, her green eyes shining. "I believe that was the first time you ever touched me."

"It was, and nothing's ever been the same since." He touched her chin, tilting her face up to his so she wouldn't look away. "I didn't know . . . if someone had told me then I could love someone as much as I love you, Rose, I wouldn't have believed them."

"No more than I love you, Max." She took his hand, pressed a fervent kiss to his palm, then rose to her feet. "Come skate with me?"

"How can I refuse you, when you ask so prettily?" But then, she always did, didn't she? Rose might be a duchess now, but despite her grand title, she was the same kind lady he'd fallen in love with, and he could refuse her nothing. "I suppose I'd better learn, in any case. Basingstoke and Montford will laugh themselves sick if I fall on the ice, the scoundrels."

Their friends would arrive in Fairford a few days before Christmas Eve and would remain until after Twelfth Night. He and Rose had spent a good part of the spring and fall in London, at his townhouse in Mayfair, but as the autumn faded to winter and the morning frost had covered the grounds of Hyde Park, they'd found themselves longing once again for Fairford and Hammond Court.

So, they'd come home, and spent every moment of the lazy, sun-filled fall days alone together, wandering the pathways between Hammond Court and Grantham Lodge until the sun set in a brilliant glow of pink and gold. Then they'd return to their cozy fireside, where they played chess, or read to each other, and whiled away the long winter nights in their bed, entwined in each other's arms.

It had been his idea to hold another Christmas party this year, but not at Grantham Lodge this time. This Christmas, and every year afterward, they'd celebrate at

Hammond Court, which had now been restored to its former glory. For Rose's sake, he longed to see it come alive once again with love and laughter.

And for Ambrose's sake, as well. Together, he and Rose had made a vow to keep as many of Hammond Court's traditions as they could, as a way of honoring him.

But there would be some new traditions of their own, too.

Hers, and his.

"Skating is the easiest thing in the world, really, as the ice does all the work." She slipped her arm around his waist and guided him toward the center of the pond, where the ice was smoother. "It's rather like walking, but lean forward a bit, and when you're ready, let your foot glide over the ice."

"Like this?" He tucked her into his side, then took a step, and another, until he fell naturally into a gliding motion as the blades on his skates took over.

"Just like that, Max. One step at a time. Lift one foot up while you glide on the other. Push off against the ice to propel yourself forward. That's it. You're skating, Max."

Against all the odds, he was.

One stroke of his foot blended into the next until he was sliding smoothly over the ice, picking up speed with every turn until they were gliding together, with her laughing breathlessly as she struggled to keep up. "Dear me, you have very long legs! I can scarcely keep up with you."

He tightened his arm around her and smiled down

into her eyes. "You don't suppose I'd leave you behind, do you? Never, Your Grace."

They went along, the scrape of their blades a soft hiss against the ice, the wide, endless winter sky above them. A gentle breeze sent sparkling clouds of snow drifting down from the branches to dust their shoulders as they passed, their bodies pressed close together as they made their way to the other end of the pond, then turned clumsily, both of them laughing, and returned to where they began.

"My goodness, you're already quite good at it, and it's only your first time." She reached up to brush a lock of dark hair back from his forehead. "Perhaps all the footwork with your fencing helped you along."

He stilled at her touch, and at the soft gleam in her green eyes. "Or perhaps I simply had a very good teacher." He settled his hands on her waist. "A lovely, entrancing teacher, with golden hair and green eyes, and a laugh so beautiful I couldn't help but fall in love with her."

"Max," she whispered, her cheeks flushing.

He still had the ability to make her blush, and he hoped he always would.

"Rosamund Elizabeth." He traced his thumb over her soft, pink lips. "My love. Teach me to spin as you do."

And she did, her hands tucked into his, her head thrown back, her face tilted toward the sky, and a dreamy smile on her lips, spinning just as she had when she'd taught him what it meant to embrace joy—to open your arms to it, and let it take you.

Only this time, it was different.

This time, he was spinning with her.